To Harry

The Mind's Eye

Miles M Hudson

Miles H...

Ⓑ PENFOLD BOOKS

Published by Penfold Books
87 Hallgarth Street
Durham DH1 3AS
England

Author's website:
mileshudson.com

ISBN: 978-1-83812-588-2

Copyright © Miles Hudson 2021
Design by Mecob

The right of Miles Hudson to be identified as the author of this work has been asserted in accordance with the Copyright Designs and Patents Act 1988.

This book is a work of fiction. Names, places, organisations and incidents are either fictitious or they are used fictitiously. Any resemblance to actual events or places or persons, living or dead, is entirely coincidental.

All rights reserved. No part of this publication may be reproduced, stored in or introduced into a retrieval system or transmitted in any form or by any means electronic, photomechanical, photocopying, recording or otherwise without the prior written permission of the publisher. Any person who does any unauthorised act in relation to this publication may be liable to criminal prosecution.

Acknowledgements

The inspiration for the audiopt surveillance series of stories was a TV interview with Edward Snowden.

Amazing help and support in turning it into this finished book came from: Kirsten Crombie for the most amazing proofreading work (twice, again); all my beta readers, especially my mother; great editing work from Gary Gibson and Philip Purser-Hallard; wonderful cover design work from Mark Ecob; and all those who pledged support up front, especially the ever incredible Stacy Miles.

About the Author

Miles Hudson loves words and ideas.

He's a physics teacher, surfer, author, hockey player, inventor, backpacker and idler.

Miles was born in Minneapolis but has lived in Durham in northern England for 30 years.

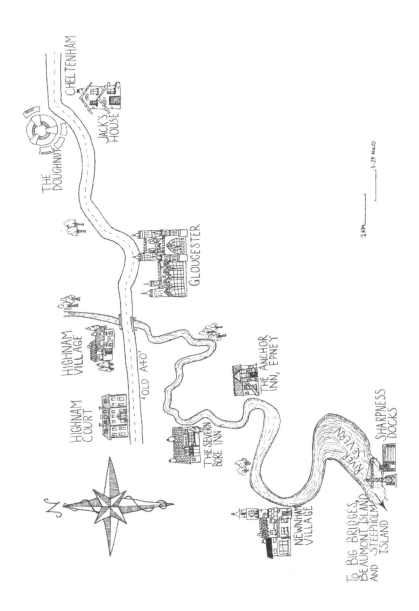

The Covenants of Jerusalem

1. Nothing will be hidden or secret.
2. Everyone will act for the benefit of all.
3. Actions will be judged by everyone.
4. Local population groups will be self-determining.
5. No influence over more than 10,000 persons will be permitted.

Signed into law as the new global constitution, 11th November 2040.

Prologue
31st January 2091, 11.40am
The Doughnut, Cheltenham

Dira had seen a man carried off a jetty by the wind and into the swollen waters of the Severn. He never resurfaced. Dira hadn't personally witnessed it – he had watched the audiopt surveillance images from thirty kilometres away, on a screen in his workstation at the Doughnut. The audiopt feeds from two Newnham residents showed the man fall into the dark water passing the village landing stage. Aluen had asked Dira to come and watch that same footage with her. She had said something seemed 'off'.

From a first floor corridor window, he looked out to see wet leaves helplessly drawn into a vortex. Wild air swirled around the courtyard inner circle of the Doughnut. The giant building had a perfect wind trap in its centre. The constant rain had been hurled against the long windows for three days. Dira realised his hands were gripping the steel handrail tightly. He blinked away the memory of a screen showing the man falling in and turned from the rain-streaked windows to walk into Aluen's office.

'What's up, boss?' Dira breezed.

She smiled – Dira was at least thirty years her senior, and neither of them considered Aluen his boss. He had been a technician supporting Newnham's sifters since the days of her predecessor's predecessor.

She had a huge space all to herself. In its historic GCHQ days, this had been an open plan office for thirty analysts. Now, Aluen wallowed alone in the middle, and the rest of the room was pretty much bare. As with most sifters, she used a horseshoe of twelve screens, in three rows of four, half

THE MIND'S EYE

wrapped around herself on a big semicircular desk. They masked her view of the computer terminals piled up behind, which operated the screens, and she used only one keyboard for all of it. She also had a gestures input gizmo, which meant she worked much of the time without needing to touch the keyboard. Voice commands worked well but, as her work involved near-constant watching and listening, Aluen preferred silent control of the systems. When she was in full flow, hands and arms waving and swinging, head bobbing up and down and turning left and right, Dira regularly thought she looked like a seated dancer.

'The algorithms have sent me these audiopt feeds about a probable death in Newnham, but there's a lot that I don't really get. I'm hoping you can help me to corroborate it.' Her job was to monitor the public surveillance system to report potential crimes back to the village of Newnham – her home Kangaroo.

Aluen sat in an oversized office chair that could swivel and roll around easily to be able to peer at any of the screens as needed. She had chocolate hair, which she always wore in a functional ponytail. As Dira approached, Aluen's dark eyebrows contrasted with her pale face. They were crumpled together in concentration, eyes flicking up and down between two screens.

'OK, what are you looking at?'

'Right, watch this one first.'

Aluen played a piece of video showing an average-sized man with short hair standing near the end of a boat jetty. It was the Newnham jetty location he'd watched previously – he'd guessed correctly. Dira recognised the Old Ferry Crossing pilings and boardwalk. The jetty was short but, at the time the feed was recorded, the tide was full, and the water roiled around and under it.

The audiopt playback screen identified the first feed as having been detected in Roy Lu's auditory and optic nerves two days previously. Aluen and Dira could see the events on the jetty unfold precisely as Lu had observed them through his own eyes and ears. He saw the jetty man bend and then stand up straight. The wind gusted strongly, and the man on the jetty was blown off into the water. Mr Lu ran out on to the jetty himself but could not see the man in the water at all. The wind was still gusting powerfully, and Mr Lu backed carefully along the centre of the wooden walkway, so as not to suffer the same fate. He was shouting and calling the whole time. He clearly did not know the unfortunate drowned man as he only called in generic terms, never using a name.

'Looks like an accident, I don't think you'd need to report that in the KangaReview. It's a sad incident, but there's nothing for the Kangaroo to rule on in terms of criminal actions.'

Aluen continued scrutinising a different screen on which playback was paused. She spoke without turning from the still image. 'Right, yeah. So, now look at this one.'

She pointed away from the paused screen to another one above the first video feed. The same story played out, except this time from the point of view of a different witness, a man called Anton Belling. The only real difference was that Mr Belling stayed put in his fishing spot on the bank adjacent to the jetty. He saw the unidentified man fall in the water, stood up to see better, and then watched Roy Lu race onto the slippery wooden planks to aid the one who had fallen in. Mr Belling clearly knew Mr Lu, as he called for him to be careful, using the name 'Roy'.

Dira looked to Aluen and expressed little surprise at the feeds, but his voice tone did suggest confusion as to why

THE MIND'S EYE

Aluen had asked for help. 'OK, same circumstances, different eyes, but I still don't think there's anything to report in this.'

With each community running its own affairs, the events that constituted criminality in each varied with the mood of that particular group of people. The weekly Kangaroo court was thus legislature and judiciary at the same time, creating precedent case law on a weekly basis. Usually, they only bothered to rule on items submitted by the sifters.

'No, on the strength of those, me neither. But you see that girl there?' She pointed, on the now still second screen, at a third person standing on the bank, initially next to Roy Lu.

'Yup.'

'Watch her feeds.'

Aluen played the screen next to the newly frozen one. The rolling timestamp at the bottom showed it as being the audiopt surveillance feeds from one Liss Peng. The timing was the same as for the first two views. Through Ms Peng's eyes, they watched Mr Lu rush out along the jetty and, like Mr Belling, she called to him to take care as it was very slippery.

'Sorry, I don't get it? What's your question?' Dira slid a hand through his hair. It remained as dark and thick as the day he'd first wandered into Gloucestershire, more than thirty years earlier.

'Watch again. Watch Liss's view of the guy going into the water.'

Aluen waved a hand near the same screen and it reset to play from the start of Ms Peng's feed clip. Peng's attention was initially focussed on Anton the fisherman, but her peripheral vision stretched as far as to encompass the entire jetty. The timing for all three clips was identical, but the dark-haired man on the jetty never appeared in Liss Peng's view. Where he stood on the planks over the water for both Belling and Lu, she saw nothing but empty air.

Aluen played all three simultaneously and pointed at the same spot on the jetty in the two clips from Mr Lu and Ms Peng. One showed the man and one did not.

'That is pretty weird. Does this...' Dira looked again at the timestamp. '...Liss Peng... have some sort of vision problem?'

'No, look. The far riverbank is clearly visible on her screen at the point where the man should have occupied some retinal space. And I've watched about twenty minutes of her before and after this. She's walking with Roy – they're out enjoying the wild weather – and she often looks him in the face. There's no blind spot in her sight.'

'Right.' Dira sat, thinking. 'Still nothing that needs reporting though. You don't think there's a crime, do you?'

'No. At least, I don't think so. But there's more.'

Dira looked at Aluen's small rounded cheeks and snub nose. He wondered how life might have played out if he had ever had a daughter. 'Go on.'

'The man on the jetty.'

'Yes?'

'He doesn't exist.'

'Sorry? What do you mean?'

'Well, I can't find any record of anyone being there at that time. You can see in the images that he's wearing an armulet, but there's no armulet locator recorded at that location at that time.' Aluen pointed at the man's forearm device on the frozen screen that showed Belling's view.

'This is peculiar.' Dira looked at the screen and then focussed on Aluen for a long time. When he realised the stare was making her uncomfortable, he turned his head back and pointed at the mystery man on Lu's feed, which was now paused. 'Broken armulet, I'd assume. I take it you haven't been having any issues with the infonetwork around this part of the town?'

'No, nothing. And the armulet locators for the other three report in perfectly throughout this. So, it's not an issue with the network radio masts.'

'Yep, must be this guy's one has a problem.'

'And because we've got no idea who he is, and no locator to ID him, I haven't been able to find his feeds record either. They'll be getting detected by the masts, even if his armulet's broken, but without knowing who he is, I haven't been able to find his audiopt record.'

Dira shrugged. 'Well, no, of course not. But until somebody reports him missing, we don't really need to worry. You'll not be missing a crime for KangaReview, and when somebody does report him missing, we can then find his feeds and show them what happened. Or maybe even find him alive. In fact, I bet that's why nobody's been reported missing. He's escaped the river, staggered home, given his family a shock, but then, after a hot cup of tea by the fire, everyone's forgotten about the whole thing.'

Aluen's face scowled in unhappiness at having to wait for answers. Dira knew she'd find it sloppy and inconclusive, but it was the only approach he could offer in the circumstances.

'How did you come across this anyway? I'm surprised the algorithms would have sent it to you without a crime, and more so without offering you that guy's feeds as part of the suggestion package.'

With the audiopt surveillance system recording what everyone saw and heard at all times, the quantity of feed information was enormous, unmanageable. The sifters had to be guided by pre-sifting algorithms. These suggested events that might be criminal but needed a human sifter to make the decision as to whether to submit them to the Kangaroo meeting.

'Mmm. Yeah, it was the algorithms, they sent me the feeds from Lu and Belling. A bit after what I've shown you, they talk for a few minutes and Belling asks if Lu thinks the man is dead. I expect that's what was picked up. It is strange that the system didn't catch all feeds from nearby to send as part of the suggestion package. It didn't include her feeds either, I had to look them up. Probably as she doesn't talk about the death of the man. In fact, maybe I should show you that conversation too. I only picked up on her not seeing the man because when they talk about whether he might be dead, and where his body might end up, she's asking who they're talking about and insists she didn't see anyone.'

'I didn't know the algorithms would preclude sending feeds from people who say they didn't see a crime.'

'Usually they don't, they include everyone who might be involved, including witnesses. I don't really get why she was left out of it.'

'Ha, that's good news! Otherwise people could avoid being reported by the computers if they just kept repeating a mantra. "I'm not stealing anything here. There's no crime happening here."' Dira was laughing, although he didn't make much sound.

Aluen's face remained serious. 'No, that wouldn't beat the system. At least, it shouldn't. I can't see any reason why she's been left out here, except that she doesn't see the man at all – he's clearly invisible in her eyes – which is the most bizarre part of it. But confusing the algorithms is not really my question here. I'm worried about that man; we need to find him.'

Dira shrugged – the look of a jaded surveillance worker who'd seen twenty-five years' worth of life and death on the screens crossing his face, although, as a technician, watching wasn't really part of his job. Aluen gave him a stare – the look of someone incredulous at his callousness. Finally, he said, 'OK, sorry. What can I actually do to help?'

'Well, firstly, I just wanted you to tell me that I wasn't imagining things.' Aluen looked up at Dira. 'But mostly, could you go and check over these feeds and confirm whether there were any transmission problems at the time? And, I guess, confirm the perfect working order of the network masts in the area and these people's armulets. You can do all that remotely, right?'

'Yes, all easy tasks. I'll do diagnostics for the whole thing and let you know. Probably less than an hour, I'd reckon. Unless something is broken, in which case I'll tell you that and investigate it a bit further.'

'Thanks. I'm going home at noon, but tell Luka if you find anything useful. I've still got several days before Kangaroo, so I'll have time to add it into the review to send to Sunday's meeting, if it turns out there is something to report.'

Dira left the room and headed to the staircase down to the basement. He was deep in thought about the detection and transmission of the audiopt feeds. Incorrect transmission of actual sights and sounds was a pet project of his, and this case study backed up everything he had researched. As he walked across his workspace, Dira worried about what had just gone on with Aluen. She had definitely come across a real problem. He felt his stomach tighten around the possible ways this had come about.

Chapter One

20th March 2091, 6.30pm
Kangaroo Hall, Highnam village

Tony pointed an outstretched finger up to the part-finished mural on the back wall of Kangaroo Hall. 'What in the name of Malthus is that?' His other hand was held up to his chin, musing by touch on his sage white beard.

Marisa Leone turned from painting a small woodland creature sitting on a tree branch. She scowled at him from ten feet up on a wheeled platform, but it was faux offence as her face immediately brightened and she teased, 'It's a squirrel, silly! Come on, it can't be that bad?'

'No, not that... that.' Tony straightened his pointing arm to emphasise a position in the large frieze about four feet below where Marisa had been finishing off the squirrel. 'The big thing with the pointy ears.'

'That's Brighton. It's a dog I used to play with as a girl. You remember: Ellie Smith's Norwegian sheepdog.'

Tony's head moved backwards ever so slightly, and his eyes opened a little wider. 'Whew, I suppose. That dog was a great big ball of fluff. But that was years ago; do you think the rest of the Kangaroo will recognise it?'

Marisa shrugged, making her dangly earrings jangle. 'I don't care if they don't. It's not supposed to be a real picture, just something nice for decorating the hall.' Everything she said came with a cheeky smile.

Tony turned to Lloyd Lloyd, Highnam's larger-than-life Spokesperson. 'I told you we should have had it planned out first.'

'I heard that,' Marisa called down, her back to them as she continued with the thin paintbrush.

THE MIND'S EYE

Tony and Lloyd Lloyd smiled at each other and Lloyd Lloyd answered, 'I think it looks great. As she says, there's no need for figurative accuracy, just something pleasant to improve the ambience in here. Thank you for what you're doing, Marisa. I'm sure everyone will love it.'

Highnam's Kangaroo meetings were held every Sunday in the largest room in the old Highnam Court manor house. After the Times of Malthus, the entire building had been unoccupied, and the community had chosen it as the best option for their meetings.

For just over fifty years, and through the tenures of six Spokespersons, the building had been maintained by the community and used for myriad Kangaroo activities. To celebrate the tenth anniversary of Lloyd Lloyd's Spokespersonship, he had decided to co-ordinate a big refurbishment. With the promise of a big, decennial summer party, he had been able to secure the volunteer services of many of the villagers in various working parties. Looking again at the mural, Tony smiled as he remembered being the first to volunteer and relived the pride he had felt when his son had volunteered to lead the outdoor work.

Although the once-incredible ornamental gardens had been returned to their former glory by Lloyd Lloyd's predecessor, they were another of the main elements of the current refurbishment programme. Tony had suggested that the party should take place mostly in the gardens. If only half the town turned up that would be a couple of thousand more people than Highnam Court itself could hold.

The wind bustled noisily into the building. Asa banged his way through the Hall's vestibule and dumped an armful of broken wood pieces onto a pile of rubbish just inside the main room. He walked over to his father and the Spokesperson, gathering and retying his long ponytail whilst walking and taking in the mural.

'That's that rotten gazebo destroyed. I'm thinking the refurb out there will take a bit longer than we thought. Should still be finished in time for Kangaroo this Sunday, but it'll be close.'

'Shouldn't be a problem, either way,' Lloyd Lloyd said. He looked up at the little stage and cast an assessing eye around the rest of the Hall. Marisa's platform had been built up all across the half-dozen wooden doors that slid aside to open one whole wall to the gardens in the summer. When it was finished and the giant doors were fully opened, her mural would seem like the garden scene extended right up to the ceiling. She wanted to paint a sky on the ceiling, but the jury was still out as to whether the refurbishment committee would agree to that idea. 'We'll still be able to function even if it's like this. Besides, half-finished will give me a chance to emphasise to everyone how much work this has been and remind them how much we need the volunteer support to keep coming.'

Tony commented, 'There's not as much space as usual with the rubbish and the platform and that pile of soft furnishings. Hopefully, it'll mostly be out of the way by then, though. We've still got five days.' He sniffed the smell of paint in the air and worried whether that would be long enough.

'Only four really – let's not count Sunday; best not to be expecting to get anything done on the day itself. I might put out a message that we're a bit limited on space this week, and anyone who has the slightest issue should attend via armulet. Fingers crossed, there won't be too much for us to rule on from the KangaReview.'

THE MIND'S EYE

Asa watched Lloyd Lloyd and asked, 'Do you think the Sunday Kangaroo is the best way we can organise running our community?'

Tony shot his son a glance to say, *Keep your mouth shut on that.*

Lloyd Lloyd looked bewildered by the question. 'I'm not sure what you mean. How else could we be self-determining, and decide if everyone has been acting for the benefit of all, and ensure that actions can be judged by everyone?' He was quoting the Covenants of Jerusalem mechanically.

Tony shook his head nervously, almost imperceptibly. Asa saw his father, but continued, 'I don't know, I'm just not sure the constant watching by the audiopts gives us all the feeling of security it's supposed to. We don't have any real crimes, so I'm just thinking that maybe we don't need to be shaming people in public for trivial things.'

Tony looked up at Marisa, remembering a time she had suffered such a humiliation at the hands of a baying mob in that very room. He remembered the shouts of 'Shame!' that had reverberated across the Hall and was saddened by how often that kind of barracking was heard at Kangaroo. Tony was pretty sure Marisa could hear Asa and was pointedly keeping her back to them.

His thoughts were interrupted by a slight, dark-haired man, who charged in through the doorway, kicking a chair out of his way. He shouted, 'Vive la revolution!' and threw flaming cloths wrapped around sticks into the hall. One landed right in the middle of a pile of new curtains, and the other slid down the side of the pile of wood rubbish. They ignited immediately, either side of the entrance. It was also the only useable exit, and the intruder turned back and fled through it.

Tony stood and stared at the empty doorway. The events he had just seen didn't make any sense at all. He wondered if he had somehow imagined the whole thing, until flickering at the edge of his view confirmed real flames. Even though he could see the fire, Tony still couldn't take in what was going on. He gazed at the wisping smoke, mesmerised.

Lloyd Lloyd screamed, 'Hey, that's Jack Smith!' and he charged off after the fugitive.

Asa and Tony looked at each other for a moment, before Asa ran off after them. Tony felt stuck to the floor. He wondered how the man could have failed to recognise any of them. His eyes had seemed unfocussed. How had Jack Smith escaped his island exile? That confusion was superseded by confusion as to why Smith would set fire to the hall. Tony couldn't believe he really had such enmity for his own Kangaroo. His crime had been a statement against the audiopt system as a whole, but the Jack that Tony had known had loved Highnam.

As the flames took hold of the pile of broken gazebo wood, the noise of combustion brought Tony back to reality. He looked up to see Marisa starting to clamber down the side of her scaffold. She turned to him and shouted, 'You go get him, I'll put that out.'

'There's two extinguishers by the door here.' Tony pointed at the red canisters as he ran to join the chase for Jack Smith.

The moon was just new and, even with the few lights from around the village, it was darker than usual. Tony spotted Lloyd Lloyd's armulet torch beam waving wildly a little way down the road to Highnam's marketplace. He chased after the light.

At the entrance to the marketplace, Tony caught up with Lloyd Lloyd and Asa. The village Spokesperson was a portly

THE MIND'S EYE

man with a big, blond mop of hair. The three of them shone their light beams around the empty space, wet mud was all they could make out. There was no sign of Smith, and none of them had seen him after they exited Kangaroo Hall.

'That *was* Smith, wasn't it? You saw him, too?' Lloyd Lloyd asked.

Asa was first to realise that the chase was now less important than the blaze. 'Fire! Fire!' he yelled, running all round the edge of the marketplace to roust the villagers that lived on the square.

Tony's stomach tightened in fear as he turned back to see flames licking out of the windows. 'Fire at Kangaroo Hall! Help! Everybody help!' He ran a lap of the marketplace, shouting alongside Asa, and they all ran back towards the building.

The community had equipped their meeting place with fire extinguishers taken from old, abandoned buildings in Gloucester. There should have been more than enough, but for the fact that the extinguishers were at least seventy years old and had not been maintained since. More than half of them failed to do anything when their triggers were pulled.

The three men struggled to even pass the vestibule of the main hall as thick smoke poured out, and only one extinguisher started spraying. Tony shouted himself hoarse trying to find Marisa, but they couldn't get back in to check that she had escaped. With his shouting in the smoke-filled hallway, Asa soon had to drag his father outside for fresh air. Dozens of villagers had arrived, and despite his weak protestations, Tony couldn't force his way back in past Asa. Sitting on the hard ground, he stared up at the smoking building.

'She got out, didn't she?' Tony gripped Asa's arm but did not look away from the battle against the fire. He continued at barely more than a whisper. 'She told me to chase after Smith. The fire was only small then. I thought she'd be OK with the two extinguishers by...' His voice tailed off.

'It's not your fault, Dad.' Asa put his arm around Tony's shoulder. He made a show of looking around them. 'I'm sure she got out.'

The failing extinguishers meant that it took a lot longer to get the fire under control than it should have. Even through squally rain, sometimes turned to sleet or briefly snow, the fire continued. Wind gusts caused the flames to spread more than the wet damped them down. The unpredictable movements of the fire occasionally caught people out. One woman ran from the front, screaming as her shirt burned bright in the dark. She jumped in the lily pond and several people went to her aid.

Firefighting villagers pushed the spread of flames back, but the occasional extinguisher failure led to a flare-up that forced them to retreat. They had numerous small battles. Fire took hold on small supplies of fuel – a door for example – and then a poorly equipped firefighter struggled to stop this spreading through the adjacent plasterboard or timbers to another significant spot.

They took turns catching their breath in the cold, wet night. This building, and others in the village, had extinguishers, but nobody had ever thought to bring any other equipment like breathing apparatus. The forefathers of Highnam's current population had not included any firefighters. They were all learning on the job.

Asa was leaning forward with his head between his knees. Tony could smell only smoke. Both had breathed in more smoke than was good for them. Asa sat up again and turned to his father. 'How are you? Shall we go and find where Marisa is, check she's OK?'

THE MIND'S EYE

Tony turned to look over his shoulder at the milling crowd. His stomach knotted again. They both jumped up and started walking around the groups of villagers. Tony became more and more anxious, and their pace quickened. They split up. Tony looked in the faces of the people tending to others. Asa ran forwards and scanned the ones close to the building who were throwing water and wrestling to make extinguishers work. Marisa was not among those fighting the flames or those supporting them by bringing water. Nor was she helping to guide the two firehoses back to the pumps at The Lake. They met up again at the medical station. It had been set up on the concrete pad where Asa had removed the gazebo structure.

'She's not here.'

'No, I can't see her anywhere.' Tony was squeezing one hand in the other.

They found Lloyd Lloyd being treated by his wife at the periphery of the medical area. He wasn't obviously injured but had probably taken in too much smoke too. He was pale, and his whole body wavered as he sat.

'We're not thinking straight!' Tony shouted in Asa's face and pushed him. He pointed at his armulet and used it to search for Marisa's location. His heart quickened as it showed her back inside. 'She's not showing any audiopt feeds, but her armulet says she's alive. Its locator has her in the hall still!'

Asa grabbed a blanket from a pile at the impromptu nursing station. He dragged it through the lily pond, and they ran for the main entrance. After shouting to their neighbours that they had to search for Marisa, both hoses were aimed at the main entrance. Its flames were already extinguished, but the heat still suggested a sudden flare-up could come at any moment.

Tony was afraid as smoke choked him again. He clutched the wet blanket in tight fists and held it above both of them as they moved gingerly forward, blind from the covering. Asa used his own armulet to move towards Marisa's location. Both knew Kangaroo Hall's geography well enough that they quickly got inside to the redecoration area. In the large open cavern of the hall, the fire was not as oppressive as they had feared. The lack of significant flame kept the room fairly dark. They could see by the light from a few bright embers but had to move slowly. Tony held the blanket above them both whilst Asa searched under debris. His armulet torch cast many shadows across the wreckage, and Tony found the light more blinding than helpful.

'There!' Asa stuck a pointing finger out in front of his father's face. Tony's heart leapt, eyes scanning for what his son might have seen. Marisa's curly, brown hair splayed like a discarded mop from the top of her head, but the rest of her body was hidden under a pile of roof plaster and planks, including two of those that had formed her painting platform.

Asa was strong enough to shift the detritus alone, allowing Tony to continue to hold the wet blanket over them all. He was desperate to reach down and help her, but had to hold the blanket with both hands. Marisa had numerous small cuts on her face. Asa shook her arm and shouted, but her body wobbled, limp. He rested a hand on her head and wiggled it a little, but still she did not react.

Asa looked up, eyes wide. 'Should we move her? If she fell off the platform, she might have a broken back.' Tony's throat rasped as bile surged up over the smoke damage already there. He was frozen, staring at his friend's body. Asa shook his father. 'Dad!'

Tony pulled back the blanket a little so they could look around the room. A blackened beam leaned in the air above them, still part-connected at ground level, but hanging at a precarious angle. The sight of this beam stopped discussion.

THE MIND'S EYE

Asa pulled a complete plank from the rubble, and they slid her onto it as urgently as a potential broken back would allow. They shouldered the plank and staggered forward. The blanket formed a shroud, stretching from the father's head to the son's, and then draping down on either side.

As they shuffled back to the exit, the beam above creaked loudly enough that it was the only noise they could hear above the wind, the flames, and even the water hoses. Tony moved his free hand back to lift the blanket and look out. He glimpsed the charred oak support juddering. Flecks of charcoal shook off and flew up into hot convection currents. It creaked again and slipped down at them. He forced them all forward as much as he could, and braced his free hand over his head, expecting to be struck at any second.

Tony opened his eyes, realising that they had not been hit by the beam. He sneaked another glance from under the blanket and it was right there. It had stopped falling with inches to spare. The beam stuck diagonally across the room at an angle of barely 30°. Tony couldn't see what had stopped its fall, but he didn't linger to look.

Father and son got the rag doll body of Marisa out to the nursing station and stood watching as the village doctor and her assistants tried to revive her. Seeing his wife there, Jonty Leone ran out of the crowd of villagers. 'Nooo!' he screamed, but the wind dragged his cry away into the night.

Chapter Two

Several hours earlier – 20th March 2091, 3pm
Steep Holm island

Jack Smith's armulet beeped three times. He dragged a numb finger to tap on the screen strapped to his pale forearm and silenced it. The nearest seagull cried at the shrill disturbance. Jack struggled up to a kneeling position on the frigid rock ledge. The alarm told him that he needed to get back inside or freeze to death. His stomach told him that he had to take at least one egg or hunger would overcome him.

The gull shrieked at him from four feet away on its nest. He was not fit to fight the bird, or even kill it, which would have made for a feast. Below, the icy waters of the Severn estuary were slapped against the cliff by a gusty March wind. Jack swung his walking stick around, and the gull avoided it by flying straight at him. He had learned to make the stick's arc finish on the clifftop, so that as the squawking attack unbalanced him, the swinging momentum made him fall back to the relative safety of the grassy edge of the cliff. He was at the limits of cold and exhaustion and barely managed to reach out and grab an egg before the bird came swooping back at him.

With his stick held overhead to ward off the enraged mother, Jack crawled away, treasuring the first food for two days. He desperately wanted to crack it and suck out the contents immediately but couldn't dare to lose any in the thin snow cover. He wasn't sure that the deadened fingers he was trying to hold it with would even be up to the job of breaking the eggshell. The angry gull, despite support from shrieking comrades scattered all along the clifftop, gave up the chase and tended to her other eggs as they would be cooling quickly.

THE MIND'S EYE

England's winters had become much colder than the gulls had evolved to expect.

With the triumph of the egg in his hand, Jack eventually managed to stand up. He staggered across Steep Holm's upper plateau towards his cottage, leaning heavily on the stick.

Jack, and the island as a whole, were running out of firewood. He had to keep the stove burning continuously. He had no means of igniting a new fire until the sun next came out and he could use the magnifying lens he had removed from a pair of binoculars. Jack had been sleeping in the kitchen since autumn so as to reduce his use of fuel. Heating the whole cottage was a waste.

He drained the shell carefully at the counter in the cottage kitchen and mixed in some water to maximise his dinner. For this banquet, he put a large, partly burnt log into the base of the stove, wafted the embers aflame and huddled close to soak up every wave of heat it produced. The thin egg-water mix cooked quickly in the small metal tin he placed on the stovetop, forming a dark orange solid. Although most of the water did not mix and simply sat around the omelette, Jack made sure he ate the lot, knowing from experience that the water would aid his starved digestive system. The meal was delicious, albeit salty in flavour. He knew that the strength it delivered would wane quickly and decided to set out in search of more food. Jack had never been well-built but, at just thirty-one years old, starvation had left him with the skinny body of an old man. He knew he had to build on this sustenance, collecting more eggs, but his main aim was to catch a gull to eat; an adult bird might last a week.

His body movements on the way out and back that morning had given his armulet a little more battery charge, and he tried to call up some of the computer coding he had been teaching himself. The device strapped around his forearm projected its screen into the space in front of the kitchen sink.

Highnam Kangaroo had banished Jack to Steep Holm, with no armulet being a part of the punishment. However, the old pub building, on the shingle beach a hundred feet below the upper flat part of the island, had contained a pair of skeletons. Lying on top of each other in the restaurant kitchen, with a carving knife between the ribs of the upper one, each had had an armulet wrapped around the ulna and radius. His friend Vicky had taken one of them when they hid here previously. Early in his exile, Jack had managed to revive the remaining armulet but had avoided re-registering it.

The nearest infonetwork masts were in Weston-super-Mare, on the coast five miles away, but this distance worked well for Jack. They were too far away to catch his auditory and optic nerve signals, so the only audiopt surveillance for him would be what his own armulet picked up. As he had not re-registered it, whatever his armulet intercepted would not be flagged as his feeds. A sifter might spot an audiopt feed coming from Steep Holm, but it would be listed as belonging to the previous owner. With no mirrors on the island, he wouldn't be spotted even if somebody followed the feeds for some time. They'd see what he saw, but not his actual face. Jack liked to tell himself that he had infonetwork access 'under the radar'. In 2091, few people knew what radar had even been.

With a number of hand gestures, Jack flipped through the armulet filing system to find the latest coding exercise. As with his physical strength, he expected that his brain would be in good order for only a brief time, if there was no further food that day. It took a little over the allotted five minutes for Jack to complete a small programming task.

THE MIND'S EYE

He watched as the armulet searched the audiopt feeds from his home village of Highnam for anyone reading a book. It was a trivial task, but few people actually knew how to write the code that powered the audiopt surveillance system. The algorithms he had worked with in his former life had been written fifty years earlier, and there had been no call to change their functionality since.

Jack smiled at the fact that the only person in Highnam reading at that exact moment was his friend, Vicky Truva. She was reading an armulet projection of a book, but he accepted this as close enough. The village had a population of over five thousand, and with the weather as it was, he had expected more people to be sheltering indoors. He wondered if he had biased his coding subconsciously so that it found his friend. He decided, with a chuckle, that this was impossible. The code just functioned; it couldn't make secret or subjective judgements. Jack then wondered if there was some other connection between him and Vicky that could not be explained scientifically. Again, he chuckled with delight at the way he felt when he thought of her.

He remembered growing up on Grannie Ellie's smallholding. She was a pragmatic, distant woman. Jack had known that she loved him but could barely remember any occasions when she had expressed that. Ellie was his entire childhood family and, at fifteen, he had gone to the Doughnut to become one of Highnam's sifters, a lonely job at best. Jack knew that he was an amateur at emotions. That lightness in his stomach, beyond any hunger, he had come to recognise as the feeling he got when he thought of Vicky. She always lifted his mood.

His other treasure from the old pub had been an empty notebook and several pencils. As he didn't have his own armulet, Jack preferred to record his journal the old-fashioned way in the thick, plastic-bound notebook. Starting from the back, he had used it for practical notes like the way to cook new things, or reasons he could think of why some things had failed to grow despite his gardening attempts. Starting from the front was the real journal. Jack looked at its first page.

Why did I blow up the Doughnut?
Well, just the server room. It was never any kind of big symbolic gesture, the servers were the important target.

He wondered if he had ever thought of the explosion with any kind of revolutionary manifesto in his head. He was convinced that he had no drive from his heart. It had been logic and his knowledge of history that had set that course in motion. But had that been enough to justify his act of terrorism? Over his time on Steep Holm, Jack had made a conscious effort to write out the background of ideas that had driven him to the explosion. Beforehand, he had never lifted his reasoning up to the level of articulation. Jack had just known what he must do. Maybe that was what being driven by the heart was. The action of writing out his justifications, after the fact, had only cemented more strongly in his mind the need to get rid of the audiopt surveillance system. Jack was certain he had been right all along. The people just couldn't see it – they still hadn't seen the full picture.

He shook his head, lifted his big coat from the hook and took up the walking staff. The path to the cliffs was short, maybe only a hundred yards. The journey took Jack past a jerry-rigged, polytunnel greenhouse which stood empty of crops and in an ever-worsening state of repair, as the winter storms battered the little rock-plug island. Even though nothing new had grown in it since November, the greenhouse had been a successful build. It had been stiflingly hot during the summer months, and nothing had grown then either, offering just a small window of harvest. He had had some tasty raspberries and blackberries in the autumn, along with a few carrots, and an accidental crop of mushrooms inside a barrel that supported one end of the structure.

His life in exile had started out as an interesting, if arduous, experiment in total self-sufficiency within a limited resources environment. For most people in 2091, subsistence farming was a way of life. Land was plentiful, and the new climate was good for crops, albeit sometimes different ones from traditional English crops. Jack, though, had only experienced a life supported by others. After growing up eating food provided by his grandmother, he had moved to working long hours indoors as a sifter. The job was well-respected, and Highnam's villagers contributed to their sifters' livelihoods; but this had left him with a gap in his knowledge. Jack's abilities to research farming were not enough to replace real experience tending to plants.

His struggles against pangs of hunger had often reminded Jack of the stories Grannie Ellie used to tell about the Times of Malthus. He wrote these vignettes into a section in the middle of his journal. Ellie had assiduously passed on their family's oral history, with tales of growing up in Brighton at the turn of the century, and the difficulties in feeding Jack's mother during the Times. Clara had been born right into famine and had never really recovered from her childhood malnourishment, to the extent that Ellie always said it was the reason she had died giving birth to Jack.

As a slight man, who'd spent his adult years in a sedentary job, he'd felt a real sense of achievement when he had carried several large, rounded rocks up from the beach. These he had used to create a makeshift laundry in the water storeroom in the big barn. The large sinks had actually made it fairly easy to attempt laundry, but with no means to make any soap, he had found it difficult to really clean anything. Scraping with stones helped a little, but he'd never found the results satisfactory. Washing his own body without soap seemed to work much better – his skin felt as clean as he might hope for, but his clothes always felt dirty. Eventually, he had become so desensitised to it that he no longer noticed his clothes feeling itchy.

Rewiring and reinstalling the few solar cells that were not broken had been much more successful. Jack had been able to set up enough electrical power generation to light his home at night. The few working battery stores were small and did not hold enough energy to heat the cottage, or even to run the large refrigeration unit in the old pub. Cooking and heating had to be done using fire in the old kitchen stove.

Managing the island's vegetation sustainably was more difficult than the videostories he watched had claimed it would be. Everything seemed to grow very slowly in the thin soil of his windswept island.

During the intensely hot summer of 2090, Jack had cleared the upper plateau of Steep Holm of the wild brambles and nettles. There was a huge pile of dried vegetation in the big barn, but it burned so quickly that it was rarely worth using in the stove. The effort of cutting and carrying mounds of the stuff was usually more work than the heat it produced. Soon, he would have no choice.

The island's stunted trees were small and thin-limbed, and he had cut and burned far too much of the tree stock before realising how quickly it was running out. In the first few months Jack had spent on the island, he turned the odd tower-like building adjacent to the derelict pub into a smokehouse and built up a good stock of smoked fish. One of the pages at the back end of his journal showed a badly drawn sketch of Jack sitting on the beach eating a fish, with the tower in the background releasing a spiral of smoke. Despite the poor artistry, the image undeniably imparted his wallowing happiness and pride at the smoking of the fish.

This food reserve had lasted him the first winter, but Steep Holm had not had enough trees to try it again for the second winter. The greenhouse had not provided anywhere near enough food to cover the loss of the smoked fish. He had caught and eaten the last rabbit on the island in late December. Insects were a decent enough food source, but he had not been able to find them during the winter.

Luckily, the well had never run dry. This was a constant surprise to Jack as the island was small and in the middle of the Severn estuary where it was very much saltwater. That the well could reach down to a freshwater aquifer connected to the mainland seemed unlikely, but he was also sure the island had not received enough rain that summer to keep the well in water.

Jack stood at the cliff edge, again, incurring the complaints of hundreds of gulls, and stared down at the beach. It had been water right up to the pub wall and the surrounding cliff base only an hour or two earlier, but the water had receded rapidly and far. The disgusting smell of dead fish and sulfur that he associated with low tide was briefly at Jack's small nose, but a gust of wind whisked it away.

More than half the beach was now visible: over a hundred yards of shingle in a large crescent moon shape. The prompt of the shape caused Jack to look up to the churning, grey clouds, but there was no chance of seeing the real Moon.

He imagined that the winter's cold might be abating. Jack had suffered a month of near-constant numbness, with snow, sleet and hail. Never very heavy or settling deep, the surrounding estuary kept the temperature wet-snow warm. That wetness in the wintry conditions meant he always felt achingly cold. Jack had tried to work through his conflicting needs – stay inside to keep dry and warm and hungry, or suffer the bone-chilling winds and find some food – but he knew the experiment would soon end if his winter famine continued much longer.

The gulls' noise was continuous but was less directed at him than when he first walked over. In one swift movement, Jack surprised himself by swinging back around blind and cracking the nearest bird right in the face with the tip of his stick. The roundhouse motion knocked it and its nest several feet onto the snowy grass and its head lolled, neck broken. *Bird and eggs in "one fell swoop".* Jack grinned and picked up the nest platter.

THE MIND'S EYE
Chapter Three
20th March 2091, 10.30pm
Kangaroo Hall, Highnam

From the building's porch, Tony could see several friends being tended to for minor burns or recovering from breathing in smoke. The darkness of night made it easier to spot each new ignition. He tasked those who were up to it with dousing the smouldering embers again, in the hope that reduced residual heat would stop the fire rekindling overnight.

Tony felt his way along inside to the hall to survey the damage. He had disconnected the electric lighting in the early stages of fighting the fire and nervously switched the circuit breaker back to 'On'. A few lights were not operating, but he could neither see nor hear any sparking. A proper check would need to be done in the morning, but Tony decided that, for now, he could get away with a five-minute quick look.

Beyond the curtains and the rubbish pile, Kangaroo Hall had not offered too much in the way of fuel. Most of the furniture had been removed to the old stables during the refurbishment. The building was basically intact, if charred. In the main room, the air was still heavily laden with smoke. Tony scanned with his armulet torchlight. He reckoned that Marisa had tried to reach the exit but falling pieces of ceiling had crushed her platform and the wreckage had just caught her as she was crawling away. A quick check on her audiopt record bore this out. He watched her view as she turned up from looking at the floor to the noise of crashing lumber and winced in surrogate pain as the record went black.

Tony's heavily bearded son, Asa, appeared and stopped at the threshold. As he heard the crashing sound from his father's armulet, and saw its screen go dark, he put his hand over it and his other arm around Tony's shoulder. 'She'll be alright, Dad.'

Lloyd Lloyd had organised a stretcher party to take Marisa to the clinic, although the doctor was already at her side. Doc had said she did not expect there was much more to be done, except to keep Marisa comfortable and hope for the best. She could treat the obvious injuries, even some pretty serious ones, but the village clinic was not equipped for major intensive care cases.

Tony and Asa did their best to keep the assembled townsfolk out of the hall. Many areas were too dark to be able to confirm the extent of the damage, and, with the gusty winds, they did not want any further injuries if more of the structure fell down. Apart from their nosey interest, the people, most of whom had played some part in helping to extinguish the fire, were not enjoying waiting in the cold weather outside. At the exit, Tony switched off the main circuit breaker again and told the assembled villagers Lloyd Lloyd would be along in a minute to give them an update.

Back in the vestibule of Kangaroo Hall, Tony looked to his son and spoke quietly. 'What happened here? What was that? I didn't think Jack Smith was like this.' He stretched his arms out to indicate the destruction around them and frowned in confusion.

Asa nodded. 'I know. I mean, I don't know. I agree, this is not what Jack wants. He wouldn't hurt anyone. And burning down Kangaroo Hall isn't going to achieve anything.'

'It is kind of a statement.'

'Yes, but this isn't his way. He's a thinker; he's not violent.'

'Are you forgetting he blew up the Doughnut and completely destroyed the infonetwork?'

THE MIND'S EYE

'Yes, but that's the actual target. And he was very careful to make sure that no people were injured in that attack. And then tonight, he did see us in here before setting this fire.'

'Do you think he was targeting Lloyd Lloyd?'

Asa shook his head and scrunched up his eyebrows. 'I just can't see it. He's not a violent man. And this doesn't help towards getting rid of the surveillance. If anything, it'll make people believe we need the audiopts more than ever.' Asa held his finger up in the air and then pointed it at his armulet. He called up his own audiopt feeds record for earlier in the evening, from the time they first saw Jack. The record clearly showed that they had not misidentified Jack Smith. The man they all thought was in exile on the island of Steep Holm had rushed in, shouted, and thrown the flaming torches. Father and son looked at each other.

They heard Lloyd Lloyd calling before they could see him. As he walked back towards the hall's main entrance, their Spokesperson appeared as a faint silhouette against the dim horizon. He reported to them immediately on arrival in the doorway, 'Marisa, she's in a bad way. Doc's with her at the clinic, but it's not looking good.' Tony and Asa looked at each other again and then back at Lloyd Lloyd. 'That was Jack Smith, wasn't it? I didn't imagine that it was him?'

'It was – we checked on my audiopt record. I don't get it, though. Why would he do this?'

Lloyd Lloyd looked up at Asa, surprised. 'We threw him out. Banished him for life on some crappy hole out at sea. Eighteen months of that could send anyone over the edge. And he was pretty unstable from the start.'

Asa frowned. He shook his head slowly. 'I'm not so sure. I think there must be...' His father's hand on his arm silenced Asa.

Tony took up the conversation. 'We need to catch him. Do you think the Bristol Brigade would be best for this?'

Lloyd Lloyd nodded vigorously. 'Oh yes, Halthrop will get him. They caught him last time, and they know all about how he thinks and where he might hide. And the infonetwork is on this time, so there shouldn't be any problem at all.'

'Why don't you go home and call Major Halthrop. I'm sure your family want to see you after all this.' Tony kept his hand on Asa's arm, holding him still until Lloyd Lloyd had moved into the open to address the little crowd. When he let go, Tony held his arm horizontal and tapped at the screen of his armulet.

'What?' Asa asked.

'Let's see where he is. If we can get to Jack before anyone else, we might be able to find out what's actually going on here. I really hope he hasn't gone crazy like Lloyd Lloyd says.'

Jack Smith's audiopt feeds were not available. The last entry that Tony could find was for the day that the Bristol Brigade had dropped him on Steep Holm, eighteen months previously. After they'd moved away from the island, and their armulets were out of range, there was nothing further. Asa tried his device as well, but neither of them could find anything for Jack.

Asa spoke quietly. 'That's impossible. Isn't it? He was here tonight. It was definitely him, definitely, within range of both our armulets and the infonetwork masts around here.'

Tony rested his grey-bearded chin in one hand as the other hand supported that elbow. 'I certainly thought that was impossible.'

'Has he developed a way to mask his feeds or to block the audiopts?'

Tony shrugged.

THE MIND'S EYE

'Please, everybody, can we have some quiet.' Outside, Lloyd Lloyd oscillated both hands palms-down in front of twenty or thirty members of the Highnam village community.

He had to speak loudly, sometimes even shouting as the wind whipped his words away. 'You've seen the destruction here, and Tony, Asa and I all saw Jack Smith appear in the hall and set the fire. I'm expecting we want to engage the Bristol Brigade to find him and bring him to full Kangaroo, but I need some sort of mandate from the village to confirm that.'

'For Malthus' sake, Lloyd Lloyd, Marisa's nearly dead. Get on with it, man!' It wasn't clear who had spoken, but with the nodding and muttering agreement, it didn't really matter.

'Right, thank you, that's all I needed. I'll call Major Halthrop now.'

'I told you at the time something like this would happen. First, he killed Bailey, and now Marisa.'

'Alright, Truvan, we all know you'd like to be first in line when we catch him, but remember the Third Covenant. We must follow our system, otherwise there's no system and we'll be back to the Times of Malthus.'

'His audiopt feeds are off, he's clearly messing around with the infonetwork again. I don't think there can be any doubt about his motives or his criminality.' A couple of 'hear, hear' calls of support emanated from the group, but it wasn't unanimous or overwhelming. Most people just wanted to go home out of the cold.

'How are his feeds off?' another crowd member called.

'I don't know,' Lloyd Lloyd admitted.

'We're not safe without the audiopts. How will we catch him?'

Nobody actually knew how many people had died during the Times of Malthus. Some had been killed in global rioting that immediately followed the Bitness Revelations.

Famine – caused by the broken food supply chain – had done for the vast majority. Without water or power, Pestilence hadn't been left out; that horseman did his fair share too. By 2040, the universal implementation of the audiopt surveillance system brought peace. Bandits could then be detected on approach and repelled. Whilst the population no longer had personal memories of the Times, the audiopt surveillance system was held to be the all-powerful protector of peace and security.

The village Spokesperson replied, 'I'm sorry everyone. I don't know what's going on with the audiopts. Jack Smith hasn't had any feeds since we sent him away. He's got no armulet, and there are no masts on Steep Holm. I'll ask the sifters to look into the system and see what's going on. He shouldn't be able to avoid detection here in the village. Something's wrong.'

The surveillance system detected and recorded everything a person saw or heard by remotely intercepting the nerve signals between eyes and ears and the brain. This remote brain bugging was a built-in function of the ubiquitous armulet devices, but was also done by the infonetwork masts. The two detection routes worked in parallel and in concert, so that it was rare for a person to be outside the scope of the system. If you took off your armulet, and moved to a remote location away from others, and away from network masts, you might fall off the grid, and some people lived like that, but it required a solitary and remote lifestyle. In town, Jack Smith should not have been able to go undetected.

Lloyd Lloyd reminded the crowd, 'Most importantly, Marisa is still alive. Let's keep thinking positively for her, please.'

Truvan Truva turned and stomped off into a thin blizzard of snow that the wind swirled off the ground. His stubbly

THE MIND'S EYE

beard caught some flakes. They were held far enough from his skin that the snow did not melt but ended up giving him the appearance of a white facemask. The little blue backpack reminded Tony of Bailey, Truvan's twin brother. Their twin backpacks had been their trademark. Within ten metres, Truvan had vanished into the darkness.

Chapter Four
20th March 2091, 11pm
Truva family farmhouse, Highnam

Vicky Truva could not make Turkish coffee quite the way her mother had. She fiddled with the cezve, adjusting its position on the stove to avoid boiling the brew. Simultaneously, she passed her father a small glass of water, which he put down on the kitchen table. Marmaran watched her like a hawk, always ready to mutter about the coffee-making process. Every cup of coffee reminded him of Janet.

Since her mother's death, when Vicky was eight years old, she had tried to support her father just as Janet had done. Vicky undertook nearly all the cooking and cleaning in the Truva household. Her brothers had helped, and her father was too proud to allow people to simply wait on him. But the reality had been that the men did most of the farming and labouring work, whilst Vicky undertook more traditionally female roles. All the Truvas regularly stated that Vicky was free to do as she pleased. Nonetheless, the patriarchal culture that her grandfather had brought from Truva in the old Turkey had de facto continued.

She had been feeling under pressure from Truvan and her father regarding the continuation of the family line. Bailey had died childless. Truvan was gay and, although this did not preclude him having children, the implication from him was that it would be down to Vicky to continue the Truva family heritage. Vicky was not against this per se, but motherhood did not figure in her thinking much. She already had two Turkish boys to look after as best she could: Truvan and Marma gratefully took all the mothering she offered.

THE MIND'S EYE

Vicky handed her father a small cup of black coffee and put the cezve back on the stove. It was all Marma could do to maintain his cup safely on its saucer as Truvan charged in through the back door. The wind chased in with him like excitable dogs, until he slammed the door shut on it.

'He's done it again! Jack Smith has killed Marisa now.' He pointed accusingly at Vicky. 'I told you he's no good. I told you he's a murderer. Just the same as he did to my brother.'

Vicky's eyes bulged and Marma put a hand on his son's outstretched arm. 'What do you mean?' she asked in a mouse-quiet voice.

'I've just come from Kangaroo Hall. It's been burnt down, with Marisa Leone inside.'

Quickly and loudly, she said, 'Well, they've been redecorating in there, maybe it started by accident.' Vicky stared at her brother. Her face drained of colour and much more quietly she asked, 'Is Marisa really dead?'

Marmaran let go of his arm, and Truvan started to remove his wet coat. 'She's at the clinic. Doc says she's very bad. Doesn't expect her to live much longer.'

'Oh, no. I must go and help.' Vicky slid the coffee pot off the hot part of the stove surface and moved towards the door.

Truvan stepped in the way and hissed into her face, 'How welcome do you think you'll be there? You saved Smith from execution. He'd done exactly the same to Bailey.'

'Nobody was going to execute anyone.' She shook her head and looked away.

'You just refuse to see what an evil man he is.'

'Truvan, that's enough,' Their father took a step towards the pair, but holding his cup and saucer made it difficult to physically insert himself between them.

Truvan turned to Marma. 'No, father. She needs to open her eyes.' He looked back at his sister. 'You might as well have killed Marisa yourself.'

Her head bowed, and tears streamed down her face. Vicky's hand came up to cover her mouth, and she could not move.

'Truvan, enough!' He almost shouted. Marmaran pulled at his son's arm.

Truvan turned and bent to pick up the coat that he'd let drop. There was a small puddle of water at his feet and a smaller one dripping from Vicky's face. She pounded his bent back with her fists. 'Do you think I don't miss him too? Every day, I wish Bailey was here with us. I love him so much; I miss him all the time.' Truvan staggered slightly away from the raining blows and turned to face her. 'I saw what happened. It had nothing to do with Jack. It was an accident. The river caught the boat, and Bailey couldn't swim. I was there, I saw it.'

He stood up straight. 'Well, they saw Smith start the fire tonight, deliberately too. Tony and Asa were in there with Lloyd Lloyd, and they all saw him clearly. He threw a flaming torch into the Hall and ran off.'

Vicky's hand covered her mouth again. Her head shook very slowly. The only sound was her breath, catching on every inhalation. She pushed past him and ran up to her bedroom.

Sat on the bed, Vicky cried. She also thought of Jack every day. She missed him terribly too. Not as much as her brother, but it wasn't a contest. Her childhood crush on Jack, her pre-teen fantasies of settling down with him, and raising a family together on their own little farm, seemed like a distant bad dream. The most interesting man she had ever met was exiled, persona non grata in their own village, for his misguided attempt to revolutionise society. Vicky admired

THE MIND'S EYE

Jack's dedication to his purpose, but she was conflicted every day about Bailey's drowning whilst pursuing her and Jack on the run.

If Jack had escaped the island and returned to Highnam, surely, he would have contacted her. She could not believe that he could have done what Truvan said; that wasn't the Jack she knew.

Vicky lifted her left hand and engaged her armulet. She knew she should go and visit Marisa, but she also knew that Truvan was probably right. With nobody else to blame, her family would connect Vicky and Jack and, even if they did believe she was not involved, they would not welcome her presence. The audiopt feed from Doc showed she was not at Marisa's bedside. Vicky switched to Marisa's husband, Jonty, who was there, and, through his eyes, she could see that whilst Marisa was not conscious, she was still breathing.

The next thing then was to investigate what Truvan had relayed. She was relieved to find that there were still no feeds for Jack. Since his banishment, she had often searched for them but had never found any. She knew Steep Holm was too remote. On this occasion, though, the lack of any audiopt surveillance connection meant that Jack was still out of range. He could not have done what they said.

She projected an image of him and spoke to it as if he was there. 'Where are you, Jack? Why are they blaming you for this thing?' She paused as if to let him respond. 'I miss you.' Another pause. 'Will I ever see you again?' A finger tap on her armulet screen and Jack disappeared. Vicky continued to gaze at the space he had occupied.

A new thought came to her. She lifted the armulet arm again and asked it to show her Lloyd Lloyd's audiopt record for the evening. Truvan hadn't given any time details; she had to watch a fast replay of most of the afternoon before coming across the crucial period. She stared aghast: the fire starter was definitely Jack Smith. There was no question in her mind. His appearance, height, gait, everything was Jack. It was exactly the man she remembered, exactly the Jack from the image she had just spoken to.

She searched again for Jack's feeds, frantic. Still no record of him. Vicky knew enough about the technical functioning of the surveillance system to know that it was impossible for one person's feeds not to be recorded when they were so close to another whose were. The First Covenant of Jerusalem stated that 'Nothing will be hidden or secret,' so Jack's feed could not have been hidden or deleted. Vicky did not know if it was even possible to delete a portion of someone's audiopt record, regardless of the fact that it was not permitted to do so.

She watched the feeds that confirmed Tony and Asa had seen the same thing. Marisa had not seen Jack, but his cry of 'Vive la revolution!' she had heard clearly. When Lloyd Lloyd had shouted, she had turned, but any arsonist had already run away, and the rubbish piles were ablaze. By the time she climbed down, the whole room was full of smoke, and the flames made escape impossible. Both extinguishers failed on her. Vicky watched anxiously all the way through until Marisa lost consciousness on the floor.

For the hundredth time, she called up the audiopt feed from Major Halthrop the day that the Bristol Brigade had left Jack in the kitchen of the little cottage where they had been caught. She remembered the fight between Truvan and Jack that had occurred in the same room, days before these feeds from Halthrop. Her brother's enmity for him still festered.

Both the memory and the audiopt record showed Jack bewildered by the events around him. She again felt sorry for him. He appeared unable to comprehend why the world did

THE MIND'S EYE

not share his vision for an audiopt-free life. As Halthrop's eye-view turned away from Jack and walked back out past the well and the barn, tears again flowed down Vicky's cheeks. That was the last time he had registered an existence. She froze the feeds and stared up to the ceiling in her room.

How could Jack have come to Highnam, started the fire and run off, but recorded no feeds the whole time? Could he hack the surveillance system and hide himself? How could she find him?

When she and Jack were caught on Steep Holm, that had been because the Brigade had seen and followed their audiopt feeds to catch them in the cottage. The Brigade's own armulets must have provided the detection then, as Jack and Vicky had discarded theirs. Since his banishment, there had been nothing. She had checked Jack's feeds daily since he was abandoned there. He had no armulet, and the feeds had worked until about two hours after the Brigade had left him.

Jack's lack of an armulet was nagging at her mind. Vicky remembered the skeletons in the pub by the beach of Steep Holm. She had to do some research about the last inhabitants of the pub. It wasn't terribly difficult; it took her ten minutes or so to identify the couple that were the last to run the place, back in 2062. The records suggested they were probably the last people on the island until Jack and Vicky swam ashore in 2089.

Having identified them, Vicky watched the bloody argument that formed the last feeds of the husband. He was drunk and that infuriated his wife. They had screamed at each other for several minutes, he had hit her, she had grabbed a kitchen knife and stabbed him in the chest. The man's dying action had been to grab his wife's wrist to stop the stabbing. As he had lost blood and strength, he had collapsed on top of her on the kitchen floor. His eyes closed and the feed ended.

It was a horrible story, and Vicky was upset at the sights and sounds of the fight.

The audiopt feed record then pinged at her, asking if it should replay the next feed from October 2089. She stared at the insistent screen on her forearm. Her finger hovered over the play button, and she saw Jack's forearm as he shook it vigorously with the old armulet strapped on. It was unmistakably Jack's hand. Vicky was convinced she'd recognise even just his fingernail. She gawped at the projection in front of her. Jack never spoke, and she guessed he was evaluating the usefulness of the stuff the ill-fated couple had left behind. Cooking pots, cutlery, glasses: everything one might need to run a pub. After twenty minutes of that first appearance of Jack's undercover audiopt feed, she switched to the time of the fire.

The first instant she called up from that afternoon showed the swinging tip of a stick bash the skull of a seagull. The stick moved out of view, and the gull and its entire nest were picked up and carried away from a cliff. Again, the hands were obviously Jack's. She recognised the island's vegetation and topography even with the thin covering of snow everywhere.

Vicky checked and double-checked against Asa's record. At the same moment, Jack was cooking a gull on the little kitchen stove in the cottage on Steep Holm, whilst also being clearly seen in Kangaroo Hall only a few hundred yards from where she sat. It was not possible; the two places must be nearly a hundred kilometres apart.

In her mind, Vicky played Devil's advocate – what would Truvan say about the domestic scene on the island? The feed never showed Jack himself, just his hands, and occasionally a boot. The feed was officially attributed to a man called Andrew Gallian, whom she had watched be stabbed to death and would be very old if he still lived. These were tricky points. She knew Jack's hands; she had held them lightly and sometimes tightly. She remembered clutching Jack's fingers when her brother, Bailey, had been lost in the river.

The location finder for Andrew Gallian had him listed as being on Steep Holm continuously since October 2089; nowhere else, ever. No trips to Highnam, or anywhere else.

Downstairs, Vicky could hear her father and brother talking but their conversation was muffled through the floor. She could make out none of the actual words, but Truvan's voice occasionally ratcheted up in volume. She spoke aloud to a framed picture of her mother. 'Oh, Mama, I wish Truvan could come to terms with it. I know twins are always really close, but his fixation on Bailey's death has gone on too long. He needs to move on. I can't get him to listen, and I'm scared he'll do something really bad if Jack really has come back. I don't want to lose Truvan as well. Or Jack.' She felt a pang of conflicted guilt at the addition of Jack's name. Vicky stifled a sob at the vision of Truvan attacking Jack and then being sent away by Kangaroo as punishment for his violence. *If you're listening, Mama, do whatever you can to help him. Or tell me what to do.*

She wiped a tear from her cheek and packed a small backpack with warm clothes. In the kitchen, she filled all the remaining space in it with a bottle of water and any food she thought would survive the journey. Jack had not been visible, but his skeletal fingers gave away his malnourishment. As she headed to the stables in the dilapidated old barn, Vicky sent her brother and father links to the feeds she had just watched. With Juniper saddled, she set off towards Weston-super-Mare to find a boat. She guessed it would take about six hours to ride to Weston; in the dark and cold, maybe longer.

Chapter Five

21st March 2091, 8.20am
Briefing room, Bristol Brigade headquarters

Major Frank Halthrop rapped the edge of his plastic lectern. Darren let Terry out of a headlock, and they both sat up straight to look at their boss. Halthrop stroked his moustache without speaking and waited. His finger moved with the grain, so the hairs felt soft. He looked at his armulet: 08:22. Darren and Terry both looked at theirs, although Terry just glanced down whilst Darren raised his right up and peered at the screen. Terry's closed lips edged up into a slight smile at how idiotic Darren looked. Halthrop sighed and slid the small lumps of chalky rock along the lip of his lectern. He looked back out at his corporal and lance-corporal, just as Terry punched Darren in the upper arm.

Before Halthrop could complain, Jane burst in through the door, scooted down to the front of the mini lecture theatre and hurled herself into the seat next to Darren. 'Sorry, did I miss anything?'

'You mean apart from the oh eight hundred muster time?' Halthrop's tone was even and only barely indicated this as a question. It was rhetorical and caused a confused look on Jane's face. She opened her mouth to respond, but he cut her off, 'I hadn't started, as we were waiting for you. Again.' More quietly, he muttered, 'It's not enough that we do our best; sometimes we have to do what's required.' In his thoughts, Halthrop reminded himself, *Churchill could soothe frustration, frustrate seduction, and seduce the masses*.

To avoid any further delay, he stepped away from the lectern and waved an indicative arm towards a map drawn in chalk on the board behind him. 'You'll all remember Jack

THE MIND'S EYE

Smith, the Doughnut bomber we apprehended on Steep Holm island.' The map showed a crude outline of the River Severn with Steep Holm at the far left, their Bristol Brigade headquarters partway upriver on the south side, and then Highnam and Cheltenham marked at the right-hand side. 'It appears he has not learnt from his previous mistakes. This time, he has burnt down the Kangaroo Hall in Highnam. One woman is very seriously injured.'

'Are we going to get him?' Darren asked loudly. His beaming grin separated rounded, ruddy cheeks.

'All in good time. Remember, save your questions till the end, please.' Terry wagged a finger in Darren's face. Halthrop wondered if he remembered their ages correctly, or if they were actually children. All three of his soldiers were in their early to mid-twenties.

'Lloyd Lloyd, Highnam's Spokesperson, has asked us to catch Smith, but there is something of a complication with this. The audiopt feeds from three witnesses have him at the hall last night at 18:35. He is clearly seen setting the fire and running away.' With a wave towards his armulet, Halthrop played them thirty seconds of Lloyd Lloyd's audiopt feed. They watched intently, and Jane's mouth opened at the sight of Jack Smith hurling the flaming torches.

'Seems pretty straightforward to me,' Terry said. 'What's the problem?'

Halthrop held up both his palms towards the audience and moved them up and down slightly with each word. 'Questions. At. The. End.'

Darren wagged his finger at Terry who batted it away.

The officer continued, 'That's the crime clearly committed. So, we have cause to go and capture Smith. However, his audiopt feed is not transmitting, so we don't know where he is.' He looked at the three young members of his militia and saw a gathering of confused frowns, with the occasional glance to each other. They looked up at him silently.

The major stood right beside the hand-drawn map and tapped his fingernails on the wooden frame of the board. The staccato sounds rattled around the small room. 'OK, questions?'

Jane raised her arm, and Terry blurted out, 'How can that be? Has he sabotaged the masts around Highnam?'

'It's not clear, exactly. If he has managed to sabotage the system, it is only affecting his own feed. Everybody else in Highnam is being recorded normally.' He let the sound from his previous answer die away for a moment. 'Jane?'

She appeared to be still processing his last statement, but eventually asked, 'How is that possible?'

'As I said, nobody's really sure it even is possible. Which is quite a conundrum in itself. One of the infotechs at the Doughnut volunteered to look into it for Lloyd Lloyd. Chap by the name of...' Halthrop consulted his armulet. '...Dira. One of the infotechs for the neighbouring village of Newnham.' Jane raised her hand again. 'Yes, continue.'

'This was actually my first question.' She paused. 'If he has no feed, is his locator off too? And if so, how are we going to find him?'

'We caught him last time with the entire network down.' Halthrop smiled under his blond moustache. 'When he blew up the Doughnut servers, that buggered info, navigation, calling, and the audiopts: the whole works. This time, we're only missing the audiopts. And only Smith's feeds.'

'The most important bit for us,' Terry muttered quietly but audible to everyone.

Halthrop ignored the interruption and continued, 'So, a bit of that old-fashioned asking people and following where

THE MIND'S EYE

he's been is going to be needed again.' He paused to make sure the insubordination had finished. 'I'm glad you asked, though, as this brings me on to the plan and itinerary. Immediately after this briefing, we'll get the quad bikes ready. The original plan was to depart at oh eight thirty, so we'll now have to make that oh nine hundred. Head off in convoy up to Highnam and interview the three witnesses. I expect we may find something useful at his grandmother's house. Lloyd Lloyd tells me it's still unoccupied – he may well have used it as a base to hide out and launch his attack from. That will be our first stopping point, and we'll re-assess from there.'

Jane raised her hand again. Before Halthrop could give her the floor, Truvan Truva crashed through the door at the back corner of the room, bringing with him a smell of sweat and horses. The room had four rows of five chairs and an area at the front for a lecturer. It was not a large space, and briefings could be given in a regular speaking voice. Any interruption dominated the room. Truvan ran down the short aisle, blue backpack swinging wildly, and shouted all the way, 'He's done it again. Smith's abducted my sister. I'm coming with you to get him.'

Frank stepped down from the little dais and got Truvan to sit down at the first chair on the front row, leaving an empty chair gap to the other three soldiers. The group leaned in as Halthrop tried to calm him and find out what new element of Jack Smith's criminal life they would have to accommodate.

'He's got her under some sort of spell. She can't see him for what he is.'

'Please calm down, Mr Truva. What exactly has happened?'

Truvan explained how the argument at their farmhouse the night before had concluded with Vicky sneaking off and claiming that Jack had been on his exile island the whole time.

She was adamant he could not have committed the Kangaroo Hall arson and had left to find him and prove it.

He projected the feeds that Vicky had linked of somebody listed as Andrew Gallian on Steep Holm. Halthrop drew up a spare chair and quizzed Truvan about this other resident of the island. They all became more and more confused about these feeds that Vicky had sent.

Terry interrupted the conflicting conversations, 'Why don't we see where Vicky is? If she's gone to find him, we can follow her to him. Maybe they've arranged a meeting, so we might well catch him, even if he has hidden his own feeds somehow.'

Truvan pulled up Vicky's live audiopt feed and projected it between them all. The images showed hands on the steering wheel of a small boat. It was approaching the beach of Steep Holm with the abandoned pub and its tower and the adjacent pretty, albeit derelict, little house. The tide was nearly full, as the shingle crescent of the beach was almost completely covered with water. The waves splashed against the wall that protected the buildings, although their real protection was that they sat a few metres above the high tide level.

Behind the pub, a track hugged the very steep bank that formed the only side of the island that was not vertical cliffs. About halfway down the path, a figure stood looking down at the boat. Vicky lifted one hand slightly to wave. The swell and the waves were large enough that she had to hang on to the wheel tightly with the other hand. As she approached the landing, which was nothing more than a section of shingle that raised out of the water and a big metal ring set into the wall at the very left-hand end, Vicky pulled the motor lever back, so she was just drifting. Both her hands lifted in a manual shrug. They heard her shout, 'How do I land? Come and help me?'

THE MIND'S EYE

The figure had run down the rest of the track and jumped up on a table outside the little house to observe the boat and the tiny section of dry beach. It was clearly Jack Smith. He cowered slightly as a squall of wet wind gusted through.

'That's him,' shouted Darren. He jumped up and pointed straight at the video projection.

'OK, shut it off,' Halthrop instructed. When the image vanished, Darren was left standing like a statue whose context was only ever in the sculptor's mind. 'Sit down, Darren.

'Now, that is definitely Smith, and your sister going to meet him on Steep Holm. What time did you say she left?'

Truvan looked baffled. 'What does that matter? We know she's there and breaking the terms of his banishment. Let's go and get her before he gets her into more trouble. I'll take Vicky home, and you can catch Smith and take him back for trial.'

'I think you said 11pm, didn't you?'

Truvan squinted and nodded. 'Yes, but…'

Halthrop interrupted, 'She's just arriving, and he's already there, and she left, what, about three hours after the fire? So, it is easily possible that he could have committed the arson and then headed back to the island. With his feeds hidden, however that happened, he could claim he was on the island the whole time.'

'We know he set the fire. Here, let me show you the feeds of it. Lloyd Lloyd clearly sees Smith.'

'Thank you, we've just seen those feeds.'

'Then what's the holdup? Let's go!'

Major Halthrop looked at his militia, the three of them, and they looked back expectantly. 'Agreed.' He stood up and stepped back away from the group to address them. A slight touch of his moustache gave a pause before speaking. 'Change of plan and itinerary: we'll decamp from here in the next five minutes and take the same convoy as previously detailed. Firstly, though, we head south to Weston-super-Mare, where we will get a boat and head to Steep Holm to apprehend Smith.

'Jane: you are responsible for monitoring Vicky Truva's audiopt feeds to keep track of him. If they leave the island, we need to chase appropriately, so report to me every five minutes.'

'Yes, sir.'

'Mr Truva, we worked together previously, and you did not operate usefully with us. Indeed, despite your assurances, all you did was attempt to harm our prisoner. I cannot have that. I suggest you head home, and we will bring your sister back with us as well.'

Truvan shook his head. 'Not going to happen. I hate Smith, but I won't get in the way. You get him, I'll get Vicky. But whatever you say, I'm coming along.'

Halthrop had anticipated this response. 'Darren, you are responsible for ensuring Mr Truva keeps his word. By force as necessary, and forcibly leaving him behind at any stage if that's necessary.'

'Yes, sir.' Darren saluted. Halthrop blinked at this.

'What should I do?' Terry asked.

'Navigation. You were pretty good handling the boat around the islands last time.'

Terry nodded.

THE MIND'S EYE

Chapter Six

Earlier that morning – 21st March 2091, 8am
Steep Holm island

Jack woke in the kitchen chair by the stove. He shivered at the cold and looked in to see that the fire was out. He had enough dried brush in the barn to be able to light it again relatively easily, assuming the sun would come out at some point and he could use the lens. He worried that the wintry weather would mean that even a cloud-free sun would be too weak to ignite the kindling. However, all remaining wood was down by the smokehouse in the tower next to the pub. That would be a cold journey in the early morning.

He recognised a whistling sound: it was the wind as it blew through a small gap between the window frame and the glass. The gust whipped up snow and dust in the barnyard outside the window. The sky was brighter than the previous day, but still overcast.

Having roasted the gull and saved half of it along with the other two eggs from the nest, Jack no longer had the constant gnawing in his stomach. That remaining food would probably only last one day – careful rationing was always easier in the planning than the execution. He pictured waking up cold the next morning with nothing but water to sustain him. He had even finished the last of his elderflower drink, but, having had a decent sleep and a good meal, he had enough energy for this day.

In recent weeks, he had been moving slowly and stopping for frequent rests. The demons of solitude would undermine his confidence about being able to survive. Whether it was fear of hypothermia or the cramps in his stomach, the rest periods were seldom actually restful.

Jack unwrapped the blanket, stood up, and replaced it with his coat. A bracing morning walk to collect the wood would give him a chance to revel in the anticipation of an egg for breakfast. He chased away the idea that he might have to eat it raw. A positive mindset was the target he set for this journey.

To engender this, he took out his prized possession. He had found the combat knife at the bottom of one of the duffel bags that Major Halthrop had left him. A heavy plastic handle balanced perfectly with the blade, nearly six inches long and with large serrations on the spine. The metal was top quality and must have been forged before the Times of Malthus. It had come with a small sharpening stone and Jack had found it worked to cut just about anything, as long as he kept it sharp.

Shaving always put him in a good mood and would have been difficult, if not impossible, without the knife. Jack had no mirrors but checked the shave was complete with his fingertips, gently caressing his drawn cheeks and neck. He rinsed off the blade, dried it carefully and returned the beloved knife to its sheath and then into his coat pocket. A final splash of his face, and he smiled to the world outside his kitchen window.

Jack wondered briefly about the possibility of surviving the day on one egg, then banished this thought with a plan to go and catch some more gulls. As he strolled along the plateau top of Steep Holm, he even considered trying to get his makeshift fishing net back into action.

He stopped about halfway down the path and surveyed the beach, wondering whether his lack of real fishing success had simply come from casting the net from a poor location, or at the wrong tide. He had always tried casting it from the wall surrounding the little house in the middle of the beach at high tide, when the water was right up to the wall. It was easy that

THE MIND'S EYE

way, although he rarely caught a fish and never more than one. He didn't really like getting wet, so wasn't keen on the idea of wandering in the shallows with the net, especially with the March water temperature of about eight degrees celsius.

As he looked around the seawater, from the high tide lapping the walls protecting the buildings, and then further out, a dark spot a few hundred yards away became steadily larger and boat-shaped. He watched as it clearly plotted a course straight for him. Even in the grey morning light, bright reflections off the solar cells on the small boat's upper surfaces were unmissable.

Jack fretted about the arrival of visitors. Nobody had landed in the eighteen months since he had been banished to the island, and he wasn't sure about people coming to visit him. Highnam's Kangaroo had not made clear any of the details of the rules of his exile. They probably hadn't even thought about them; he was the first person ever to be given that punishment by Highnam. On that basis, Jack reasoned, he couldn't get into any trouble by receiving guests. He figured it would be a fishing boat out of Weston; the crew most likely wasn't even aware he lived on Steep Holm. Jack often saw boats passing one way or another, but they never came this close, nor on a direct course for the landing beach.

The boat had come close enough for him to make out one person at the wheel. They waved at him. He wondered if he was easy to spot against the cliffside and looked around at the vegetation. He walked down the path, trying to get a better look at his visitor. As she got within fifty yards, he stopped. Jack peered from a slightly hidden vantage point between the house and the little tower. Could it really be Vicky? He thought that she would surely get into trouble for visiting, but his heartbeat felt like it would pop his coat buttons open, and he couldn't help smiling.

He ran around to the front of the house, and she shouted at him something about trying to land. Jack jumped up onto a wooden table behind the sea wall and looked about for how she could moor the little motorboat. There was only one big metal ring on the seawall, perfect for tying up, but the wind was gusting, and he expected the boat might keep banging into the wall.

'Have you got an anchor?' he shouted over the wind and wave noise. Vicky shrugged and looked around. She was drifting, waiting for them to work out what to do. He pointed. 'You could speed onto the dry bit there, the water never gets up that high.' She manoeuvred back and forth a little, lining up a run onto the exposed shingle. 'Wait!' She looked over and froze theatrically. They both grinned. Jack continued, 'The tide's as high as it ever gets. If you ground the boat now, we may never refloat her. Tie the front to that hook, and I'll tie the other end to this table. Should be heavy enough for that little boat. Are there two ropes?'

As she pushed forward, the boat grounded a little anyway. None of the prow was high and dry, but she seemed stuck fast. Vicky threw Jack the dockline and almost danced to the front of the boat to tie off. He invented some knot to tie to the table, and she leapt onto the patio area to meet and hug him for the first time in nearly two years.

Vicky's armulet started ringing with a video call coming from Truvan. She dismissed it and looked at Jack. She made a show of sizing him up. 'I looked at your feeds yesterday – you seemed frozen and struggling.'

His eyes widened and his body tensed. 'You found my feeds?'

She nodded with another little smile. 'Remember, I've been here before. Including in the pub kitchen with the skeletons.'

THE MIND'S EYE

Jack visibly relaxed and took her hand. She looked down at the hand-holding and then up to his face.

'Come. Help me carry some wood up to the cottage and I'll cook you some breakfast.'

'Seagull?'

He turned quickly, paused and smiled. 'I was thinking just eggs, but I'll make whatever you want.'

'Bacon sandwich?'

'OK, whatever you want out of eggs or seagull.'

Via the tower smokehouse wood store, they headed up to the little cottage kitchen. Jack looked out of the window, hoping for sunshine.

'Hmm, this may not be as easy as I'd hoped. I need the sun in order to restart the fire.'

She rummaged in her brown knapsack and produced a flint and steel on a little orange lanyard. Jack knelt to get the fire going, while Vicky sat in an armchair and watched. After a minute, she shuddered and reached out to touch Jack's back. He turned, continuing to waft the dried bramble kindling, which smoked without flame. The smoke smelt dry and homely.

'Jack, they think you burnt down Kangaroo Hall.'

He stopped fanning the fire and twisted round. 'What?'

'Kangaroo Hall. It burnt down last night. Marisa Leone is very badly hurt, and she might die.'

'Well I didn't do it. Why would they think it's me? Why don't they look on Marisa's feeds to see what happened?'

'Jack, you did do it.'

He stared at her.

She continued, 'I mean, I can't understand what's going on, 'cause you're here. And I saw your feeds from yesterday, so you couldn't have been in Highnam. But you were in Highnam – I've seen the feeds that show you were there.'

Jack swivelled completely round on his knees. 'Do you think I would hurt Marisa? Or anyone?' He fell back to sitting on the floor.

'I mean, I know you didn't, I saw your feeds here. But you did do it. The feeds from Asa and Tony and Lloyd Lloyd all show you clearly there and throwing the flame in.'

'What do you mean? I've never left here. How can they have seen me there?'

Vicky started to cry. 'I don't know, Jack. You're here and you're there. At the same time. I can't explain it, but it's definitely you.'

He silently lifted his hand up onto hers but made no other movement. Jack looked aside to the hearth. He felt her kneel beside him and put her arms awkwardly around his neck. He turned his head, so they were nose to nose, eye to eye. 'I didn't do that.'

Breakfast was forgotten and, as they sat in front of the smoking kindling, Vicky showed Jack the four sets of feeds, three from Highnam, plus the phantom Andrew Gallian's from Steep Holm, all from the same time. Twice more, she dismissed calls coming in from Truvan. They sat side by side on the cold stone floor. After they'd watched the last one, Vicky started to speak again, 'The trouble with that last one is that whilst I recognise your hands in the view, there's…'

He interrupted, 'It doesn't clearly show it's me.'

'No.' They sat in silence for another minute. 'And if they use my feeds as evidence, the fire was more than twelve hours ago – you could have made it back here before me. But how could it be you? How could you appear on their feeds if you weren't there? Could it be some sort of mass hallucination?'

Jack shook his head. 'I don't know, but that doesn't sound very likely. Or very believable for the folks at

THE MIND'S EYE

Kangaroo. "It wasn't me; they just imagined it was me." That's not going to be believed by that lot. I wouldn't believe it.'

The window whistled, and they both looked up sharply.

'How about hypnosis? Could somebody have made them imagine they saw you?'

Jack considered this. He first wondered who might want to frame him in such a way, before realising, 'Ah no, that's not how the audiopt surveillance works. It intercepts the radio waves produced by the tiny electrical currents in the optic and auditory nerves, so it can't produce an image like that unless their eyes actually detect light reflected from my body. But that's not possible either, because I wasn't there.' He was silent for a minute. 'Which also rules out hallucinations as an answer too. I have no idea what's happened.'

The stove fire rather unexpectedly took hold of a damp log. To take some time and think it through a bit more, Jack made Vicky a banquet of a breakfast. She was starving after her overnight journey and pulled bread and cheese from her backpack. Jack himself could not eat much, as he'd starved for so long that his body couldn't cope with too great a quantity.

Whilst he nurtured the fire and cooked up gull meat and eggs, they discussed what they should, or could, do to prove Jack's innocence. The way Vicky approached this made Jack confident that she thought he was indeed innocent. He smiled to himself with his back to her.

They agreed that, with the strong evidence of the audiopt feeds from the three witnesses to the fire, the only way anything would change people's minds would be for Jack to actually appear, to defend himself and answer questions. The fact that this would be in contravention of his banishment order would complicate things. In the end, they decided it was the only way.

Jack was also hoping he might be able to work out what had actually happened and be able to prove his innocence, rather than just argue about it and hope he could win over the Kangaroo court. Solving it was not possible stuck on Steep Holm.

'In any case, we've eaten the last of the food.' Jack confirmed that their decision must be to take the boat and head to Highnam.

'They're gonna catch you as soon as you get back in range of the infonetwork. Probably before you've even left Weston.'

'Well, let's make it so they have to actually come and catch us, then. Let's take the boat all the way up the river. It's probably a bit slower than the road, but it also means we don't need to find bikes or horses.'

'My horse is there already,' Vicky initially argued, then immediately backed down. 'She'll be OK, I guess. We'll need to bring the boat back eventually, so I'll pick up Juniper then.'

'OK, good. Actually, they'll be able to find us right now with your armulet. If you leave it here that'd give us a little bit of a head start. I'd really like to try and work out what's going on before Halthrop takes me out of circulation. I doubt I'll be able to find out anything more after that. I'm assuming it's the Bristol Brigade they've sent, is it?'

'It is. And bloody Truvan's with them again. He thinks I can't make decisions by myself. Idiot. For all he knows, I could be here to take you in myself. There'll be quite a bounty for you this time, I expect.'

'I doubt it could be more than last time,' Jack retorted with a snigger. Vicky's face fell, and Jack stifled his mirth. He guessed that she connected his previous time on the lam with the death of Bailey. Not his fault, but he could see why she

THE MIND'S EYE

wouldn't find it funny. He squeezed her hand to try and show some sympathy.

Vicky changed the subject. 'I can't leave my armulet behind. We'll need one.'

'You forget that I have one. And an incognito one at that. I'd be very surprised if anyone else could do the same research as you did to find it. You only guessed I had it because you'd actually seen it. Most people would imagine this island as utterly devoid of any technology.'

She was troubled but unbuckled the leather strap and laid it on the kitchen table. The smartphones of the early 21st Century had rapidly been replaced by a wrist-worn device, once the need to touch and look at it had been largely removed. The Armulet brand had launched in 2026, with the ability to accept both voice and gesture commands, as well as holographic projection of the screen. They had been so universally successful that the brand name became equivalent to the object itself, and no competitors survived. With ubiquity, the price tumbled, and they became a leveller across the world.

'There's plenty of them in Cheltenham – we can pick you up a new one, no problem. Probably some in Gloucester too, I just don't know the place so well.' He paused. 'In fact, I wonder where Grannie Ellie's went to. That should be in the house somewhere.'

Jack pictured the interior of his grandmother's farmhouse on the edge of Highnam, but he couldn't remember seeing her armulet. He shook his head and berated himself for having run back to his sifter work at the Doughnut so quickly after her funeral. Nobody would have questioned if he had asked to spend a week, or a month, sorting her things out. The other local sifters would have covered for him. Aluen on the floor below could probably have done her job and his without trouble.

'The tide's going to be against us some of the way. If we leave now, we may get to the bridges, or possibly further, before it really runs back. I expect we'll have to tie up during the fastest ebb. Three hours probably. We should get all that back again when it returns and drives us forwards. I don't really know, but I'd guess it's maybe twelve hours to Highnam by boat?'

Jack nodded and grabbed a meagre handful of clothes to bring along. He stuffed them into one of the green duffel bags Major Halthrop had provided when he left Jack there. Vicky filled a water bottle and handed it to him for the bag. As they made for the kitchen door out to the barnyard, there was a moment of embarrassed confusion as they both went for the doorway at the same time and collided. Vicky took Jack's hand and surprised him with a kiss on the cheek. Before he had time to process how to react, she leapt for the exit, pulling him behind.

As he made to close the door, her armulet sounded from the table. Its bleep resonated in the old wood. She stepped back inside and looked down without touching it. There was a message from Truvan. She intended to turn away and continue outside, but her eyes could not miss the first few words. It told her that Jack had attacked the Highnam Spokesperson, and there was a link to Lloyd Lloyd's feeds from back in the village that morning.

She grabbed it up and played the feeds, again showing him. They watched in silence. As clear as looking at Jack there in the cottage, the man's audiopt view showed him attack Lloyd Lloyd on Lassington Lane in Highnam. The timestamp said half an hour earlier. She scrolled the player backwards, and they watched a second time.

THE MIND'S EYE

'Oh shit, I do hope he's all right.' Vicky had stopped the replay at a moment when Lloyd Lloyd looked down and saw his own blood mixing with the mud on the ground. She raised a finger and started twirling the hair that fell down by her right temple. She stared at Jack, wide-eyed and bewildered. A tear ran down each of Vicky's cheeks.

He took the armulet from her hands, laid it back on the table and led her outside. 'Something is definitely wrong. At least for this one I've got you as a witness that I was here all the time. Who the hell is doing this to me? Does Truvan have computer skills?'

'Wait!' She pulled her hand out from his and stopped. 'You can't think he would do those things. He's mad at you about Bailey, but he's mad at you, not Lloyd Lloyd or Marisa.'

'Somebody is doing this, and it isn't me. But it looks like me. So, somebody must be disguising themselves as me. Who would want to make the world mad at me? I can only think of Truvan.'

'Stop! Stop!' Vicky put her hands on either side of her head, willing the world as a whole to stop. She couldn't reconcile the conflicting emotions. He was right that she could think of nobody else who hated Jack enough to commit such horrible crimes in his name, but she refused to believe that her own brother would do such things. In the end, Vicky deflected, 'That's not a disguise, Jack, that's actually you.'

He took a step towards her but faltered. 'You know that isn't me. You were here with me right then. All this morning.' They stared at each other. 'Look, we don't know what's gone on, and we won't work it out here. All we can do for now is go back and try to find out some answers where it's all happening.' Jack turned and headed off across the yard.

He was nearly out of sight before Vicky chased to catch up.

Chapter Seven
21st March 2091, 9.30am
Highnam village

Marmaran Truva was walking towards Kangaroo Hall. Ahead, he could see Lloyd Lloyd muttering to himself in the grey morning light, as he walked back from the clinic, also towards the Hall. They would intercept in about fifty metres. Marma had an urge to tease their Spokesperson about never being able to stop talking even when he was alone. He listened in on his audiopt feeds and changed his mind, when he realised that the village's head man was cursing himself for the injuries to Marisa Leone.

Highnam needed to organise a working party to plan the repair, or potentially rebuilding, of Kangaroo Hall. Marma was on his way to this meeting, and so he decided he would engage Lloyd Lloyd in conversation about that instead. He was about to call and wave when he saw a man step from a gap in the hedge in front of Lloyd Lloyd.

The man's body language was obviously aggressive. Marmaran stopped and hesitated for a moment. The man leant forward and punched Lloyd Lloyd in the face, and he fell to the ground. Marma started to run forwards, and it became clear that the assailant was Jack Smith. He shouted at them, but Smith didn't look up from concentrating on his prone victim.

He proceeded to kick Lloyd Lloyd several times on the floor, before running away, back through the gap in the hedge and out of sight. Marmaran went a few steps past Lloyd Lloyd to try and see where Smith was heading. The man was not visible in the vista through the gap in the hedge. Marma rushed through and looked all around the open field. It was completely empty.

THE MIND'S EYE

There were two gates in the hedges on two sides across the big grass space, but they were further away than anyone could run in the seconds it had taken Marmaran to arrive. He crouched suddenly and looked left and right to see if Smith was hiding in the hedge close by. He couldn't make out anyone anywhere, so he moved out into the field a few yards to scan further up and down the vegetation all around the boundary. Still no sight of the man. 'What the hell?' he murmured. Marma did a full 360° turn and could see only empty field.

He frowned and returned to Lloyd Lloyd. The Spokesperson was groaning and pushing his hands on the ground. 'Take it easy. Don't try and get up.' At the sound of his voice, Lloyd Lloyd flinched and put his arms around his head. The older man squatted down. 'It's OK, it's me, Marma Truva.' He put his hand on a shoulder. Lloyd Lloyd initially flinched again, but then looked up through his protective arms. He sat up and spat some blood onto the muddy lane. 'What was that about?'

Lloyd Lloyd looked up. One eye was puffed up already, and there was blood seeping from the corner of his mouth. 'He said to me, "This is for ruining my life." That's it. Ruining his life? I'd say he'd done a good enough job of that himself.'

Marmaran squeezed the shoulder gently. 'Well, you represent everyone at Kangaroo that sent him away. If he blames anyone for that, you'd be the focus for his rage, I'm sure.' They were both silent for a while.

Lloyd Lloyd wiped away more blood and winced as he did so. 'Where did he go? We need to get people out to catch him.'

'He just seemed to vanish. I was into that field five seconds behind him, and I couldn't see him anywhere. But there's nowhere to escape to from that field. It was like he disappeared into thin air.'

'Just like last night.'

'It was dark last night, it's not surprising he got away. But here, there's nowhere he could have hidden. I don't know how he did it.'

'Call some people. Get them out here. We'll find him.'

Marmaran patted the Spokesperson's shoulder lightly and called the group they were supposed to be meeting. Whilst Marma was straightforward about what had happened and calm in suggesting they leave the Hall to start a search, Lloyd Lloyd raged in the background. He cursed Smith and urged them to hurry.

Marmaran agreed but qualified it by telling them to be careful. 'He was totally focussed on hurting Lloyd Lloyd. Make sure you stay together, in pairs at least.'

'And call others – get the whole village out after him.' Lloyd Lloyd's booming voice had returned.

Marmaran disconnected the call and stared at his friend. 'I wonder if he meant to catch you in the fire last night.' Neither man spoke for a minute.

Lloyd Lloyd shook his head slowly. 'Poor Marisa.'

'How is she?'

'Not good. She's still never been conscious.'

Big Bearded Bill and George Kendrick came running down Lassington Lane and stopped by the other two. They helped Lloyd Lloyd to his feet and insisted that he had to go to the clinic.

Marma volunteered to go to Kangaroo Hall and explain to the others what had happened, and Lloyd Lloyd instructed them that Tony should run the search. Tony was one of the most senior men in the village, mainly through dint of having lived there his whole life, being aged, and also still very active and alert.

On his way, Marmaran watched the audiopt feeds that the infonetwork had recorded from Lloyd Lloyd. The fight was exactly as he had watched, and he had been right: it was definitely Jack Smith.

He called his son to find out when the Bristol Brigade was going to arrive at Highnam to catch Smith. Truvan explained that they were on their way to get a boat from Weston to catch Jack on Steep Holm island.

'He's here in Highnam right now. This happened ten minutes ago. Tell them they've missed him there and need to get here right away.' Marmaran paused the call to search for Jack's exact location. There were no feeds from him whatsoever. He scowled at his armulet and returned to the video call. 'But his feeds are off somehow. I don't know if he's managed to hide them or block them or something. Everybody else's are on though, so he hasn't sabotaged the whole infonetwork like last time.'

'Dad, look at Vicky's feeds right now. She's on Steep Holm and she's looking right at him. Have a look. We're gonna catch him. I reckon we'll be on the island by lunchtime. We're about to leave for Weston now. I'll tell Major Halthrop about the attack, but if you can't find his feeds anywhere in Highnam now, then we're still following the best course. Even if he's messed with his feeds somehow, we'll still find Vicky.'

The gusting and cold wind bustled Marmaran along. He cut the call. *How can Jack be on Steep Holm? I just saw him here.* He was confused at Truvan's claim. One of them must have made a mistake, but he was sure he was right. He'd even watched Lloyd Lloyd's feeds again to double check. His daughter's viewpoint did indeed show her walking a path following what, from the back, looked like Smith. Marmaran didn't recognise the location, but Vicky's armulet locator claimed to be on Steep Holm island. Again, Truva senior muttered to himself, 'What the hell?'.

Inside Kangaroo Hall, Tony and Asa were already co-ordinating the search, each on live calls to several other villagers. They also watched the attack from Lloyd Lloyd's point of view and searched, without result, for any feeds from Jack Smith. Tony was troubled, more about the man than his apparent magical disappearance. 'This is not his way.'

Asa replied with a query: 'Look again at this altercation. That does look exactly like Jack Smith, doesn't it?'

'Yes. That's exactly as I remember him.'

'Yes.' They both stared at the frozen face hovering in front of Asa's armulet screen. 'Exactly as I remember he looked too. And we haven't seen him in eighteen months.'

After two hours, the entire village had been searched, with people reporting in from every street and smallholding. The original working party had returned to Kangaroo Hall and Tony suggested they all get a cup of coffee and take a seat around the only table that had survived the fire. Marmaran wasn't keen on the idea of a coffee. The small café kitchenette didn't have the equipment to make proper Turkish coffee and the alternatives were uninspiring at best. At worst, he would have to drink tea instead. Neither coffee nor tea grew well in England, despite the changing climate, and even in the hothouses locally built for cultivating them. The drink quality was always poor, but society's rituals remained. The five men and one woman took turns mixing up brown brews of one sort or another and sat round the table, mulling over how lovely Ellie's grandson could have turned out so bad.

Ellie Smith had been a long-time stalwart resident of Highnam. She was a generation ahead of Tony and Marmaran and had died nearly three years earlier. Her vitality and zest

THE MIND'S EYE

had meant that, when she died, most people in the Kangaroo could not believe that she had actually reached eighty-eight years old. Marma had assumed she was only slightly older than himself. This confusion was probably added to by the fact that she had raised Jack as her own son, after her daughter died in childbirth.

He wondered at how Ellie had never seemed to grieve Clara's death. Vicky and her brother had helped Marma through the grief when Truvan's twin, Bailey, had died. His children had been the one thing that kept him going when his wife, Janet, had been taken from him in a blizzard. There had been nobody else in the house to support Ellie. Marmaran felt a twinge of guilt. The raising of a new-born baby might have been all-consuming enough to distract Ellie from the darker places, but could he have done more to help?

He knew that Truvan continually struggled to contain the anger inside him. His fiery temper had gained even more of a hair trigger, and Marma could see his son hurting every day. He worried that this new trouble with Smith could be dangerous for Truvan. Marmaran checked his armulet to see where his son was: still close to the Bristol Brigade headquarters. Hopefully, Major Halthrop would be able to keep him from doing anything stupid.

Tony waved an arm around the table and then around the room. The whole place remained damp from the firehoses. Everywhere was a mess of broken walls and windows, with burnt debris scattered around. He tried to bring the group back to the work on the building and gardens. 'Lloyd Lloyd is getting treatment, and Jack seems to have disappeared. The brigade is out searching for him. I don't think we can do any more towards that ourselves. I suggest we get back on to the jobs we need to do here.' Marmaran focussed. The chatter silenced, and Tony continued, 'I'm assuming we'll just have to take the whole refurbishment back to square one. Rebuild first, and then go through the whole programme again.'

Asa nodded. 'I'd like to think we could redo Marisa's mural as she'd planned it. Partly because it was very nice, but also as a kind of tribute.'

Marma interjected, 'I hope she'll redo it for us.'

'Yes, yes, of course. I'm not sure she'll be up to the task for a fair while, though. But I dare say we can simply leave the wall as is until she's ready to work on it again.'

Big Bearded Bill waded in with his baritone. 'Let's not assume too much for her. She may come through this and never want to set foot in here again. Bad memories and so on.'

Everybody nodded and remained silent for a moment.

Tony began again. 'Right, well how about we work on the rebuilding? Making sure the place is safe, cleaning up and so on, and work out the refurbishment plan later.'

Again, there were nods. Waving up at the mural wall over their heads, Mali said, 'I think we should repaint this wall. That way Marisa has a clean blank canvas to repaint onto.'

George Kendrick added, 'Also, it won't immediately remind her of the fire. Fingers crossed at least.'

'Oh, I know Marisa. She don't raise her petticoat after peein'.'

Marmaran had never been able to place Mali's accent exactly, but, at this, he settled on Welsh as a best guess. She was the blackest-skinned person he had ever seen, with the most wondrously lilting voice. Marma wondered if the incomprehensible language she spoke with her husband was Welsh. He concurred with Mali's point of view: Marisa was a tough woman. He expected that she would not be cowed by any traumatic experience, even such a near-death one as the fire. Ever since the Times of Malthus, people had become significantly more pragmatic than previously. The cycle of life was embraced, and people got over things and got on with life with little fuss. Marmaran worried about Truvan again. He didn't seem to be managing to move on from losing Bailey.

Bill said, 'Why are we discussing this now? We need to catch Smith before he hurts anyone else.'

There were murmurs of assent and Tony attempted to pacify the group and remind them that they had just searched the whole village. Whilst they discussed it again, Marma looked to his armulet screen to see what Vicky was looking at. Her audiopt feed had gone blank, but her armulet locator still placed her on Steep Holm. Marmaran frowned. How could his daughter's feed be off? She wouldn't be asleep at ten in the morning.

He tuned back in to the conversation as Tony said, 'Well, the fact is he got away. His audiopt feeds are not on, so how would we find him, even if we choose not to wait for the Brigade?'

Marmaran said, 'He was on Steep Holm earlier. Vicky was there, and I saw her feeds looking at him. I don't know how he got here so quickly, but I'd guess he's headed back there.'

George asked, 'Vicky's with him? I thought he was supposed to be in exile?'

Marma was glad that George was so delicate with this question. Vicky definitely had broken the terms of Smith's banishment, and he doubted that the Kangaroo as a whole would be too happy about that. He decided honesty would have to be the best policy. 'Yes, I'm not sure why she went there. Maybe to accost him about the fire. She's totally against violence, and I think she thought he was too.'

'He is.' Asa muttered it, but everyone heard.

'I think there's a bigger problem. I don't know why exactly, but her feeds are off at the moment, and his have been off all the time. There's nothing from him since we sent him away. But he's been here twice now, setting the fire and assaulting Lloyd Lloyd. But everyone else's feeds are running as normal. So, somehow, he's managed to mess up the system so we can't track him, and now he's done the same with Vicky's feeds too.'

The group mulled this over for a minute. Marmaran decided not to mention the link to Andrew Gallian's feeds that Vicky had sent him. She claimed they actually belonged to Jack, but Marmaran couldn't tell why she thought so. They hadn't seemed to show anything useful, and were no longer on.

Mali asked, to nobody in particular, 'Isn't Steep Holm past Cardiff? How long does it take to get there?'

There were some shrugs, but Tony answered, 'Yes, it's a long way. I'd say a day's travel, probably. Including maybe an hour on the river.'

Asa shook his head and commented, 'It's like he was in two places at once.'

Bill said, 'Well, he won't be there anymore. If he can change the audiopt feeds, then there's no reason for him to stay there. He's probably been hiding out round here somewhere for more than a year.'

The group again paused to consider this new concept.

George was first to speak again. 'Well, if he can change the feeds, we've got a real problem. I mean, how long has he been doing that? Was he changing things before, when he was a sifter? Were his KangaReviews actually true?'

The idea dumbfounded them. Marma could see the cogs in their heads working through how much of their world had

THE MIND'S EYE

been fake all these years. But nobody actually knew if this was even possible.

It did not pass Marmaran by, though, that he had been standing next to George Kendrick, at Kangaroo, when George and Marisa had been shown to have had an adulterous affair. That had been in Jack Smith's last KangaReview before he'd blown up the Doughnut. The two had accepted their punishments, served them, and the community had moved on. Forgiven, and mostly forgotten. Marma did not comment on the coincidence of George raising this point.

Tony tried to bring the conversation to a conclusion. 'OK, I think the computer work required on this is beyond the likes of us, so we'll have to get the sifters to investigate what Jack may or may not have done to the audiopt records. For now, we can't really think about chasing him, as he's vanished, feeds and all. So, we should get on with what we can do here.'

Marmaran offered, 'My son is with the Bristol Brigade looking for Smith, so I'll give you any updates as he lets me know.'

Mali agreed, 'Good to hear that there's a posse on the needles. Let's get cleaning up, shall we?'

Chapter Eight
21st March 2091, 10am
Bristol Brigade HQ

The Bristol Brigade trundled their bikes up the steep concrete drive at the front of their HQ building onto the road. Darren and Terry both had quad bikes; the rest were on two wheels. All were electric. Truvan Truva tagged along, second in the group, beside Major Halthrop. The road was damp, and the air smelt of wet mud.

The Brigade was one of the few groups left that wore anything approaching a uniform. Most other remnant militia groups had given up on uniforms over the decades since the Times of Malthus. Halthrop considered it one of the few ways he had of shoring up his troops against the casualness inherent in 2091's society. He wasn't against an informal approach to life, per se, but he needed to run an efficient unit.

The three younger soldiers wore black boots, black trousers and camouflage-pattern jackets over green shirts. When necessary, they also had camouflage-pattern caps to protect against the sunshine. When riding the quad bikes, it was generally too windy for a hat. Halthrop had been very pleased to find a treasure trove of military equipment stored in a warehouse by Cardiff's old airport since before the Times. This had supplied the green and brown camouflaged backpacks that Darren and Jane also carried. Camouflage was not of much use with the audiopt system in place, but he felt that it instilled a military mindset.

As one or two of them mounted up, Truvan took a call from his father. The major could plainly see and hear the discussion. He could even see Marmaran's face on the armulet screen most of the time. The news disturbed him. Marma

THE MIND'S EYE

explained all about the assault on Lloyd Lloyd and insisted that the Brigade should go to Highnam immediately. With the information that Smith had again disappeared, Halthrop was sceptical. He looked up Vicky Truva's feeds and played the video projection in front of Truvan. His father would be unable to see, but the posse could all see Jack Smith clearly. They were on the island, and she was following him along the path from the cottage towards the big barn with the water storage tank. Halthrop remembered it well, despite his two times there being only very brief.

Jack Smith still had no feeds to see. Halthrop was irked. He could see Jack's face through Vicky's eyes, so his feeds should be recorded too. He mused that Jack must have manipulated the computer system somehow. This irked him further, as he had researched the whole surveillance and infonetwork system extensively as part of his own Brigade training and knew this should be impossible. The system was supposedly impregnable. That had been the point, when it had been rolled out globally to support the signing of the Covenants of Jerusalem in 2040.

As they knew where Smith was, Halthrop instructed Truvan to tell his father they were going to Steep Holm and would apprehend him there. When they returned him to Highnam, Kangaroo could investigate what had gone on with the assault on Lloyd Lloyd.

The posse had travelled a little over three kilometres when Dira videocalled Major Halthrop from the Doughnut. 'Sir, I've managed to track down Jack Smith. He's at his grandmother's old house in Highnam.'

Halthrop scowled. 'Are you sure? How did you locate him?'

'He is definitely masking his feeds somehow. I haven't managed to get to the bottom of exactly how yet, but I've been able to watch them intermittently. I'm locked out again now, but here's what I recorded from five minutes ago. It's video only, I'm afraid.'

He transmitted a thirty-second stretch of moving images, which the major watched on his own forearm screen. Having seen it right through, he then projected and played it again for the rest of his group to watch.

'Thank you, Dira, we'll head up to Highnam right now.'

Truvan poked at his own armulet. 'No, they're on Steep Holm.'

Halthrop took his sunglasses off and wiped the back of his hand across his moustache. Before he could start arguing with Truvan, the man's demeanour changed and gave him pause. 'What is it?'

'Her feeds are off. They've vanished.' He banged his hand on the armulet vambrace. 'She was just there, what, ten minutes ago? Smith really is messing with the feeds. We'd better get there as fast as we possibly can. Her locator is still registering as being there.'

Frank Halthrop leaned over to look at the absence of action on the man's wrist. He looked up again and stared into the distance, vaguely in the direction of Steep Holm. Everyone watched the major thinking. His features twitched a little towards a frown and then returned to unfocussed blank thought. Another twitch and then he spoke. 'I wonder if what we were watching before was some sort of recording to lead us astray.' As he scanned his soldiers, they all shrugged.

When his gaze got back to Truvan, Vicky's brother shook his head and said, 'No, he's just switched them off. They're still there, I can feel it.'

Terry stepped off his quad bike and scuttled into the discussion. 'You've just seen him at the house. We went there before – that's definitely the old woman's house, up in Highnam.'

Darren jumped in too. 'Yeah, I remember it.'

Major Halthrop held up his right palm. 'Mr Truva, you've just seen the feeds for yourself. Why are you arguing?'

'Look, there's no feeds from him or Vicky, but I've got her locator in the cottage on the island.'

'Firstly, that's not his locator, it's your sister's. And, secondly, actual live pictures are more convincing evidence in my book, than just the locator. What if she's taken it off and left it there? With no feeds to verify, we can't tell.'

'She's with him. She wouldn't let him leave the island and stay there by herself!'

Halthrop gave the slightest shake of his head. Jane did the same, and then she pointed out, 'We never saw Vicky in the feeds from Jack in Ellie's house. Maybe she didn't go with him.'

Halthrop held up his hand again. 'We can't trust any of the info coming from either of them, whether that be feeds or even the locator info. If he's altering the feeds, I assume the locator would be just as easy to rig.

'We can only trust what Dira has managed to uncover at the Doughnut. The decision is to head back and carry on up to Highnam. We've only gone ten minutes in the wrong direction, so we should be able to make Highnam in a couple of hours. You can come with us or not, as you like.' He turned away from Truvan and gave Darren a nod to lead them off back the way they had just travelled.

The Big Road, as the old M5 had come to be known, was still in pretty good shape. Although the wind was still gusty, so the cyclists had to proceed with care, the rain had stopped, and the clouds were clearing. They made swift progress, and just over two hours later, Halthrop stood in the garden of Ellie Smith's farmhouse. The bikes had been left in the lane and they had slipped through the gate as quietly as possible. The others were behind him in the shadow of the arbour over the garden table.

Jane and Truvan would collect Vicky, whilst Halthrop assigned himself and Darren to tackle Jack. Terry was to remain in the garden, ready to catch anybody who fled the house.

Frank patted his short haircut, for once ignoring his moustache, and checked Vicky's feeds again. Nothing. The major checked her armulet; its locator put it in the cottage on the island, but she was still not showing up any feeds. He assumed she must either be asleep, although it was the middle of the day, or Jack really was controlling their audiopt signals.

Still no feeds from Jack himself either. Halthrop's head tilted to one side. *Surely, Jack can't have been asleep the whole time we've been looking for him? Unconscious, perhaps?* He shook his head to clear away the distracting thoughts. They'd seen Jack first thing in the morning, running to meet Vicky. And a sleeping man couldn't start a fire; they'd seen him do that too. It had to be external interference with the computer system. *But that's supposed to be impossible.*

He scanned the group and stepped forward. Jane skipped quickly out from the arbour and pulled Darren's arm along with her. They all walked forward, purposefully but slowly. A movement at an upstairs window caught Halthrop's eye. He held out an arm, and they all paused. The glass looked dark, and his vision could not penetrate. The breeze blew again, and a tree shadow flicked across the window. False alarm.

He stepped forward again, and they processed through the main doorway and fanned out inside the big, open lounge room. It was dusty and smelt old. Without further instruction, all four continued to spread out and search the building. On reporting back to Halthrop five minutes later, they all had nothing of use. It was clear to Frank that nobody had been in the building for a long time; probably since they were last there, some eighteen months before.

The untouched appearance of the inside of the house did not match with the audiopt feed of Smith in there that they had watched two hours earlier. Halthrop called Dira, the infotech. There was no reply, so he left a message about this conflict of evidence and asked if Smith had maybe doctored the feed record that Dira had found. The weather had warmed up, and the sun had appeared.

They convened at the garden table to consider the next move.

'I told you they weren't here,' decried Truvan impatiently.

'It looks like that footage we saw was fake,' Terry said.

'I told you. What if he can mess around with the audiopt records but can't change armulet locators? That makes more sense, because sifters can access the feed records, but how would you hack somebody else's armulet remotely?'

Nobody answered him.

'Look, Vicky's locator is still where it was when we left. Let's get back there and catch him.'

Again, nobody spoke. The junior ranks were all looking at their CO.

Halthrop fiddled with his own armulet briefly, confirming that there was still nothing to go on. He pulled his lips in so that his mouth made a grim line. His fingers rapped on the wooden table. The fir trees behind the house answered with a rustling.

Darren went to his quad bike and returned with a large sandwich. He was chewing noisily as he slumped in the chair at the end of the table. Everyone else watched as he munched through it with complete focus.

'OK, here's what we'll do.' Attention immediately moved from Darren's mastication to Halthrop's plan. Even Darren looked at the boss and chewed a little slower and more quietly.

'We'll head straight back to HQ, get something to eat.'

Through his last mouthful, Darren agreed, 'Good plan.'

Halthrop scowled at the ruddy-faced young man. 'And we'll need to switch the bikes for the others back there. The charge on these probably won't get us all the way to Weston-super-Mare from here. And certainly not back again afterwards. If we put these on to charge when we switch bikes, then these ones should be OK to bring Jack and Vicky back up to Highnam once we've got them.'

'What if they're not there?' Terry asked.

'They're there.' Truvan leaned back in his chair and nodded with a smile.

'I'm not sure, Major,' Jane said. 'We were sure they were here, and nothing. We're not sure they're on the island. Are we just wasting our time heading out there?'

Halthrop nodded. 'It wouldn't surprise me at all. But if you think through what we've got to go on, we've actually no idea at all. So, we might as well go and have a look. If we don't find them, they may have left clues. It's pretty obvious nobody has been here, so there's no clue about where they might go. We know he's been on Steep Holm recently, so maybe he's left some indication of where we might find him. Hopefully unwittingly.'

'Do we, though?' Terry asked.

'What?'

THE MIND'S EYE

'Do we know he's been there recently? It seems like we may know nothing about where he is or where he's been. The last thing we can know for certain is the day we left him there.'

Halthrop shrugged. 'You're right, but that still means the last thing we know for sure is he was on Steep Holm.'

They all looked around the group at each other. Darren stood up and said, 'Come on then. We're gonna be really late for lunch. Let's go.'

Terry and the major connected the bikes to the huge battery power store in the vehicle garage outside their HQ building. Jane and Truvan were transferring the last of the equipment into the storage panniers on the new bikes. Darren had gone straight inside the main house to prepare food for everyone.

As they stepped out of the shade of the shed into the now blinding sunshine of the compound's driveway, Frank was lifted into the air and flew backwards. The air was punched out of his lungs, and an incredible bang slammed his ears. He felt groggy and opened his eyes, only to have them shut again by themselves, as he was looking straight up at the blinding sun. Halthrop put his hands to his face to feel that his sunglasses were no longer there.

His ribs and back ached. His shoulder blades were particularly sore, and the major lifted himself up to sitting to relieve them from pressing on the ground. He looked around – shattered debris was everywhere. Other people were raising themselves from the floor too. Halthrop's ears were ringing, and he struggled to make out what Terry was saying to him. He pointed to his ears, and Terry nodded and did the same. Jane mouthed 'I'm OK' and gave a thumbs-up sign.

Truvan was flat on his back and appeared to be unconscious. Frank's chest surged with pain, his heart thumping at the sight of Truvan's body. 'Don't be dead!' Halthrop shouted. He leaned over and shook the man's foot. Truvan roused and put his hands to cover his ears.

Rubble and splintered wood laid a trail back across the large yard towards the remains of their HQ building. The large, old house had been constructed in two halves on either side of a wide main door with an unenclosed porch. The left-hand side had been pretty much destroyed. It was a pile of rubble and broken timbers. A pall of grey smoke twisted up from flames licking out of the upper windows on the right-hand side of the building. Dust of brick and cement filled the air and clogged breathing. The rocky taste filled Halthrop's mouth. He coughed and spat and saw the others doing the same.

On the right-hand half, the building was standing, but alight. The flames were relatively small, little fires dotted in many places. Splintered planks could be seen under the eaves and through broken windows. They seemed to point themselves towards the warmth of the flames, begging to be taken up. Major Halthrop's office was the room that most appeared to be on fire. Frank winced at the thought of his tiny library of military histories; the compendium of Churchill's speeches, a leather-bound *Art of War* from the 18th Century, his signed first edition of *Assassination*. The books were his pride and joy. Halthrop's distress at this threat to them surged adrenaline through him.

'Come on, get up!' He leapt up to organise the firefighting. With a little wobble of his legs, the major turned and repeated his instruction as a shout. Jane was already on her feet, and his yell pierced the ringing in their ears and pulled everyone into action.

Jane responded, 'Darren was in there!'

THE MIND'S EYE

They all started at a run and stopped very quickly. How to access the building safely to find him was not obvious. Halthrop directed Jane and Terry to get the firefighting equipment from the garage. There was a storage cage devoted to it, equipped with hoses and buckets and extinguishers of all types.

Halthrop had no time to consider or feel anything – he simply acted. Frank and Truvan were able to help each other in through a rear window, which was in the room adjacent to the kitchen. Halthrop worked on the assumption that Darren would have been preparing food in there, so it was lucky that the safest-looking entry point was close to it.

They used a wooden table as a shield and battering ram to knock down the door to the kitchen. It wasn't blocked, but it was smouldering, and the handle was too hot to touch. Inside, most of the little kitchen was unscathed. The narrow rectangular room was a lot of stainless steel surfaces, a large metal oven and two large, solid fridges. Darren was unconscious on the floor in the centre. He was partly covered with ceiling tiles and the door from the other end of the room, which the explosion had blown in. The strength of the kitchen's furniture and Darren's own stout frame had saved him from significant injury. As they dragged him back through the small dining room towards the broken window, he revived and, albeit groggily, was able to help them help him out.

Once all the fires were out, they all sat on the ground back by the garage, staring at the damage. Major Halthrop considered that they were lucky to have been at the compound when the bomb went off, so they had been able to begin the firefighting immediately. They had not been able to save most of the books. *Like Alexandria*, he thought.

They had found a mostly destroyed backpack during the battle with the flames. None of the group was any sort of explosives expert, but the backpack reminded Frank of the way Jack Smith had blown up the Doughnut server room. He bottled his anger up – as commanding officer, he had to remain calm and rational or mistakes could be made. He believed that to lead people well required an outward appearance of being completely unflappable.

Even restraining his emotions, Halthrop could not avoid worrying that Smith might well be planning an even bigger attack. He found it difficult to put himself in the mind of a dangerous enemy. For all his study of military history, the major realised this was the first time he might need to be able to imagine various tactical scenarios and devise ways to counter them. He stared at his hands and listened to the muffled ringing in his ears, disappointed that life had only been able to offer him a role as a mere bounty hunter. *A man is great by deeds, not by birth.* He stood up and clapped his hands together to induce action.

The drab green and grey of the building was blackened in spots. Behind them, the separate double garage building that they used for the Brigade's vehicle store was unharmed. This meant their various bikes and other equipment were undamaged, and the large electricity batteries were all housed there safely too. Most of the solar cells to power them had been on the roof of the main building. Recharging the battery stores would not be possible until after rebuilding. Halthrop did a check on the instruments and calculated how much power they had left. If the pursuit of Jack Smith took more than the current recharge and one more, their bikes would all be out of juice.

'We need to stop him.' Truvan had walked up behind Frank. He wondered if the man had been careful to be quiet or if his hearing was still impaired. They had all reported that their tinnitus had subsided but, to differing degrees, their

THE MIND'S EYE

hearing still seemed fuzzy. Even Darren seemed to be able to hear sufficiently to function.

Unsure how loud his voice really came out, the major replied, 'Agreed.'

'They're still on Steep Holm. How long were you reckoning it'd take to get there?'

'Assuming Weston provide a boat with no delay, a bit more than two hours from here.'

He beeped everyone's armulet so they knew to assemble at the vehicle garage. The entire group were charged up to chase down Smith and bring him to justice.

Halthrop kept his orders brief to avoid delay. 'We've still got no feeds from Smith or Miss Truva, but her armulet locator is still showing in the kitchen at the cottage on Steep Holm. We depart in five minutes. Same vehicles, same equipment, same packet order, all as we originally planned. Let's catch these two…'. Halthrop paused as he saw Truvan bristle at the suggestion of catching his sister. '…And get Smith back to Highnam for Kangaroo.'

Chapter Nine
A couple of hours earlier – 21st March 2091, 10am
River Severn

Jack took over piloting the boat. In fact, Vicky let Jack take control of the boat, so she could get some sleep. Steep Holm had not even fallen out of sight behind them.

Before lying down completely, she looked back up to him, on her elbows. 'Is it possible, do you think...' She paused. 'Um... I'm wondering, maybe, do you have a twin?'

'What? Don't be absurd.'

'Think about it. Your mother died in childbirth – far more likely that the stress of twins might cause that. And then Ellie was left on her own to raise the baby. Well, if that was babies, she might very well think about giving one up to another family.'

'But why wouldn't she tell me? Surely there would be no secret to it. I don't see a mystery twin being the answer.' They both sat watching the prow cut through the river. The sun was gaining ground over the rainclouds of the previous two days, and the only sounds were the wind and the water. 'Although, admittedly, I don't have any kind of answer.'

'I wonder if my father might know. He and Ellie were good friends in later years. I'll wait until we get there so I can ask him face to face.'

Jack screwed up his face in uncertainty. He imagined that he should be feeling more emotion at the prospect of an unknown brother. Excitement maybe, or anger at Grannie Ellie that she had kept this secret from him, and then died and taken the secret to her grave so he might never know. All he did feel was a logical certainty that a mystery twin was not the solution. 'Yeah, the other question would be why he'd be doing these things, and why now? He said, "You ruined my life." We should ask Lloyd Lloyd if he knows anything about a twin. I still don't think that's it, though.'

He went back to watching the whitecaps on the river surface as the wind gusted. Vicky reached up, squeezed his hand. 'I'm going to try and get some sleep,' she said, and lay down on the small deck in the slight shaded rectangle provided by the starboard side of the boat.

The tide had turned and was coming back at them increasingly hard. Added to the current flow after two days of rain, the boat struggled to maintain its position, let alone move upriver. Jack pulled the boat into a rocky eddy, part-bounded by one of the structural pillars of the big bridge over the Severn. It had been inset with metal rings, so he moored up to wait out the tide.

He struggled to reach his hand to the mooring ring and bumped the port side slightly against the concrete column. Vicky opened her eyes and pulled herself sluggishly up. The tide had only offered her a couple of hours sleep. They sat on the bench at the stern end of the little boat. Both the front and back ends had mini decks on which solar panels had been mounted. Jack tried to lean back, but the panels were too hot to touch, so he had to sit pretty much straight up.

As he fidgeted on the wooden seat, a distant boom of thunder came from the southeast. They both looked towards the sky in that direction. There were a few clouds left, but they were scattered and much whiter and fluffier than the previous two days of rain, sleet and snow. Even that prolonged rain had not included thunderstorms, and they could not see any evidence of one in the sky in any direction.

The old city of Bristol still had a few thousand inhabitants. Above the mostly derelict urban centre, a spire of grey smoke grew up. Jack looked at his armulet – it was exactly 12pm. Vicky yawned, waved her hand side to side and lay down again. 'I wonder what that was,' she said as her eyes closed.

Jack looked back up at the plume of smoke. He scowled and muttered under his breath, 'Vive la revolution!'

The sun gradually became stronger, and Jack and Vicky napped together on the deck. In the late afternoon, Jack untied them and set off again. He let Vicky sleep and watched her face twitching in the sunlight.

He spent nearly three hours playing both defence lawyer and detective rolled into one. His arguments went along the lines of *If I had done those things, how could I have managed to be in both locations? And how could I have avoided audiopt detection?*

He thought through some of the computer programming he had taught himself over the last year or more, and went on to wonder whether any of his ideas about spreading a virus in the surveillance system could have any applications toward these things that had happened.

In the angled and heavily reflected setting sunshine, he was now feeling very hot. They had not brought much water to drink, and his thoughts seemed to be going round in circles. Jack could not come up with any direct answer, a way that somebody might have falsified the records. He thought back to his explanation earlier about how the audiopts worked. They could only record him being in Highnam if somebody actually saw him there; the feeds recorded only what their eyes and ears actually signalled, through the nerves, to the brain. He knew he had never left Steep Holm, so a record of him in Highnam was definitively impossible.

THE MIND'S EYE

Vicky's question about a twin played on Jack's mind. Could it really be possible that Ellie had never told him about a brother? *No. Absolutely not. She'd have nothing to gain. And other people would have known.* The First Covenant was so deeply ingrained nowadays. Even if Ellie tried to maintain such a secret, nobody else would even think to, and they certainly wouldn't agree to some village-wide conspiracy. Since the Times of Malthus, such behaviours were anathema to people.

Jack shook his head. But his thoughts would not be still. He remembered back to the story of his father. Jack had enjoyed such a secure and supportive childhood that he had never suffered the urge to investigate deeply into his parents' background.

He had watched some of the records of the life of his mother, Clara. He remembered a waif-like, blonde beauty with the biggest smile imaginable. Ellie had told him about his father, a travelling tailor who had left town before anyone knew Clara was pregnant. Again, Jack had watched some of the records of his father courting his mother. Nothing had been strange or surprising, or in the least bit contradictory to the way Ellie told the story.

In post-Malthus England, society was such a melting pot of orphans and refugees that the villages just looked after everyone in their midst, without too much concern for parentage. Many people did not know their parents but grew up happy and healthy in a supportive community. The whole Kangaroo shared parenting responsibilities, in exactly the same way human villages had always done for thousands of years.

Jack now wondered, though – might his father have taken a twin brother away and raised him without their knowledge of each other? In the same way that so many children grew up happily without specific knowledge of their parents, might Ellie and his father have simply not thought to tell the twins of each other's existence? Could it be that it was just not relevant to the lives of any of them? If his father and brother had settled somewhere far away, they would likely never meet anyway. Jack didn't really believe this line of argument, but he considered it possible.

He had a vague recollection that Ellie had told him his father was from a far-flung part of England. He couldn't remember the details beyond that. Jack wasn't even certain she had told his childhood self any more information. He wanted to look up his father but couldn't remember the man's name. He and Ellie had not spoken of him for probably twenty years. And it had been merely a passing interest then. 'Here's the story of your father,' was a phrase he distinctly remembered in Ellie's soft voice, but none of the actual story itself.

It would be a bit of a jump-around research task, but Jack reckoned he'd be able to find it all out if he searched his own historic audiopt feeds for Ellie telling him the story. Simpler, though, he decided that he should watch his own birth, and see whether Clara had borne twins or not. Apart from anything else, he knew the exact date and time to call up on Ellie's audiopt record.

'Why did you blow up the Doughnut?' Jack nearly leapt overboard. He had been totally focussed on visions in his mind of Clara suffering contractions and not noticed Vicky stirring on the deck of the boat. She lay there squinting up at him, her question hanging between them.

'What?'

'I know what you told me, but did you really think you'd achieve it? Did you honestly believe that everyone would agree to switch off the audiopts?'

Jack was floored. 'I thought you believed in it too?'

THE MIND'S EYE

She sat up and held her hand to shield her eyes from the brightness. 'Well, yes, probably, but that's not what I'm asking. It's been our way of life for fifty years. Did you think people would suddenly want to change it all?'

He shrugged. 'Well, you did, so why not others?'

'But you didn't know what I thought before you did it.'

'No-o,' Jack agreed. 'But it's still the wrong way to live. I still think that given half a chance to understand what it is, most people would say we should change it.' Jack surreptitiously pressed the screen of his armulet to stop his mother's labour. 'As a sifter, what I know, that most people don't realise, is that it's simply not necessary. Surveillance all the time doesn't benefit society. We should use the audiopt records to solve crimes, yes. That'll keep the security benefit of it, but the rest is not in keeping with the Second Covenant.'

'Surely that means: keep the surveillance on, but restrict who can watch it, and when. Which breaks the First Covenant, no?'

Jack shifted slightly on the bench seat. He looked out at the river. 'They can work out the details, it's the principle that I'm trying to get across.'

'You *are* trying to get across? Are you still doing something? Have you done something?' Vicky shifted backwards slightly on the floor of the small boat, until she was up against the side wall. She faced him, and Jack couldn't tell if she was scowling at him or because of the light from the sun.

He pondered on the coding he'd been teaching himself, and what purposes it might be possible to put that to. He thought through Vicky's point about suddenly changing the minds of everyone in Highnam, or even everyone in the country. His gaze was unfocussed, towards the deck, as Jack ran through the possibility of a broadcasting hack. He wondered if he would be able to program the system to send information out to everyone's armulet explaining some of his ideas.

Jack jumped a little in his seat again. He almost believed he had heard a bell in his mind. It had not been used in over a generation, but he remembered that the system already had a local alerts function. When the audiopts had first been introduced, in the late 2030s, one of the main problems they aimed to solve was local banditry. A Kangaroo could send an alert to all its population that a danger was coming from some direction and muster a defence force to repel the attack. The system had been so successful that banditry was now unheard of in England. In fact, most bandits had quickly discovered that joining a community was an easier life than trying to fight them. The new security system had sealed the deal.

'Hey, are you listening to me?'

Jack parked the idea of hacking the alerts system to send out his information and ideas, and turned to answer Vicky. He shook his head slowly, pushed out his lower lip a little, and replied, 'I haven't done anything specific, but it is still my aim to get them to change things.'

Vicky looked at Jack. 'The last time you and I were escaping in a boat together, my brother died.'

He moved his hand, attempting gesticulation, and stuttered but got stuck on the first syllable of every word he tried.

She continued, 'Jack, I believe in you, I always have. But you must include me. I'm on your side, let me help. Talk to me about your plans and ideas.'

He still couldn't form any coherent response, but Vicky did not mean right there and then. She was asking more generally and in the long term. The notion of the long term future flustered him more than any indecision about what to tell her of his, as yet half-formulated, ideas for pushing society into a happy revolution.

She held his gaze for fully sixty seconds, and then lay down again and turned on to her side.

Chapter Ten
Just before the explosion – 21st March 2091, 11.50am
The Doughnut

Dira spoke loudly as he exited Aluen's workspace. 'Not a problem, I'll get it done before you arrive tomorrow. I'll be in the basement if you need anything else. I've gotta go and carry on with that Highnam thing for the Bristol Brigade.' He limped, albeit quickly, down the staircase to the basement. Her reply of, 'OK, but I'm going home in ten minutes,' was barely audible, as he had already made it two flights down.

The basement office Dira had created for himself was ostensibly comprised of the standard infotech workbenches, with shelves of old equipment to be cannibalised, vices and toolboxes, plus more delicate work areas for electronics soldering and wiring. However, at the very back, inside a metal cage, he also had a horseshoe of screens and servers exactly like the sifters used.

The sifters spent twelve hours a day analysing the audiopt feeds for crimes and misdemeanours within their geographic region. Aluen worked the midnight to noon shift for Newnham and was effectively Dira's manager. Most sifters and infotechs didn't view the working relationship that way though: the sifters needed the technicians to provide working hardware for them to be able to do their jobs, whilst the infotechs felt duty bound to make sure that their hometown's sifters had adequate functioning equipment to keep up with the work.

It was an honour to be able to protect your own Kangaroo by supporting the sifters with the technical work of keeping their computer systems functioning, but it could be a highly frustrating job at times. The hardware being recycled

THE MIND'S EYE

was often more than sixty years old – the Fifth Covenant of Jerusalem meant that no organisation was manufacturing technological equipment. With the loss of so much population during the Times of Malthus, though, a huge amount of old equipment remained to be salvaged. And the sifter workstations were generally set up with plenty of redundancy.

Dira had been supporting the sifters of Newnham for nearly thirty years, Aluen in particular since she had arrived in 2080. They had developed a good working relationship, although everyone at the Doughnut worked pretty much independently. She messaged what she needed, and he generally completed the tasks whilst she was off shift. The infotechs worked six to six, so each sifter and each infotech overlapped both the other shifts. As the old lag in the place, Dira's workflow systems were generally those that all four of them worked with.

One of his most notable achievements was that he had set up a complete replica of Aluen's workspace. If anything significant went wrong with one of her twelve screens or servers, he could simply swap the whole section out and repair it at his own pace. This also meant that Dira had a serious computer research centre at his disposal anytime he wanted to use it.

As Dira had been there throughout the time that Jack Smith had worked on the floor above Aluen, Major Halthrop had quickly accepted Dira as an ideal person to investigate Smith's location. He had also asked Dira to try to offer some explanations about what had gone wrong with, or been done to, the feeds surrounding Jack during his arson attack on Kangaroo Hall. They had not been friends, or even close acquaintances, but Dira knew Jack well. Within the last hour, Halthrop had just added an extra similar task to examine the feeds around the assault on Lloyd Lloyd.

MILES M HUDSON

Dira typed in a password on one of the four keyboards and this unlocked his twelve screens. Audiopt surveillance had rendered password security obsolete, but Dira maintained it on his replica sifter workstation.

The bottom row of four screens showed live audiopt feeds: Truvan Truva was on the very left, then Major Halthrop, Jack Smith – Dira had discovered Andrew Gallian's armulet feed – and Vicky Truva was on the far right. Her screen was black, but her name scrolled along the bottom to identify that it was her and that it was live. Dira unstrapped his own armulet and laid it down between two keyboards.

Behind the middle keyboard, underneath the lowest edge of the bottom row of screens, was a small photograph. About ten centimetres square, it showed a head and shoulders shot of a blonde woman. Her hair was shoulder-length, a bob that had a couple of month's growth. The big smile was all white teeth and rose pink lips, and it glowed from the old frame. She held a glass of white wine up to the photographer. Dira remembered that the home-made wine had tasted awful, but nothing could have spoilt the joy that they felt that day. As he did on most days, Dira wondered what madness had overcome him to leave her, and her village, and go wandering off across England. He remained disbelieving and annoyed at the fact that the day of bad wine was the last time he had seen her.

Dira drummed his fingers on the front edge of the wooden desktop and decided to listen to Jack. He smiled, as it seemed Jack was socially uncomfortable. His view showed that he was sitting at the back of a boat on the Severn, right beside the big bridge, and he was fidgeting on the seat as he watched Vicky sleep on the deck at his feet. Dira clicked a key, and Jack's audio was played from the desktop speakers.

THE MIND'S EYE

Jack was steering the boat haphazardly and broke off the distraction of looking at Vicky. He was headed for a concrete bridge column and had to swivel the steering wheel back and forth and reduce speed rapidly. He was not quick enough, and the boat scraped its edge into the concrete. The rasping sound echoed around Dira's cramped room.

Vicky's screen lit up as she looked at mostly sky, with Jack's face in one corner. The combination of Jack's armulet recording and the infonetwork masts on the shore meant that the audiopts captured everything she saw and displayed it to Dira. The white concrete bridge deck cut across her view. The bridge was huge, and the supporting column dwarfed their little craft. She sat up, blinking a lot, and moved beside him, so her screen was focussed on Jack struggling to tie up a mooring line to an embedded metal ring, which he couldn't easily reach. He finally sat back next to her, and their faces filled each other's screens.

There was a distant sound like thunder, and both viewpoints turned to observe a thin spiral of grey smoke emerge above Bristol. They watched in silence for a moment, and then Vicky must have moved back to the boat deck; suddenly, she was looking at the sky again.

'I wonder what that was,' Jack heard Vicky say as her screen blacked out.

Quietly, but clearly audible on Jack's feed, he muttered, 'Vive la revolution!'

Dira looked at the timestamp at the bottom of the screen: 12.01.

He quite regularly talked to himself. It was fairly common practice in the Doughnut where everyone worked individually. 'Just like before, eh, Jack? Bombs set to go off at exactly noon, with you far away and with a good alibi. I'll bet they're exactly the same construction as you used last time. Why change a sound working practice?'

Both Vicky's brother's and Major Halthrop's screens were also black now. After another minute, the major's eyes reopened, and the sound from his feeds was muted, slightly fuzzy, but basically just lower volume than normal. His own voice could just be heard, urgently saying 'Don't be dead!' Halthrop's hand was then visible, reaching out to shake the foot of Truvan Truva, whose body lay stretched away from the major. He saw the man's eyes open and Truvan's hands move up to his ears. Halthrop looked further around. Terry pointed at his ears, and Halthrop saw Jane's lips move to say, 'I'm OK,' but she produced no sound from the speakers on Dira's desk. Frank's eyes finally returned forward, to take in the half-destroyed building, and flitted to the spots of flame jumping around from different windows and holes in the building.

Dira was strangely calm as he added a row of screens showing the feeds from the other members of the Bristol Brigade, and he watched them all for ten minutes through various locations and activities of firefighting. The technician monitored everything closely, but he did not call anyone, or send any messages to engage additional outside help for the brigade.

He was not a sifter, but Dira knew that one of the rules for the job was that you should never watch live events. The desire, on the part of the sifter, to intervene was a slippery slope to their becoming shadowy Watchers. He remembered comforting Aluen in tears one day early in her tenure. She had seen the feed of an old man fall from climbing a gate and had videocalled the man's neighbours to go and help. Nobody had made any sort of complaint, but Aluen knew she had broken the rules, and her inner conflict had been severe enough that he found her sobbing on a bench in the Doughnut's central courtyard.

When Halthrop's screen landed on the body of Darren under debris in the small kitchen, Dira squeezed his own thigh. The healed femur was often still painful, and the doctor in Cheltenham had told him he would probably always limp. He had chastised Dira for not getting medical attention earlier.

The day that Jack Smith had blown up the Doughnut in 2089, Dira had been walking out of the server room where the bombs went off. He had been caught by falling rubble and had dragged himself away in agony. In his own basement workspace, he had strapped up a workable splint, but it was several days before he could stand the pain enough to move out. The metal cage of his workstation blocked the transmission of radio waves. The audiopt search system had not been able to pick up him or his armulet, and it had marked his workspace as 'empty'. No human search party had bothered to double check.

He had equipped the place with supplies of food and water, and a bed, for the days he stayed over at work. Dira regularly joked with Aluen that he lived in the basement. In fact, this was more often true than not. He did stay in a house in the suburbs of Cheltenham, but it held very little for him. His life at the Doughnut was everything he'd had. And then Jack blew it up.

Since then, Dira struggled to work out how he felt about the place. He still often stayed overnight, but on many occasions, it was to avoid the pain of limping home and back the next day.

He wasn't certain if the doctor had believed his story of falling down a staircase, but Dira had wanted to avoid getting involved at all in the case surrounding Smith. And he had achieved that very successfully.

'So then, Jack, let's see you planting those bombs, shall we? Halthrop's gonna catch you soon, and I can't see Kangaroo letting you off so lightly this time, can you?'

Dira shuffled the Andrew Gallian recording of Jack back, but it just showed him watching the course they had taken upriver from Steep Holm. With it being registered as the feeds of a man who would be nearly a hundred years old, but never seeing Jack's own face, the recording would never make great evidence for Kangaroo. Dira knew the townsfolk always wanted simple. One old sifter had once told him of their work: 'Keep the narrative simple, and the populace will do the right thing.'

'They'll never do the right thing with this,' he muttered. 'And bloody Vicky was asleep the whole time. She wakes up just long enough to show you that you're a violent thug as well as everything else, and then she's away with Morpheus again.'

Dira stared at the ceiling. He looked at all the screens and then paused everyone. Following Jack's frozen view, which looked under the big bridge and up the Severn to a partly cloudy sky, he continued his one-sided conversation. 'So how exactly did you get the boat into Avonmouth docks, tie up, sneak to the brigade building and plant the bombs, and then get away back on to the water, without being seen, or waking Vicky, until you were back in the middle of the river? Hmm, how could you have achieved that? Without being seen by anyone... that's good going, Jack, young lad. Good going indeed.'

He stared at Halthrop's face, frozen on Truvan's screen, the blond moustache full on his lips and still coiffured perfectly, despite a gust of wind having caught the mousy hair on top of his head. Dira looked up at the ceiling again.

'And that business with setting the bombs is nothing compared with how you got back to Steep Holm from

THE MIND'S EYE

Highnam so fast, after assaulting Lloyd Lloyd. In fact, that one really is impossible.' He shook his head and leant back in the chair staring at the black screen for Vicky. He exhaled hard through his nostrils and shook his head again.

Dira still avoided contacting anyone about the explosion he'd witnessed. The Bristol sifters would have a lot to work through, and he wanted to think about how he might be able to help with the missing feeds and providing KangaReview evidence for those Bristol sifters. Others could catch Smith, but Dira was a techie – he would work on Jack's missing surveillance feeds.

He stood up and re-attached his armulet before wandering out of the metal cage back into the workshop area. Dira picked up a printed circuit board with several tiny capacitors dangling by only one leg. He scrutinised them closely and screwed the green plastic square into a small vice.

MILES M HUDSON

Chapter Eleven

21st March 2091, 2pm
The old M5 motorway south to Weston-super-Mare

Major Frank Halthrop monitored the time carefully. The surface of the Big Road south was pretty much the same level of quality as it was towards the north. The posse made swift progress, and an hour later, Halthrop stood on the beach at Weston-super-Mare, negotiating to borrow a boat for the journey. He had dealt before with the large woman, who acted as Weston-super-Mare's Spokesperson. She disliked the thought of such a violent criminal coming through her Kangaroo, but Halthrop insisted he would be under guard and would pass by smoothly, just like the previous two occasions.

As they plied steadily across the five kilometres of water towards the island, Halthrop sat on the boat's rear bench and worked on a plan for the arrest. They would arrive at about 4pm. The tide would be a bit higher than halfway and rising rapidly. Terry should be able to land well up the beach, but he would have to stay with the boat and move it forward as the tide rose, in order to avoid them losing access to it and getting stuck for the best part of six hours. The other four would advance up top, probably straight to the cottage. Jane and Truvan would collect Vicky, whilst Halthrop assigned himself and Darren to tackle Jack.

Terry argued that Darren might still be groggy from the explosion and that he should stay with the boat. It was clear Terry was excited about the prospect of some action, and it was this over-excitement that made Halthrop confirm Terry must stay with the boat. The Bristol Brigade didn't see much real action on a regular basis, but Terry had a history of trying to justify making hot-headed decisions, as if he had analysed the tactical situation carefully.

However, the major also worried that he might indeed be pushing Darren into a situation he was not fit for. The young farmer was a bull of a lad and followed orders without question. Halthrop didn't have enough bodies for the operation he wanted to employ. *I'll have to go with the plan that 'Darren's body is simply impervious and will just keep going' as the least worst option.* He was unconvinced by his own convincing and fearful that they might underestimate the enemy.

Despite his previous feelings that Jack was a cerebral and reasoning man, Halthrop could not forget the devastation of HQ. He closed his eyes and remembered the flames playing out of his office window, as they destroyed his irreplaceable library. Anger burned in his chest. Eyes still closed, he clenched his fists on the edge of the bench. The way their building had been blown up – bomb in a backpack – was exactly like the Doughnut two years before, and Smith had readily admitted to that explosion. They had to stop him before anyone else got hurt.

Frank stroked his moustache and checked on Vicky's feeds again. Nothing. He checked her armulet; its locator put it in the cottage on the island, but he was troubled by the absence of any feeds. He told himself to accept the usual scenario that she must be asleep.

The major stood up and took in a deep breath of salty air. The Severn estuary was so wide, it was probably better called the Bristol Channel at that point. Not quite the Irish Sea, but Halthrop felt he could call this lungful 'sea air'.

As they approached the half-covered beach shingle in front of the old house and derelict pub, Halthrop heard a distinct scrape of rock on the hull. All of his team turned to look in the direction of the sound, but there was nothing to see. Terry shrugged to them and began manoeuvring as close as he could get them to dry land. They splashed ashore, and Terry backed away a bit.

Halthrop had already briefed the landing party, and they rushed up towards the cottage. The path was so steep that Major Frank stopped them all behind the big barn so they could catch their breath and be ready for whatever might come at them inside the house. Truvan was edgy and unwilling to wait. Halthrop had to physically hold the man's upper arm. He didn't actually need to restrain him, but the tangible contact was the only thing penetrating Truvan's extreme focus.

As planned, they headed around the barn in pairs in opposite directions. Halthrop and Darren made it through the back door before the sprinting Truvan burst in the front. The house was empty. The major's hand on the stove felt the heat still emanating from it. The stove was designed to hold its fire and heat for very long times, but it was clear that the fire had been alight earlier that same day. Just as they had watched.

Truvan found Vicky's armulet on the kitchen table, but there was no sign of Vicky or Jack. He immediately checked their audiopt feeds. Both were still off.

Halthrop organised as complete a search as they could manage with only four people. The ubiquitous gulls screamed and divebombed the humans as they disturbed nesting sites all over the island. It could not be totally conclusive, but after an hour going through the various little buildings and old gun emplacements scattered around the kilometre-long plateau, all agreed that the fugitives were not there.

Jane piped up, 'Oh, Malthus! You know what we missed?' The others looked at her. 'Where's her boat? Her feed showed her tie it up by the house on the beach, but I didn't even think about it when we landed. It wasn't there.'

THE MIND'S EYE

Darren chimed in, 'She's right, it wasn't.'

'Bugger,' was all Major Halthrop could muster. The anticlimax of the fruitless search had left him even more frustrated and concerned than before they arrived.

Truvan said, 'Hey, you know what? What if this was the trick he's managed with the audiopt system? They were never here, but he somehow put that feed in, so we'd follow her here, whilst he's off… shit, I bet he blew up the Bristol Brigade building.'

Halthrop nodded. 'I had wondered about that.'

'Yes, that all makes more sense than anything else. In fact, I wonder if those images of Vicky seeing him as she arrives here are just a recording that he's cut and stuck in again for us to find.'

Halthrop shook his head. 'That can't be done. And in any case, how would he know when we'd be looking? Or even who would be looking. No. Well, maybe. There's something altogether wrong with the feeds, and I just can't fathom out what it is.' His mouth was a horizontal line, and a finger slid across the hairs of his moustache, right side then left side. 'Bugger,' he said again. 'Right, let's get back to HQ, and see what can be salvaged. Truvan, you monitor your sister's feeds all the time, please. When she wakes up, I want to know where they are.'

'No, no, wait!' It was Jane again. The group were standing in the barnyard by the low, circular wall protecting the large opening of the water well. She ran into the cottage kitchen door and emerged again seconds later. Dangling from Jane's small left hand was Vicky's armulet. 'This is definitely hers, is it?' Truvan nodded. Jane turned to her boss and held it out to pass over. 'She was definitely here, so presumably Smith too.'

Darren stepped forward and spoke as Halthrop examined the device. 'Where could they have gone to from here? She had a boat, and we definitely saw them here at, um, what time was it this morning?'

Jane called up a projection of Vicky's feed recordings from the morning. She played them fast through until Vicky went to sleep on the boat deck at a few minutes before 10am.

Truvan spoke through barely separated teeth. 'I just kept looking for her live feed. I didn't think to look at what had gone before. I assumed he had tampered with her feeds as well. I never thought she'd go to sleep.'

Halthrop nodded. 'Sleep has always been the easiest way to defeat the audiopt surveillance. The system only picks up what you see and hear, so if you're unconscious, black silence is all it'll record. The timings you gave us mean she must have travelled through the night to get here. It makes sense that she'd be tired enough to sleep.' Truvan looked into the distance through the space between the house and barn.

Darren stepped forward another step. 'So, where do we go to follow? They've got six hours on us.'

Jane found a few brief moments where Vicky woke up again. They watched as she looked up from the boat deck and saw the towering bridge column rising vertically above her. She had looked at Jack Smith and then turned towards the sound of a distant explosion. All four watched intensely. Vicky's eyes closed again, but after the projection went blank, Jack said something.

'I know where that is,' Darren boomed.

Major Halthrop held up his hand. 'Yes, it's the old M4 bridge. Jane, can you play that sound again and turn it up loud?'

'Which sound?'

THE MIND'S EYE

'Just after she closes her eyes, he says something. I couldn't make it out though. Play it again.'

They heard Vicky muse, 'I wonder what that was,' and the video went black. Almost inaudibly, Jack muttered something afterwards.

Halthrop shook his head slightly. 'No, again.'

She adjusted the playback controls and his voice came out clearly. 'Vive la revolution!'

Darren shouted, 'That was when the bomb went off. Look at the timestamp!'

Jane looked up at the major, who just nodded. He also muttered, 'Vive la revolution.' Halthrop's nodding stopped and turned into a single shake of his head.

'Frank, we gotta get him,' Darren said in a much quieter voice.

They all looked at the leader, waiting for him to make a plan and get them on the chase again.

'Let's get down to Terry. That was twelve o' clock at the bridge, and they were tied up to it. We've got the run of the tide now, but not for much longer.' They jogged down to the beach, and Terry pushed forward enough that they could leap aboard from the beach wall by the old house.

'Fast as you can, Terry, to the M4 bridge. They were tied up to one of the support columns at noon today. If we're lucky, they're still hiding out there. How long will it take us?'

Terry looked at the instrument panel. He scanned each dial a few times before he just shrugged. Jane was working on her armulet, and at Terry's shrug, she spoke up, 'The tide will slow down but shouldn't turn against us before we get there. At top speed in this thing, we're over an hour away.'

'It'll be dark by then,' Truvan said.

Major Halthrop remembered the last time they had chased Smith on the river in the dark. They had lost him several times. With the feeds off, it had been impossible to see enough or work out where to go. He looked out at the endless water in front of them and his hand pulled thoughtfully at some of the hair just above his forehead. 'No. Terry, take us back to Weston. We'll never find them on the water in the dark. They must be heading upriver somewhere, and we'll make faster time on land. Back to the bikes as quick as you can.'

'Yes, boss.' Terry gave an exaggerated salute.

'Easy does it, Terry.' Jane was at the prow of their boat as the posse arrived back at Weston-super-Mare's harbour boat launch. The concrete ramp down into the water also had mooring ties, but they were too far apart for easy tying up of such a small vessel.

'I've never arrived here with a boat before. We landed straight onto the beach last time, if you remember.'

'It's not that bloody hard,' Darren scoffed.

'Right, you do it then.' Terry stepped away from the ship's wheel. They were travelling directly towards a big wall.

Truvan leapt forward to grab the wheel and turn them quickly away. He manoeuvred the boat round rather jerkily but pulled up into a corner where the ramp turned a right angle and then descended into water. He placed it so the boat sat idle even without any mooring ropes. Major Halthrop stepped off, and by the time he looked back, his three juniors were also behind him on the jetty. Nobody had thought to tie the boat up, and Truvan was left on board. Halthrop waved towards Jane at the rear of the group, but before he could tell her to tie it up, Truvan pulled the boat away with a little wave.

Halthrop called, 'Hey, Truvan, pull forward, and Jane will tie the mooring ropes.'

'Sorry, Major, I'm off to get my sister. Malthus knows what Smith's capable of.'

THE MIND'S EYE

Halthrop shook his head. 'I've borrowed that boat from the Spokesperson here. You'll have to come with us.'

'Sorry, no. I'll drop it back here for you though. I saw Vicky's horse over there. She can ride him, and I'll use that bike you lent me. Leave it for me.'

'You don't even know if they're still there. You'll never find them in the dark!'

Halthrop watched him motor slowly towards the marina access channel and the estuary.

Once up on the open concrete parking area, still home to a couple of rusting and ancient vehicles, Halthrop barked, 'Double time!' and they broke into a jog.

It was fifty metres to the place they had left their bikes under a small shelter. The junior brigade members lined up in front of their senior officer. 'Right, men, we need to go and apprehend Smith. This has gone too far. He is very dangerous and must be stopped before he hurts anyone else.' Everyone watched him silently. Halthrop looked at his armulet and then tapped it a few times. 'It's 17:21, and Smith's audiopt feeds have now come back on. He is piloting that boat upriver. They're just beyond Sharpness.'

Jane added, 'They must be in range of infonetwork masts again. Even if they dumped their armulets, the radio masts can do the audiopt system's work on their own.'

'So, what are we going to do?' Terry asked.

Halthrop glared at him. 'I would estimate that they are heading for Highnam. Maybe Miss Truva has a bigger hold over him than I gave her credit for. He can't expect to escape us in range of the audiopts. We'll head up the Big Road now, and we can keep monitoring their location as we go. I anticipate we can intercept them wherever they land.'

Chapter Twelve

Several hours earlier – 21st March 2091, 2pm
River Severn

Jack let Vicky sleep. The sun gradually became stronger, and he watched her face twitching in the sunlight. He wondered why just looking at her made him smile.

He fiddled with the old armulet, pulling up a lot of information about the programming language that drove the audiopts system. It had been difficult for Jack to learn even the fundamentals of coding, as it was outside the sphere of experience for people in 2091. It wasn't terribly complex, but the system ran itself, or at worst the infotechs knew enough to fix any problems he'd encountered whilst working as a sifter.

He liked to have the information presented as a projection of an old style leather-bound book. A hand gesture that mimicked turning a page made the projection turn the page. However, the system was more powerful than simple projection.

He was using a learning module that could move the information from the book simulacrum through the air to appear as it would on a computer screen, so the learner could see it in the real context. Then the book could make little programs run as they would on a real system. And it had an emulator that allowed the student to alter code and see the differences in outcome.

Jack loved learning, and this course had kept his attention enough on the island so that he had never worried about the lack of freedom or human interaction. The latter had been barely worse than in the life he had lived as a sifter, and that had been of Jack's own choosing. He looked back down

THE MIND'S EYE

at Vicky and frowned. *What have I missed out on all these years?*

One of the simplest exercises that Jack had set himself in programming was to see whether he could hide his own audiopt detections from being displayed in the records, or in the live feeds.

He looked at Vicky sleeping and wondered if that could be a route towards the solution. The audio still recorded during sleep, but the video was always black. He had heard that a person who slept with their eyes open would show their surroundings in their audiopt feeds, but he'd never seen it happening.

Jack muttered to himself, 'No, I need it to work from the other end.'

He looked back at the coding textbook and an idea floated across his mind. He gestured at the projection, moving little bits of text and typing new bits in the air at the back of their boat.

The emulator suggested that his hack would work, but he would have to test it in real life to be sure. There was no reason not to try it immediately, but access to the audiopt code could not be obtained from an armulet. He would only be able to make the test from within the Doughnut.

Jack assumed his old sifter workstation would have the necessary access. In the past, he had never had cause to try and alter, or even look at, the underlying software code in the system. But the First Covenant meant it would not be hidden.

Who might have authority to make changes to it was an interesting conundrum for the Covenants. He was planning to try and make his own feeds hidden, which would contravene the First Covenant. But restricting access to the code would contravene both the First and the Fifth Covenants. He checked again that it could not be altered from his armulet. Maybe that was simply a technical problem rather than a mass-influence one. In checking again, Jack realised that the solution to the conundrum was that, in fact, he was trying to break the Second Covenant. Access would be available to all, but they would not be expected to change the code.

Jack laughed out loud. 'Maybe that really is a conundrum.'

The tide had turned. Jack reckoned that the boat would now be able to make some headway up the river. He quietly untied the boat from the ring in the concrete column and pushed them away from it. The water around them was virtually stationary, but he still managed to stagger slightly, on stepping past Vicky's prone body to take the wheel. He set the motor to the lowest speed setting and moved them into the main channel between the bridge stanchions.

The river flow and incoming tide were close to balance, so the boat cut through the water quietly and easily. Vicky continued to sleep.

Jack's face was facing forwards, but he was unfocussed, concentrating on the ideas and images in his mind. He had barely even registered that the sun had set, or that Vicky had stirred awake.

'Jack, look out!'

He came back to the boat on the river and could just make out that they were heading at high speed towards a very ruffled area of water. There was obviously something just below the surface, although he couldn't tell what it might be. The disturbed area was huge, so probably a sandbank.

As he steered to the left to avoid it, Jack realised that this was the location that had seen the *Skinny Jean* overturned and Vicky's brother, Bailey, drowned in the surging waters. He looked at her, but her face was shrouded in shadow. Having stood up and warned him of the danger, she was then turned, watching the sandbank area behind them. Jack decided not to speak.

The tide was running fast like that day again, and the river narrowed sharply up ahead. Jack shifted the motor power to its lowest setting. The water flow rate increased surprisingly quickly. He held the wheel with both hands and worked hard to keep the boat in whatever appeared to be the safest course. He could not really navigate along any best route; just keeping her in control was difficult enough. The narrowing of the banks forced the water through even faster, and it churned with eddies and debris. Several logs banged the hull alarmingly, but they shot away as fast as they had come.

The flow tide took them seven miles in less than an hour. Into darkness. They were moving too fast to attempt to land without light. His armulet torch would not be enough. Jack just tried to keep re-adjusting towards the middle of the fastest channel. He hoped this would avoid hitting any submerged obstacles.

At one point, Jack thought he heard someone shout his name, but looking back at the bank, he couldn't make out any person. A building was dimly lit, and a variety of shadows interweaved all around. He focussed back on steering, but it was mainly by feel that he guided the direction. And the benefits of navigation were probably more in his mind than any real improvement in their chances of surviving the river surge.

Vicky stood next to him, trying to point out things to avoid. 'Jack, what's that noise?' The churning of the water and the river-borne debris around the hull made quite a racket, but a noise even above this could now clearly be heard. It sounded like a stampede around the bend behind them. Stealing glances as best he could, Jack kept looking back. The sound got steadily louder but there was nothing to see. It became a rushing, like an ever-increasing wind in a forest.

After five minutes, Vicky squeezed his arm. He turned to see a huge wave galloping up behind them. The new moon had set but had provided no light anyway. The churning wavefront was just about visible in the night's dark, a wall of white splashes. The wave created a vertical maelstrom, creeping up behind them.

Jack pushed the throttle right forward, and they shot along. The river was following a large curve to the right and still narrowing all the while. The Severn bore wave edged closer behind them. Jack could see Vicky's knuckles, white as she clung to the dark top edge of the low windscreen. Her permanently askew little finger was unable to grip as well as the others on her right hand. His own knuckles were also bright, gripping the wheel. The banks showed up dark against the frequent white splashes all over the river surface. To maintain course and avoid obstacles, Jack made many little jigs left and right with the wheel. They clung on, ever faster, the jaws of the bore snapping at the stern.

They had been edged closer and closer to the bank, and a huge branch loomed up in front. Jack hurled the wheel to the right. The boat turned too much, and the wave crashed on the rear of the starboard side. The boat was flipped, and Jack and Vicky hurled into the water. The rolling boat didn't hit them, but they tumbled along in the surge.

Jack felt something punch him in the stomach. The air was knocked from his lungs. He flailed, trying to see the surface. The water was black all around. It spun him this way and that. Once, it threw him half out above the surface, and Jack drew an almighty breath. He went under again, but now had some orientation. He swam as best he could towards the bank. He could see abandoned buildings by the side and a step ladder down to the water. Jack lunged for the ladder's handrail but missed it. He did hit the rocky bank just beyond and clung onto to a submerged bush. Steadily, he hauled himself onto the rocks.

He looked back to the river for Vicky, but she was nowhere to be seen. Jack clambered back across the rocks to the ladder and climbed a few steps. From there he could see Vicky, twenty yards further upstream and also clambering up the bank. She was barely a silhouette in the gloaming.

At the top of the ladder, Jack collapsed on his back on the grass. A sign above him, written in peeling paint, blurring black on white, read 'Severn Bore Inn Beer Garden'. He closed his eyes and tried to regain regular breathing.

'Are you OK?' Vicky arrived and sat beside him.

'No. How about you?' She laughed. They sat, and lay, for several minutes, recovering.

'Where are we?' she asked eventually. Jack just pointed up at the sign. 'OK, but where's that?'

'I've no idea.'

'Well, you're the one with the armulet. Have a look.'

Jack lifted his arm to see if the armulet was still there. He nodded and sat up. 'Um, this is Minsterworth. What's that, about five miles from Highnam?' Vicky laughed. 'What? It is. Look I've got the map up on the armulet here.' He tapped the screen on his forearm, and a projection of the local map appeared in the air in front of them.

'No. Look! This is where we picked up that boat when we were escaping the Brigade last time. Nature seems to have reclaimed one at exactly the same spot.'

Jack looked around them and up and down the river. 'It wasn't here.'

'Well, OK, over there, then.' She pointed to a low wall that backed off the next big shadow of a building. The river was marginally lighter than the rest of the surroundings, and the wall silhouetted against it. 'But near enough.'

'I guess we should be able to find our way back in the dark then.'

She took his hand and hauled Jack up to standing. He didn't let it go, and they stood awkwardly facing each other.

THE MIND'S EYE
Chapter Thirteen
21ˢᵗ March 2091, 6pm
The old M5 motorway north to Epney

Major Halthrop brought up the rear of the convoy, as the Bristol Brigade made quick progress along the old M5 road. It had numerous potholes and cracks, but, for electric quad bikes, it was expansive. They could race, avoid surface damage, or even just meander erratically around the wide carriageway. The weather had improved significantly too, so they could pretty much drive as fast as was possible. Night fell quickly, which meant that their bright headlights showed up the route well. Terry drove in the middle of the convoy, whilst Jane rode his pillion and monitored Jack Smith's live feed constantly.

Halthrop took the occasional opportunity to check on Truvan Truva chasing Jack and Vicky on the river. Truvan was constantly projecting Jack's live feed too, so when Halthrop watched Truvan, he could also see what Jack was up to. Watching the watcher was slightly confusing, but effective once he dissembled the scene each time.

They saw the sun go down from the embanked height of the Big Road. After three days of rain, the skies had cleared, and sunset was a glorious, pink sight.

A little less than two hours later, Halthrop estimated that they had overtaken Jack and Vicky on the river. The two fugitives were travelling a large meander, the short end of which the Brigade had simply cut across. The bike convoy turned onto a smaller road to Epney where the river narrowed significantly and came right next to the road. They pulled up in the garden of the Anchor Inn, still fully operational as a rest stop for travellers after more than three hundred years in business. Frank Halthrop arranged an evening meal for the four of them with Artur, the landlord, and went back outside to wait at a picnic table with the others.

They were all staring at the river, and Jane was also showing a projection of the view that Smith had from his boat. Smith's view of the river showed it as definitely wider than at the Anchor. The audiopt locator put him just out of sight round the nearest bend in the river. The group was tense, and the major hoped the food would come quickly and distract his soldiers. He knew a build-up of tension could make people react with less thought. He had read that it was the body's way of releasing the stress as quickly as possible.

Halthrop did not have a plan. He would attempt to communicate with them from the bank and encourage them to land and give themselves up. If they ignored this, the posse would have to follow along on the banks. The boat landing at the pub was empty, so there were no vessels to commandeer. However, he was happy enough with this plan. As the feeds were functioning, Jack could not escape, like he had the last time round, simply by being unseen. Even if they landed on the opposite side of the river, it was just a matter of time before Frank and his men caught up with them. *This is exactly why the audiopts were put in place.*

He hoped that would be before Truvan caught them. He considered getting the man to stop and pick the Brigade up again, but he preferred to avoid working with him. Previously, Vicky's brother had proven to be mercurial at best. Halthrop checked the man's feeds again. Truvan seemed to have a slower boat, as he was not closing the gap at all. If anything, he was slightly further back, but it was difficult to tell exactly with the twists and turns of the river. However, that was not very far behind, perhaps one kilometre. Frank mused, and then decided that one kilometre on the river was actually plenty of distance between them.

THE MIND'S EYE

Artur's food was excellent. The Brigade members were so engrossed in defending their food from Darren's attempts to steal extra that they nearly missed Jack and Vicky motoring past. It was also a result of the fact that not only had the sun set, there was no moon to offer any help. The pub garden was illuminated, but little of that light spilled onto the river. The compact boat was visible for a total of about a hundred metres as Jack piloted it round the bend in front of the garden. By the time Major Halthrop had leapt up and run to the bank to call Smith ashore, they were already past. He had seen two figures standing near the front of the boat but couldn't even make out which was Jack and which Vicky. Neither responded to his shouts.

Perhaps five minutes later, Truvan shot past. Frank called to him but again got no reply. He could have videocalled but, even if he asked Truvan to stop, and Truvan agreed, it would be impossible with the rushing tide.

'Darren ate your food,' Jane informed the major. He stared at the chubby, blond man. Darren struggled to restrain a burp. Halthrop reminded himself that he was not running a military outfit with the kind of ethos it might have had a hundred years ago. He knew he had to accept those who were willing to work for the Brigade. And he consoled himself that the lack of interaction with the two boats had spirited away any appetite he might have had.

'What happened with the boats?' Terry asked. 'Didn't look like they took any notice of you.'

Major Halthrop nodded. 'No.' He paused and looked at the state of the plates. His and Darren's were clear, but Jane and Terry still had some to finish. Halthrop sat down. 'They either couldn't hear me, or couldn't see me, or both. Once you two have finished, we'll set off again. We've got two more bends we can cut off, so we'll easily get ahead of them again.'

Darren was sent in with the empty plates, and the posse packed up and prepared to continue. When he returned, he stopped and looked around. 'Do you all hear that?'

The rest of the group stopped still and listened. Terry frowned and shook his head, looking at Darren with disdain.

Jane said, 'Yes. Yes, I do.' They all listened again.

Frank strode over towards the riverbank, and the others followed. He turned his head slightly to the side and opened his mouth a little. Jane mimicked him. Darren and Terry looked at each other and then also copied the boss. There was a sound like distant thunder, except that it was continuous. Quiet, but the volume was growing.

'It's the bore,' Halthrop said. 'No wonder the tide is moving so fast today. New moon.'

They waited, and the sound like galloping hooves grew louder; the stampede was approaching. Eventually, a broad band of white spots appeared in the furthest part of the visible river. It approached much more slowly than the expectation induced by the noise. But it did move. The chaotic wave steadily came into clearer focus. As the white wall surged upriver towards them, Halthrop realised they were standing exactly at the bend in the river. The bore could easily breach the bank when it hit. He grabbed arms and bustled the group away from the danger spot, and they watched as it sloshed around the curve. They would not have been in danger but would have got wet.

'Wow,' Darren said. 'It's larger than I remember.'

'We're further upriver than last time,' Frank replied.

Jane added, 'I hope those boats will be OK. Neither was very big, and the bore will be even bigger by the time it reaches them.'

THE MIND'S EYE

'And they're none of them used to boats. Right, we'd better follow along then. It may turn out that we can catch Smith by pulling him out of the river.'

'Dead or alive,' Terry said.

'We want him alive,' Halthrop snapped.

They ran to the bikes and set off up the lanes that weaved closer and further from the river. The headlight beams were funnelled within hedges on both sides for about a kilometre and then burst out across open, overgrown fields on both sides. Far to the left, the vegetation ended and indicated the riverbank. The shape of the winding river was clear from this shadow boundary, and they could see it approaching the road.

When the little convoy reached the point where the water's edge next abutted the road, they stopped to look out. The feeds from Jack Smith and Vicky were off again. Those for Truvan were showing as only just downstream; he should have been physically visible. Once again, Halthrop heard the bore wave approaching. The river route had been more than five kilometres longer than the road route. The foaming white band across the dark river was higher than it had been at The Anchor.

They spotted Truvan's boat. It was stuck in the trough at the base of the front of the wall of water. The boat was surfing the wave. In the light from the bike headlights, they could see Truvan hanging on to the steering wheel. He squinted into the sudden brightness. As the river turned, he did not appear to see the change in direction. On closer approach, he raised one arm to shadow his eyes. The bend came too fast. Truvan failed to turn as the banks forced the bore around the curve. The boat was broadsided and rolled. Truvan flew forwards into the water and under the capsizing boat. The boat rolled twice before settling into being dragged. And then the wave pushed past, and the boat continued much more slowly behind it.

'There!' Jane was pointing to the black water. Truvan's body was floating fast, face down. The tide pushing behind the bore still dragged everything along. He was already past them.

The stretch of road by the riverbank continued for only another thirty metres. Darren was the only one who had stayed sitting on his bike. He shot off along the road until he was ten metres ahead of Truvan. He leapt straight into the water. He was caught immediately by the current.

Jane and Frank ran along the road beyond Darren's bike. Terry followed quickly on his bike and set it to illuminate as much river as he could. They spotted Darren hanging on to Truvan like a floating log. He had turned the man, so his face was at least up to the air.

Halthrop grabbed a small tree trunk and leant out. He was not going to reach the two in the water. Terry jumped from his bike and ran down into the water beside Halthrop. He held the major's outstretched hand and reached as far as he could.

Jane shouted to Darren, guiding him to catch Terry's arm. She lay down in the shallows to avoid being swept away. She then reached out and gripped Truvan's leg. Darren let go and grabbed Terry. The sudden weight ripped Terry's grip from Frank's hand, and the two of them fell into the swirling water. Halthrop and Jane dragged Truvan ashore. The boys were invisible. They had been swept beyond the light from the headlights.

Halthrop turned Darren's bike so the light fell on Truvan. Jane did her best to implement the first aid they had all learnt. Truvan responded quickly. He recovered consciousness and appeared not to have swallowed much water. She continued to tend to him as Halthrop moved Terry's bike forward as far as he could.

The road turned away from the water, but the ground that followed the river was passable for the ATV. Another fifty metres upriver, he came across Darren and Terry. They were both on the grass out of the water and arguing.

'You both OK?' Halthrop had to shout the question a second time to gain their attention. They were silent and clambered up to the boss. 'You two walk back, I'll light up your way.'

He pulled a slow circle and drove behind the shuffling pair.

They brought the three quad bikes together, and each of the men who had been in the river sat on one. Jane and Halthrop stood facing them.

'Is everyone OK now?' Jane asked. 'All going to be able to carry on?'

Darren said, 'Yes.'

Truvan and Terry followed up simultaneously. 'Yes.'

'What about you, Frank?'

Halthrop stuttered slightly at her question. 'Uh, yes. Yes. Did you see them, Truvan? What happened to them? They were ahead of you, but their feeds went off.'

Vicky's brother answered, 'I missed them completely. I saw their boat on its side in the reeds at the water's edge back there, but I couldn't stop. I could hardly even steer.'

Halthrop swivelled to look back downriver. Everything was darkness. 'How far?'

Truvan held up both hands. 'Where are we now? I've got no idea how far I got dragged.'

Halthrop looked to Jane as she tapped through screens on her armulet. Its brown leather strapping was sodden and loose on her forearm. 'Still nothing,' she said. Her fingers continued dancing on the screen. 'They were last showing on the other side after getting out of the water. That was about twenty minutes ago, but the feeds are off now – they went to sleep in a building in Minsterworth.'

'Where?' Halthrop stepped back slightly to look over her shoulder.

She looked up into his face, whilst pointing between them, back downriver. 'About halfway round the big bend that we cut off, and on the other side of the river.'

'Is she OK?' Truvan asked, whilst also calling up Vicky's feed.

Jane didn't answer as she saw the same view she was watching appear on Truvan's wrist. Instead, she asked the major, 'What do we do?'

Halthrop paused. He looked into the darkness of the river where Jane had pointed. 'We keep going up here.' He pointed in the opposite direction to the way he was looking. 'They'll be headed to Highnam, so we catch them there; or, if they sleep long enough, we go 'round and catch them where they are. The next bridge is probably five kilometres from here, right by Highnam.'

THE MIND'S EYE
Chapter Fourteen
22nd March 2091, 6.30am
The old Severn Bore pub, Minsterworth

After landing up in the beer garden, Vicky had forced the back door of the pub open to try and get them warm and dry. The place was long abandoned, and there was no heat or lighting to be had. They'd hung up their wet clothes and huddled together shivering for a few hours, trying to sleep.

Jack started. 'I lost my coat. It was on the bench at the back of the boat.'

'You won't need it today. Look at the sky – it's going to be glorious.' Vicky pointed out of the pub window. The black sky was punctuated with stars.

He was watching his feet. 'It had my journal in it.'

'Journal? What was that?'

'I found a notebook in that old pub. A real book. And some pencils. I was writing down all my ideas.'

'Small book, was it?'

Jack stared at her in the dimness. Her teeth shone – Vicky was grinning at him. His voice whined a little. 'It's not funny, that was important.'

She put on a mock serious expression. 'Oh dear. You can get it all back from Andrew Gallian's audiopt record, can't you?'

He wobbled his head in resignation. 'Yes, but it won't be the same. It took me weeks just to learn to write by hand. I'd got a lot of my ideas written out in coherent statements, rather than just the vague notions in my head of what I think I should do. And I'd done some sketches too. They'll never look the same on the recording.'

Vicky's voice was laughing as she spoke. 'How can they not look the same? It's a recording of exactly what you saw.'

Jack scowled at her again. Vicky was not giving this problem the importance he wanted her to. Another realisation distracted him from his upset at her.

'Malthus! It had my knife in it, too.'

Vicky looked sideways at him. 'Do you need it?'

There was another long pause before he replied, 'Hopefully not, but I really loved it.'

Vicky put her arm round Jack and gave him a squeeze of reassurance.

After another hour, Jack became sufficiently impatient that he convinced Vicky to put the cold, wet clothes back on and head out into the night to keep moving ahead of the posse. She could cope with the physical discomfort but was confused about what they were doing other than simply avoiding capture. They couldn't keep that up for long. Jack obfuscated every answer he gave her. She allowed him to take the lead for the moment. The exercise warmed them up, but he was still preoccupied.

The sky was clear and, an hour after dawn, it had become totally blue and the Sun's rays worked wonders on Vicky. She warmed and her mood lifted. 'I'm glad of that sunshine.'

'Yeah, I might get dry in another eight hours.' Jack was unusually sarcastic, but Vicky took it as a sign that morale was improving. Especially when he continued, 'I might even work out where we're going, and why, if it keeps warming my brain.'

'Have a look and see where my brother and the Brigade are. I'm not sure what to suggest if they're catching up on us, but it'd be nice to know.'

THE MIND'S EYE

'Halthrop's feeds show them riding the road just out of Highnam. Shit, they'll be here in just a few minutes.' Vicky stopped and stared at Jack. He asked, 'You still wet enough to swim the river?'

'Well, yeah, I guess so. You think that will help?'

'Either they'll have to swim across and leave the bikes, so then it's a foot race, or they'll have to go back round through Gloucester to the other side again.'

'A foot race to where?'

'I'll tell you when we get there.'

Vicky often found that Jack kept his ideas and plans close to his chest. It annoyed her, and she demanded, 'What, why?'

'So our feeds don't give it away. Let's get swimming, and I'll tell you what we'll do when we get there.' As soon as he stopped speaking, Jack ran down the grass embankment and leapt into the water.

The tide was now right out. It was shallow enough to stand at the edge, but the bottom was sucking mud. He started swimming, although the river was only ten metres wide at that point. Vicky splashed in behind and overtook him easily on the short swim. She was panting, hands on her knees, when he clambered out, but they both set off at a brisk pace across the field towards the nearest little road.

She could accept the argument about avoiding the feeds, but she still felt like he wasn't keeping her in the loop enough. Vicky was putting herself on the line to support him and needed him to involve her more in the decision making. 'OK, why are we going, um, wherever we're going?'

He again gave a reasonable answer that imparted no actual information. 'I need to work out how to prove my innocence. And to do that, I need to find out exactly what's happened to the audiopt system so that it could give false records like it has.'

She puffed, 'OK, but where do we start with something like that?'

As they moved onto the easier running surface of the little lane, a cart pulled by two horses rattled to a stop just behind them. Vicky's face was a picture of horror – disbelief that they had been apprehended so quickly.

'You don't know me.' the driver stated. An oversized coat, hood up, was swallowing him. They looked at each other, both certain they knew exactly who it was. Vicky even recognised the horses.

Silently, they clambered aboard, three abreast on the front bench. He pointed forwards so they both looked ahead. 'Don't look at me,' he said, putting on a husky, gruff accent to disguise his voice. He had already urged the horses forward.

'Um, OK,' Vicky said, 'but where are you taking us?'

'Take us to the place your dad dropped me off sixteen years ago,' Jack interjected.

Vicky turned to stare at him. Without looking back at the driver, she asked, 'Why are you helping us? You are helping us, aren't you?'

'Aye,' he grunted. In the ridiculous accent, he continued, 'Dunno how it was done, but I know that weren't Jack who started the fire.' He broke into a coughing fit brought on by disguising his voice.

'Wait, I know I didn't do it, 'cause I know I never left Steep Holm, but I can't see why anyone else wouldn't believe the audiopt records from the fire. Why don't you believe them?'

'Those feeds don't show you. They show Jack Smith from before. It looks exactly like you did at your trial.'

THE MIND'S EYE

'Of course.' Jack nodded slowly. After another minute, he held up his armulet for Vicky to watch and played Lloyd Lloyd's feeds from the fire again. Jack hadn't changed much at all, but it was just enough to be obvious when you were looking for it.

'We should close our eyes, so they can't follow where we're going.' Jack followed his own advice.

Vicky also did as she was told but was confused. 'But they'll just follow his. Wait, they'll know it's you that helped us from your feeds.'

Jack didn't let the mystery driver respond. 'Only if they know whose feeds to look for. I assume you left your armulet at home.' They heard no response but didn't dare look to see why not. 'Without your own armulet to indicate the source of the feeds, the system rests on triangulation between masts, which is not particularly accurate. Especially if you're moving at high speed. Fingers crossed they've not discovered this one yet.' He shook his arm in the air, but only the driver could have seen it.

'Oh, no.' Vicky put her hand on his arm. 'I sent your feeds on Steep Holm to Truvan to make him believe it wasn't you that set the fire.'

'You mean the feeds from this armulet?' Jack didn't wait for an answer. He unstrapped the leather vambrace and hurled it from the moving cart.

'Marisa Leone died this morning.' Their hooded accomplice stated this flatly.

Vicky put her hand to her mouth, but kept her eyes closed.

'The poor woman,' Jack said. 'How is her death going to be of benefit to anyone? Let alone everyone. I wish I could think who might want to do this.'

'You think somebody has done this?' Vicky asked.

'It's too bizarre and complicated to be a malfunction. And a software glitch can't start a real fire that way. That had to be a real person, but manipulated to look like me. Although I still can't think how somebody could hack the system like this. Or why. Or, like I say, who might want to. In fact, the only person I've ever had upset with me in a way that might lead to this is Truvan. And I don't see it being how he'd do it. Take a boat to the island and bash me with a rock is more what I'd expect from him.'

Vicky reached to grab his hand again and, moving blind, caught Jack round the wrist. 'Stop it. Of course it's not Truvan. He's got over his anger. He still grieves, but he's not consumed by it like those early days.' She knew this claim might not be wholly true, but Vicky refused to believe her brother could have committed these terrible crimes.

Jack did not reply, but he slipped her grasp to take her hand and squeeze back.

The three continued for the remaining half hour without speaking.

When the horses pulled up, Jack and Vicky climbed carefully down, maintaining their self-imposed blindfolding. They both thanked the man, who responded with 'Vive la revolution!' and drove the horses away smartly.

'What did he mean by that?' Vicky asked. She put her hand up to blinker Jack's view as he turned to stare after the man.

'I, I'm not sure I know why he would say that.'

'OK, how are we going to get in here?'

'It's about an hour to sifter shift change, so we'd better get going sharpish. There'll be quite a lot of movement right around midday. I'm thinking we just go straight in. The place is barely occupied. Even with all the sifters from half of England and all of Wales, they rattle around. The building was originally meant for five thousand people to work in. I doubt we'll even see anyone.'

'And there's nobody checking who comes in?'

'Why would they? That's what the audiopts are for. Besides, what damage could you do if you got in but weren't supposed to?'

'I know somebody who once blew the place up.' They both smiled.

'Nonsense. Look, it's still standing. I barely scratched at it.

'In any case, there's not really a 'not supposed to be here' thing. The sifters do their work, the infotechs do their work, and if somebody else fancies wandering around in there, why not? Remember, one of the guiding principles in the formulation of the Covenants of Jerusalem was an embracing of anarchy. Nobody is allowed to control anybody. Come and go as you please. Here as much as anywhere.' He was leading her by the hand towards a double door in the nearest portion of the curving Doughnut. 'Nothing will be hidden or secret.'

She thought his tone was almost mocking the Covenants and pulled her hand back out from his. 'OK, once we're in, then what?'

'I'm hopeful that my workstation will be unoccupied. Whoever replaced me will more than likely have set up their own space. Most of them have a quite particular personality.'

'Don't they just.' Vicky brightened again, and they both smiled. He held the door open for her to pass through. She looked left and right along empty glass and stainless steel corridors.

'Straight ahead, and up to the second floor, up those stairs.' Jack didn't lower the volume of his voice. They nipped across the empty space and into the relative security of a stairwell. 'Actually, who did replace me?'

'It was Ali Dally.'

'Really? He was the subject of KangaReviews I sent in on a couple of occasions.'

'Yes, I half think he was voted into it to get him out of the village.'

Jack didn't reply but let out a bellowing laugh.

'Shhh!' Vicky was now leading him, and she pulled him into a doorway. He put a hand over his own mouth but was already back in control of himself. Jack gave her a signal to indicate that he would be quieter.

'OK, so have his KangaReviews been any good?'

'I suppose so. We've had the meeting every Sunday, and there's been a variety of things in them. How would we tell?'

Jack didn't reply immediately. He wondered what the metric for a good KangaReview actually would be. 'Well, I guess you can only tell on a negative: if he misses something. If there's been a problem, which the Kangaroo discovers should have been sent to the meeting but never was. And there's two of them doing the job anyway.'

'Did you ever miss anything?'

'Ha. Not that I know of. Discounting my own bombing of this place, I suppose!' He was walking behind Vicky and reached up to turn her shoulders to walk in through the next doorway on the right.

As predicted, his old workspace was empty. He had not predicted, but had only hoped, that it still also functioned. Jack pressed the power for each of the terminals, and they leapt into life as if he'd never been away.

'I'd guess we've got, what, half an hour? Maybe an hour? Then the Brigade will be here, and I doubt you'll get much more chance to research after that.'

'If everything I've thought of to look for gives us nothing, then I'll be finished in less than an hour.'

THE MIND'S EYE

'Anything I can do to help?'

'Just keep an eye out for anyone coming. There may be some movement at shift change, but the most likely is an infotech going past and spotting us in here.'

Right on cue, Vicky clucked her tongue loudly. It was a sufficiently strange thing to do that Jack looked over to her. She had her back pressed to the wall behind the open door to the corridor, and she was waving frantically for him to duck down. Jack managed to both duck down and lift his feet up, so that everything was obscured from view through the door. All the screens had their backs to the doorway, so an observer would need to be pretty sharp to spot the handful of little lights on various bits of equipment. And, most of those were also obscured.

Footsteps paused right on the threshold. The pause lasted so long that Jack's stomach muscles ached and started to shake, as he maintained a horizontal pose lying out across his seat base. He grimaced and felt his face flush with the exertion. The footsteps pottered away, their owner singing, 'Vi-cky, Vi-cky, give me your answer do, I'm half crazy, all for the love of you. It won't be…'. The sound disappeared as the singer descended the stairway at the end of the corridor.

Vicky hustled over and hissed, 'Did you hear that? What was that about?'

Jack was upright again, and frowning. 'That was Dira. He's Aluen's infotech, and I've no idea why he was singing that.'

'He knows we're here.'

Jack nodded. 'It would seem so. Maybe he didn't want to accost a dangerous criminal like me.'

'So why taunt us if he wanted to avoid any danger?'

'Yeah, I don't know. Let's have a look at his feed.' Vicky stepped round behind the horseshoe of screens to watch.

'That's strange.' Jack was clicking repeatedly on a keyboard.

'What?'

'He has no audiopt feeds.'

'Huh?'

'Well not live right now. And his armulet locator is not functioning either. It's like he vanished.'

THE MIND'S EYE
Chapter Fifteen
22nd March 2091, 9.30am
The Doughnut

The screen Dira had set to show Truvan's feed had been the most exciting of all. His wrestling with the boat as it surfed the Severn bore wave had been a vicarious thrill ride, which had gone into overdrive when he'd finally been tossed in, and the Bristol Brigade had saved him with their human chain. Dira often enjoyed watching the feeds of people who were rock climbing, or surfing, or similar things, but Truvan and the rest had been genuinely in danger. The second-hand thrills had been doubly exciting.

Major Halthrop and Truvan had a history of conflict where Jack Smith was concerned, and Dira was intrigued to see how the latest episode would play out. He was disappointed when he finally found the moment that Truvan had dropped them at Weston-super-Mare docks and made off with the boat. Dira had hoped for something more exciting. He wanted to see Halthrop in a real fight. The man had historically been annoying to Dira, as he directed events so that very little actual physical conflict occurred. *Where are the fights?* Halthrop was supposed to be a major, CO of the Bristol Brigade. Dira could not see much of the military in the man.

However, as he zoomed through Truvan's boat ride of the previous night, the excitement that Dira had wanted came through in copious quantities. He almost giggled as the boat went over and Truvan was hurled into the churning water. He didn't find the events particularly funny in themselves, but it was more the coincidence that Vicky and Truvan's brother, Bailey, had been lost to the Severn bore during the previous chase after Smith.

'What would Vicky have thought of you if Truvan had died in the river as well, eh, Jack?'

He'd also found it intriguing to watch the way Jack managed to evade the posse, despite the audiopt system making it impossible to avoid detection. At least now he was back on the mainland, always in range of infonetwork masts, his feeds would always be visible.

'Well, well, Jack, what are you two up to now?' Dira was sitting in his basement cage. The live feeds from Jack and Vicky and Truvan and Halthrop were running beside each other on the bottom row of his set of screens. The screen above Jack's had a frozen image of a man in a big overcoat, with a scarf around the lower part of his face, and his hood up. The screens for both Jack and Vicky had since gone black.

They had slightly outmanoeuvred the Bristol Brigade by swimming across the river again, minutes before Halthrop's posse caught up with them. With the river to cross, Major Halthrop had been skewered on the dilemma Jack had designed. Either chase by swimming across, losing any equipment they had as they'd have to leave it with the bikes, or follow back up to the next bridge and try to chase them again on the south side. Perhaps an hour's delay. Dira had entertained himself watching this by mimicking Halthrop, as the major stood considering and stroking his moustache.

Jack and Vicky walked fast across a field onto a small road and started running, albeit slowly. The strange man, whose disguised face was frozen on screen, had picked them up on a cart and started driving the two fugitives. He had a severe cough, and Dira wondered if he was ill. Dira was annoyed about the man – he did not know many of Highnam's residents by sight and could not identify this man from the feeds he had so far reviewed.

THE MIND'S EYE

'The place his father took you sixteen years ago, eh? Well, that was here. I can't imagine anything more significant than your journey to start work as a sifter. Closing your eyes isn't gonna help.' Dira had been talking out loud and finished with a 'Ha!'.

'Ah, now, if I can find the date you started here, I can see who your driver was on that trip, and this mystery helper will be unmasked.' Dira started clicking and searching, watching the screen beside the still image.

The route Jack and Vicky's mystery driver had taken was roughly north east from the point he picked them up. This almost immediately took them out of the path of the posse returning from Minsterworth to intercept them. By the time Jack and Vicky opened their eyes at the Doughnut, and the Brigade could identify where they were from their audiopt feeds, this put them nearly an hour away.

On Dira's screen, frustration was writ large on Halthrop's face. All they could do was turn around again and head for the Doughnut. Jane was unerringly positive, but, watching Terry's body language, Dira thought he'd had just about enough of the whole thing. Darren appeared not to notice that they'd been run a merry dance thus far. Dira made a mental note to later look through a few of the Brigade's apprehensions and see how long it normally took the team to catch people.

At that moment, though, Dira had something else to do. He froze all the screens, picked up a screwdriver and a circuit board and headed upstairs. He went past Aluen's floor and on up to the second level. Along a short stretch of corridor, Dira kicked his shoes down hard with every step. When he arrived on the threshold of Jack's old workspace, he paused and looked in. He could not see anyone, but the screens and servers all had the little lights on to indicate they were working.

He started singing, 'Vi-cky, Vi-cky, give me your answer do, I'm half crazy, all for the love of you.' Still singing, he turned and wandered away down the corridor and down the stairs again. Within a minute, Dira was back in his basement cage, watching everyone on his horseshoe of screens.

He watched Jack and Vicky frustrated at having worked out who had been singing but being unable to locate him. 'You see Jack, I can do anything you can do, and I can do it better. We'll get you this time.' He smiled and typed a few things into the far right-hand keyboard of the four in front of him.

He watched Jack and Vicky get excited and confused in equal measure and then run out of the building.

The Bristol Brigade arrived forty minutes later. They had barely been inside the Doughnut before. Halthrop had previously visited a ground floor office close to an entrance, but the architecture repeatedly cycled around the large circle. His previous visit could not help Halthrop navigate inside. They didn't even know where Jack's sifter workstation was located. All five, including Truvan, entered about a third of the way round the giant building from the correct office, which was also two floors up.

Dira added the three junior posse members' audiopt feeds to the live show, putting them on the top row of screens. He smiled as he watched them all get more and more confused by the identical appearance of each part of the building.

Some places had sifter workstations, some were just derelict. Changing floors did not help; it all looked the same. People they asked for directions were the worst help possible. Everyone knew who Jack Smith was because he was the man who had blown the place up. This meant everyone thought they knew where he had worked but, in fact, they only had vague ideas. And the building was huge. Perhaps two hundred offices had been used since the Times of Malthus, out of some three thousand across three levels.

Dira's armulet could not receive a call from Halthrop, as the metal cage blocked the signal. Dira saw Jane stumble into Aluen exiting the stairwell, late to leave at the end of her shift. They were on the ground floor, and he watched Aluen lead Jane back up the two flights of stairs to show her Jack's old office. Jane messaged all members of the posse, but even with the location name and approximate directions, they took some time to find it. Truvan and Darren arrived simultaneously, but from opposite directions, after ten more minutes.

Jane and Halthrop had established that it was definitely the right place – there was a photograph of his Grannie Ellie, which Jane recognised from their search of Jack's house eighteen months earlier. At that time, they had all been surprised that anyone would still have old-style hard copies of photos.

All Jack's electronic equipment was off, but Dira nodded encouragement at the screens as Terry pointed out that the computer housings were warm. Halthrop sent Darren downstairs to confirm with Aluen. He came back quickly with the information that nobody else ever used the room.

Dira could see on Halthrop's feed that he spotted Aluen hovering in the doorway. 'Thanks for your help,' the major called over.

She was hanging on to her dark ponytail, which was slung forwards over her left shoulder. Aluen smiled and asked, 'Is Jack OK?'

Dira laughed out loud, the sound echoing in his cavernous basement den. 'OK? OK?' he was almost shouting at the video monitor. 'There's nothing "OK" about Jack Smith! Guess again, girl!'

He re-directed his commentary to the Brigade major's image. 'Go on, you tell her, Frank.'

On cue, Halthrop replied, 'To be honest, I don't really know. We're trying to catch up with him to find out about those serious crimes in Highnam, but he's managed to elude us thus far. Vicky is with him, and the audiopt feeds for both of them are off at the moment.'

Aluen frowned. 'Off? There's not many places round here where the masts have a blind spot, and their armulets will fill in those gaps. Are you sure they aren't just asleep?'

Terry interjected, 'They ditched their armulets on their way here.'

'Oh.' She paused, her eyes seemingly unfocussed, in thought.

'Come on, Aluen, you explain this to the nice soldiers,' Dira said to himself, downstairs.

'Well, if they've been here recently, then they definitely aren't out of mast range, so must be asleep.'

Major Halthrop had been fiddling with his moustache. He stopped to reply. 'But that just seems so unlikely.' He projected the last records of the two of them. 'Look, they were here until about an hour ago – right here, in fact. Then both their feeds go blank, whilst they're standing here. No lying down to sleep. Cut off in mid-sentence.'

Aluen checked the same piece of feed recording and scowled. She checked her own audiopt recording and it passed straight through the same timestamp without a hitch. 'Right, that's supposed to be impossible. I was here an hour ago, but I didn't notice them enter or leave. How they've done this to the feeds, I don't know.'

Truvan jumped in. 'Smith's done it. Vicky is no saboteur; she's under his spell and going along with him. We need to get her away from him.'

THE MIND'S EYE

Aluen threw her ponytail back over the shoulder and stepped forward to the workstation. 'I'll have a look on his system and see what I can find out, but I suspect this may be a more difficult job than I have the skills for. I'll get Dira up to come and help though. He's still on shift till 6pm.' She sat down in Jack's chair and started up the computers.

Halthrop had not switched off the blank feed for Jack. The armulet projection jumped back into life with an image of Vicky Truva standing in the air in front of the major. Leaning back, Dira put his hands behind his head and watched the show going on upstairs: he watched the posse, themselves watching a projection of the female fugitive. They saw through Jack's eyes as he looked at Vicky outside on a minor road. He was talking to her about heading to the Leckhampton bunker he had previously recced as a possible hideout. In his feed, life-size in the open space in front of Halthrop, Vicky nodded and apologised for having given that hideout away previously. Jack's viewpoint showed his own hand reach out and take Vicky's. He told her not to worry as it meant that they could use it this time.

Downstairs, on Dira's other screens, Jack was beside Vicky, as they rode along a different road out of Cheltenham.

Halthrop left the projection running but turned his head to look at Aluen. Dira had added her feeds to the top row of his screens, above Halthrop's screen, and as the two of them looked directly at each other, Dira's eyes flicked up and down.

The major's voice boomed from the loudspeakers in Dira's little cavern. 'Whatever you did, well done.'

Upstairs, Aluen scanned the screens in front of her, and back to the major. The scenes Jack was seeing, as projected in the office space by Halthrop's armulet, were exactly replicated on one of Aluen's monitors. She raised both her hands in mild confusion, acting out leaving the computer keyboard alone, as if it was operating by itself. 'I don't think that was me, unless, well, I guess maybe he's set his feeds to be hidden unless he's at his workstation. Doesn't make much sense, but I don't know how else that might have happened. But I still don't know how any of this is happening. You can't escape the audiopts – that's the point of them.'

Truvan stepped over and grabbed Halthrop's arm with a tug. 'What are we waiting for? Come on, let's go. Even if the feeds go off again, we know where they're going.'

Major Halthrop looked up the Leckhampton bunker on his armulet.

Dira shouted at the screen for Halthrop. 'Go on, go get him!'

THE MIND'S EYE
Chapter Sixteen

About an hour earlier – 22nd March 2091, 11am
Jack's old office, The Doughnut

Jack tapped at a keyboard. With no sign of a feed from Dira, Jack left that screen running blank and called up the feeds for Halthrop and Truvan on the two adjacent screens. Both were heading towards the Doughnut. They were on the road from Gloucester, probably still half an hour away.

The screen monitoring Dira lit up. He was walking in the sunshine and had just crossed the old A40 road bridge, over the River Severn, on his way towards Highnam. Jack and Vicky stared at the screen. They looked briefly at each other and then back at Dira's view of the road. He was still humming the old ditty that he had sung on the threshold to Jack's office.

'Now then, where exactly is Ellie's house?' They heard him quizzing himself and could see Dira's view as he fiddled with a map on his armulet screen.

Without turning from watching the screen, Vicky hit the table with a fist. 'How did he get there so quickly?'

Jack could not look away from the monitor either. 'I've no idea. Could you get that far on a quad bike in…' He pointed at the screen's timestamp digits ticking away the seconds through 11.14am. 'Surely not?'

'How long ago was he here? It must have been no more than ten minutes, you think?'

Jack shook his head in confusion, and they both remained mesmerised. The picture turned off from the road onto a woodland path. The way Dira's view of the world swayed with his lumbering gait was slightly asymmetric. Jack tipped his head from left to right to watch it happening from different angles. He couldn't pinpoint it, but there was something odd.

After another five minutes of the humming and wobbling viewpoint, they saw Jack's grandmother's old house come into view. Jack felt Vicky squeeze his arm a little, and then she tugged it to turn Jack to face her. 'Do you think we should chase him and find out what he's up to?' Her face managed to look both eager and worried at the same time.

'Why would he go to Ellie's? Nobody has been there since I left.' Jack felt the way Vicky's face looked. He needed to get some answers, but Dira unsettled him. Jack had known the man, albeit vaguely, for years and had never noticed it before. Jack decided Dira just came across as a bit strange because he was introverted. He nodded to himself with a little smirk, dismissing the worry. *Yeah, I get that – just like you, Jack Smith.*

Vicky replied, oblivious to Jack's internal musings. 'Well, he's not to know that. Maybe he's looking for you – looking in the best-guess place you'd go.'

'But he was just here and almost certainly knew we were here too.'

'Hmm. Maybe he thinks he'll find some background information or something. Reasons why you might commit such crimes.'

'I didn't commit any crimes.'

'I know, but until we show him the proof, he's not to know that.'

'He's definitely after something. In fact, I wonder if he's gone there because he knows for sure that we're here, so he can look round the place undisturbed. That's why he rushed so quickly from here.'

'Look for what?'

'I have no idea.'

THE MIND'S EYE

'OK, let's go, but how are we going to avoid my brother and the Brigade? We can't close our eyes all the way there.'

'Well, no. And they'll have seen this so know where we're going.'

Vicky had let go of Jack's arm and was twirling her left forefinger in her hair, winding up the locks, letting them fall, and then winding up again. After a few moments, she said quietly, 'Maybe now is the time to give ourselves up. Dira could show them that it wasn't you who committed those crimes, and then Major Halthrop will be able to help us work out who really did them and how.'

Jack shrugged. 'How's he going to know I haven't done the crimes? Or show them that? Even we haven't worked out how to *prove* I didn't do those things.' He had come to the same conclusion about their next step, though. 'OK, let's head out to Ellie's place. They'll probably intercept us on the A40 or, most likely, be there before us.'

'Of course they'll be there before us. It'll take two hours to walk there.'

'I was thinking we take a couple of the bikes from outside.' Many of the sifters and infotechs at the Doughnut cycled to work and, with zero crime, they never locked the bikes.

Vicky gave Jack an angry frown. She gave off the impression that he was only making things worse for himself by committing more crimes in the pursuit of clearing his name. He was amazed that, simply from her look, he could understand exactly what she felt. Neither spoke. Eventually, she stood up to go.

As Jack had expected, the shelters outside held a number of electric bikes waiting to be stolen, most with plenty of battery charge too. Some sifters were arriving, just before their shift. A few were entering by the nearest door, but none came close enough to Jack and Vicky to notice them.

Vicky expressed a worry that somebody might recognise Jack, especially in light of his current crime spree. However, all the crimes had been committed in Highnam, and most sifters had little time to be interested in problems in other Kangaroos. Jack wondered if this was a sufficiently high profile case that it might have done the rounds of the sifter workstations, especially given his previous history with the Doughnut. They cycled across the vast, old car park as fast as the bikes could get them away from the risk of recognition. Despite knowing that they were likely to be heading straight into the path of the posse, Jack felt lighter as they rode away from visible people.

His relief was short-lived. As they cruised along, there were quite a few people out on the roads. The low population in 2091 meant that the roads were always only sparsely used. However, as this was the first fine day for a week, many had taken the chance to get out and catch up on errands. Vicky reckoned that the foot traffic was probably double that of an average day. Each person they passed gave a cheery wave or nod and usually a spoken greeting as well. Every time, Jack felt a knot in his stomach. He was convinced their gazes lingered on him too long. He couldn't bring himself to reply to anyone, but Vicky answered for both of them. Grannie Ellie's house was on the nearside of Highnam, but he still worried that somebody would recognise them before they got there, especially as they got closer – everyone in Highnam knew Vicky. The real interactions with people en route delivered a much stronger feeling of dread than the imagined Sword of Damocles of Halthrop's militia following their audiopt feeds to intercept. Even picturing them approaching from all directions on their quad bikes didn't trouble Jack as much as each 'Hello' or smiling wave.

'Where do you think Truvan and the others are?' Vicky's voice shook Jack from his reverie, and he wobbled slightly on the bike.

'I'm guessing they're just heading straight there.'

'I'd look on my armulet, but somebody made me leave it on a distant island.' She smiled at him.

Her levity soothed him. 'Well, I'd look on mine, but I threw it from a moving cart.' They rolled up the hill towards Grannie Ellie's small farmhouse. Jack estimated they might be thirty minutes behind Dira. The garden path wound up to the main entrance, which was a pair of French windows. No other vehicles were there. They'd seen Dira walk the final stretch, but Jack had assumed the posse would ride right up to the garden fence.

Jack walked in front, up the broken paving pieces that formed a winding footpath across the overgrown lawn. 'Heeelloooo,' he called. There was no reply.

Nobody was visible through the large glass pane in the main door. He pulled the door open slowly and leaned inside. He saw nobody. He also could not see any sign that anybody was present in the house: no coats, no bags, nothing. The place looked exactly as it had when he and Halthrop left together eighteen months before.

Jack and Vicky wandered around his late grandmother's house. It had been unoccupied in the nearly three years since she died.

'It does look like someone's been here. All the dust is messed up. In fact, I'd say it looks like several people have been here.'

Jack returned to the main lounge room where Vicky was examining footprints in the dust on the wooden floor. 'What the hell happened to the Brigade? I can imagine we might have missed Dira searching for whatever he thinks is here, but there's no way Halthrop would have left us alone, and they were closer than us.' Jack felt he knew Halthrop well. He couldn't understand how the man could be so inefficient. Since the cart ride to the Doughnut, he and Vicky hadn't tried to conceal anything from the audiopts. So, where were they?

'Should I mention again about having to leave my armulet on Steep Holm?'

'Ha, no thanks.'

'You're right though, it is pretty weird.'

'Hold on.' Jack bolted from the room. He headed towards his grandmother's old bedroom at the back of the house. He sat on the edge of her bed and opened the drawer of the bedside table. Vicky appeared on the threshold. 'She died in her sleep.'

'Yes, I know.'

Jack turned his head to look at Vicky. Her slight frame was silhouetted in the weak light from the windows across the front of the house. The shadow form highlighted the skew little finger on her right hand as it stuck out at its bizarre angle.

'She always took her armulet off before going to sleep.' From the drawer, he removed a leather wrist strap with the device clipped in and started shaking it. 'I don't have to tell you how old fashioned she was.'

'I do that too.' She smiled. Her face wasn't well lit, but Jack always thought Vicky's smile illuminated her face from within. Just like Ellie's had.

They walked back into the main lounge and sat beside each other on the old, green sofa. Jack stopped shaking occasionally and then had to continue when the armulet told him it still did not have enough charge. Once it agreed to start up, he strapped it on to Vicky's wrist.

THE MIND'S EYE

'Why am I having it?'

'In case I have to go on the run again.' He gave her a theatrical wink and then continued to shake her arm. 'Besides, I think the leatherwork looks better on you.'

'It is lovely. Do you know where she got it?'

'I never believed her, but she claimed it was from the very early days back in Brighton. She said people used to hold armulets in their hand, and they moved to wearing them on an arm when she was a young girl. It always struck me as unlikely that with everything she'd been through, it could last that long in one piece.'

'Well, I'll do my best to look after it – just don't make me throw it away!'

'Hopefully, nothing like that will be necessary again. Call up Dira's feeds and see where he's gone to.'

'Sorry, I'm gonna check on Truvan first. You want first say, put it on your own wrist.' Jack shrugged nonchalantly, but he revelled in Vicky's teasing.

She projected the view from her brother's eyes: he walked in to meet the rest of the posse in Jack's work area at the Doughnut. They saw Jane point out a photo of Ellie that sat in a frame on Jack's desk. He and Vicky both looked up to a copy of the same photo on her sideboard. Jack commented, 'She only put that up in here because I liked it so much. It took me ages to convince her. "Why would I want a photo of me in here?" she'd always argue.'

'It's nice.' They stared for a moment at Ellie Smith in her sixties, sitting, windblown, by The Lake.

'See where Dira is now.'

Vicky made several gestures at the armulet. 'He's not showing any feeds.'

'What?' Jack leaned in to look at the screen itself. 'Again? Something is buggered up here.' They both looked back at Ellie for inspiration. She smiled down from the picture frame but offered little more than that implicit support.

'I'll see when they went off again. Maybe we'll catch some of what he did whilst he was here.'

She was confounded by the search system. It refused to offer any records at all for Dira for 22nd March.

Jack's expression became more confused as Vicky continued to gesticulate towards her forearm. 'Wait, how is this possible? There's no records at all since this morning? We both saw it, didn't we? He was walking along near here and searching for Ellie's house. You did see that too?'

She stopped waving at the device. 'Yes.' Vicky's voice was quiet.

'Wait, OK, try this. Look back at my feeds, for the time when we saw Dira's feeds showing him coming here. Ch- check if I really did see that.' He stuttered slightly.

Her voice was barely audible. 'Jack. You've got no feed record either.' She waved her fingers some more. 'Neither have I.'

There was silence for a long time.

Jack was first to speak. 'Does anybody have feeds? Maybe the whole system's gone off. Check back on Halthrop.'

'I just showed you Truvan's.' She paused. Jack stared at the armulet screen and waved his hand for her to proceed anyway. 'OK.' Vicky called up Frank's audiopt view. He was at the Doughnut, in Jack's old office.

'Jack.' She looked at him wide-eyed. 'I'm scared. None of this makes any sense. What's happening?'

He put one hand on her free one and pointed at the armulet to refocus them into action. 'I think we may need to call Halthrop directly and arrange to meet so we can work out together who's doing what and why. But just before we give ourselves up, let's watch the mood there. I want to make sure your brother doesn't railroad them into simply handing me to Kangaroo. We'll never get any answers if that happens. Is Truvan still with him?'

Jack and Vicky saw that Halthrop was watching an image in Jack's workspace, with Aluen at his station in the background. The projected image showed Jack looking at Vicky, outside, and talking about going to Leckhampton bunker. In Ellie's lounge, Vicky slowly raised her arm and moved her finger to point on her screen at the timestamp scrolling along the bottom of the holographic image Halthrop was watching. It purported to be the audiopt feed for Jack Smith, and it purported to be live.

'Malthus! There's buggered up, and then there's this!'

She turned and grabbed his arms. She was shaking, and it made him shake too. Her voice was now louder than normal. 'What's going on, Jack?'

Chapter Seventeen
22nd March 2091, 12.40pm
The Doughnut

Halthrop scratched his head and then moved his hand to touch his moustache. As bizarrely as it had appeared, Jack's audiopt feed went off again. The posse had watched him and Vicky discuss heading to a place they referred to as 'Leckhampton bunker' as a hideout.

'Come on, let's go!' Truvan picked up his little, blue backpack and headed for the exit from Jack's large office space. Terry was on his heels.

'Just a second, where exactly are you headed? Do you know this place? Where is it?'

Truvan stopped and turned back to Halthrop. He looked slightly confused. 'Well, Leckhampton is just outside Cheltenham, isn't it? South side of town.'

Jane chipped in. 'Leckhampton is. It's not even two kilometres from here. Actually really close to Smith's old house in Cheltenham.' She continued fiddling with her armulet.

'There you go. Come on, we're wasting time.'

Halthrop held his left hand up, palm facing Truvan and Terry. The air conditioning buzzed quietly. 'Just a moment. With Jane, there's always something more....'

He looked at the short, young woman. She stood to the side of Jack's horseshoe workstation, still swiping and tapping the screen on her forearm. Jane projected a picture of a crumbling concrete building. It was single-storey, very rectangular, and had a wooden-framed door hanging open, attached by one last hinge.

THE MIND'S EYE

She looked first at Terry and then back to the boss. 'Leckhampton is very close, but the bunker is actually on Leckhampton Hill in Ullenwood. That's getting on for 10k. Probably just under half an hour away.'

Major Halthrop smiled. He looked at the two near the doorway. 'OK, Jane will navigate. Let's get going.'

Nobody ran, but the group bustled down the stairs in a considerable rush. As they went out through steel and glass double doors to the bike shelter, the bright sunlight suddenly blinded. The tinting on the building's glass was supremely effective. In many corridors, it was actually solar p-v plastic that helped to generate the electricity that powered the building. Bringing up the rear, Frank got his sunglasses on before stepping outside. He watched the others standing at their bikes, all waiting for their eyes to readjust, having also donned sunglasses. The sky was blue, but, being March, the midday temperature had still only reached about twenty-five degrees.

Although nowhere near summertime temperatures, the heat outside, compared to the environmentally controlled interior of the Doughnut, made for a hot and sweaty cycle to the bunker. As Jane had estimated, it took them twenty-eight minutes.

Halthrop worried as they approached that he had not organised the convoy order. He had not even thought through what he wanted in that regard. He cursed himself for being hurried into this chase. He remembered, *Whoever is first in the field and awaits the coming of the enemy, will be fresh for the fight; whoever is second in the field and has to hasten to battle will arrive exhausted.* Out loud, he muttered, 'Sun Tzu, you'd better be wrong.'

They continued up to the chainlink fence surrounding the building at a distance of about twenty metres. It had a double gate, also chainlink, which was in a similar state to the entrance door. Each gate was lazing at a heavy angle, whilst the main double doors looked rotten around the edges. They were dark wood, thick frames around large panels of glass with security wire criss-crossing through it. The right-hand door was wide open, stuck against the crumbling concrete ground for so long that grass had grown up between the door and the entrance it was supposed to block. It also leaned at an ungainly angle that defied its hinges.

Despite there being no difficulty to passing inside the perimeter, everyone had dismounted outside the big gates. In the few seconds that it took the major to arrive at the milling group, he shook his head, took a deep breath, and cajoled himself, 'If we open a quarrel between the past and the present, we shall find that we have lost the future.'

Darren leant his bike against the fence and asked, 'Is now a good time for lunch?'

'Is there never anything else? I haven't even brought any food,' Jane retorted.

'An army marches on its stomach,' Darren replied. He looked at Major Halthrop, with a hand on the pannier at the back of his bike.

Halthrop leant his bike in front of Jane's and scanned the group. 'I take it that is the main entrance?' He looked at Jane but pointed at the brown door, hanging open.

She answered, 'Yep, and the way I read this, there's no other entrance. It's a real labyrinth inside, though. And still no audiopt signal from either of them.'

'Darren, you stand guard, and make sure nobody escapes. You can eat your food, but pay attention to the doorway all the time. In fact, once we've gone in, you stand right in the doorway, please.'

THE MIND'S EYE

Darren was already inside his pannier, and replied, 'Sure thing, Frank.' Halthrop frowned.

'I'll go point, then Terry, Jane, and Truvan, you follow at the back, please.'

He stepped through the gap between the gates and strode towards the doorway. The place looked like a derelict primary school from videostories Halthrop had watched about the Times of Malthus.

In 2091, children were educated in people's homes. Usually in groups, so you might call it school, but the requirements of education were left up to each individual Kangaroo, and they generally devolved details, like the curriculum, to those individuals who volunteered to teach classes. All human knowledge was available on the infonetwork, so teachers could easily follow systems of education that had been recorded online, many from before the Times. That wasn't often popular; some people believed that the education systems in place eighty or so years ago had led directly to the start of the Times. For the most part, the volunteer teachers tended to weight their lessons towards the history of the Times. Often, they would start before the Bitness Revelations, but it was rare to continue much beyond the signing of the Covenants of Jerusalem.

Halthrop entered, and the primary school image fell away. Almost immediately, there was a concrete stairway with a red-painted steel handrail that headed down into darkness. Armulet lighting helped them down safely. The major had to avoid a variety of debris, fixtures and fittings that had not survived the ravages of time.

Silence took over the group. Terry touched Halthrop's back, and, with his other hand, he pointed to smashed glass splinters on the ground that had once been an old light tube. The torch beam from the armulet pointed wherever his finger pointed. They were at the bottom of the staircase, and the corridor went away left and right into the dark.

There was no need to be quiet. However, even when he spoke, Halthrop's voice was a whisper. He directed Jane and Terry to the left and took Truvan to the right.

He had not noticed any solar panels on the roof of the ground level, but they came across a wall of transformers and circuit breakers. There seemed to be no change in the power supply when Truvan turned the fuse box handle to 'ON'. Certainly, no lights came on.

They continued along the narrow underground corridor until it opened into a cavernous room. On each side, there was a giant metal engine of some sort. Both were smooth, painted in a cream colour. At the far end of each machine, there was a big rectangular tank with a pipe feed leading into the back end of the machine. This detail, combined with the bits of writing in various places, led Frank and Truvan to conclude that these were electricity generators, but the old kind, powered by oil of some sort.

The fuel tanks boomed ominously when Truvan banged the sides. The place had been designed as an emergency shelter, so would originally have had numerous stores. Halthrop knew that even if there had been any fuel, it would have long since degraded beyond use.

He had heard of people in Texas still pumping up oil on individual farmsteads, but no fuels were available in England. He imagined an old style cowboy standing at the tank and filling it with a thick, black liquid poured from a wooden barrel on the man's shoulder. The daydream proceeded with the generator starting up with a rumble, and a cloud of black smoke, and then whistling like an old steam train.

'Major?' Truvan tapped his arm and stepped forward towards the next doorway. Halthrop realised that they didn't

THE MIND'S EYE

need power. The little light they had would suffice to find anybody hiding in these subterranean rooms. He checked the audiopt feeds again but still nothing for Jack or Vicky.

Frank was distracted looking at his forearm and standing still, when Truvan shouted, 'Vicky, stop!', and tried to run back past the major. Halthrop turned and saw two shadows running off down the corridor towards the exit stairs. He followed Truvan in the chase. Their torchlights did not catch on the two people, and they seemed to be carrying no light source either. The clattering of footsteps was the only thing that made Halthrop believe he had not simply imagined the phantoms he wanted to see.

He shouted ahead to try and pull Jane and Terry back to intercept. They arrived at the bottom of the main staircase at the same moment that Halthrop did. Truvan was a dozen stairs ahead already, bounding upwards. They all chased up too.

The light outside blinded them again. Darren was sat right across the threshold with his back against the door frame. Truvan was outside but had stopped. Jane leapt over Darren's legs. Terry tried the same but caught his toe and sprawled over his seated comrade. Halthrop stopped to wait for the young man to get up again. This was swift as Darren pretty much hurled Terry outside one-handed.

'What are you doing, you idiot?' Darren shouted. He was rubbing his thigh with one hand and cradling a large sandwich with the other. Fortunately for Darren, his giant hand was even larger than the sandwich, so no part of it was lost.

Halthrop bent down and put his hand on Darren's shoulder. 'Shh. Accident.' He stepped over Darren's legs and saw the other three facing in various directions, all breathing heavily. The smells of damp grass and pollen on the breeze were a shock change from those of concrete and wet decay in the underground tunnels. He inhaled deeply.

Major Halthrop turned back to Darren, who was staring at the rest of the posse in the bright space outside. He bent down again and rested his hands on his knees. He was also out of breath and spoke quietly to the sentry. 'Where did they go?'

'Who?'

'They must have run right by you, right over you. How could you not stop them?'

'What are you talking about, Frank?'

'Stand up.' Halthrop took Darren's upper arm and impelled him to rise. 'Two people came running up the stairs ahead of us. Look. From the top of the stairs to here, the only way they could exit is over where you were sitting. We chased them up the stairs. You must have seen where they went.' Darren stared at his CO's face. 'Well? Which way?'

Darren's ruddy, round face appeared to be made of jelly. 'Honestly, nobody came past me. You lot went down, I stood in the doorway till your lights all disappeared, then I sat down.' He looked down and pointed at the floor where he had been seated. 'Then you all came running up.' He looked around the others, who were all watching and listening, and back to Halthrop. 'Nobody else.' His lips wobbled as he said the last phrase.

Halthrop folded his arms and turned slightly to face everyone. He closed his eyes for a second and then re-opened them, focussed on Truvan. 'You shouted that it was Vicky. I wasn't able to see who they were. Are you certain it was them?'

Audible only to Halthrop who was closest, Darren sighed as he stared at the ground, 'Nobody.'

Truvan stepped forward and announced, 'Yes, I saw her well enough to know it was Vicky. I didn't see the other one more than just a figure, but it must have been Smith. Who else would it be?'

THE MIND'S EYE

'Where did they go?' Jane almost wailed towards the perimeter fence.

'Did you two see them?' Halthrop waved a finger at her and Terry.

Terry answered, 'I didn't actually see them, but heard the footsteps running up the stairs to Darren.' Silently, Darren shook his head. His mouth opened and closed.

Terry turned to look at Jane. She shrugged. 'No, like Terry said, just the noise.'

Halthrop knew he had heard footsteps running away from him in the dark corridor. 'And you two were away the other side of the staircase from us all the time?' He'd also seen them arrive at the base of the stairs from the opposite direction, but it was possible that everyone had been chasing others from their own group. Strange things happen in the dark. Disorientation would be easy. Jane's hair could easily be mistaken for Vicky's when held in a ponytail. But Jane was much shorter, and it was Truvan's own sister. Together, Jane and Terry answered, 'Yes.'

She continued, 'There wasn't anything to see up that way. A kitchen area, some showers and toilets, and a dormitory of bunk beds. What did you find your way?'

'Terry, you and Jane go back inside and check there's no possible other way out or hiding place. Maybe a door on the stairs. See what you can find. Darren, you guard this door properly this time. Nobody comes out unless I agree. Got it?'

Darren's lips trembled again as he breathed, 'Yes, sir.'

Terry shoved past his much larger colleague, and Jane followed Terry inside. She stared at Darren all the way in passing. Darren scowled and stepped onto the threshold. He braced his arms, hands on hips, shoulders back, so as to fill the space as much as possible.

Halthrop's armulet rang for a videocall. He tapped the screen and heard Jack Smith's voice. 'We need to meet.'

Jane and Terry had not descended far enough to miss Jack's statement. They turned and headed back. Darren stood still. 'Get out of the way!' Terry ordered.

'Nobody comes out till the major agrees.' Terry tried to push Darren aside, but he was bulky enough to be able to withstand the skinny man's best efforts.

Halthrop had been distracted from the call by the squabbling soldiers. He had not said anything in response. 'Cut it out you two. This is important.'

He turned back as Truvan arrived at his side to watch the little screen. 'What have you done with my sister?'

Vicky's face had been the one on screen all the time. 'I'm right here. We're together at the Doughnut. But he hasn't kidnapped me or anything.' She smiled at Halthrop.

'The Doughnut? How did you get there so fast? In fact, you two have been managing to travel impossibly fast a lot.'

Jack's voice sounded again. 'That's kind of what we need to talk about. Meet us at my old office in the Doughnut as soon as you can. And Major…'

Halthrop jumped in, 'Yes?'

'Under no circumstances should you believe anything you see on any audiopt feed. I'm not just talking about those crimes that look like I'm committing them. All audiopt feeds are compromised.'

Vicky's brother had to speak. 'Don't think you can tell us what to do, Smith!'

Halthrop raised his other hand to silence Truvan. 'What do you mean "compromised"?'

'We're not sure exactly what's going on or how it's being done, but somehow false images are being played into the feeds system.'

THE MIND'S EYE

'How do you know?' Truvan demanded. He turned to look at Halthrop and spoke more quietly. 'This is just a smokescreen to put us off.'

Jack interrupted, 'Why are you at Leckhampton bunker? Because you saw me and Vicky discussing how we should go there to hide out. We watched you watching that on a projection in my office. But when you were watching that, which said it was live, we were in my Grannie's old house, and we've never spoken about Leckhampton since the last time we saw each other, eighteen months ago.' The videocall was cut off.

Chapter Eighteen
An hour earlier – 22nd March 2091, 1.30pm
The Doughnut

Dira sat at his workstation at the back of his cavernous workshop. The walls were concrete, painted white. Above ground, the construction included limestone and granite, but the basements had not been built to look pretty. Behind the office chair he wheeled around on, a small living space was Dira's second home. He had a metal framed bed against the back wall, an old armchair and a small, low table.

He sipped a black coffee and put the mug down on the desk at the limit of his reach. Over many years, he had worked out the least-risk locations for placing food and drink by his computers. If he could barely reach the coffee, he would struggle to knock it over accidentally.

The central screens were the two showing Jack and Vicky's feeds. Dira was typing some code on the two below them. He had both audio feeds on but very quiet. His subconscious caught Vicky speaking the word 'stairs' and scrambled his brain to concentrate. The two of them were descending towards his basement location. They had just passed Aluen's level and were continuing down. Dira pressed a two-key combination on the keyboard and all the screens went blank and silenced.

He moved as fast as his limp would take him through an adjoining door into the destroyed server room. Dira wasn't ready to be found yet. His long hands closed the door and, as quietly as he could manage, rolled a large block of broken concrete behind it. He made to look at his armulet, and his body jerked. With a stab of horror, he realised had left it on the workstation desk.

THE MIND'S EYE

There was a centimetre gap at the bottom edge of the door. Again, moving as stealthily as he could, Dira laid himself flat out so that his ear was at the gap.

He heard Jack and Vicky tinkering with tools, which banged metallically. Their conversation was sometimes clear and sometimes muffled. He put his finger in the ear away from the door to try and improve the sound detection of the open ear.

The dusty, rubble-strewn floor was uncomfortable but Dira was intent on shifting position as little as possible. He didn't want to miss any conversation and didn't want to make any noise.

After the Doughnut explosion, the infotechs repairing the network, including himself, had decided that the simplest approach would simply be to repurpose a different server hall to run the audiopts. The software was easily transferable – Jack had not destroyed all the computers in the world. All around Dira sat the shattered remains of the hundred or so that he had blown up.

Dira concentrated on the sounds coming from under the door. His eyes were left scanning this permanent museum to the revolution that never was. He often thought about how, apart from this damaged room, his damaged leg was the only long-lasting result from Jack's bombing.

Jack and Vicky discovered the replica sifter workstation. They also found his armulet and the coffee cup that was still hot. The presence of the workstation confused them slightly but was not an extraordinary surprise. He heard Jack reconcile it as probably useful for any infotech.

A squeaking sound told Dira that Jack was sitting in his chair. He imagined Jack trying to crack the password protection, whilst Vicky wandered around picking things up and dropping them down on his big repairs table.

'You see this metal framework?' Vicky's voice was clear.

Jack responded but didn't sound like he was actually concentrating. 'Uh-huh.'

'It's got a load of hooks for tools out on this part, but I can't see the need for it go all the way around where you are. And especially all the way around that little living area.'

'Uh-huh.'

'Are you listening to what I'm saying, Jack? Why has he built this cage around all that?'

Vicky stopped, waiting for Jack to answer. In the silence, Dira could hear the chair creaking again, but no clattering on the keyboards.

'Jack!'

'Sorry, I'm struggling to work out how to get these terminals to let me in. What?'

'I asked why you think this metal cage is here. Would that block radio waves? Is this why his audiopt feeds go off some of the time?'

He was uncomfortable; there was a rock sticking in his ribs. Dira tried to pull it out from under his chest without moving his ear away from the door. It scraped. He stopped. There seemed no response from within his workrooms, so he completed the movement of the rock. He could not see what he was doing as he placed it on another couple of smaller rocks. The three of them toppled and fell making a small crash. Dira froze, listening intently.

Vicky heard it. When she asked Jack, he had still not been paying enough attention to the noises around him to identify the crash as special. She said she would investigate and Dira heard Jack grunt. He felt panic as he heard her footsteps approach.

THE MIND'S EYE

Without moving from his prone position, Dira pressed both palms above his head against the wood of the door. Vicky tried to open it. She pushed hard. Sweat slid down Dira's cheeks as he exerted as much force as possible against the door. He tried to breathe deeply without making any sound, but it was a struggle. He felt the door push again and re-tensed his arms. They were shaking and hot. He pushed his head and neck against the concrete block he'd pushed against the door. Dira thought the door moved, but the pressure ceased. He had managed to hold it fast enough to convince her.

'I can't move this door. Do they sometimes lock doors in this place?' Vicky called across the space on the other side of the wood that separated her from Dira. She was still only centimetres away, and his heart was pounding.

Dira couldn't hear Jack as well as before, but he said something negative in reply. Dira shook his head a little and mouthed the word 'No' in agreement. He thought she gave up a bit easily but was glad to relax his arms. They ached. He didn't dare lower them but wiggled his fingers in a feeling of release.

As her footsteps moved away from the door, Vicky asked Jack what he had discovered. Jack confessed to having achieved nothing – the computers were locked down. Dira smiled. He had to bite his lip to stop himself chuckling out loud. He whispered, 'Oh, my dear Jack, you'll kick yourself when you hear the password!'

'I don't think there's anything else we can get from down here, then. Come on, let's go back up to your office.'

The chair stopped squeaking. 'He's left his armulet here, but it won't work for me either. I think he's set some sort of biometric lock on it too. It won't even tell me what it wants to see to open up.'

'What do you mean?'

'Well, you can make your armulet lock up, and it'll have to do a retina or fingerprint scan to open again and start working. Or something like that – there's loads of possibilities like ear scans or palmprints.'

'How weird.'

'Still, even if we knew, it would need his body to open it.'

Dira smiled to himself in his hiding place.

Jack said, 'I'll take it upstairs and see if Aluen has any ideas.'

'No, leave it here. I think we may be making too much of all this. If that cage'll make his feeds disappear, then that could be a perfectly innocent explanation. He might need computers to be shielded from the infonetwork signals for some electronic engineering reason, when he repairs them. Hence the cage. And then the audiopt blocking is just an extra consequence of him doing his job.'

Dira sniggered silently.

He heard Jack argue. 'Don't you think this is all rather strange? He goes snooping through Ellie's house, he has this metal cage, which happens to block his own signals, and he leaves his armulet in it.'

Vicky countered, 'He's been assigned to help find you. I'm not at all surprised he went to your Grannie's house. The rest may be a bit odd, I don't know. He's an infotech. Like I say, maybe the cage helps with tech problems. And leaving his armulet here won't stop the infonetwork masts from picking up his audiopt feeds. We don't know what any of this stuff is for. What I do know is that none of it is criminal. Didn't you say he's one of the most well-respected techs in the place?'

Jack's voice faded as they left the basement. 'That just means that…'

THE MIND'S EYE

Dira responded out loud, albeit only to himself, 'Don't go thinking you can make them believe I committed your crimes, Jack.' He struggled to remove the concrete blocking the door and squeezed through the tiniest of gaps, before continuing the monologue. 'Oh no you don't. I can go under the radar of hidden audiopt feeds too, you know.'

He collected his armulet and it unlocked at his touch. He tapped the screen in a quick medley of instructions.

'Right then, Dira, what do I need to take?' He looked around the small living space and put a few provisions into his dirty brown backpack. The bottles of water made it heavy, so he put some back, but kept the small amount of food he had put in. It was mostly fruit, so he figured he would eat it on the way.

Dira's plan was to head back to his house in Cheltenham, pick up a few more things and then head to Leckhampton bunker. He grinned to himself at the thought of it and put on a funny voice, an attempt to mimic Halthrop. 'It would be terribly embarrassing for a tracker as good as Major Frank Halthrop to have to return to a place already cleared.'

At the base of the staircase up to the world, he checked the feeds on his armulet. The posse were leaving Leckhampton bunker and on their way back to the Doughnut. Jack and Vicky were ensconced in Jack's office.

Perfect. The detour back to the house will take me out of the Brigade's way, just as they pass by, and then I can get back on the quickest path. The scooter should be OK on the Ullenwood road.

He tapped away at his armulet again, reviewing the footage of the arson at Highnam Court, the assault on Lloyd Lloyd and the explosion at the Bristol Brigade HQ. 'That is a catalogue of evil crimes. He'll get the death penalty this time; justice needs to be served.'

Chapter Nineteen
22nd March 2091, 3pm
The Doughnut

Halthrop arranged for the three younger Brigade members to enter Jack's office from the far side, whilst he and Truvan went up the stairs past Aluen's office. They all entered simultaneously and found Jack and Vicky seated in front of his horseshoe of screens. Five of the screens were set to show each posse member's audiopt feeds. The rest were blank.

'Got him!' Truvan shouted and pointed. 'Let's take him back to Highnam.' He stepped forward towards the side of the workstation where Vicky sat. In a more normal voice, Truvan said to his sister, 'Why do you let him fool you all the time?'

'Oh, Malthus, do be quiet!' She swivelled the chair around so that her back was facing him.

Major Halthrop took charge. 'You two cover that door.' He pointed at Darren and Terry to stay beside the far entrance to the room, across the large open office space. 'Jane, you've got this one.' He waved behind at the door through which he had just followed Truvan.

'OK, Jack, you've got one chance to tell us about what you've done to the audiopt system, and then we're going to take you to Highnam for Kangaroo.'

Jack reclined in his high-backed chair. It creaked like the one in the basement, and he put his hands behind his head. 'Well, first off, I was not the one who committed any of those crimes in Highnam. I think Vicky sent you the link for my feeds record on Steep Holm, which shows me there when the crimes were committed.'

THE MIND'S EYE

Truvan interjected, 'You're not in any of those records – I've watched it all. And it's not even you anyway. The link she sent is for someone called Andrew Gallum.'

'Gallian. That man died in 2062. And he's been using that armulet since he got there, without re-registering it,' Vicky retorted. She looked at Halthrop, keeping her back to her brother.

Jack's relaxed pose was less comfortable than he had hoped. He took his hands back down from behind his head and rested them in his lap. Jack looked at everyone, then continued, 'If you look closely at the recordings from those events, the man who appears to be doing the crimes looks exactly like I did eighteen months ago, the last time I was on a known feed recording.'

Halthrop nodded, a finger touching his moustache. Jack had been thin when they had captured him previously. Now, he looked positively unhealthy – gaunt was an understatement.

Jack continued, 'Whoever has produced those fake feeds has used my image from then to make them. You can watch them and see what I mean. But I think we've got bigger problems than that.'

'What do you mean, 'bigger problems'? Marisa Leone died because of you.' Truvan emphasised the word "died".

Jack did not even turn towards the man. 'As I said, I was on Steep Holm when that fire was set.'

He looked set to continue, but Halthrop urged him on anyway. 'What *do* you mean, "bigger problems"?'

'You watched Vicky and me, right on here.' Jack waved at the screen in front of him. 'You saw a conversation we never had. So somebody has worked out how to insert fake records into the infonetwork and make the system believe it's real.'

'Nobody believes that the records of those crimes don't really show you. There's no fake records. It's not possible to fool the system.'

Vicky swivelled back to face her brother. Her skin burned much redder than its normal olive oil brown colour. 'Will you shut up! I saw that conversation you saw us have about Leckhampton. I watched it live, but I wasn't having it. This is real. Open your mind, and your ears, and listen to what's going on. If we can't stop this, much worse could happen. Whoever is doing this could do anything they want and get away with it.'

Jack grimaced and put his hand out to Vicky. She turned back to face him. 'I think there's actually an even bigger problem with the audiopts. Not only can we not trust them, but we need to dismantle the whole system.'

Terry spoke up from the back of the room. 'Not this again. Frank, this is all just another excuse to get the whole system taken down. I wouldn't be surprised if he'd done it all himself.'

Jack smiled. 'Had I thought of it, I probably would have done this. I don't think I've quite learnt enough coding to be able to manage it though. But I can show that the system is not impregnable: I managed to hide mine and Vicky's feeds earlier.'

'See, I told you. He's the criminal here, he's...' Vicky turned again and shot her brother such a look that he stopped talking.

Major Halthrop stopped stroking his moustache to get the discussion back on course. 'What do you mean, Jack? What's the big problem? If you managed to hack into the system, then it sounds like we need to get some techs working on protecting it. Surely, that'd be enough?'

THE MIND'S EYE

'I don't think so. Whoever is doing this can do more than just fake records. We watched you lot at Leckhampton: you saw two mystery people down in the bunker, right?'

Halthrop gave a little wave of his hand for Jack to keep going.

'If you look on Truvan's feed, it definitely is Vicky he sees. It's probably me too, but the first person isn't so clear.'

Halthrop said, 'What do you mean "probably me too"? Surely, you know if you were there?'

'This is the point. Vicky and I know we were not there. You saw a vision of us. It wasn't really us, but you were made to see us. Just like the witnesses of the Highnam crimes. They really think they saw me, but I was not there.'

'I can confirm Jack and Vicky have been here since at least 2pm.' Nobody had noticed Aluen hovering at the doorway. Jane had been concentrating on the conversation, making sure nobody escaped, rather than stopping extra people listening in. 'Since I spoke to you earlier, I stayed in the Doughnut, and I've watched all of you the whole time. What Jack says looks to be true.'

Halthrop asked, 'Hold on. You're saying that this isn't just manipulating the digital records that are stored in the basement? What I see in real life isn't necessarily real?'

There was a long silence. 'That is what I'm saying, but I can't get my head around it,' Jack finally answered.

'It isn't possible,' Aluen concurred. She had stepped past Jane to a point almost within the conversation circle. Her dark ponytail swung a couple of times and settled. 'But it does answer all the inconsistencies in the records of those crimes.'

'But wait.' Halthrop stopped, trying to reconcile conflicting thoughts. His delivery came a sentence at a time, with pauses between each new idea developing. 'That means we cannot trust anything we see or hear. Even this conversation might not be totally real. One of you might be somebody else, disguised somehow. And I might be hearing things you're not saying. And you might not hear my responses.'

'Exactly! Like I said, can't get my head round all the implications.' The room fell silent again. 'But I'm pretty sure that the solution is in the audiopt surveillance system. Or I should say, the problem is in the surveillance system. So, the solution, or at least a mitigation to allow us to investigate without having more visions interfere with what we're doing, is to switch the audiopts off.'

'It's very convenient that you know the answer, and that it's to switch off the system that you tried to destroy last time you were here.' Terry's tone was sardonic. 'I tell you, Frank, this is a ruse. He's planned the whole thing.'

Halthrop spoke. 'Well, look. Even if he did do those crimes in Highnam as part of some big plan to get us here and convince us to switch off the system, we definitely saw the two of them at the bunker, and Aluen definitely saw them here at the same time.'

Terry pointed out, 'Aluen watched her screens to see them here. And it looks like the records on screen can be messed with.'

'No, I came down and peeked in here,' Aluen said. 'I wondered exactly that at the time. I saw them sitting where they are now.'

Halthrop added, 'And they were back here so fast after escaping the bunker that something impossible has happened.'

'Wait!' Vicky blurted out. It was such an ejaculation that everyone turned to her. Even Darren, who had been slouching against the door jamb at the back, stood up to listen. She swivelled towards Jack. 'The audiopts work by intercepting nerve signals from our eyes and ears, right?'

THE MIND'S EYE

'Well, I'd probably use the word 'detecting' – the signals aren't affected, so you still see and hear everything, but so does the surveillance system.'

'Alright, *detecting* the nerve signals. And you said that those fake records couldn't be there if we didn't actually see and hear the things because of that detection?'

'Yes, but I'm not so sure now. We've seen so many strange things going on that it looks like maybe the records can be manipulated.'

Vicky looked up over his head at some indeterminate point on the far wall. She was twiddling with the hair at her temple, twisting it up repeatedly. 'OK, tell me if this would work: instead of detecting those nerve signals, could the system be reversed, so that it transmits signals to the optic and auditory nerves, so you see and hear stuff that isn't really happening?'

Halthrop said, 'That would seem as real as if it actually happened.' He paused and thought some more. Looking back and forth between Aluen and Jack, he then asked, 'What about that, sifters? Could that explain what we've been seeing?'

Jack looked at Aluen. Her eyes were closed, so he spoke. 'I think that could work. The signals would have to be encoded so only specific people would see the fake images. You couldn't blanket transmit it, or the images would be out of context. The background wouldn't work with what you were looking at, for example. But the system will have detailed enough records of every individual's nerve signals to do targeted encoding. It'd be easier to single out those who have their armulet on, but even that wouldn't strictly be necessary – I'm sure the infonetwork masts can transmit strongly enough to do the job if you're in range. It'd be really difficult, though, even to co-ordinate images for just a couple of people at once.'

'Is that why Darren didn't see them come out of the bunker?' Jane asked.

At his name, Darren came to life. 'I told you nobody had escaped. I was watching.'

Halthrop held up a hand. 'OK, Darren.'

Aluen spoke. 'I can't see how it could be done though. We don't have any control over the system – it's completely isolated.'

Jack answered this. 'It's taken me eighteen months, but I've learnt enough coding to be able to work out how to mask my own feeds. That's not nearly the same, but it shows that the system is not impregnable. But...' His voice trailed off.

'What?' Halthrop poked.

'I could only do it with the access to the system you can get from here. Inserting the necessary code needed direct access to the servers here. I couldn't have done it from anywhere outside the Doughnut. And I couldn't do it on my armulet even from here.'

'Are you saying...'

'A sifter's done this.'

Vicky spoke quietly, 'Or an infotech.'

Jack added, 'That does make some sense though. The computing power required to pull off these fakes, in real time, with several participants, is... well, unimaginable. But, if there's anywhere that would have that amount of computing power, it's this place.' He waved his arms around.

Halthrop said, 'Well, that cuts down the suspect list quite significantly. Will you be able to work out who it was?'

Jack looked at Aluen. She gave a shrug. He said, 'I don't know.'

Aluen countered, 'Actually, we know a few instances where there's been a fake vision for sure. There's the witnesses in Highnam, and these two in the bunker. Do you think we

THE MIND'S EYE

could find the software code that related to them and then that would show who had put it in?' It was Jack's turn to shrug. 'I'll ask Dira to have a look into it. He really knows everything about everything when it comes to the whole infonetwork system.'

Vicky spoke up. 'No, remember, somebody that works here is responsible. We can't trust any of them. In particular though, we're not so sure about him. His feeds keep disappearing.' She pointed at one of the blank screens in front of them. 'This is live-streaming him, and nothing for at least an hour. Well, most of the day actually, but we haven't been here all day.'

'Really?' Aluen came around the horseshoe of desks and looked at the screen. The timestamp at the bottom confirmed it was Dira and live feed. 'He's on shift right now. He should be in the basement or working somewhere around here.'

Halthrop instructed the three junior Brigade members to go with Aluen and find Dira and bring him to Jack's office. Once they had gone, he asked, 'Do you think we can trust Aluen? Might she be the culprit?'

Jack said, 'To be totally certain, I don't think we can trust anybody here. I feel like she's not the one, but I wonder if we can somehow confirm that. But, actually, it's more urgent than finding out who's behind it all.'

'What do you mean?'

'Until we shut down the whole system, they can keep sending false visions. This could make us do things wrong in every possible way. This very conversation could be unreal, imagined. I could be looking at the computer system trying to search for the hacking code that's been inserted and see a vision that it was Aluen who did it, when in fact that's not reality. I'm seeing it, but it's not what the screen is actually showing. We can't trust anything we see and hear whilst the system is still running.'

Halthrop frowned. He looked left and right at the floor in front of him. He exhaled hard, like a horse blowing its lips. 'I'm not sure I'll be able to swing that. This is going to affect every Kangaroo. Most of which haven't even heard of the Highnam crimes. I can't see them believing me with this tale. Especially when they hear your name associated with the whole business.' He waved in the direction of Truvan, who had moved to stare out of the panoramic window. 'They'll think exactly like him.'

'I really don't think we can proceed with the system on. At least over quite a large area around here, much larger than Highnam.'

Vicky said, 'If we can do the investigation from here, don't we only need to switch it off for the Doughnut?'

Halthrop turned to Jack. 'That's true.'

'Um, maybe. I think we should extend a bit further, so none of the masts nearby can affect us in here. But if we find out who it is and try to catch them, we might need to chase outside, so we'd need to have authority to shut down other areas too. Actually, you could tell them all that we'll only do it temporarily till we catch whoever it is. The other slight problem is that I'm not even sure how to shut down the system. I assume we can find infotechs who would know what to do.'

'This all started with them trying to frame you for the fire, and the assault on Lloyd Lloyd,' Vicky said.

'And blowing up our Brigade HQ,' Halthrop added.

She continued, 'So this is clearly about you. I don't see this being somebody random like the sifter for, I don't know, Swindon, say. This is going to be somebody that knows you. We just walked in here. You said yourself there's no control over access to this place. Surely it could be anyone, although they'd have to actually be here.'

The other four trooped back in. Jane reported, 'He's not in any of the places Aluen thinks he might ever be.'

'You mean your eyes didn't think they saw him,' Jack said.

'Well, whatever, we couldn't find him.'

Halthrop decided that he needed to set up a properly organised mission plan. He told them all to get something to eat, rest, and he would brief the newly enlarged posse at 16:00 hours.

Truvan briefly argued about this being beyond what Highnam had tasked the Bristol Brigade to do. The instructions from Lloyd Lloyd had simply been to apprehend Jack. Terry argued alongside Truvan, almost to the point of insubordination.

Frank struggled to work out how to argue against them, as he wasn't sure what the new mission was actually going to be. Finding Dira would be a good focus to start them off, but he was careful to remain open-minded – they had no real idea who the culprit might be, and Aluen's infotech might not have an immediate solution at his fingertips.

With Vicky's support, and a Brigade promise that Jack would always be supervised, her brother was brought onside. Or at least he stopped refusing. Begrudgingly, and probably only temporarily, in the end, the entire group was at least willing to listen to Halthrop's briefing.

He decided to split the group into a specific task and a more general task: Jack and Vicky and the major would enlist Aluen's help to find Dira and see if the lot of them together could counter whatever hacking had gone on; the others would sweep the entire building looking for anything suspicious.

Truvan insisted that Vicky should go with him on the building sweep. She agreed, so Halthrop switched Jane into the hacking-specific group. He convinced himself that the balance of militia-trained personnel in each team was better that way.

Both groups would have to work without believing their eyes and ears, which made a mockery of the whole plan. A search where you can't believe it when you find something struck Frank as total madness. He was at a loss, but wondered what else they could do. *'Men occasionally stumble over the truth, but most of them pick themselves up and hurry off as if nothing ever happened'.* Oh well, *'We are still masters of our fate. We are still captains of our souls.'* A smile played across his lips, beneath a finger stroking his moustache.

Jack and Aluen agreed that they might be able to turn off the audiopt system so that the searches could proceed with more confidence, but they weren't sure. They further agreed that infotechs would definitely know some way of doing so.

'Not including blowing it up, though.' Halthrop said, deadpan.

THE MIND'S EYE
Chapter Twenty
22nd March 2091, 4pm
The Doughnut

Jack jumped in his chair at Jane's shouting.

'There he is!' Jane pointed at the huge second floor window. Her arm was angled downwards towards a point in the Doughnut car park.

Jack and Aluen had been working on the screens at his desk, with Major Halthrop looking over their shoulders. The major spoke gruffly into his forearm. He told Terry and Darren to get their group out to the car park immediately.

'Jane, you run down and join them in catching him. You're sure it's him?'

'He looks just like that picture she showed us.'

'OK, let's go.' He ran across the room and followed Jane out of the doorway and into the chrome, steel and glass stairwell.

Jack called after them. 'Wait – it might not be real.'

Aluen hushed him. 'Let them go, they've got to follow something. If we assume everything is fake, we'll never catch whoever's doing this, 'cause we'll never try to catch anyone.'

'I know, but it's just so annoying that we can't trust anything we see.'

'Ummm. Would it be right to think that if we see something real, we will actually see it?'

'What do you mean?' Jack looked at her with his head tilted sideways.

Aluen said, 'Well, say we were looking for Dira and we really happened to find him.'

'OK.'

'We'd see him as normal, right? We might see things that aren't real, but we will still definitely see real things as real.'

'Oh, yes.' He paused. 'No, yes, definitely. Like you say, there could be fake extra things, but you can't make yourself invisible in real life. Malthus, I hope you can't!'

They watched the screens showing the live feeds for Jane and Halthrop. They were a hundred yards behind Dira and chasing him across the large expanse of crumbling asphalt that once parked several thousand cars. Jane wore no sunglasses, and the afternoon sun made her squint and look away. An adjacent screen showed Vicky's view, running out of the building behind Truvan, and from the right, she saw Terry and Darren joining the chase from another set of doors.

Jack and Aluen watched the scene, a screen set for each person. Dira's feeds had come on, and they saw him cross the old A40 into abandoned suburban Cheltenham. He appeared to be picking paths to run along at random, despite having worked in the Doughnut for nearly thirty years. It was difficult for the pursuers to monitor their armulets and run at the same time, so Jack relayed verbal directions to the various pairs. He found it confusing as Aluen was talking beside him.

'He's only ever been nice to me.' She banged both fists gently on the table edge. 'Ever since the first day I arrived, he's been totally helpful and supportive.' She banged again slightly harder. 'I can't believe he could have done anything bad, let alone this.'

Jack sensed that she had turned to look at him but couldn't turn his focus from the screens.

'What do you think, Jack? Wasn't he always nice to you?' She grabbed his chair and shook it.

Jack jerked his arm up and held out a flat hand to silence her. He was constantly commentating to the militia members about Dira's movements. Despite the infotech cutting across

THE MIND'S EYE

overgrown old gardens, side alleys and back streets, Jack was able to help the posse reduce the gap fairly quickly. Dira was older than the rest and had a pronounced limp. His pace was not nearly enough to outrun them.

They finally came to the cricket pitch at Hatherley. It was well maintained – pretty much the only area they had passed where the vegetation had been kept in check by human gardening. On Dira's screen, Jack and Aluen saw a scuffed boot kick the pavilion door open. He entered and turned to jam it closed again. He had broken the latch, so he piled three chairs from the first changing room in front of it and ran to shut himself in the last room on the tight corridor.

Jack explained all this to Halthrop, who set up a group to stay outside and catch the man if he exited the building some other way. Dira was an unknown quantity. They had no reason to be sure he had done anything wrong, but his flight from the Bristol Brigade made the major very wary, especially in combination with the intermittent appearance of the man's audiopt feeds. At worst, this could be the criminal responsible for assaulting Lloyd Lloyd. He did not want any casualties amongst his own men.

In the pause as the chasers regrouped outside the pavilion, Aluen nagged at Jack's dirty shirt sleeve again. He looked straight at her. Jack's voice was stern. 'I hardly knew him before, but I'd say his behaviour has been erratic at the very least.'

She banged the other fist down very hard and jumped up to stand at the same time. 'No! It can't be Dira. I won't believe it!' She was shouting, and Jack put a hand over the microphone slot on the terminal he was using to broadcast to the group.

Jack kept using the sharp, serious tone. 'Look, we just don't know. But why would he run? What's going on here, if he's just a sweet, old man?'

'Stop it!'

Jack reckoned Aluen was more upset with herself, that she'd been duped, than actually disbelieving. He tried to distract her back onside. 'I need to keep helping the Brigade. Can you see if you can find the plans for Hatherley's cricket pavilion on the infonetwork? Halthrop may find it useful if you send it through to him.'

She sat down to start a search on an empty screen, but continued chuntering. 'You'll see. It's not him. I promise you.'

Halthrop and Darren barged through the chairs barricade and ran along the corridor straight to the end. Darren was a dutiful soldier, and as he ran first along the corridor, barely wide enough for his stout body, he screamed and shouted. It was an incoherent, guttural noise.

The major followed him and joined in the shouting. His battle cry was clearly the man's name, with the final vowel sound extended all the way until they were both in the last changing room. 'Diirrraaaaaaaaaaa!'

Jack could see both bodies tensed for a fight, turning and looking at the whitewashed walls. The room was empty. As the men had screamed, Dira's feed – a view of the compact changing room with wooden benches – had blanked out again.

Halthrop alerted the external guards who had spread out so one person could see each aspect of the pavilion building. Dira did not emerge. Halthrop and Darren conducted an interior sweep to make sure he had not moved and hidden in a different room. There was no sign of Aluen's infotech.

Before leaving, Darren stopped in the toilet. Jack saw Aluen smile at the sighing sound the big man made, the relief of emptying a full bladder. She seemed to settle a little. Jack commented, 'Probably the adrenaline made it all the more urgent.'

'Wasted adrenaline, though.'

THE MIND'S EYE

Jack shrugged but then spotted something in Darren's peripheral vision. He wound the feed back five seconds to look again, double-checked on the plan of the building that Aluen had called up, and then called Major Halthrop.

On closer inspection, Halthrop agreed that the manhole cover in the concrete floor of the toilets room was disturbed. It was only barely off at one end, but it was not properly seated in the groove. It was quite possible that it had been left like that for years, but they decided to investigate. Halthrop sent Jane and Terry, the smallest of his brigade members, down to see whether there might be an escape route.

'How can he have just vanished?' Aluen seemed to be blaming herself again.

'It seems to be the way of things just now.' Jack wondered how to lift her mood. 'You know the feeds often don't work so well underground.'

She shook her head and sat staring at the blank screen that had shown Dira's feed.

Jack continued, again attempting distraction as his best idea at a ploy to comfort her. 'Let's get back on to searching the code for clues. We might find how to get Dira back on that way.'

She turned her focus to the work screen and muttered, 'It better not be Dira. I'll kill him myself if it is.'

They left the feeds running but focussed back onto trying to find some software hacking code. Neither was a programming expert, and even Jack's recently learnt knowledge didn't help much. They didn't know what most of the code did normally, so it was difficult to search for bits that shouldn't be there.

Aluen changed tack. She set up an algorithm to filter the feeds for people inside the Doughnut, to see whether there had been any visitors that were not sifters or infotechs. Prior to that day nobody unexpected had entered the building in the previous three months.

She then tried monitoring Dira's feeds for the same three-month period to find out how much they went off and on. She tried to connect these with her memories, but she had never made any mental notes about his movements, so this approach turned up little. The important result was that his feeds were very erratic. They always went off as he approached his replica sifter workstation in the basement.

The two of them went downstairs to poke around. He was supposed to be on shift, but there was no sign of him, and they discussed whether he really had been chased out to the cricket field. Had that all been an illusion?

The basement workshop tools and bits of computers gave no clues. The large desk with the horseshoe of screens and servers was right at the back of the space. There were racks and boxes of further bits of scrap equipment and tools, held up on a big metal racking system that pretty much enclosed that workstation and sleep space.

Aluen gripped a part of the metal cage with both hands. 'This must be why the feeds go off. Radio waves won't penetrate this cage.' Vicky had made the same suggestion earlier, but Jack realised he had not paid enough attention. He followed the metal latticework all around the space to see it was almost a complete box. Aluen continued, 'Do you think it's intentional? Or is it just chance that this metal racking was useful, and he set up a complete enclosure without realising what effect it would have?'

'It's difficult to imagine that he wouldn't have realised, even if he didn't construct it deliberately to mask his feeds. Vicky thought it might be to avoid radio interference when repairing computers. I don't know if that's necessary for such repairs or not. Any idea?'

THE MIND'S EYE

She shook her head. 'No, I leave all that tech stuff to, well, to Dira. My other infotech would know, but she's the night shift, she's not here now.' She was leaning against one side of the cage, with her fingers hanging through the metal squares that the latticework created. She shook it with increasing ferocity until Jack just stared at her. She stopped. 'Sorry, it just makes me so angry. These terrible things came from here. Well, from the Doughnut, even if it's not actually Dira, but I just hate that somebody could be so terrible. That woman who died in the fire, and the attack on your Spokesperson: we're supposed to stop all that. It's just so… '

Jack wondered why she had tailed off. He had been thinking that her rant might make Aluen feel better.

She began again, her speech speeding up. 'Hold on. No. No, no, Vicky's wrong.' Aluen had her nose pressed right up to the copper-coloured wires to peer through at Jack sitting at the workstation of screens and keyboards. She turned her head to look around the main room, without letting go her fingers. She turned back to speak to him and shook the fence more gently. 'This can't be for shielding to help with repairs. The only thing inside are all those terminals. Repairs would be done out here on this big table with all the tools.' She released one hand to point at a printed circuit board clamped in a vice on the work bench behind her.

Jack nodded and tapped at two of the keyboards. 'You're right. And this is no accident either. Look.'

Aluen stepped around to look at the screens. All twelve were demanding a password. 'Wow, I've read about password security, but I've never seen anyone use it. It's almost impossible to keep it hidden from the audiopts.'

'Unless you're sitting in a metal cage.'

She walked past Jack to the sleeping area and picked up the photograph from the little bedside table. 'He never spoke to me about any family. Who do you think this could be?' She turned the frame so Jack could see the blonde woman with the glass of wine and the vivacious smile. 'Looks like she'd be about the age of a daughter I'd guess.'

A jolt shot through Jack. The sight of the photo sent his stomach whirling. He staggered out of his seat and grabbed the picture. Jack held it at arm's length with both hands. It was about six inches square. 'What's he doing with this?'

'What? Who is it?'

Jack couldn't turn his eyes away from the bright face in the photo. 'This is my mother.'

'What? I thought Ellie was your mother?' Jack had enlisted Aluen's help to cover for him for three days leave when Ellie had died. He didn't respond, just stood transfixed by the image. Aluen put a hand on his shoulder. 'Jack. This isn't Ellie, is it? I'm sure your picture upstairs isn't the same woman.' She raised her voice. 'Jack?'

'No.'

'No, what?' Aluen kept her voice loud. 'Jack, tell me who this is.'

Finally, he turned to look at her. 'This is my mother. Ellie was my grandmother. This is Clara. She died giving birth to me. Ellie raised me, but Clara was actually my mother. Ellie is Clara's mother.' After a moment, he corrected himself. 'Was.'

'So why does Dira have a picture of her?'

'I don't know.' He held out a hand to steady himself, holding on to the edge of the computer desk. His knees were wobbly. How long had Dira been stalking him? Angry bile bubbled up Jack's oesophagus but confusion reigned supreme over the anger or anything else.

Aluen had to drag Jack back upstairs to meet the returned posse. He clutched the photo all the way and then stood it beside Ellie on his old desk. Jack sat in his swivel chair and stared at the two pictures. Aluen explained what they had seen.

Vicky pushed her brother aside. She stepped to Jack and put her arms around his neck and head. It was awkward as she was standing, and he was sitting. Her right hand held his cheek, which meant that the skew right little finger rested under his chin and touched his throat. 'They looked so alike,' she said. Jack leaned his head into her hip.

Major Halthrop offered nothing to solve the mystery of the picture of Clara. Instead, he seemed more interested in their failed chase. 'The sewer Jane and Terry entered quickly opened up into a very large pipe under the road across from the cricket pitch. After some fifty metres, they found a fully open manhole cover, but there was no sign of Dira, or which way he might have gone, and by then his feed was off again.'

Jack came to life. 'We discovered that his feed always goes off when he goes to the workstation downstairs, but he wasn't there, so he must have a way of turning it off remotely.'

'I thought you said that wouldn't be possible. It would have to be done from here.' Truvan badgered Jack.

'That's what I thought. I guess if he has a system for masking his feeds, that could be triggered to operate on a remote message from his armulet. He'd have had to set it up in here somewhere – in the basement presumably – but once the code is in, you can probably set it running from somewhere else.'

Vicky also spoke. 'And that's assuming it was him you chased and not a fake Dira, a phantom.'

Halthrop pointed out that a phantom wouldn't need, or be able, to shift a manhole cover, so it'd be a huge coincidence if that cover had, by chance, already been open.

'Or pile up the chairs behind the door,' Darren added with a big grin.

Everybody was silent, thinking through the possibilities and implications.

Terry finally spoke up. 'If he's doing this, and can control it remotely, but it's actually working from here, could we stop it if we destroy his system down in the basement?'

Jack looked up at Aluen, who shrugged. 'I doubt that would work. His servers down there don't run the whole system, so they might be part of triggering it, but it'd need to be in the whole system. We'd need to destroy the central servers.'

'We're not doing that,' Halthrop interrupted.

Terry asked again. 'OK, would it hurt anything if we destroyed his set up down there? If we've got nothing to lose by it, we might just happen on the solution if we do. Do you think?'

Aluen said, 'We still don't know Dira is actually behind this. He's done a lot of weird things here, but I've known him for years. What we're suggesting is all totally out of character for him. I still can't believe it's him. He's the guy they were looking at when they wrote the Second Covenant.'

Major Halthrop decided. 'I agree with Terry. If you say it won't hurt anything, Jack, then let's destroy Dira's equipment. If we're wrong, we'll help him rebuild it when this is all over, but for now, needs must, let's try it.'

Vicky told them that she and Jack would wait in his office. The rest of the group all descended to the big workshop space. With all of them showing on Jack's screens, he and Vicky were effectively there with them.

Halthrop tasked Terry and Darren with smashing everything in the cage. Terry picked up a large spanner, at least a foot long, thick and heavy. He slammed it down onto things

THE MIND'S EYE

with gusto. Darren simply hurled stuff at the concrete floor. He then picked up smaller pieces and threw them down too.

Halthrop asked Aluen if anything outside the cage might be involved. She could barely hear him over the crashing and smashing that immediately started up. She waved over the workbenches and shouted over the noise, 'No, none of this stuff is connected up.' After a moment and a few more loud crashes, she added, 'And the stuff in there...' She pointed into the cage where the two young men were having the time of their lives. 'The stuff in there can only communicate out of it by wire.' She picked up a cable from the floor that led back into the cage. She pulled it from a socket in the wall. 'Now it's completely useless,' she said. 'They can stop.' Jane shouted in at them to stop. Aluen pulled another few cables from wall sockets. 'Can't believe it took them smashing stuff up to make me realise the simple answer.'

Everyone trooped back up to Jack's office. Halthrop instructed that they would split up and return to the tasks they had been at before the chase out to the cricket pavilion. This time, though, he and Jane would join the group sweeping the building. It was coming up to shift change for the infotechs, so they would quiz anyone they saw about Dira's whereabouts.

Vicky prodded Jack, bent down to give him a kiss on the cheek, and left with Truvan. Jack had fallen into another reverie, staring at his mother and grandmother. He seemed oblivious, even to Vicky's kiss.

'Come on,' Aluen said. 'Let's see if we can find some hacked code.' After a moment she also said, 'Here, do you know how to set up a search that looks for recent changes in the system's code?'

Jack realised what she had said. 'You know what? I think I might be able to do that. What sort of timescale, do you reckon?'

Chapter Twenty-one
22nd March 2091, 6pm
The Doughnut

Jack felt her poke him in the ribs. He turned his head from tapping at the keyboard, engrossed in the central two monitor screens. He saw Aluen's face in profile with the dark ponytail proud behind her head. She kept poking but kept looking forward.

He followed her gaze to the doorway to his office. The glass door had been propped open all day. Leaning against the metal door jamb was Dira.

Aluen stood up. 'Dira, what on Earth is going on?' She stepped around the desk, took one or two steps forward and paused. 'Why are your audiopt feeds off a lot of the time? And what did you find about the Highnam crimes?'

He kept his casual leaning pose and smiled. 'I didn't find out anything we didn't know already – Jack Smith, here, is a vicious criminal. He needs to be stopped at all costs.'

Jack leapt up to standing and Aluen looked back and forth between the two men. 'What? I've done nothing. And if you've been investigating it, you should know that well enough.'

Aluen stepped further from both of them. 'I'll go and get the Brigade.' She backed out of the room by the rear doorway.

Jack sat back down as Dira limped over towards the workstation. With three rows of screens between them, as well as the big desk, Dira kept appearing and disappearing. Jack could see through small vertical slits between the columns of screens, and there was a similar horizontal gap all along the bottom row, above the computer terminals. Jack flicked his eyes to the screen that was set to follow Dira's live audiopt feeds. It was blank.

He was tall, despite the slight hunch induced by his rubble-damaged leg. His swarthy complexion was exacerbated by dark hair and a thin beard. Dira's eyes matched the hair colour, and his forehead stretched high above dark eyebrows.

Once the man was fully visible to the side of the screens, he said, 'Welcome back, Jack.'

'I could probably say the same to you. I may have been away a bit longer, but you've been absent from your post for most of the day. Where have you been?'

'Oh, round and about.'

'If you think I committed all those crimes, why did you run from the Brigade?'

Dira waved his hand dismissively. 'I don't know what you're talking about. I didn't run – I was never there.' He gave Jack a conspiratorial grin.

Jack's stomach was doing backflips. He felt so queasy, he put a hand to his belly to try and calm it. 'Why was this photograph in the basement?' With his other hand, Jack held up the small frame they had relocated from Dira's den.

Dira did not reply for more than a minute. 'I've been investigating you for the Bristol Brigade – any clues as to where you might have vanished to could have been important. I found it at your grandmother's house as part of my investigation.'

'That's not true. Vicky and I were there earlier, and I saw it was still there.'

'She was a wonderful woman. So full of life, nothing but fun.'

'You clearly didn't know her very well. Ellie was much more than just fun.'

'I was talking about Clara.'

Jack was struck dumb. He had to press harder with the hand on his stomach, but finally stuttered, 'You… knew my mother?'

'Very well.' He smiled broadly. 'But that's not important right now. The real question is how long you will remain a free man. You've left the island you were exiled to, in order to commit a number of very serious crimes. Highnam Kangaroo will want blood this time.'

Jack squinted his eyes half-closed. He couldn't work out what Dira wanted, or what the man thought he knew about the crimes. Jack knew that Dira was the most experienced infotech at the Doughnut. If anybody could have found out what had happened with the audiopt feeds hack, it would be him. So why did he still think Jack was guilty? Jack worked through the things he'd seen of Dira in the last few hours. 'They will indeed, but it won't be my blood they're after.'

Dira winced, almost imperceptibly, and bent forward enough to lean a hand on the desk. 'Oh, I think you believe in your own capabilities too much. Just like you did with the explosion here. I should have done the job of teaching you properly.' He punched his own thigh and winced again.

Jack stared at the older man. His gaze shifted to blankly watch a point on the far wall. After some silence, he eyed up Dira again. 'I'm not sure I know what you mean.'

'Well, you failed to destroy the audiopt surveillance system, and you failed to avoid hurting anyone.'

'I didn't hurt anyone. Then, or now. I've had nothing to do with the recent series of crimes. And nobody was hurt in the explosion.'

Dira lurched forward, shouting. 'Why you arrogant, little…' He stopped shouting as he started flailing his fists. The attack caught Jack by surprise, and he took two punches

THE MIND'S EYE

directly to the face before he could raise his arms to try and fend off the blows.

Dira's next move was to grab the seat of Jack's chair with both hands and, with a big heave, he threw the chair over onto its back. Jack's head struck the solid floor, and he was knocked unconscious. He woke to feel excruciating pain in his left leg. Dira stood over him wielding a large metal bar. He rolled sideways and fell out of the chair seat to the floor. The landing sent another shot of pain just below his knee. Jack was hazy; only the pain kept him conscious. The next time he opened his eyes, Dira was gone. His eyes closed again.

Jack came round with a shock. Vicky's face was very close to his, so close it took him a moment to recognise her.

'It's OK,' she soothed. 'It's just me. It's Vicky.' He felt her hand take his. She knelt beside him and used her other hand to stroke his cheek. Aluen appeared in his line of sight with a medical kit in her hand. Terry appeared and grabbed the kit. Jack tried to sit up, but Vicky held him down and whispered close to his ear. 'You're really hurt, Jack. Stay where you are, and Terry will fix it up.'

'D-Dira. He was here. He did this.'

'Sshhh. OK, lie still. We'll find him.'

Terry had to start by cleaning and stitching an open wound on Jack's shin. He cut his trouser leg open, making an almost circular hole in the fabric. The whole operation was incredibly painful, and Jack kept losing consciousness. His leg was broken, and the medical pack contained a flexible, inflatable splint. It fitted like a long boot and immobilised Jack's leg from toes to thigh. Once splinted, Jack felt somewhat better and a few minutes later, they sat him up with his leg outstretched.

During the course of his treatment, Terry told Jack that, once Aluen had called them up, the posse had arrived within five minutes. They had found Jack alone and injured on the floor.

Halthrop wanted to debrief him and find out what he might know that could help them catch Dira. Jack found it difficult to get the major to believe how little he had learnt in their short conversation.

Jack insisted, 'No, I'm telling you, he seemed to blame me for everything and then got really angry when I denied committing the crimes. And that was it. The next thing I knew, Vicky was waking me up.' He thought for a minute. Halthrop looked frustrated at the lack of useful information. 'Is there anything from my feeds or Dira's for the attack?'

Halthrop shook his head. 'Are you still sure turning the system off is the best plan now?'

Jack struggled to sit up straighter. All movements hurt, but it was bearable. 'Yes. We're not getting anything from the ones we need to anyway, and we must make sure that there are no more... I don't even know what to call them... fake feeds, I guess. Except, I don't mean fake records, I'm talking about the hallucinations in real life – that's the big problem. It'll be impossible to convince people to ignore them.'

Halthrop said, 'And to work out which ones to ignore. What is real and what is fake?' He gave a nervous chuckle. 'I wonder if it was even Dira who attacked you!'

Jack tried to smile, but the pain turned it to a grimace. 'I don't think Truvan has the technical knowledge to hack the audiopt system to that extent.' He looked around. The three junior members of the Bristol Brigade were leaning against the huge glass of the panoramic window. Jack could not see anyone else. He made swivelling attempts with the office chair, but his trussed-up leg restricted his movements.

'What do you need?'

'Where are the others?'

THE MIND'S EYE

'Who do you mean? Aluen is downstairs still. Vicky and Truvan went home.'

'What, why?'

'Well, actually, I sent Truvan home. He was wanting to do you more harm. Kept muttering about how Dira should have finished you off.'

'And Vicky?'

'She said that now we know it's not you committing the crimes, she would take Truvan home to keep him from making trouble.'

Jack looked at one of the keyboards in front of him. He looked at the wall. 'Was that all she said?'

'Uh-huh.' Major Halthrop stood up and walked over to his soldiers.

Jack stared after the major. Terry gave Jack an artificial grin and turned to listen to his CO. The Brigade grouped together, and Jack could not hear what they were saying. Jane left by the main doorway and headed down the stairs.

Jack looked at his empty wrist. He called up Vicky's audiopt feeds on a monitor. She was sitting on her veranda, talking to her father, Marmaran. Truvan was standing at the base of the veranda stairs, his head at about Vicky's knee level, and listening to the conversation. She was explaining the events to her father, as he sipped occasionally from a small, white china cup. Vicky kept stealing glances at the screen on her armulet – it was set to show Major Halthrop's audiopt feeds.

Aluen appeared at the threshold to Jack's office, and everyone left with her. Jack put Halthrop's feeds on another screen. They had gone down to her office, which was immediately beneath Jack's. She had a similar workstation set up, and they all gathered around it. Another woman was already there, seated and typing vigorously at a keyboard. She was working with code displayed on three of the screens on the bottom row of the horseshoe of twelve. Jack recognised her as Aluen's other infotech, the one who worked the alternate shifts to Dira. He couldn't remember her name. The timestamp showed 18:48.

The woman confirmed she was ready, and Frank Halthrop nodded. Aluen used a different keyboard to dial in several people on a joint videocall across the remaining monitor screens. Jack listened, staring at the ceiling, as the major explained the situation several times. On the screens, he recognised only Lloyd Lloyd.

Aluen had to confirm the technical possibilities repeatedly before the Kangaroos' Spokespersons understood, and also believed, what they were being told. Lloyd Lloyd remained quiet throughout the call. She made reassurances that the audiopts would only be down temporarily, until the culprit was caught.

One Spokesperson asked, 'How will we keep ourselves safe without the audiopts?'

Jack thought Halthrop's reply a bit haughty. 'Well, this is only expected to be a short outage. We're aiming for no more than…' He looked to Aluen and then across to the infotech. Both gave him no help, as nobody really knew. 'Twenty-four hours. I'd hope that your Kangaroos are not dangerous places where there'll be a sudden descent back to the Times. Maybe just don't tell anyone what's happening unless they ask you. Obviously don't keep anything hidden or secret, but don't go shouting about it if you're worried about the criminal element in your village immediately coming to the surface at any opportunity.'

Aluen helped ratchet things down a notch. 'Only the surveillance system will be off. The infonetwork, and calls, and general armulet functionality: none of that'll be affected.

THE MIND'S EYE

So your people can always call each other for help, or whatever.' She followed up by emphasising that it would have to be all audiopt detection. The network masts and the armulets would stop collecting any auditory or optic nerve signal information. After some discussion amongst themselves, all the Spokespersons agreed. They put a caveat on it: another call should be convened in twenty-four hours to confirm that the system was back on.

This videocall process was repeated twice more for a number of other local Kangaroos, to a radius of about thirty miles from the Doughnut. After the third call reached agreement and was disconnected, Halthrop's voice boomed through Jack's tinny computer speaker, 'Confusion to our enemies.'

Aluen's night-shift infotech started to speak, and with a click on her keyboard, she was cut off in mid-sentence. Jack looked back down to his workstation. All screens were blank. His office was silent.

A minute later, the Brigade trooped back in. They all looked to Major Halthrop, so Jack did too. The major cupped one elbow in his hand. The other hand supported his chin.

'What now?' Jack asked.

Halthrop put his hands on to the top of the bank of screens. He looked down at Jack from behind the barricade. 'We're going to take you to Highnam, for Lloyd Lloyd to look after.'

'What? How will that help?'

'It's what we were commissioned to do. You're in no shape to do anything, and you should get proper medical attention. I'm sure Vicky will come and visit you at the clinic.'

Jack frowned. He couldn't work out which of Halthrop's points caused him the most discomfort.

The Doughnut's elevators had not worked for several decades. It was difficult for the group to manoeuvre Jack down the stairs without pain. He helped a little, but mostly he berated Darren and Jane. They were doing their best to carry him, but Darren was much taller than she was.

Outside the nearest set of exit doors, Terry pulled up in a horse-drawn cart. The back end of the wooden cart had an old sofa forming a rear passenger seat. Terry had a large, luxurious, old car seat to drive from. There was a makeshift bed laid out across the floor, but Jack insisted on sitting up on it with his legs flat out. He made them re-arrange the bed so that the pillows supported his back against the springy rear sofa. Halthrop took over driving, and the three younger members rode their quad bikes, which lit the darkening road. They had to keep a tight formation as the cart had no lights.

The sun was sinking and the temperature dropping with it. Jack pulled the blankets around himself. The wind from the cart's movement added to the chill and made enough noise that he could not attempt any conversation with Halthrop.

He thought of Vicky and went over the conversation he had just witnessed her having with her father. They had been talking about the trouble with trying to work out what might be real and what might be faked from audiopt feeds transmitted directly into your brain. As with everyone, Marma had struggled to accept that such a thing could happen at all. Jack had silenced the feed in favour of Halthrop's after the Truvas had begun to discuss the philosophical implications of what it meant for something to be real.

Jack scowled. Vicky had not used the recent Highnam crimes as examples of how witnessing an event might not represent true reality. She had only offered up hypothetical examples along the lines of 'I might not even be here talking

THE MIND'S EYE

to you'. Jack shuffled in the makeshift bed in the cart. His leg shot with pain.

After an hour, just as the dark circle of the moon set, they pulled up at the building Highnam used as a medical clinic. It was barely two hundred yards from Highnam Court, and they had to pass it en route. He twisted his neck as they went past, trying to spot the fire damage. There was not enough light for Jack to see the blackening, and the building's silhouetted outline looked exactly as it always had.

Chapter Twenty-two

About an hour earlier – 22nd March 2091, 7pm
Truva family farmhouse

Vicky felt like tugging at her hair. 'For Malthus' sake, Truvan, will you listen to yourself. You are talking rubbish just because you hate Jack. You know very well that he didn't commit those crimes, but you insist on continuing with this.'

'I can't believe you're defending him. We don't know he didn't do it. He claims he didn't, but the most important thing we've learned in the last day is that the feeds can be faked. And, he has the skills to do that. So, the records you found from the island could easily be anybody. Or nobody, just made up.'

Truvan stood at the base of the flight of five stairs from the front garden to their farmhouse veranda. Vicky was seated on the sofa, next to her father. The old man wore a cream linen suit over a lemon-yellow shirt, open at the neck. He held a white cup on a matching saucer and occasionally drank the black coffee Vicky had prepared for him. She watched his face at each sip. Usually, it was inscrutable, but every so often, he gave away a little expression. Vicky was annoyed that half the time it was a tiny wince, and half the time there was the flicker of a smile. He always insisted it was fine, but she knew nobody's coffee lived up to the memory of that made by her mother.

Marma had listened intently as his children bickered, but at this point, he interrupted. 'Stop. You two need to bring me up to speed. What are you saying about the feeds being faked?'

The two dived in immediately, both talking simultaneously. Neither wanted to let the other put their slant on the situation. After a pause, they both spoke again.

THE MIND'S EYE

Marmaran Truva was a lifelong smallholding farmer; born in Highnam, he had spent all his fifty-six years there. He had been five years old when the Covenants of Jerusalem were signed, and he knew no life other than that with the audiopt surveillance to maintain security. Vicky remembered him telling fireside tales of the earliest times, when the villagers had used the feeds to protect Highnam from intruders and thieves. Such excitement had never occurred in her lifetime. She expected that her father understood little of the technology behind the surveillance system. He could use his armulet as well as anyone and attended weekly Kangaroo religiously, but knowing how to use the system was not the same as understanding how it worked.

Vicky and Truvan agreed to take turns explaining little parts of the events of the previous day, since the time Marmaran had gone to help fight the fire at Kangaroo Hall.

Vicky started with the tale of guessing that Jack had restarted the found armulet in the old pub on Steep Holm. 'You should have seen him, Dad. I don't know if he would have lasted another day if I hadn't brought him some real food. He'd been living on seagull eggs and could barely stand. There was only enough firewood left for a couple of days. When I arrived, he was on his hands and knees.'

Truvan spoke up. 'He seems to have recovered from death's door pretty quickly. When we caught up with him, he swam the River Severn in the bore tide. Of course, that was after blowing up the Bristol Brigade's headquarters building. Did you hear about that up here? Course you did. Sorry, I told you, didn't I?'

'That wasn't Jack! Truvan, stop it.'

'Not only is he on the records as setting it...' He held his hand up to thwart her interruption. 'I know, I know, faked feeds, blah, blah, blah. But they tested the chemistry of the explosive, and it was exactly the same as the one he used on the Doughnut. That's too much of a coincidence for me.'

Vicky tensed to speak up, but her father put his hand on her thigh. 'Go on, Truvan.'

He explained the waterborne chase, of which Vicky had been mostly unaware. She knew he had followed them, but she had not previously known about his fall into the Severn, and the struggle to survive the churning currents. Vicky had seen Truvan's twin, Bailey, disappear in a similar fall into the river. Bailey had not been able to swim and had suffered a knock on the head as his boat capsized, but she was shocked and scared to hear that Truvan could have gone the same way.

'I'm so sorry.' Her hand was held to her heart. 'I had no idea that had happened.'

Marma added, 'Please don't go in the river ever again. Either of you.' He looked back and forth to each, and they solemnly nodded.

'Who was it that helped you and Jack get away from us there, though? Did she tell you, Dad? They got a carriage ride from somebody hiding their face and disguising their voice, and they both kept their eyes closed so we couldn't follow where they were going.'

Vicky shook her head and told a lie of omission. 'Jack knows, but he wouldn't tell me.'

Marmaran asked, 'Couldn't you follow their armulet locators?'

Vicky put her hand on his. The armulet locator had found her mother dead in the snow, when Vicky had been only eight years old. And then they finally found Bailey the same way. In fact, the locator told them where he was, but his body was never recovered – by the time the infonetwork system had come back on, he had been far out to sea.

THE MIND'S EYE

Truvan shook his head. 'No, she left hers on Steep Holm, and Smith threw his from the carriage as soon as they got on.'

Marma turned to look at his daughter. She gave him a cheeky grin and squeezed his hand. Vicky took up the story and explained the strange events at the Doughnut, how she and Jack had seen themselves on a live audiopt feed saying things they were not really saying. The thought of it made her shiver.

'Who is this Dira, then?'

Vicky described the dark-skinned, dark-haired man who had been Newnham's infotech for more than a generation. 'Aluen, that's one of Newnham's sifters – Jack's known her since quite a long time – has total faith in Dira's technical abilities, but she was surprised to think through how little she really knows him.'

Her father mused, 'And you say he had a photo of Clara on his desk?'

'Yes, it was weird. Jack has the same photo, but Dira had it down in a basement sleeping area. It looked like he lived there. It wasn't exactly hidden from everyone, but right out the back where nobody would ever go, only one way in and one way out.'

Truvan added, 'Right next door to the server room that Smith blew up.'

Vicky had Ellie's armulet on, displaying Major Halthrop's feeds with the sound muted. She wasn't exactly trying to hide it, but just looked briefly and occasionally.

Marmaran said, 'OK, darling. You mentioned seeing that fake record of yourself and Jack, but you said there was even worse to deal with. What was worse than that?'

Truvan interrupted, 'I'm not sure I believe this. Smith has just made it up to excuse anything he wants to do.'

Vicky glared at him. She struggled to keep her voice to a normal speaking tone. 'You thought you saw me in Leckhampton bunker, when I was in Jack's office the whole time. How can you deny the hallucinations?'

'Hallucinations?' Confusion paraded across the old man's face.

'Yes. They're still trying to work out how it's being done, but somebody has hacked the system so they can make you see things that aren't real.'

'What?'

'Well, exactly. That's why the witnesses thought Jack burned Kangaroo Hall and attacked Lloyd Lloyd, but it wasn't him. Same with the explosion in Bristol.'

'But the hall did burn. That was no hallucination, I was there, I threw buckets of water myself.'

'Yes, sorry, but it wasn't Jack who did it.'

'I saw him attack Lloyd Lloyd myself. It was definitely Jack Smith.'

She held his hand tight again. 'No, Dad, it was an illusion. Like I say, they're investigating how it's done, but somebody definitely has the capability to create these hallucinations. We think it's some sort of reverse engineering of the audiopt surveillance system.

'Truvan, tell him what yours looked like.'

Vicky's brother shrugged and climbed a couple of the stairs. 'We were in Leckhampton bunker. It's like these underground concrete corridors, very dark. I could barely see anything. I felt people rush past. As I turned, I thought I saw Vicky in the darkness. We chased after them, and by the time we got up to the exit, they'd vanished.'

'We?'

'I was with the Brigade at the time. We were following her and him.' He pointed at his sister.

THE MIND'S EYE

'Why did you run away from Truvan?'

She banged his hand on his thigh. 'That's just it! We were never there. It was a hallucination. Jack and I were in the Doughnut. It's like this conversation: you could just be imagining that Truvan and I are talking to you, when in fact we're somewhere else.'

'Why would I imagine that?'

'Well, I guess it's not really *imagining*. We think the hallucinations are directed by somebody. So, you could be seeing and hearing me because somebody's putting the visions in your mind. You know how the audiopts detect your optic and auditory nerve signals when you see and hear stuff?'

'Yes, OK.'

'Well, Jack thinks that it might be possible to transmit signals that those nerves pick up, so you think you're seeing and hearing something, but it's not actually real. So I might be in the Doughnut, at a computer, sending messages to the system to make you see and hear me here when, actually, I'm not here at all and not really saying these things.'

'Right, but why? What would be the point in that?'

Truvan interjected, 'It's Smith's way of claiming he didn't commit any of the crimes. Despite being the only person in the world who has any kind of gripe with Lloyd Lloyd or the Bristol Brigade or our Kangaroo, this is his claim to get away with it all.'

Marmaran put his cup and saucer down on the floor beside the end of the dirty-red outdoor sofa. 'But Jack's been hurt, is that right? How did that happen? Or was it one of these hallucinations?'

'Good point, Dad. I bet it was another made up story to get sympathy.'

Vicky saw her armulet go dark as Halthrop's feeds shut off.

'No.' Vicky stopped and looked at her blank armulet again. 'Um, hmm.' She found her train of thought. 'No, he's definitely hurt, one of the Brigade had to sew up and splint his leg.'

'But...' Truvan smiled.

'Well, as soon as he came round, he said it was Dira that had attacked him, but what if it was another hallucination? What if somebody else had done it and made it appear to be Dira?'

'Or he smashed his own leg.'

'Don't be ridiculous!'

Truvan wouldn't back down. 'There's nothing on his or Dira's records. They've both been off most of the day. Convenient situation if you're going to frame somebody. Turn the poor fella's feeds off and say he did it. Aluen doesn't think Dira did any of this.'

'That's not what she said. She said it would surprise her.'

Marmaran held his hand up for quiet. 'But he's back in Highnam now, is he?'

'Nobody knows where he is. It's true that his feeds have been off most of the time.'

'I meant Jack. Are they bringing him back here?'

Vicky nodded. 'Oh, yes. They're taking him to the clinic. They're going to keep him there till Kangaroo on Sunday. Hopefully, Major Halthrop will explain about the hallucinations at Kangaroo. They'll have to postpone doing anything until they can work out what has gone on. I'm assuming they'll be able to search through and find out what was real and what wasn't.'

'And if not?'

Vicky looked at her father. His eyes were gentle and inquisitive. 'If not, we're all screwed. The entire system is useless. But worse than that, you can't even trust what you see as being real. Halthrop has just arranged with all the local Spokespersons to shut the whole system down for a few days while the sifters and infotechs investigate.'

Truvan jerked up his hand and started tapping at his armulet.

Marmaran watched his son but did not look at his own device. He looked back to Vicky. 'Why are you wearing Ellie's armulet?'

She eyed up her father. 'Like Truvan said, I left mine on the island. Jack and I were at his Grannie's house earlier, and he gave it to me. It's lovely, isn't it?

'Tony's finest work, that.'

She stared at the intricate leather strap work. 'Ha. She claimed to Jack she'd brought it from Brighton, from before the Times.'

It was Marma's turn to laugh. 'Haha. She was a coy one, old Ellie.'

'Truvan, can you go inside? I need to talk to Dad.'

He looked back and forth between them. 'Whatever it is, Dad, you tell her no. No way. He's got the same charms as his grandmother. Although, I can't tell how he's managed to. I could see it in Ellie. Jack's just an idiot, a weak, pathetic idiot.' He trudged in through the front door and slammed it shut.

Vicky jumped in her seat at the slamming noise. She looked at the door. They could hear Truvan banging about inside the house. He was always so angry. Vicky wondered how she could help to bring back the happy brother he'd once been. She couldn't understand why he was unable to move on from their brother's death. She felt like she'd lost both of them, when Bailey went overboard.

'I'm so sorry.' Marma held both his daughter's hands and stared down at them. 'Are you sure it's really true about the hallucinations? I watched Smith punch and kick Lloyd Lloyd. It wasn't someone else, it was him.'

She shook her head slowly and looked into his face until he turned to look back at her.

He argued more. 'It can't have been a hallucination. Lloyd Lloyd was really hurt. A hallucination can't do that. I might think I see a fight, but Lloyd Lloyd wouldn't have any injuries – it wouldn't be real. You're wrong.' His voice got louder as if he was convinced of his rightness, but the tone was whining, imploring.

Vicky and her father spoke for ten minutes more. Marma got up, handed her his cup and saucer, and departed down the little staircase. He was quickly enveloped by the darkness beyond the pool of light from the one veranda bulb.

As she watched him go, Vicky was sure she saw a movement in the shadows at the edge of the front garden. She leant with both hands on the porch rail, straining to see to the left into the dark. Her vision could not penetrate it, but she heard a scraping sound at the side of the house. She walked the length of the veranda to look. There was a cracking sound in the dark. Animals and birds making noises were common at night. Vicky felt this was different, almost more accidental.

The side section of garden was even darker. No light from the front filtered around the corner. She leaned over the rail and shone her armulet light around the lawn. The light played through bushes and tree branches making shadows dance everywhere she looked. Vicky went down the steps and then walked back around to the side of the house. She stopped halfway across the lawn, trying to force her vision into the dark bushes. The noise had ceased. Had she scared an animal away into the night? *This is pointless*, she thought.

Vicky felt a sharp pain in the back of her head. The vague veranda light disappeared as she blacked out.

THE MIND'S EYE
Chapter Twenty-three
A couple of hours earlier – 22nd March 2091, 7pm
The Doughnut

Dira had a new plan.

He had previously offered to help the Bristol Brigade find and catch Jack so that he could be taken back to Kangaroo for trial. In the end, that had come to fruition, but not as Dira had envisioned it. Some people had developed a sympathy for Jack. A sympathy he did not deserve.

In Dira's opinion, Jack had gone off the rails and become a dangerous man. The explosion at the Doughnut was the ultimate demonstration of this. The pain in his leg ached daily, and every time it did, he would clutch at his quadricep and remember that day stuck under the rubble. If any crime deserved a death penalty from Kangaroo, that had been it. But Jack had been tried in Highnam, which was not Dira's Kangaroo, so he had only been able to watch the proceedings remotely; he could not attend or participate.

Barely more than a year later, Jack was now held by the Brigade for even worse crimes. Directly malicious attacks, in which a woman had died. Surely, the good people of Highnam would see sense and punish Jack appropriately this time round.

A vision of Ellie Smith entered Dira's mind. He shook his head to send her away and clambered up from the smashed concrete on which he sat. The server room Jack had blown up had not been repaired, other than a few vertical props to shore up the structural damage. Dira selected a lump of concrete twice the size of his fist and carried it next door to his workroom.

He checked on the Brigade. They were upstairs with Aluen and Dira's infotech counterpart for the nightshift. He watched for a moment as Major Halthrop was engaged in a videocall discussion with a number of local Spokespersons about turning off the audiopt system for a few days. Dira listened in, whilst he put a couple of bottles of water in a bag, along with one of the foodpacks from under his bed. He had discarded his brown backpack in the chase away from the cricket pavilion. The new bag was small, and he had to reshuffle things so the concrete could go in without squashing the food. He clicked the computers on to password-locked and limped back out and up the stairs.

Dira's unsteady leg did not have enough mobility to ride a bike, so he had taken to using an electric scooter for any journey he needed. The Doughnut's bike shelters were equipped with solar panels and plug points for all manner of electric conveyances. The scooter had a long range for little charge, but it could be very difficult on fractured roads and poor surfaces. Dira had become increasingly annoyed with having to carry it half the way on his most common journeys. A quad bike would make more sense, but they took a lot more charging up.

The route to the Truva family farm had mostly good footpaths, but significant sections were muddy. This was another problem with a scooter. Dira cursed when he realised that his new plan could not possibly function with a scooter. He abandoned it in a hedge on arrival at the outskirts of Highnam.

He knew the Truvas had horses. He thought about commandeering one. His leg would almost certainly not make it feasible, and a strange horse could not be relied upon to play the game either. Dira dragged his limp through several gardens before he found a house with a quad bike he could borrow without asking. It was only half charged, but his plan would only involve a couple of trips within the village, so that would be enough. Quad bikes ran silent, so he was able to slip away into the night without alerting the householders. The wooded paths around the village were utterly dark. He switched on the headlights as soon as he had moved away from the owner's home but had to switch them off again within minutes, to avoid being seen on approach.

Dira parked up at the side of the Truva garden, hidden by the boundary trees and bushes. The smell of fir trees enveloped him. The lights from the house sprayed beams like searchlights from half a dozen windows at different heights and in different directions. Between the light beams, the night sucked everything in.

Dira took up a position at the side of the house to listen in on the conversation on the veranda. Vicky was explaining the audiopt hacking to her father. Truvan made several important contributions, although Vicky shouted him down pretty unfairly. Dira was impressed with their father though. He seemed reasonable, and he considered things impartially. Or so it seemed in this conversation; Dira had never had any previous dealings with Marmaran Truva. He suddenly felt very sorry for the man.

Under his breath, Dira paraphrased the Second Covenant, 'We all have to make sacrifices for the benefit of all.'

He made a mental note of the technical errors Vicky made in explaining how visions could be produced by the audiopt system. There was a crucial difference between simple hallucinatory visions and visions hiding physical actions: the former were an easy hack and could work with quite a large number of people at the same time; covering for some physical action was much more complex programming. The audiopt vision had to exactly disguise the sight and sound of the act's perpetrator from all angles, overriding all witnesses' actual vision and hearing. Jack Smith had been witnessed setting fire to Kangaroo Hall. Dira felt this was his crowning glory from thirty years' technical work at the Doughnut. In comparison, programming deletion of somebody's audiopt feeds in real time, or replacing them in the records, with some alternate reality, was child's play.

Dira was very pleased to hear Vicky report that Aluen supported her infotech as not responsible for the current series of crimes. Jack had gotten what karma he deserved; only Jack could be responsible for that.

Dira heard the door slam and Truvan banging around inside the farmhouse. Vicky's conversation alone with Marma was held in whispers, and Dira could not make out any of it. The audiopt feeds were off for everyone now. He toyed with the idea of crawling along right under the front of the veranda, but it was far too likely they would discover him.

When Marmaran left, Dira slipped back to the edge of the lawn and moved into the trees. He tripped on a low bush, and the branch he grabbed broke off in his hand. As he cursed himself and got to his feet, he could see Vicky leaning out over the rail, straining to see him in the bushes. Dira froze absolutely still.

As she came down and round the lawn, Dira looked to the sky and thanked the bright stars for his good fortune. He could see her struggling with still-blinded retinas trying to regain their night vision. Grinning, Dira felt invisible as he glided across the grass behind her. The lump of concrete felt solid in his hand, and Vicky crumpled silently into his arms with a single strike.

Dira was strong, but his enfeebled leg hampered carrying her back to the quad bike. He imagined Jack's slight frame would make lifting her just as difficult for him and smiled. He had nothing to tie her down, so he laid Vicky over the pillion space and drove slower than a walking speed to ensure she was secure and did not wake.

Although the progress was slow, he was only heading for Ellie Smith's old house, so they reached it in ten minutes, and Vicky was still unconscious. The path from the Truvas brought him to the back of Ellie's place, but none of the doors were ever locked, so he carried Vicky in the back entrance and placed her on the floor.

A thin rope from the main store cupboard by the rear door was perfect for trussing her up. Dira tied Vicky's hands together behind her back, and her ankles, and then strung a third rope between the two bonds, so that she would be able to half-kneel, half-sit with feet beside her. He found one of Ellie's colourful, thin scarves, and it made for a perfect gag. Another from the same drawer, but slightly thicker, worked well as a blindfold.

Vicky had not stirred throughout the manhandling, and Dira checked her pulse and breathing to check he hadn't hit her too hard. No, she was alive.

Lights skewed and turned in through the large windows across the front of the house. Dira stood sideways by the main door. The headlights from three quad bikes parked up, shining straight into the garden at the front of the house. He quickly checked his armulet, before remembering that the audiopt switch-off had happened, and so there would be no clues as to who was visiting him. This was not the way he had planned things. He grabbed the small framed photo of Clara.

Dira carried Vicky over his shoulder across the overgrown vegetable garden and through a thin hedge towards the tractor shed. Ellie had had a number of outbuildings around the property, but the tractor shed was the largest. As he squeezed the two of them through the side door of the wooden building, small mammals scuttled. He sat Vicky down on the dry earth floor, released her feet and used the rope to tie her hand bond to the rear of the tractor.

Half an hour later, he returned to the main house. Dira moved stealthily all along the back of the building, to see what was going on inside. The window glass felt cold against his cheek. Clear skies meant that the temperature had fallen rapidly. His armulet told him it was eight degrees and not even 10pm. He wondered how the two of them would fare through the night by the tractor. He couldn't afford to have Vicky die on him.

Ellie's house was occupied by the Bristol Brigade. They spread themselves right out through all the rooms. One boy was asleep on the sofa; the other slept in a bed; the young woman made a bed of cushions on the floor, leaving Major Halthrop the other bedroom.

Having set up their beds, the team were roused again and held a meeting in the kitchen. Dira could not watch through the window for fear of being seen, and he could not make out the conversation. From beside the back door, he heard somebody rifling through the big larder. At one point, the back door scratched open. Dira held the concrete lump tight in his fist, but nobody emerged. There was some even more muted discussion going on, before the door closed again. He relaxed and decided that it would be wisest to retreat to the shed. It was clear that the Brigade were in for the night.

That meant Jack must be unguarded at the clinic, but Dira had not planned on using the tractor shed for the next part of his new scheme. As he wandered back across the vegetable plots that Ellie had once tended daily, he heard a wheel skid in mud and saw the lights of one of the quad bikes disappear, back the way that they had arrived.

THE MIND'S EYE

Vicky was still out cold and Dira pulled a tarpaulin from one corner to wrap around her as best he could. He pulled the blindfold off and slipped it around his own neck.

Dira cradled the photo of Clara, staring at her bright smile. Despite leaving her pregnant thirty-two years before, Clara remained the love of his life. *I'm so sorry for your pain, my love. Soon, Jack will pay for taking you from me.* He placed the picture on the ground, a metre or so from Vicky.

Dira took another tarpaulin and wrapped it around himself and sat down on the chilly floor. The dirt at his fingertips was dry and thin, dusty. He leaned up against one of the big rear tractor wheels. The wheels had solid rubber tyres. The rubber was much warmer than when his back touched the metal hub, but the rubber was thin. It was difficult to find a position where the temperature at his back was comfortable and where he was still just out of sight of Vicky's tied location.

Chapter Twenty-four

A couple of hours earlier – 22nd March 2091, 8pm
Highnam village

Haltrhop spotted Lloyd Lloyd as the clattering wooden cart approached. Highnam's head man stood outside the village's medical clinic, and three lights brightly illuminated its entrance area. His rotund figure and big hair cast a shadow the shape of a snowman, as he loitered several metres in front of the wide double doorway.

Once he had reined in the horse to a standstill, Major Halthrop jumped down and shook the Spokesperson's hand. The man was not bouncing and beaming in his trademark fashion. The handshake induced a grimace, and Halthrop released it gently.

The major had previously explained that, although they would hand Jack over to the Kangaroo, he had suffered a serious assault and would need to be held at the clinic until Sunday's Kangaroo meeting. Lloyd Lloyd himself had spent much of the day at the clinic, as a patient. During Halthrop's videocall, he had offered no sympathy for Jack's injuries.

Frank had flagged up in his own mind a question mark about the situation. He should assess Lloyd Lloyd's state of mind before releasing his prisoner into the man's custody. Would Jack be safe there if the Brigade did not post a guard? He wanted to give Darren, Terry and Jane a good night's sleep. In truth, Halthrop himself needed the rest too. He was sure that the next few days would involve a lot of work. They might have to chase down a suspect, and probably without the support of the infonetwork.

Lloyd Lloyd was polite but curt. He pointedly did not look at Jack at all. They had already discussed the state of play in the investigations, but Halthrop reiterated that the transmitted hallucinations meant they could not be sure who had assaulted Lloyd Lloyd. It was clear that the man himself was convinced Jack had done it, but the major decided that he was not a threat to Jack. A combination of weakened physical state – Lloyd Lloyd held a hand to a pain in his side throughout their conversation – and the man's years of duty to the process of Kangaroo gave Frank an acceptable balance of probabilities.

The situation was both complicated and eased when Lloyd Lloyd introduced the village medic. Doc lived next door to the clinic and came out to meet her new patient. As Jack had lived away from the village for more than fifteen years, the doctor did not know him. Despite Jack's incapacity, she was aloof with him. Doc was a small woman of Algerian heritage, and aloofness came easily to her. She spoke perfect English, French and Arabic so, when she said nothing, it was pointed. It had been only a day since Marisa's body was removed from her charge.

However, once they assisted Jack into the overnight care bed, Halthrop could see the professional approach the doctor took. There was also a nurse on shift for the night. The nurse jumped straight in, removing the inflatable leg splint and assessing the wound dressing. He laid out a variety of cleaning tools and liquids and new dressing materials that would replace the first aid one that Terry had applied.

Jack winced and moaned in pain throughout the nurse's ministrations. Terry had given him no pain relief, and it did not appear that Highnam clinic felt it was a necessary evil either. Halthrop wondered if the clinic had any drugs. Some places would use chemicals that had been left over since before the Times of Malthus, but their degradation over time made them dubious at best. He had read occasional reports of serious illness being caused by the use of old drugs.

Ever the student, Frank took the opportunity to discuss drug availability with Doc. She had been in medicine for a lifetime, and in Highnam for the last ten years. Doc was very much of the opinion that the human body was its own best friend. Halthrop listened quietly as she expounded the ideas of natural healing. The philosophy seemed to be founded in a naturalistic, back-to-evolution set of beliefs.

The major tried to broach this in the most diplomatic way he could. He wanted to point out that early man had died young of relatively simple things. Doc was well-versed in the arguments, tired of them almost, and she countered with a compelling simplicity. She told Halthrop that with a good knowledge of anatomy and healing, it was relatively easy to give the patient an environment in which they would recover as well and as fast as was humanly possible. She took Frank's hand and pressed it flat onto Jack's good leg, in the same location as the damage to the other one. He couldn't comprehend how Doc thought this would confirm her explanations, but he nodded. At the moment of the touch of his fingers on Jack's leg, Halthrop felt an ache in his own leg at the same position. He stared down at his trousers and retracted his hand sharply.

Halthrop knew that since the Times there had been pretty well zero medical research. This meant that much of what Doc was claiming would be based on her own experiences. It also meant that there was no scientific argument against what she declared.

He looked at Jack and could easily accept Doc's suggestion that the pain would adrenalise the recovery process. As long as they offered his bones the best positioning for repair, and combined this with active recovery, she prophesied that Jack would be playing cricket again within weeks. Halthrop smiled as he wondered if Jack had played cricket before, but checked himself before blurting out the question.

The major shrugged. *Safe hands, I guess.* He bade them all good night and went out to talk to the rest of the Brigade about his plans for their night.

Lloyd Lloyd had not entered the clinic but stood outside talking with Terry and Darren. Jane and Halthrop walked over, and everybody fell silent. They were gathered around the three quad bikes, behind the cart. The light strained to reach them from the front wall of the clinic. Faces were partly in shadow, sounds muted. It reminded Halthrop of a gathering of ne'er-do-wells in some olden days smugglers' rendezvous. Even the atmosphere seemed to suggest double-crosses and secrets within secrets. Normally, he would have laughed it off.

'We're going to spend the night at Smith's grandmother's house. I hope that's OK with Highnam?'

Lloyd Lloyd shrugged. His normal gregariousness was distinctly absent.

Halthrop continued, 'I haven't mentioned it to Jack himself, but I think he's got more important things to worry about. We shall leave the place as we find it.'

'Fine. Good night.' Lloyd Lloyd shook the major's hand, gave a cursory wave around the group, and wandered away.

Frank stroked his moustache and tried to lift the mood. 'Right, folks, we may have a lot of work to do in the next few days. So, before that begins, we're going to get a good night's sleep, a wash and yes, Darren, some food.' They all looked grim. He assumed they must be tired. The chase had started thirty-six hours previously, and they had not slept since.

The sound of shouting made everyone turn to the clinic entrance. The door was just closing on the back of a svelte man with a thick mane of grey hair and a beard of equal size. The shouts were silenced as the door closed completely.

Halthrop ran back inside. In the overnight room, the man was speaking loudly without shouting. He had placed himself between Lloyd Lloyd, who was ranting at the top of his voice, and the bed that held Jack Smith.

The doctor and nurse waited in the corridor. Halthrop rushed past them, but the rest of the Brigade waited in the corridor too. He positioned himself beside the bearded man, but Lloyd Lloyd did not appear as if he would need physically restraining.

'Please stop,' Doc said in a normal speaking voice. The volume of the voices in the bedroom meant she was unheard except by Halthrop. Unperturbed, she continued, 'You'll just hurt yourself more.'

Halthrop finally placed the older man assisting him as Tony, Highnam's main leatherworker. In fact, he was Highnam's only leatherworker, apart from his son, Asa. Tony said, 'Save it for Kangaroo. If he's guilty, we'll punish him there.' Although his voice was slightly raised, it was his hand on Lloyd Lloyd's chest that focussed the head man on what Tony was saying. 'Come on, you know this isn't our way.'

Lloyd Lloyd's head drooped loosely, probably looking at Tony's arm. He took a massive breath and exhaled noisily. He remained stationary, seemingly catatonic. Tony took his arm and turned the man around. Halthrop stayed in place, watching for any sudden moves to get back in the room. None came. Tony led him away along the corridor, and Frank heard the outside door swish open. He waved at his junior ranks to follow outside.

'I hope you're going to leave a guard to protect me overnight.'

THE MIND'S EYE

Jack's voice sounded almost smug. It caused a rising ire in Halthrop, but he managed to constrain it and respond appropriately. 'We're not. I'll tell the doctor and nurse to keep the clinic doors locked, and we'll take Lloyd Lloyd home and explain the situation to his wife.'

'Ha – you think she can contain him?'

'Frankly, I can't spare a man for a guard duty.' He checked the bedroom door. 'You could ask Doc if you can lock this door as well. It looks like they should have a key to do so.'

Jack looked over to the door handle and scowled.

Once the major caught up with the group outside, the big, blond man had calmed down. Halthrop explained they would take Lloyd Lloyd home before retiring to Ellie's. They left Tony in the pool of bright light outside the clinic.

The quad bike headlights shone brightly and lit up the entire L-shaped garden in front of Ellie's house. The fence did not let them any closer though, so they traipsed up the garden path for the second time in two days.

All four collapsed into the sofa and armchairs in the big main room. Jane asked, 'What are we going to do with this, Frank? Are we still chasing it up tomorrow? I'm lost as to what our mission is now.'

Major Halthrop looked at each face. They all stared at him. He didn't answer.

'Frank?' Terry prompted.

'We are going to continue tomorrow. At a minimum, we need to find out who blew up our HQ. Even if no Kangaroo has commissioned us directly, that one is for us. But I've got quite a strong feeling that if we solve that, we'll actually solve all the rest. I think it's either confirm it to be Smith, or exonerate him. I can't see different people being responsible for different parts of this.'

Again, nobody spoke for some time. When Darren started snoring, Jane and Terry got up and headed for the kitchen. Halthrop's thoughts of possible strategies for the morning's activities were punctuated by Darren's noises.

Jane called through, 'There's tea and coffee back here. Everything else has been infested.'

Halthrop stood up and went to join them. Jane was shaking a bag of flour and insects into the kitchen sink. Terry assaulted the insects with jets of water from the tap. 'The water's good,' he said without taking his eyes off the insect drownings.

'What food have we got in our kit bags?' The inventory was brief, and he decided that they would need to secure provisions for breakfast. They could go and get something en route back to the Doughnut in the morning, but Halthrop figured it would boost morale a bit to have a team breakfast at Ellie's alfresco dining table. 'I'll see if I can get some food from the neighbours. You two feel free to go to bed.'

Ellie's house was in a wooded area. Her land stretched down to the River Leadon in a long narrow strip. Those fields were much more open, but the neighbours were in the other direction, through the woods. The darkness was intense.

Halthrop mounted a quad bike. The electric motor was ready, but before he started moving, he heard a noise. He wasn't sure how far away it was. A few dull thuds, a bit of scraping and a bang. He didn't point a light in the right direction in time. The silence had returned as he twisted the quad bike left and right to sweep the light into the woods. It could have been close up and fairly quiet, or very loud, but a long way away.

THE MIND'S EYE

With nothing to see, and nothing more to hear, he headed off along the woodland path towards a light several hundred metres away, in the hope of scrounging enough food for breakfast for four hungry soldiers. He wondered if bacon would be a possibility. Halthrop loved bacon. *I like pigs. Dogs look up to us. Cats look down on us. Pigs treat us as equals.* He wasn't sure quite how Churchill's quote could be reconciled with wanting bacon for breakfast, but it was the first thing all evening that had really cheered him up.

Chapter Twenty-five
22nd March 2091, 10pm
Grannie Ellie's tractor shed

Vicky felt a throbbing pain in the back of her neck. It wrapped around her skull to be intensely painful in the temples. She was in a seated position, leaning against something cold and ridged and uncomfortable.

Tentatively, she opened her eyes just a fraction. She could see almost nothing. Everything was dark. The air was cold, but she could hear that she was separated from the breeze inside the walls of some sort of room. Her hands were bound at the small of her back and fixed to something back there. The ground under her legs was cool and smooth. She couldn't work out whether it was just cold, or also slightly damp.

A cloth gag was tied around her head and across her mouth. It was not too tight – she could breathe easily – but it was discomfiting. Vicky rubbed her head against the solid ridges behind. A wave of nausea rolled over her, and suddenly the gag was oppressive. In conjunction with opening and closing her jaw, she managed to work the gag off so that it fell loosely around her neck. She sucked in a deep breath and exhaled hard.

'Owwwww.' A man's voice loudly disturbed the dark space. She could not see anybody else, but she could not see much of anything. The sound had come from the other side of the large, solid lump she leant against.

'Who's there? Who's that?' Vicky demanded.
'Who's that?' the man answered.
'I asked first.'
'Ha, sorry, my name's Dira. Who are you?'
'I'm Vicky Truva.'

THE MIND'S EYE

'Are you tied up as well? I'm stuck fast, and I can't see much of anything. Where are we?'

'You're tied up? I am too. Why are you tied up?'

'I got knocked out and woke up here. Did you see who brought you here?'

'No, I didn't, but they cracked me good and hard on the head.' Vicky paused as another wave of nausea blurred her vision. 'I've got a real headache, and I can't feel it to check, but I think that's dried blood on my neck.'

Vicky didn't speak further but twisted and turned her neck to try and see Dira. She reckoned the object between them was a huge wheel, and she could just about make out the outline of one of his feet on the floor to her left. She wriggled a bit more, trying to check whether she had any blood from a head wound. She couldn't identify any for sure, but the pain was overriding most other sensations. She closed her eyes and sat still for a moment in the hope it would subside.

Dira continued, 'I can only think of one person who might do something like this. It must have been Jack Smith that brought us here.'

'No.' Her answer was immediate, and then she paused. 'I didn't see the person who did this. I was in my garden, and that's the last thing I remember. Ooh, ow.' Leaning her head back to rest on the thin pillow of her hair eased the pain ever so slightly. Keeping still was the main thing.

She spoke to Ellie's armulet, but it hadn't yet learnt her voice pattern and did not do anything she asked. Dira said he had left his armulet in the basement at the Doughnut. That was the last place he remembered being before waking tied up. He agreed that they were leaning against either side of a tractor tyre, inside some small building, but said he had no idea where they might actually be.

'Why did you ask if Jack brought me here? He would never do something like this.'

'On the contrary, he's the only person likely to kidnap us. I don't know how it might fit into his grand scheme, but he's shown himself to be violent already.'

'You're the violent one. You broke Jack's leg, you know? What were you two fighting about?'

'What? I haven't seen Jack Smith since the day before he blew up the Doughnut. What are you talking about?'

Vicky's mind whirled. She wondered if the blow to her skull had done some real damage. Was she imagining that Jack had been hurt? Her head lolled as she struggled with pain and nausea and confusion. Had Jack suffered a bogus vision, just like when Lloyd Lloyd was attacked?

'Jack wouldn't do this. Especially not to me. And he didn't do those other crimes.'

'Yes, he did. I've seen the feeds from all the witnesses – it's definitely him.'

'They're not real, the audiopt records have been forged. In fact, people have been made to see visions of things that aren't really happening. Basically, you can't believe anything you see and hear, so those feeds don't count for anything. And what's more, I found him using some dead man's armulet on Steep Holm, and those records show he was there when the crimes were committed.'

'Now, hang on a second. First you say you can't believe the feeds at all, and then you say they show he has an alibi.'

Vicky paused. She had known as the words had come out of her mouth that there was a paradox. It was difficult to think clearly. 'OK, well, even if we don't accept the feeds from Steep Holm, we still don't have any idea who did those crimes.'

'Have you heard of Occam's Razor?'

THE MIND'S EYE

She racked her brains, but her fuzzy mind would not reveal the memory. 'I think so, but my head's not in a good way at the moment. What is it?'

'It's a philosophical principle that basically says the simplest answer is likely to be the right one. If we don't know what to believe from the feed records, then we should just believe the most obvious thing. Don't make up stuff to try and find a more convoluted explanation than the most simple, obvious one.'

'I'm still not sure what you mean.'

'People see Jack Smith commit the crimes. Ergo, he committed the crimes. Even if it's possible they were seeing mass hallucinations, why invent that answer without any evidence for it?'

'Because Jack's not a violent man. There has to be someone else behind this.'

'Eighteen months isolated on an island, without enough food, could easily send a man mad. And he wasn't very stable in the first place – don't forget he blew up the Doughnut. He just got lucky nobody was killed that time. No, for me there's enough evidence to believe he did all this. It might not be perfect evidence, but it's enough for me.'

Vicky said nothing. She scanned around the room, trying to make out anything in the dark. There was a window in one wall. It was dark outside, with only starlight to assist. The window was the source of a faint brightness. She could see the outlines of trees, and occasionally a branch moved revealing a star behind it.

'Wait! Why did you run from the Bristol Brigade this afternoon? I was there. I saw you run away to the cricket pavilion and then you disappeared.'

'Again, I don't know what you're talking about. I've been at the Doughnut all day. Mostly working in the basement but also around the place fixing up bits and pieces of hardware. The last thing I remember is being at my workbench. There was a noise and... yes, that's it, I was about to turn towards the sound, and that's the last thing I remember. Smith must have knocked me out and brought me here. Wherever here is.'

A thought pushed its way through the pain in Vicky's head. 'Hold on...' she paused. Dira grunted to indicate he was listening. 'Jack's leg is broken. I left the Doughnut just as they were going to take him to the clinic in Highnam. He couldn't walk, let alone abduct the two of us.'

'He's at the clinic in Highnam? Well, maybe they fixed him up well enough so he was able to. Do you have any idea what the time is? They could have sorted him out by now.'

Something unsettling was sneaking around in Vicky's mind, but she couldn't catch it to see what it was. It kept hiding behind the headache.

Dira continued, 'Or he might have an accomplice. There are quite a few things about the crimes that seem to be impossible for one person. For quite some time, I thought you were helping him, but that doesn't fit with the two of us being cracked on the head and tied up here.'

'Everybody else seems to think you've committed all these crimes, including attacking Jack.'

Dira roared at her. 'Shut up! It was Smith, not me. He's the one. He needs to go to Kangaroo for all this.' The space fell quiet. Vicky could hear him breathing heavily. After a minute, Dira spoke more calmly. 'You said that the audiopts were being fooled somehow. That must be the answer. Somebody must have made fictitious feeds showing me doing that attack and running away from the Brigade. I didn't do anything.'

A scratching sound came from the floor directly in front of Vicky. She guessed it was a couple of metres away, and it sounded like a mouse pottering about. She kicked a leg to try and shoo it away. Vicky was a friend to all animals, but she knew that it wouldn't balk at giving a little bite to test if she was edible. She kicked her foot again and hit something hard on the floor. She could see a small square outline by her foot. With some careful sliding, Vicky was able to move the object to the lightest part of the floor. She was unable to make out any more than its small, square shape.

Her head was pounding. Vicky leaned it back against the tyre and shifted so there was a ridge just under her occipital bulge. With careful positioning of her ponytail, she could get it to rest without rubbing the place where she had been hit.

When Vicky woke up again, the window supplied vaguely more light. It was before dawn, but the world was beginning to illuminate. The square between her feet was now clear as the photograph of Clara that they had found earlier in Dira's basement area.

Ellie's armulet was stuck behind Vicky's back and still ignored her voice commands. Her fingers felt numb; she couldn't feel it accurately enough to cause it to make a call.

She strained against her bonds to see as much of her surroundings as she could. Dira's foot was no longer visible, and he didn't respond, even when she shouted. The building was a wooden construction shed, and she found herself tied to an old tractor. She did not recognise any of it except the photograph.

Jack can't be responsible for this. It can't be him. Is there somebody we missed entirely? Jack had said that it was Dira who attacked him. So who's done this?

Jack had been so certain that Dira had attacked him. Vicky supposed that was the point of the feeds' deception. The victims would be so convinced of what they had experienced, it would be impossible to make anyone believe that their own eyes and ears were lying.

She tried again. 'Dira, are you awake yet?' Nobody replied.

Vicky's head was still painful. Sitting as still as possible, she worked through two lines of thought at the same time.

One sequence of thinking took her to wonder how kidnapping herself and Dira could possibly be of use to whomever had done all this. Whether or not it was Jack, what could they gain from the kidnapping? She tried to think through what knowledge she and Dira might have that the criminal needed to remove from circulation. Or who they might want to put pressure on with the threat to their wellbeing.

The implication from her casual conversations with Aluen was that Dira had no family that could be pressured. Her own brother and father would certainly make every effort to ensure she remained safe, but Vicky could not work out what either Truvan or Marma could offer in return. They were just a family of village farmers. They held no power in Highnam, or anywhere, and they owned nothing of value or importance.

So, was it something she knew? Now the feeds were off, kidnapping might well be an effective way to silence her and Dira. Although she wondered whether the kidnapper wouldn't have taken her armulet away too. She couldn't currently use it, but it still seemed like a bit of a dangerous oversight. They couldn't know that it wouldn't respond to her voice commands. If only she could work out what important information she didn't realise that she knew.

Vicky's other train of thought was to evaluate the situation with a view to escape. What items could she see, and how might they help to get her and Dira out of there? There wasn't much on offer in the small shed. Or at least not much visible. Vicky found her hands to be tightly bound still, with no play in the knots, and she was unable to lean very far forwards or sideways to see much further around the space. Worst of all, the movements kept causing her headache to scream at her.

The photograph of Clara nagged at her thoughts. Jack had moved it upstairs from Dira's living space, so why was it here? Had Dira reclaimed it before being knocked out, and then maybe it fell from a pocket on arrival? It was small enough to fit in a large pocket. Jack's injury meant the kidnapper definitely could not be him.

Ah, yes, definite conclusion: whoever brought me and Dira here must have been to Jack's office in the Doughnut. That's the only way the photograph could be here.

No. Damn it. Dira might have collected it, and then the kidnapper's picked up the picture along with Dira.

Come on, Vicky, think!

Chapter Twenty-six
An hour or two earlier – 23rd March 2091, 5am
Highnam medical centre

Jack's leg was painful on and off throughout the evening. The nurse came and adjusted it from time to time. Every movement caused him pain, but Jack appreciated the care being shown. Each new position was, for a time, more comfortable. Late on, the nurse told him that he was going to get some sleep, and that Jack should too.

Having spent much of the previous night shivering in the Severn Bore Inn and evading the posse on the River Severn and on the roads near Highnam, sleep came to Jack more easily than he expected. It was fitful, though. He woke many times with a yelp of pain from his shinbone, and several times from troubling dreams.

His dreams sometimes had no particular action that he could remember, but he woke with a sense of dread. Other times were clear – he would wake from being chased by all the people he knew in all the places he knew – but they worked in mismatched combinations. Aluen and Lloyd Lloyd chased him up the path on Steep Holm and around the top of the island. Later, the skinny boy and the girl from the Bristol Brigade chased him around the burnt remains of Kangaroo Hall. Dira chased him along a path and into Grannie Ellie's house. Jack hid in a dark wood wardrobe in the spare bedroom.

The wardrobe door opened, and a hooded man put a sack over Jack's head. It was a vinyl drybag, and the monster tightened the bag's neck around Jack's neck. He could just about breathe but the material kept sticking across his mouth. Jack was dragged from the wardrobe and fell on his back on the floor.

THE MIND'S EYE

The shot of pain from his splinted leg woke Jack up. He was being dragged across the floor. There really was a bag over his head. He tried to writhe and wrestle his way free, but his legs were bound together, and his wrists were also tied.

'Who's that? Stop!' Jack had tried to shout, but his breath was so limited it came out as a whispered croak.

His assailant did not reply. He was dragged through the door from his room in the clinic, and his good leg struck the frame of the door. Jack was woozy with the pain. He could not summon the strength to twist his body in order to try and escape.

He felt his head crack into something solid. It was at about waist height. The person dragging him struggled to manoeuvre his dead weight body through the main door of the clinic. The sack over his head was impenetrable to his vision, but he could see a distinct drop in the light level as he was dragged further away. The building had been purpose-built as a doctors' surgery in the early 21st Century, and he felt his feet rub across the asphalt of the small car park.

Jack had so many sensations coursing through his body, he couldn't make sense of them all: pain from his shattered leg bone, pain from where his head was banged, the friction on his back and legs... and he still hadn't shaken off the sense of panic from his night terror. He felt icy with fear. It was cold in the night-time air, but Jack was certain that the chill was coming from within himself.

The wind was knocked out of his lungs as Jack was lifted and then dropped onto something solid. It was only large enough to support his chest and stomach, so his head and feet sagged downwards, but it was high enough that they could not feel the ground. The person sat on top of him, on the middle of his back. With the tight, impermeable material across his face, and the pressure on his thorax, he struggled to breathe.

They lurched forward, and Jack realised he was on a quad bike. He passed out.

Jack woke with the bag still over his head, but he was sitting up on a cold floor. His feet were still tied together, and his wrists were now tied together behind his back and also tied to the huge solid weight he leaned back against. He pulled and shook his bonds, twisting left and right, back and forth, but he was tied fast. In a panic, Jack repeated the convulsions, more and more violently, desperate to get free.

His leg pulsed with pain, and he felt nauseous. Jack sat very still and took small, slow breaths to try and calm both his leg and his mind. The bag was slightly looser at his neck than it had been. As long as he didn't throw up in it, he should be able to breathe with relative ease.

'Who's there? Who is that?' Vicky's voice was loud and urgent. Jack's breathing quickened again, and he opened his eyes. The world outside the bag looked a bit brighter, even more so than inside the clinic.

Jack tried to answer, but it just came out as a moan.

'It's me, Dira, I'm still here with you. Are you OK? What was that moan?'

'That wasn't me, there's somebody else here. I can't see them either, but they're on the other side of me from you.'

He mumbled, 'It's Jack, it's me, Vicky.'

'Oh, Malthus, are you OK? You sound terrible.'

'My leg's really bad.' He felt the intense pain and cried out. 'Aargh! Owww!'

Vicky's voice was strained. Jack could hear the distress in it. Her speech became slurred. 'Oh, no, c-c-c-an you mo-o-oo-ve? We're tied u-u-u-p. Somebody abbbbb...' She got stuck and paused. Trying again, Vicky said, 'too-oo-k us and tied us in here. Wherever... there... is.'

THE MIND'S EYE

Dira asked, 'What can you see from where you are, Jack? Looks like we're in some sort of shed, but can you see an exit or anything?'

'They've put a bag over my head. I can't see anything. I can barely breathe. And I'm tied to some big metal object.'

Vicky started to reply, 'We are too. It's a...' but then trailed off, lost for the word. A few seconds later, she continued, '...tractor, but we're all on different sides of it, so we can't help each other. We can't even see you.'

'Have you got bags on your heads too?'

Dira said, 'No, we're just stuck out of sight round the big wheels of the tractor. Vicky's at the back, and you and I are on either side.'

'You'd better rest, Jack. That leg injury was really bad, so if you've been dragged here, it could be even worse now.'

'I was on a quad bike. They sat on my back. That's all I remember.'

'Me too,' said Dira.

Vicky added, 'They knocked me out completely, and I just woke up here. Do rest though, Jack. Dira and I will work out how to get out of here.'

'Dira?' Jack could still not shout his incredulity, even though that was the message his brain sent to his mouth. It came out as another croak.

He rubbed his head back on the big rubber tyre and tried to scrape the bag up and off, but it kept getting hooked under his chin. He had a mild ache across his chest, but he hardly noticed it, as his broken shinbone was much worse. Jack leant his head back. Wooziness slipped him into unconsciousness again.

He awoke again at the sound of Vicky's voice. 'Jack, Jack, are you OK?' Her voice sounded more normal.

'Um, yes, what is it?'

'Dira thinks he can get his hand untied. We'll get you loose soon. How are you?'

He was suddenly alert. 'Much better. My leg is still agony, but I don't feel ill anymore.'

She turned her attention the other way. 'How's it coming, Dira? Are you getting anywhere?'

'Just about there.' Jack heard some shuffling and then footsteps. 'So, Jack, let's see what a mess you've gotten everyone into.' The bag was pulled off his head and he squinted against the light. Dira loomed over him with the red plastic bag held high in one hand.'

Vicky spoke from around behind Jack. 'What do you mean, Dira? This isn't Jack's fault. Come on, untie us.'

'Oh, I will. I'm just taking a good look at our vicious criminal. The Brigade will be pleased that I've caught him. And Highnam will get their revenge.'

Jack tried to shrink under the tractor, but he could barely move. He spluttered, 'It wasn't me.'

Vicky voice was loud. 'Stop it, Dira! Whoever kidnapped us must be the one who's done it all. Untie us and let's get after *them*.'

Dira untied the rope at Jack's feet and leant over his head to reach down behind for the other knots. He stood on the broken left leg in the process. Jack wailed. His vision popped with coloured lights. Jack had only ever seen fireworks in old videostories, but this appeared like a fireworks show just for him. With his hands released, Dira stepped away around the tractor wheel to Vicky. Jack leaned forward to put his hands on the damaged leg. He squeezed at the side of the inflatable splint but couldn't bring himself to actually touch the source of the pain.

THE MIND'S EYE

Jack could see Dira standing facing Vicky. He rolled around to his left to look at her too. She looked up at Dira, her face confused.

'Come on, what are you waiting for? Untie me!' Her voice was unsteady.

Dira leant down and grabbed Jack by the back of his collar. He dragged him forward in front of Vicky.

'Take a look at your murderer.' He was grinning. 'You say Jack's no criminal, but I doubt Kangaroo will spare him when they watch my audiopt feeds as I watch him kill you.'

'What? I'm not going to do anything!' Jack's voice was loud and clear. In his mind, he did not understand what Dira meant. He had a vision of himself stabbing Vicky as she sat there. He shook his head.

Dira stepped to the corner of the room and picked up a large lump of concrete. Watching him, Jack realised where they were. 'This is Grannie's big shed.'

'Yes, indeed. I know you wanted to murder Vicky in the house, but the Bristol Brigade are in there, so you'll have to make do with here.' He grinned again and waved the concrete at them.

When Dira stepped forward, Jack saw the photo lying by Vicky's thigh. Her green dress was partly covering it, but he recognised it immediately. 'Wait, why did you have that photo of my mother?'

'Why do you think? She was the first person you killed. It took being stuck in the explosion last year for me to realise that you're nothing but malice. And it's my responsibility to fix that. If I'd been a better father, maybe you'd never have ended up like this, but I can fix it now.'

He lurched another step closer to Vicky and raised the concrete over his head, held in both hands.

'The audiopt feeds are off,' she cried.

Dira's grin closed into a simple smile. 'My feeds go on and off often. Nobody will be surprised that they happened to be on tonight.'

Jack looked up in a daze. '"...a better father..."? Father?' He was gazing at Dira, open-mouthed. He had been struggling to focus clearly ever since being attacked, but Jack's mind was now whirling out of control. He couldn't latch on to any idea or thought for even a second. He started panting, unable to catch his breath.

Vicky replied to Dira, 'They will. All feeds have been turned off, not just yours. It would be an amazing surprise for people if yours were the only ones that had been working.'

Dira stood for a moment. He looked awkward with the concrete raised over his head. 'Well, then, I'll just have to wrestle this rock from Jack's hands and kill him to save myself. I can be a witness even without the audiopt records.' His grin re-appeared. 'In fact, if they're all off, then what I witness can't have been a hallucination fed to me by someone else.'

'Help! Help! We're in the shed! Dira's going to kill us!' Vicky was shouting as loud as she could. Jack looked at her and her eyes were directed straight at Dira's.

The old man commanded, 'Shut up! Stop it, that won't help.'

'Come on, Jack, the Brigade are in the house. Shout as loud as you can!' Jack couldn't process the situation and just did what Vicky told him. Together, they shouted for help several more times.

Dira growled, 'Shut up!' He turned to look out of the small, high window that faced towards Ellie's place. In that instant, Jack rolled fully over his back and launched a two-footed kick at Dira. He caught the man right in the kidney.

THE MIND'S EYE

With the weight of the concrete held high, he staggered and fell against the wooden wall.

Jack lay in front of Vicky, twitching with the pain. He heard shouts from outside the building. And then he heard Vicky calling back to guide people towards them. Dira picked himself up and ran for the far end double door exit of the shed. He shouldered it open, and Jack watched his feet under the tractor. They disappeared into the woods, although Jack couldn't see very far anyway.

The single door at their end opened, and Asa and Marmaran ran in. Asa lifted Jack up to sitting, so that her father could get to Vicky and untie her.

'Are you OK?' Asa asked.

Jack could not respond, so he just nodded.

Vicky said, 'He's not OK; his leg is in a really bad way. We need to get him back to the clinic right now.'

There were some shouts from outside, in the direction Jack had seen Dira escape. Asa and Marma both looked towards the noises. They quickly returned attention to Jack and Vicky. Marmaran untied his daughter and helped her to her feet. She wobbled momentarily and then knelt down beside Jack.

'You saved my life.' Vicky leant forward and gave Jack a long kiss on the cheek. She followed this up with the briefest skim of her lips against his and stood up again.

Jack was mumbling. 'He's my father... father.' He passed out again.

Chapter Twenty-seven
Several hours earlier – 23rd March 2091, 2am
Highnam medical centre

Marmaran peered in through the window. He could see that Jack's leg was keeping him awake. It didn't help that the nurse had left most of the clinic lights on, although Marma noticed that the light in the room the nurse slept in was off. The outside temperature was dropping under clear starlit skies.

He walked around and opened the front door of the building. Asa came out of the shadow of a darkened room and exited so they could talk. Marma helped the door to close silently.

'I assume nothing has happened?'

Asa answered, 'No, although the nurse has only been in bed about an hour.' He raised his arm and Marmaran could see the time on Asa's armulet – ten to two.

'OK, well fingers crossed Vicky's worrying about nothing.'

Asa patted the shorter man's upper arm and walked off into the night.

Marmaran slipped through the entrance door and clicked the switches so all lights were off. Vicky had warned him that somebody might come back to hurt Jack again, and Marma knew the list of those who might have cause to do so was slowly getting longer. An hour or so earlier, Tony had told him of Lloyd Lloyd's outburst, when the Brigade had dropped Jack off at the clinic.

Much as he disliked the thought of it, Marmaran also knew that his own son, Truvan, had a loathing of Jack Smith that would probably never subside. Losing his other son, Bailey, to the River Severn had put Marmaran into the same dark place as the day he had found Janet asleep in the snow. He always used the word 'asleep' when he thought of his dead wife. He had not been able to reach her in time in a desperate blizzard at their farm. Weak and lost, hypothermic, whilst Marmaran battled the wind and the darkness, Janet had lost consciousness, never to wake up.

Both the deaths had come decades too early. In Janet's case, Marmaran blamed himself, and so he understood how the twin that survived must feel. He hoped he would not have to face down Truvan that night, in order to keep him from hurting Smith.

In a widened part of the corridor were two armchairs and a small table between them. Marmaran sat down and looked all around, up and down the corridor. He waited a few minutes for his eyes to become completely accustomed to the dark and then checked what he could see. The night was dark. He could make out doorways as darker shadows in the darkness. After a time, he was sure he could make out the few items of furniture.

The main entrance door was the easiest outline to observe, and he thought he could see if someone entered. Marma shook his head, got up and switched on the light that shone outside on the porch area. *That won't keep him awake.* The large glass panel in the door spread light just inside but little further. As Marmaran sat back down, he nodded and smiled.

He wondered if Vicky was really correct in thinking Jack might get attacked again. And he could not understand why she had not asked the Brigade to protect him overnight. He felt pleased that she had entrusted him to help, and he was especially happy that Tony and Asa had agreed to help too. Even if none of them quite understood what Vicky was thinking.

She had told her father that she expected Dira to attack Jack again. Marma could not see why this was likely. Indeed, nobody had even confirmed that it had been Dira that had broken Jack's leg in the first place. That was what he had claimed, but the injury could easily have made him delirious. However, if Truvan or Lloyd Lloyd might lose control, Marmaran would be glad to intervene and save them from themselves. Both men were bigger than he was, but he was certain that if they appeared at the clinic in the night, his presence alone should be enough to change their minds.

Vicky had been particularly concerned because the audiopt feeds were off, so somebody might think that they could get away with an attack. Marma checked the armulet locators for Truvan and Lloyd Lloyd – both were at their houses. Dira's armulet did not register.

After another ten minutes staring at the darkness of the corridor, he tapped a few times on his armulet screen. A virtual tawula board was projected in front of him, and he began to play against the computer.

A little before 6am, Tony shook Marmaran awake to take over for his shift of guarding Jack. 'How has it been? Quiet I suppose – enough so you could sleep.'

'Oh, I didn't mean to sleep.' Marmaran cricked his neck. 'Is Jack asleep?'

Tony turned and walked back the ten metres along the corridor to look in on the patient. He did not switch on any lights but shone his armulet torch into the room. He then did switch on the light and rushed into the room. 'Jack?' Tony called out.

Arriving at the threshold, Marma could see the bed was empty.

THE MIND'S EYE

They woke the nurse from further down the corridor and switched on all the building's lights. Both men had slept through Jack's departure. He had no armulet, and the audiopts were still off.

'Did he run away?' the nurse asked.

'Well, we were supposed to be watching him,' Marma admitted.

The nurse shrugged. 'He can't go far on that leg. The Brigade will catch him.'

Tony videocalled Asa to come and help, and then he looked at Marmaran. 'We'd better go and tell the Brigade.'

'They're staying at Ellie's house. I wonder if he's gone to see Vicky.' He made to call his daughter, but her armulet was on Steep Holm. There was no answer when he tried it. He decided not to call Truvan instead.

Asa arrived, and the three men went to discuss it with the Brigade. They had all walked, but they knew the village paths well. Even in the dark, they were there in less than ten minutes. It was very cold. Frosted leaves, still on the ground since autumn, crunched under their feet. The sounds were clear and loud in the still air.

They had called ahead to Major Halthrop, so the members of the Bristol Brigade had already been roused. They were fully dressed and assembled in the main lounge room when the three villagers entered the house.

'What are the details?' Major Halthrop took charge.

'Jack's disappeared,' Tony replied.

Marma wanted to say something, but he couldn't think of anything that might help.

'Where would he go?' Asa asked and looked around at everyone.

Marma now had an answer, but he still didn't think it would help. 'I'd expect him to come here.'

Halthrop clicked his fingers at Jane and Terry and pointed back through the doorways. They shot off out of sight.

'Anywhere else?'

Halthrop was looking at Marmaran, and he in turn looked at Tony and Asa. They looked at each other and said in unison, 'Vicky.'

'I couldn't call her; she hasn't got her armulet.'

Jane and Terry returned and confirmed Jack was not in the house.

Marmaran excitedly held up his left arm. 'Wait, she's wearing Ellie's, I saw it on her this evening.'

'Is it still worki…'

'Shh, everybody quiet,' Terry shouted. His sudden intervention gained immediate silence.

They heard a muffled noise. 'That's outside,' Tony said.

Halthrop held up his hand for continued silence, and they stepped as lightly as possible through the kitchen to the back door. As soon as he opened it, a shout came clearly through the night.

'Who is that?' Darren asked the group. He never received an answer as they all bundled out of the door to investigate. The shouting had stopped, so they fanned out across the back garden and moved forward to search for what was happening. Seven mini-searchlights penetrated the slowly lifting darkness. The lights wobbled and bounced from trees and bushes, dying in the depths of vegetation beyond the garden.

Marmaran heard somebody shout something. Several of the light beams started moving away from the house faster and appeared to be closing together beyond Ellie's big tractor shed. He wondered if they were actually converging on a person, or if the growth of trees in the woods was funnelling everyone together.

THE MIND'S EYE

'We're in here. Help!' Vicky's voice could be heard calling over and over.

Asa caught his arm as he ran forwards and prompted Marmaran to come along. A noise was definitely coming from inside. Marma followed. He stumbled over something and staggered for a few steps before catching the end corner of the wooden building. He walked in through the door and could see Jack and Vicky in the light from Asa's armulet.

The younger man lifted Jack up to seated and inquired how he was. Vicky told them that Jack's leg was worse than ever. Marmaran realised that his daughter was tied up. He leant over her and tried to reach the bonds behind her back. It was difficult to undo the knots. His haste made it even more difficult, and she twice told him to calm down and take it slowly.

She could not tell him enough times that she was OK. Once he had untied her hands, he hugged her tightly. After ten seconds, she pushed him back a little and leaned forward to untie her ankles. Marma went to untie them as well, but just ended up interfering in what she was doing. She finally slapped his hand away.

More shouting could be heard from outside. It wasn't clear what they were saying, but Marma interpreted the shouts along the lines of 'Over here!' and 'I've got him!' and 'this way!'. It seemed to keep going around in circles – they had him and then they didn't, and one minute he was here, and the next minute he was there.

Marma turned back to his daughter. She accepted his help to stand, and he caught her when she wobbled. Vicky stepped over to Jack and knelt beside him. She said something, but there was more shouting outside and consequently Marma missed it.

'I'll go and get one of the Brigade quad bikes so we can take Jack back to see Doc.' Asa walked out of the doorway.

Vicky was stroking his cheek, and her father stood silently, watching them both.

Asa came back in, and the two of them carried Jack out to the quad bike. They found it difficult to secure him to it so that Asa could drive them safely, but eventually they moved off at less than walking pace along the path around the side of Ellie's land. Further away in the woods, the shouting continued.

Marmaran said, 'I'm so sorry, darling. This is all my fault. Are you sure you're all right?'

She nodded.

'How did I let this happen? Stupid, stupid!' He made to hit the side of his own head, but Vicky caught his arm in the air. She opened his arm and placed it around her waist, and he helped her back into the house. Neither had realised how cold they were until they stepped inside the kitchen, and, shivering, they went and took the blankets that were still warm from the beds. They wrapped up and sat beside each other on the sofa.

Vicky's story was confusing. Dira had also been kidnapped, but then got free and tried to kill her. He'd accused Jack of being the criminal but had then said he'd get away with killing Vicky. Jack had saved her from the attack, but the Brigade had come in the nick of time, as Jack's leg would not have allowed him to fight any further. She was very glad she had enlisted her father, Asa and Tony to help.

Vicky threw off the blankets and ran out of the room. She returned two minutes later, leapt back on to the sofa and wrapped herself up again. She poked something out of the shroud for her father to look at. He took the small photograph and looked at Clara's face.

THE MIND'S EYE

Marmaran looked at Vicky. 'This is the photo Dira had? Of Clara.'

Vicky nodded.

'Why?'

'We don't know.'

'Ellie used to have this photo here somewhere. Why would Dira want it?'

Vicky started working at something on Ellie's armulet. She projected a photograph of Jack as a small boy into the air in front of their sofa. She slid the display onto another picture. They were all of Jack – she had filtered a search to just show them. There were a number of him in trees, and helping dig the garden, and so on. From the very first steps, through to teenager.

She changed the search filter to show images of Clara and started flicking through. One image came up and she stopped. Marmaran looked at the picture of Clara and a boyfriend and then looked at Vicky. Her mouth was hanging open.

'That's Dira.'

'Are you sure? I remember that man. He and Clara spent a summer together, but he was just passing through. Oh, what was his name? It wasn't Dira, I'd remember that.'

'No, it is. He looks younger than he does now, but it's definitely him. He still wears the same beard.' She looked up the image data and found that the picture was from August 2059. Those pictured were 'Clara and Taylor'.

'Yes, that's it, Taylor. Yes, it was a silly name, because he worked as a tailor. He passed through town, made some suits and dresses for some people, got Clara pregnant and then left.' He sat and ran through what he could remember of 2059. 'Neither Ellie nor Clara mentioned him later, so I never asked any more about him. I assumed they were happy with the situation. And then Clara died. I don't know that I ever thought of him again. Ellie was all the parent Jack ever needed.'

Vicky was staring at him. 'But that's Dira. Dira's Jack's father.'

'But hang on, you said he was an infotech at the Doughnut. Taylor made clothes. Are you sure it's him?'

'Why else would he have a photo of Clara by his bed?'

THE MIND'S EYE
Chapter Twenty-eight
An hour or so earlier – 23rd March 2091, 6am
Grannie Ellie's house

Major Halthrop shouted the Brigade awake. His troops were all on their feet and in the main room before he was. Through the large windows, night was starting to give way to day. The blackness had become more of a murky purple.

The three villagers trooped into Ellie's house. The oldest man's shaggy, grey hair was unkempt, and where his beard started and the hair ended was unclear. He said that Jack Smith had vanished from the clinic. Vicky's father thought the man would come to the house. Halthrop knew that nobody had entered, but he sent Jane and Terry to search the rest of the rooms to be certain.

They returned quickly and gave a silent shake of their heads. The major could not imagine Jack being able to travel easily or far with his broken leg and asked about other possible places he might go. The men were in the midst of setting a videocall to Vicky Truva when Terry shouted for quiet. There was a definite noise from outside the house. The front doors were still ajar and at first the noises – faraway shouts – sounded like they were coming from somewhere in the village. Halthrop listened carefully, and the sounds could also be heard penetrating the walls from the back garden.

He was first to the back exit out of the kitchen and, as soon as he opened the door, he could hear the commotion, closer than the main part of the village, coming from the rear of Ellie's land. They spread out across the back garden and set off away from the house. The shouting stopped, so they would have to find the source without any further guidance.

Jane shouted that she had seen someone. Halthrop headed towards her voice. He could see the bobbing torchlights getting closer together, but there was no confirmation shout.

'Jane, what's happening?'

Her call came back, 'No, I've lost them.'

'Who is it?'

'I couldn't tell.'

Darren then shouted from further to the major's right, 'Over here! I saw Dira.'

The little set of lights jiggled away towards the right, lighting up one tree trunk after another. Dawn was coming, but the lights still made a significant difference in the dark of the woods. Frank turned his off and moved as quietly as he could. He curved around trying to stay ahead of the group. He hoped they would drive Dira into him. They seemed to move for ages, and then he saw a shadow scoot between trees away from him.

He commanded the Brigade through their armulets, 'Fan out to your left, I've just seen him heading that way.'

Their lights and noise were obvious. Halthrop's plan took a few minutes to come to fruition, but the crashing, chasing group did drive the fugitive back towards him. He saw a figure without a light limping between trees.

Halthrop muttered quietly into his wrist, 'Now, slow down, and turn back towards the house. Spread slightly further apart. You're driving straight towards me, so keep that line.'

They did well. The lights moved to even positions in a line ahead, like footlights on a hidden stage lighting tree actors. One errant spotlight was waving around out of sync with the other three. One of the Highnam men was there, and they were not on the Brigade's group calling system. Fortunately, the man was slower than the others, so he was not

THE MIND'S EYE

as far up as the rest of the line, and Halthrop hoped he would not send their man away from the ambush zone.

Halthrop had lost sight of the silhouetted man. He took a few cautious steps backwards and further along to his right. 'Advance slowly towards the house.' The lights were spread at an ideal distance, so there should be no hidden spaces between them, and they started to move towards the Brigade CO. Halthrop held his lips slightly open and controlled his breathing. His whole body was tense, and he felt a gentle tightening in his stomach.

The righthand-most light arced and disappeared. There was a crash and Darren shouted, 'I've got him.' They all moved towards the sound where his light had last been. Halthrop saw the thatch of blond hair first. It was wrestling in the darkness, with most of Darren's torchlight sucked into low bushes or the ground or underneath him. The trees were dense, and Halthrop held his arm up in front of his face as he forced his way through as fast as possible.

Still three or four metres away, Halthrop saw another man appear and kick Darren off the captive. Halthrop shone his light, and Truvan turned towards it. He immediately turned back and shoved Darren from his knees and into a mass of branches.

Halthrop charged through, both arms shielding his face, and simply ran into Truvan. The two of them tumbled back, and the thick branches held them up. Halthrop took two fistfuls of the man's shirt, dragged him back into more space, stuck his leg out and twisted him over his thigh. Truvan landed flat on his back in the litter of pine needles.

Jane and Terry arrived from slightly different directions and fell onto Truvan. He struggled but they clung on, lying over his body, until he subsided and lay still.

Frank helped Darren back up. 'You OK?'

He put a hand to the side of his large chest, where Truvan's boot had connected. 'Yeah, I'm OK.' He looked down at the pile of three on the floor. 'I don't get how he managed to hit me though – I had him pinned.'

'It wasn't him.' Halthrop suddenly realised that Dira had vanished. They had Truvan pinned down, but the other man was no longer there. 'Shit, where did he go?'

They all looked around, but Halthrop got the impression that he was the only one who had seen two people there. He could hear somebody crashing through the branches, but before he could set off after them, Tony arrived, and it was clear that he had been the one making the noise. When he stopped in their group, the only remaining sound was Truvan squirming under Terry and Jane.

'Get him up,' Halthrop said.

They all had a hand in pulling Vicky's brother up to standing.

'Truvan? What are you doing here?' Tony asked. 'Marma said he didn't tell you what we were doing.'

'What were you doing?' Truvan retorted. 'Helping a criminal?'

'Well, no, we were making sure he wasn't attacked again. And making sure he didn't escape either,' Tony puffed.

Halthrop asked, 'What are you doing helping Dira to escape?' As the words left his mouth, the major wondered if in fact Dira had been there at all, or if he had suffered one of the audiopt hallucinations. He knew they had switched off the system, but the lack of comprehension on the faces of the others made him doubt himself.

He was vindicated by Truvan's reply. 'We have a deal.'

'What do you mean, "a deal"?' Tony asked. He shook the man.

THE MIND'S EYE

Truvan stared at Tony. 'I do what I can to keep you all off his trail, and he'll get Vicky away from Smith for good.'

'And what do you mean by that?' Tony shook him again, his voice louder.

Halthrop put his hand on Tony's shoulder and pulled him away from the prisoner. 'Enough. Let's get him back inside and work out what's going on. You two keep searching out here. He can't have got far.' He waved at Terry and Darren.

Terry said, 'You should get the audiopts turned back on so we can catch him easily.'

Darren added, 'Yeah, this is impossible.'

Their boss shook his head. 'No, you could see anything then. You might get a vision of him in three different places at once. The system is compromised. We've got to do this the old-fashioned way. It might be a bit of hard work, but we've trained for it, remember?'

Jane and Halthrop took an arm each, and it took them some time to get their threesome back out of the thicker forest to the lighter vegetation and finally the back garden.

They frogmarched him into the lounge and pushed him down in to an armchair. His father and sister were on one of the large green sofas, wrapped in blankets.

'What's going on?' Vicky said loudly. She held her father from standing up.

Halthrop explained, 'I'm sorry to tell you that Truvan attacked one of my men and allowed Dira to go free.'

'Is that true?' Marmaran leant forward, but Vicky's hold was secure. The sofa was soft and deep, and he was wrapped in a blanket. He let her hold him from getting up but stared hard at his son.

Truvan replied, 'Smith must be stopped.'

Vicky shouted at him. 'Stop, Truvan! Jack saved my life just now. Dira is the killer. He tried to kill me too. You sound as mad as he is. What is wrong with you?'

Truvan stared at her. 'You're wrong. He's going to get Smith away from us for good.'

'What are you talking about?'

'I can prove it. I can show you what he said.'

Major Halthrop said, 'We turned the audiopt recording system off just after dark last night. When did you discuss this with him?'

'He came to the house in the middle of the night.'

'Then, I'm afraid, nothing he said will have been recorded.'

Truvan tapped at his armulet. Dira's voice came into the room. He swiped through some of the conversation to a point where Truvan asked why he should help Dira, and the man replied that he would kill Jack Smith.

Vicky and her father looked at each other.

'I'm not that stupid, I knew the system was off, so I made a voice recording directly with my armulet.' Truvan stopped speaking for a moment and then looked up and said, 'I knew he was the one, so I tricked him into confessing. This should be good evidence for Kangaroo, shouldn't it?'

Major Halthrop stepped forward. 'If you are now claiming that you were trying to catch him all along, then why did you help him escape from us just now?'

Truvan said nothing.

Jane interrupted, speaking to Vicky. 'Wait, you said Jack saved your life *just now*. Was he here? Where is he?' She looked up to her boss.

Vicky answered, 'He hurt his leg even more. Asa took him back to the clinic to get it seen to. You realise that he didn't try and kill Jack at all, he tried to kill me.'

THE MIND'S EYE

'Rubbish, why would he do that?' Truvan rocked back and forth slightly in the armchair.

Major Halthrop nodded to Jane, and she headed out of the front door. Every time a blast of cold air from outside entered the house, it wafted away the musty, old smell of the furniture. The smell wasn't noticeable, until it was cleared by incoming fresher-smelling air and the difference became obvious. Halthrop closed his eyes and rubbed his forehead. He just wanted the whole thing to be over. He asked himself, *Why has this become so complicated?*

Vicky answered her brother. Her arms emerged from the blanket so she could wave them up and down to emphasise her point. 'Because he's not right in the head. He said Jack was going to kill me, and he'd have to kill Jack to save himself.'

Truvan nodded, 'Exactly, so it was Dira that saved you.'

'No, you idiot. As he said all that, he was standing over me with a huge rock, ready to smash it down on me. He was going to make it look like Jack had done it. Jack kicked him away and saved me.'

'I don't believe it. That's not what we agreed.'

Marmaran's eyes bulged, and Vicky stared at Truvan.

In his head, Major Halthrop continued to wish they'd never been called on for this mission. He misquoted Chanayaka. *Through association of evil even one without vice becomes evil.*

The major spoke with a sigh. 'We're going to have to go and catch him. We can pick this one up at some later time. I'm sure Kangaroo will be interested to find out what he did agree, but I assume Dira will be chasing after Jack back at the clinic.'

'I'll watch him here,' Tony said.

Frank called the other two back from the woods. He had reached the big patio doors when Vicky said, 'Major.' He turned and she followed up, 'Dira is Jack's father.'

Halthrop scowled all the way out to the quad bikes. He stopped Darren and clambered on behind him.

Chapter Twenty-nine

Half an hour earlier – 23rd March 2091, 6.30am
Grannie Ellie's woods

Dira was held down by one of the brutes from the Bristol Brigade. He was twisting and trying to throw him off, but the young man was heavy and strong.

Without warning, his captor flew off, and Dira could crawl into hiding in the undergrowth. Truvan Truva had appeared, but was immediately charged into by Major Halthrop, and the two went tumbling into dense branches.

Dira did not look back. He took the opportunity to escape into the dark woods. Back at the tractor shed, he could hear voices inside and stole a look in through the window. Vicky and her father were walking towards the door, so Dira moved around to the other side of the building. He saw the lights of a quad bike slowly moving away down the path to the main village.

Following the quad bike, Dira could see Jack sitting backwards with his leg sticking out, as he struggled to hold on to the passenger handles. Dira could barely make out the driver; he was skinny and had long, shaggy hair. Maybe the same driver as the mystery one from the previous day, but it was still not light enough to be sure. He cursed that he had become distracted before he looked up who that driver might be. He felt a twinge of pain in his thigh. The running and the wrestling had aggravated the old explosion injury.

Dira guessed that they would probably need to take Jack to the clinic to have his broken leg seen to again. *I should have finished you off when I had the chance.* He followed them along the main path – the quad bike was moving very slowly. Two hundred metres or so from the clinic, Dira cut off to the left on a much narrower footpath shortcut. The sun was rising over the roof of the medical centre. He held a hand up to shade his eyes. The sunlight sent steam rising from the bare tree branches on either side of the path.

He spoke to himself. 'I'll let them give you all the treatment they like, and then I'll finish it in the care bed. It won't be the first time a person died in that bed.' Dira laughed out loud. 'In fact, the last person was Marisa Leone, who you killed, so nobody will mourn your passing that much.' Dira's intent to make everyone believe in Jack's guilt had become completely ingrained. He had come to believe his own lies. He said nothing more but remembered that it was the same clinic where Clara had died. In Dira's mind, she was another of Jack's victims.

Dira set himself up in a sort of observation hide outside the clinic. The large rhododendron bush was kept cut in a rectangular shape and stood on the corner of the main path from the village, opposite one end of the doctors' surgery. It was one of the few trees that still had leaves after the winter. Inside the bush, the space was quite open, with a tangle of low, flat branches that would support a person's weight. The thick, rubbery leaves completely shielded the hideout from external view but allowed pretty good views outwards. Dira could see both the way that the quad bike should come and the other way, along the front to the clinic's main door. He chose not to sit on a branch in case of making the whole bush appear to shake, but his thigh made kneeling painful. In the end, he had to sit on the cold ground with his legs outstretched along the inside of the leaf wall.

Jack's quad bike had not arrived when the short, auburn girl from the Brigade rode up and parked on the old car park. She got off and went inside. After a few minutes, she came back and stood at the front entrance. The girl was speaking

THE MIND'S EYE

into her armulet, but Dira could not hear what was being said. He was probably twenty metres away, and the leaves masked some of the sounds around him.

After what Dira guessed might be ten minutes, another quad bike arrived carrying both Halthrop and the fat boy that had tackled him, and then the skinny boy trundled up as well. He looked every way he could see from the bush, but there was still no sign of Jack. He strained to see through all possible gaps between leaves, in every possible direction, but the mystery driver definitely had not arrived.

Dira gripped a branch in each hand and swore silently. Jack's quad bike should have been there by now. However, even if Dira decided to go and search for him somewhere else – Vicky's house came to mind – he was now trapped in the bush with the Brigade hanging around outside. He shook his head in frustration and had to bite his lip to stop cursing out loud.

The members of the Brigade talked some more, and they turned around looking in all different directions. Dira sat very still and watched them. After five more minutes, Halthrop took an armulet call, and they mounted the bikes again and drove off.

He stepped out from the rhododendrons and walked around the clinic building. Looking in the windows, he saw the nurse lying, fully clothed, on top of his makeshift bed. The care bed that Jack had occupied was empty.

Dira looked around and was alone outside. 'Where are you, Jack?' he asked quietly. 'I suppose we're going to have to go and find out.' An electric bike was plugged into a socket on the outside wall of the clinic. It was a regular two-wheeler. Since his leg injury, Dira hated bikes. It would take too long to walk to the Doughnut, and he might get caught again on the way.

He unplugged it and headed the long way around Highnam Court to join the old A40, which went pretty much straight up to the Doughnut fifteen kilometres to the east. Dira figured that he could reinstate the audiopt feeds to find Jack's location. He needed to get to Jack before the Brigade found either of them. The plan needed to be brought together as soon as possible or it would fail.

On the way, Dira thought through some possible false feeds he could maybe send to Halthrop or to Jack himself. As everybody thought the feeds were off, they should be easily fooled, but Dira couldn't work out the best diversionary tactic.

In the end, he decided on a simple one. He would use the feeds to give him Jack's location, and then send Halthrop off on some wild goose chase far from there. As Jack was immobile, he would then be a sitting duck. Dira chuckled at the double waterfowl metaphors and weaved the bike from side to side. He always had a plan.

As if it were a perfectly normal arrival at work, he plugged in the bike in one of the shelters by a double entrance door to the Doughnut. Had he been arriving for work, he would have been three hours late, but Dira strolled in as if he owned the place. He was bang in between shift changes, so there was nobody around. With the audiopt system off, nobody could possibly know that he was coming in.

He had entered about a quarter of the way around the circular architecture from the best staircase down to his basement spot. As he walked around the outermost corridor on the ground floor, the sun was low and bright against the tinted glass window that ran all the way alongside.

He heard a murmur of conversation up ahead, like there was a low-key party going on. Dira slowed up and tried to make out what was being said. He did not recognise the voices, but there seemed to be quite a lot of them.

THE MIND'S EYE

The topics were varied and seemingly random. One voice explained how much honey they liked to add to their elderflower drinks. He heard another ask how long they might expect the audiopt system to be offline.

It took a good ten minutes of eavesdropping, but Dira pieced together that the sifters were socialising because they could not currently do any work. With the feeds down, the server algorithms were offering no suggested crimes for them to assess and add to their villages' KangaReviews for the week. He smiled at the ongoing chaos and puffed his chest up.

Rather than walk across the open doorway, Dira went back to the previous staircase and descended. This route would mean that he would have to walk through the destroyed server room that would bring a twinge to his thigh, but it was better than being seen upstairs.

He sat in his tatty, old office chair at the workstation in the metal cage and entered the password that opened all the servers and screens. The programming methodology that had been employed to switch off the audiopt surveillance system was not the one that Dira had thought up. This made it tricky to find. He spent over thirty minutes searching for the code that had done it but was stumped.

He laughed at his own stupidity. 'Of course. By Malthus, you fool!'

Dira knew that his infotech counterpart, Newnham's other technician, had been the one to help Aluen to arrange making the system go offline. The audiopt records from before they went offline were still available as normal. At least, they were from a Doughnut workstation. He looked up the records for both Aluen and the other infotech and watched the two of them as they had worked on it the night before. He saw the hack they had used, shrugged at its comparative simplicity compared to his own idea, and dived into the system to cancel it out.

As soon as the system was back online, Dira set up several of his screens to display the live feeds for Jack and Vicky and Halthrop, as well as the other members of the Brigade. When he saw who Jack was talking to, he nodded in comprehension and added a screen for Asa.

Initially, the Brigade were talking to Lloyd Lloyd, but almost as soon as Dira switched the system on, the group left his home and mounted up the trio of quad bikes again. This time, Halthrop rode pillion on Terry's bike. Dira chuckled. 'I'd avoid sharing with that fat buffoon too.'

Noone in the Brigade spoke, and Dira watched closely as they drove back up the Gloucester by-pass heading for the Doughnut. His face twitched in various ways, thoughts and plans whirling to be nailed down.

Dira mused aloud, 'Right, we need a diversion to get Asa out of his house. And that would be best if it took Tony away too. Let's see, what emergency will work for them?'

He tapped away at the middle keyboard for a few minutes, cutting and editing bits of video footage of Tony. He watched the short video message once it was complete, leaned back with his hands behind his head and smiled.

'OK, program that to send from my armulet, and we'll be in business when I get close to the house.' He picked his armulet up from the desk and strapped it on. The leather was smooth, and the place it always sat on his forearm was void of hairs.

'Right, now – Halthrop. Something different for you, I think.' He worked on some more video editing. Halthrop's screen showed him approaching the Doughnut. He was a couple of hundred metres away.

THE MIND'S EYE

The circular building was silver and gleamed in the morning sunlight. It was incongruous, large and alien at the edge of Cheltenham, which had become thoroughly overgrown over the last fifty years. With no Kangaroo proper, and a tiny population, the city epitomised nature reclaiming urban space. But not the Doughnut: the hundred metres of car park had minimised how much vegetation could seed its way to the building. And the materials, mostly glass and steel, had also proven generally impervious to Mother Nature's reclamation. As Dira watched, he imagined Major Halthrop as an actor in an old videostory, the character observing a spacecraft landed in the countryside.

Dira clicked a few buttons on the keyboard, and the major pulled Terry's back to stop. He stood up on the back of the quad bike, watching a figure limping away at the edge of the car park. One of the aliens had disembarked and was headed into the abandoned human city.

'That's him,' Halthrop shouted to the Brigade members and pointed after the disappearing figure. 'Dira's over there. Probably headed to his house.'

In the basement, the old infotech's chest puffed up again and he grinned.

The other two bikes circled round to meet up with Terry and Frank.

Jane said, 'I didn't see him. Where did he go?'

Darren agreed, 'Sorry, I was watching ahead towards the building.'

Halthrop looked at Terry who just shook his head. His view turned towards where Dira had been observed hurrying away. The place was empty and Halthrop looked back at his troops. They all looked expectantly at him.

Chapter Thirty

23rd March 2091, 8am
Highnam

Halthrop sat behind Darren as they rode through the brightening village towards the clinic. The streets were still quiet, and the sun was rapidly sending the chill away for the day. They drove slowly enough that goggles were not needed, but it was already bright enough that they both wore sunglasses.

They arrived at the clinic to find Jane waiting outside. She had already called Major Halthrop to tell him that Jack was not there. They stood in a huddle a few metres from the building and Halthrop asked for ideas as to what they thought the best next move would be – in particular, where they thought Dira might go. There were some obvious answers he already had in mind, but it was a good low-pressure moment to give the ranks an opportunity to be involved.

Halthrop's armulet rang again. He smiled at the timing. Taking the call from Vicky would give the other three time to think on their suggestions for the Brigade's next move.

'Frank, I've had a call from Jack – well, from Asa – but Jack says he's gone to hide in a safe place until you catch Dira. With the feeds off, he reckons that he should be able to keep out of Dira's way long enough for you to catch him.'

'Understood.' He cut the call without asking anything further. 'Right, plans, ideas, suggestions?'

Jane put her hand up. Halthrop pointed at her with a flat hand. 'If he's looking for Jack, I'd expect him to come here.'

'That's why we've come here. No Jack, no Dira. Other ideas?'

Jane looked at her boots.

THE MIND'S EYE

Terry said, 'If Smith's not here, then Dira would have as much idea where he is as we do. The only way to find him would be if the audiopt system came back on. So, he might go back to the Doughnut to try and fix that.' Halthrop pouted his lips forward and gave a little nod.

Darren suggested, 'Do you think he might go home? Where does he live?'

Halthrop prompted Jane for the information. She said, 'He's one of the infotechs for Newnham, but he has a house in Cheltenham. Although Aluen told me he spends most of his time in that basement space in the Doughnut.' She looked up at Halthrop.

He added, 'Just before Darren and I left Ellie's place, Vicky told us that Dira is Jack's father. Shines a different light on everything, but does that give us any more ideas about where he might go? Or indeed, where Jack might go? Or not go?'

The four of them looked at each other.

Terry broke the silence. 'Do you think he might just run? He knows we want to catch him for attacking Vicky, and he knows the audiopts are down. Perfect opportunity to get away.'

Jane said, 'I don't think so. The fact that he's Jack's father does make this whole thing different. Seems like there's something personal going on between the two of them. I don't know why that would make him want to hurt Vicky. Actually, maybe we should stay with Vicky. He could come back to attack her again.'

Halthrop put his hands in his pockets. 'I don't think so. He knows that she'd have told us about him trying to set Jack up, so I think that ship has sailed. I think he'll know that there's no chance we'll believe that story now.'

'OK. What do you reckon we should do then?'

Halthrop said, 'It's got to be the Doughnut. Not only is it home for him, his safe place, but there's the possibility of getting the surveillance back online in order to hunt down Jack.'

The younger three did not wait. They mounted up the quad bikes immediately. Halthrop pointed east and added, 'The quickest route is the old A40. We go right past Lloyd Lloyd's house, so we'll stop for two minutes to bring him up to speed on what's going on.' He clambered on behind Darren again.

As they drove, Halthrop made another call.

'Hello, Major, everything OK?' Aluen's voice was crisp, but the wind rush as the quad bike whizzed along made it difficult to hear her. He tugged on Terry to stop the bike.

'Yes, I think so. We still haven't caught Dira, though. The best guess is that he's coming back to the Doughnut to get the audiopts back on so he can find where Smith has gone. He is definitely the main suspect in all of this – he attacked both Jack and Vicky in Highnam earlier, but Jack's gone into hiding. My reckoning is that getting to him is Dira's only intention right now. And Jack isn't wearing an armulet either, so Dira will need the audiopts to find him.'

'OK, should I get people out of the building so there's no violence if he does come here?'

'Actually, probably best if everything is left as normal there. I just wanted to warn you, but also ask if you could help us. If you see Dira, give me a call and let me know he's there.'

'Things aren't normal here right now, though. With the system down, this place has a weird ship-with-nobody-steering kind of feel about it. There's people wandering the corridors and having random conversations. Middle level east has a huge game of frisbee going on in one of the empty conference halls.'

'I expect he'll try and avoid everyone. He won't know how much we've told people. So, I suppose, act as normal as you can.'

'If he gets the feeds back online, he'll know when I warn you.'

'Well, only if he's monitoring m…,' Halthrop started to reply but paused. 'Yes, are they off still now?'

On the little screen, he saw Aluen look away and then back at him. 'Yep.'

'Good. Right, let's go with a coded message. If you see Dira, send me text only that says, "Still no sign of Smith." Do you get what I mean?'

'Yep, got it.'

'Um, actually, you can also add "in his office," if you see Dira in his basement work area? "Still no sign of Smith in his office" means Dira is in the basement. OK?'

'Yep.'

Highnam's Spokesperson lived very close to the clinic; they arrived before Halthrop had collected his thoughts about what to report to him. Lloyd Lloyd came out of the door to meet them. Halthrop clambered slowly off the bike and walked around behind the other two, the long way round.

'What's going on? Smith has escaped, and I've heard nothing from you.'

'That's why we've stopped in now, to give you an update. We're in a hurry to go back to the Doughnut, where we hope to apprehend the person responsible for all this. And we are highly confident that that is not Jack Smith. He is currently in a safe house.'

'Where?'

'I can't tell you that. The fewer people who know, the safer it is.' Halthrop caught both Jane and Terry's eyes as he said this. Jane gave a little smile.

MILES M HUDSON

Lloyd Lloyd folded his arms across his chest. 'Hmm. OK. Can you tell me how much longer it will take? We need to get the audiopt feeds back working as soon as possible, or there'll be nothing for Kangaroo on Sunday.'

Halthrop stared at the man for an uncomfortably long time. 'Even in the performance of allotted duties, the master should be praised.'

'What?'

'Never mind.' Halthrop often found his historical quotes were lost on people. 'I can't make any kind of promise about the timing. The person we're looking for is currently in the wind, so it's just educated guesswork at present.'

'Well, look, why don't we get everyone on to helping. Who is it? I'll spread the word around the village, and if anyone spots them, we can let you know where they are.'

Halthrop shrugged. It was a good idea. 'One of Newnham's infotechs at the Doughnut. A chap called Dira. I don't have a picture of him, but you may well be able to find one on the infonetwork. He's been trying to frame Smith all along and may well be responsible for everything we've been investigating.'

Halthrop decided not to offer up the information that the man was Jack Smith's father, and he held up his hand towards the others to make sure they said nothing either. Lloyd Lloyd looked around the group. They all looked blankly back at him.

Jane tapped her armulet to see the time. 'Sir, we should go.'

'You're absolutely right, Jane.' He put out his hand to shake. 'Sorry, we'll catch nobody if we stand around talking all day.' By force of social habit, Lloyd Lloyd shook the proffered hand but it hurt him again. The major turned and mounted up behind Terry, who had never dismounted. Halthrop tapped him on the shoulder, and they set off again.

THE MIND'S EYE

As they turned off the road to speed across the Doughnut's big parking area, Major Halthrop again tugged at Terry to stop. Jane and Darren pulled alongside, and the major stood up on his seat.

'That's him! Dira's over there. Probably headed to his house.'

He looked towards the edge of town, where trees and buildings intertwined. A figure limped away, and he pointed towards it.

'Do you see him? Look, he's got the same limp. It must be him. Pull up to park at the building, and we'll chase him on foot.'

Ten minutes earlier, Aluen had sent a message to Halthrop's armulet: 'Still no sign of Jack Smith in his office.' The Brigade members were all briefed on what to do next, including ignoring Halthrop's loud instructions.

They rode another twenty metres, leapt off the quad bikes and ran in through the nearest set of doors. They split into two pairs and ran away from each other along the ground floor circumference corridor. Each pair descended the first staircase they came to. This brought Terry and Major Halthrop down the nearest stairs to enter Dira's workspace directly. Jane and Darren would arrive across the destroyed server hall and could enter via the adjoining door. Or stop the man if he tried to escape that way.

As Halthrop followed Terry into the workshop, he immediately saw that nobody else was there. The side door opened, and the two of them ran towards it, but only Jane and Darren entered. Aluen called.

Major Halthrop put her voice on the armulet loudspeaker. 'He put the feeds back on, so I'm monitoring where he is. I'll direct you if you want?'

'Brilliant, thanks. Which way?'

The Doughnut's architecture was basically symmetrical, with repeated connecting corridors and large office spaces around the circular shape. With some slight variations in the basement level, the same floorplan was repeated on all the four levels. This made the chase both confusing and straightforward. Following Aluen's directions made for slight delays in the Brigade's movements.

They were up on the second level above ground when they caught sight of him. Halthrop and Dira briefly locked eyes. The major saw Dira's look change, with recognition of something. Across that vast office space and past a number of smaller meeting rooms, they got to a staircase.

Aluen said, 'He closed his eyes on this staircase, so I'm not sure if he went up or down. He's on the next level, one way or the other, and continuing in the same direction we've just been going.'

Halthrop said nothing out loud but indicated with a flat hand point that Jane and Terry should go up, whilst he and Darren ran down. As they ran, he told Darren to call Jane, so they had comms across the group.

Aluen quickly came back to them. 'It's ground floor. He's almost at Doughnut due north. There's a set of exit doors there if he takes them.'

Darren shouted to Jane who was also on speaker, 'Did you hear that? Ground floor, very north doors.'

Halthrop heard her breathless reply. 'We're at the staircase for those doors now, heading down.'

Frank could see past Darren that they were one big office space away, and Dira's solid back was now within twenty metres. Before they caught him though, Terry flew into view and tackled the man to the ground. Terry was slight, but he was flying at such pace down the stairs that his tackle was irresistible. The other three arrived and surrounded the two sprawled on the floor. Nobody moved a great deal as they all tried to regain their breathing.

Terry produced an ancient pair of metal handcuffs and looked at Halthrop. The major was leaning forwards, hands on his knees, but he managed enough of a nod that Terry attempted to apply the handcuffs to Dira, pinning his arms behind his back. Dira struggled and rolled over, throwing Terry to the side. By luck, that sprawled Terry on the floor in the way of the others. Dira was able to scrabble to his feet and get out of the doors.

At fifty-three years old, and with a pronounced limp, Dira didn't even get ten metres away from the exit before Darren grabbed him. The two of them grappled, but Dira was no match for the big farmer's boy. He continued to struggle uselessly as the other three walked over, and Terry was then able to clamp on the handcuffs.

'You idiots, Smith is going to get away. It's not me you want.' He was shouting, and the Brigade members stood watching and let him rant. Dira continued in the same vein. 'Let me go. You don't know how dangerous he is. Nobody does. But I do. I've seen it. I've suffered it.' He spun left and right, but Darren and Terry had a fast grip on a shirt sleeve each. 'Get off! Only I can deal with him. Kangaroo needs to see the full extent of his evil.'

'Apple never falls far from the tree, does it?' Terry mocked Dira.

Major Halthrop said, 'That's enough, Terry. We just catch them; Kangaroo makes the judgements.' He gave a flat hand point towards the quad bikes.

Darren hauled the man forward. They plonked him down, pillion to Terry, where Major Halthrop had ridden.

Halthrop moved to sitting behind Jane, but he told them they would all wait ten minutes for rest.

As they sat, overheated in their camouflage pattern jackets, with the sun rapidly pushing the temperature above twenty degrees, Halthrop called Lloyd Lloyd to explain that they had Dira and would bring him to Highnam for Kangaroo to deal with.

Separately, Halthrop asked Aluen to put together her own KangaReview for this case, despite not being a Highnam sifter. It was still two days before the Kangaroo meeting, and he agreed to help her with the details once they had deposited their prisoner in the custody of the village.

He looked at Dira. 'History will not be kind to you, for I have stopped you writing it.'

'History will not be kind to you if you let him go free,' Dira retorted. 'You must see that he's the guilty one. He blew up the Doughnut and nearly killed me. And he did kill my Clara. And then there's the Highnam Spokesperson, and that woman in the fire.'

Frank stroked his mousey moustache. The three younger soldiers stared at Dira in bemusement. Jane spoke for them. 'You did those things. Aluen showed us that the feeds were faked. It was you, not Smith.'

Dira writhed and shook. He screamed an incoherent shout and stood up on the footrests for the pillion seat. 'Not me! Not me! It was him!'

Halthrop stepped over and, holding the man's arm to still him, unlocked one handcuff, pulled him down to seated, and re-attached it onto the pillion handle. He mounted back up behind Jane. 'Hang on tight, Dira.' He gave a forward gesture, and the convoy pulled away.

THE MIND'S EYE
Chapter Thirty-one
23rd March 2091, 12pm
Highnam village

Major Halthrop considered his prisoner and the forthcoming trial. With two and a half days until Highnam's weekly Kangaroo court meeting, the Bristol Brigade had three suspects to keep apart from each other, until the townsfolk ruled on who was guilty of what.

Vicky's tale of the shed kidnapping suggested that Dira was likely to harm her or Jack or both. From his quad bike seat, the man was ranting at every person they passed. The major felt that Dira wouldn't pause from hurting anyone, if he thought it could help him escape.

Asa had taken Jack to a secret location for safety, but Halthrop held no fears that Jack would, or even could, run off. However, he was in danger from Dira, Truvan, and even Lloyd Lloyd. As he didn't know the man, Frank also worried that Jonty Leone might be grief-stricken enough to do Jack harm. A secret safe-house made good sense, but having to maintain the secrecy even from Highnam's Spokesperson created something of a political headache. Other senior members of the community would have to back that plan in order to convince Lloyd Lloyd that Smith would be held securely and would definitely appear at Sunday's Kangaroo. Despite all the evidence, it would be hard for Lloyd Lloyd to override his own memory of being attacked by Jack.

Truvan represented another difficulty. Whilst Halthrop considered that the man had been duped by Dira, he had still interfered in the pursuit. Assuming nothing further from Vicky's brother, Frank felt inclined to recommend that Kangaroo ignore his intervention. With the audiopts switched back on, Truvan would not be able to escape. His volatility was a worry – it could put him at risk of attacking either Jack or Dira, if he could gain access to them. On balance, Halthrop reckoned that Truvan's rehabilitation would be best achieved through the love and care of his family and neighbours.

Truvan and Dira posed similar problems for Major Halthrop. He mused on whether their motivations were actually all that different. As the prisoner transport trundled into Highnam marketplace, he remembered a quote from a book lost in the HQ explosion. *A fanatic is one who can't change his mind and won't change the subject.* Halthrop stopped the convoy near Lloyd Lloyd's house to discuss prisoner holdings. He made them park fifty metres away as Dira continued to rant loudly.

'Morning, Major.' The village's head man sounded bright in the noonday sunshine, but his posture belied his words. Lloyd Lloyd's shoulders were slumped, and he held one hand to his side throughout their discussion.

Frank took off his sunglasses, preferring to make eye contact, even if he had to squint. 'How are you doing? Should we go inside?'

'No, but maybe we could sit down here.' Lloyd Lloyd indicated a bench that sat at the edge of the green in front of his home. 'I see you've got Dira, but where's Smith?'

Major Halthrop stroked his moustache and eyed up Lloyd Lloyd. 'Asa wouldn't tell me. "Safe" was all he said.'

'What? That's not on. Bring Asa here, and we'll see what nonsense this is.'

'Sir, I agree with Asa. I promise Jack Smith will be at Kangaroo Hall on Sunday, but you will not have access to him before then.' They stared at each other for a minute, neither willing to give ground by being the first to speak. Halthrop chose a diversionary path. 'Actually, will Kangaroo be in the Hall this Sunday? Or are you moving it?'

'It will be there. One thing we're adamant about is that these crimes will not make us change our community's way of life. Are you sure you can trust Smith? And Asa too, I suppose?'

Frank dipped his head slightly. 'Well, bear in mind that the audiopts are back on now, so I doubt their location is genuinely secret now. However, I don't intend to go looking for them until Sunday.'

'Unless Smith is still messing with the audiopt feeds.'

Halthrop inhaled deeply. 'As far as we can tell, he never was.' He waved a hand towards the man handcuffed to the ATV on the other side of the green. 'That was all Dira's doing. From his work with the Newnham sifter, I expect he now knows how to do that, but she tells me they are working to close the loopholes in the software as we speak.'

Lloyd Lloyd spoke quietly to his armulet and then held the device up for the major to view the screen. Jack Smith was showing no audiopt feeds.

Halthrop gave a dismissive gesture. 'He was up all night and severely injured. I'm sure he'll be asleep now.'

'I want confirmation, Major. Find him please. Detain Asa if you need to.'

The Brigade CO nodded.

'Holding Dira is a bigger issue as far as I'm concerned. Him I do consider dangerous, but our building was blown up, so we've got no holding cells available. The next nearest brigade building is in Birmingham, but my men need rest too. Taking him there is too far, in my book. I'd like to suggest we hold him at Ellie Smith's old house, although it's really not ideal.'

'Presumably there's an old police station in Gloucester. Do you know if that's still in a good enough state to take over for a couple of days?'

'Hmm. Most police stations were destroyed during the Times, but I bet we could find something appropriate there. Especially as there's no Kangaroo living in Gloucester.'

'Good. I think that's settled then, no? You'll hold Dira prisoner till Sunday, and you'll confirm on Smith's location and let me know. I'd like you to make sure he is held securely, although I understand that those two need to be kept apart, so I'll leave your best judgement as to what is needed to secure Smith.'

Halthrop responded indirectly to avoid agreeing to informing Lloyd Lloyd of Jack's location. He had a sneaking suspicion as to where he was hiding, and it wouldn't allow anyone to find him. 'Truvan Truva is another problem, I'm afraid. He helped Dira escape at one point by attacking my men. Not exactly violently, but he deliberately interceded. And I do think he's capable of violence if he finds out where Jack is. I recommend he is allowed to remain at home, but I suggest you have a conversation with Vicky and Marmaran.'

'Oh, dear. Yes, I will do, Major.'

The men got up and shook hands again. Halthrop hit on an idea. He placed a group videocall to both Asa and his father, Tony. Asa answered from the driving seat of his horse carriage along the old A40. Tony was in his leather workshop three streets away. Frank kept the call on the forearm screen but huddled next to Lloyd Lloyd so he could be involved in the call. He cast an eye across the green to confirm that Dira was out of earshot.

'Major, what can I do for you?' Asa asked.

'I see you're alone, and Jack Smith has no audiopt feeds just now.'

THE MIND'S EYE

'Yes, I left him sleeping.'

'Highnam's Spokesperson is concerned that he may escape, and it is my responsibility to make sure that does not happen. I know you're caring for his injuries, but remember he is a suspect in several crimes. Kangaroo will rule on Sunday as to what he is or isn't guilty of.'

'He's got a broken leg – he isn't going anywhere.'

Tony remained silent.

'I understand it wouldn't be easy for him, but, especially if he has help, I agree with Lloyd Lloyd that escape is possible. I know you and your father are well-respected members of the village. What I want you to commit to, and I'm asking you as well, Tony, is: will you promise to keep him caged until we collect him on Sunday morning?'

Asa grinned, and Tony continued to listen without comment. 'Major, I promise I will ensure that Jack Smith is held in a cage until Sunday. We will keep him both safe, and also secure.'

Halthrop looked sideways at Lloyd Lloyd. 'Is that good enough?'

He nodded and spoke to the screen. 'This is on you, Tony. I'm trusting you. Highnam's trusting you.'

Tony spoke. 'Have no fear. Jack will see justice for any crimes he has committed. In fact, I tell you what. Asa and I will talk to Doc about visiting to keep track on his injuries, and she can also report to you about the security of his situation. How does that sound?'

'Yes, good. Thanks, Tony.'

Halthrop disconnected the call. Lloyd Lloyd had a noticeably improved bearing since the major had arrived. They shook hands for a third time, and Frank strode away across the grass.

Gloucester's main police station had been damaged in rioting in 2029. Not quite destroyed, but it had been unused and abandoned ever since. The city's population had been in the hundreds since the Times of Malthus, and the station looked like an old office building. The Brigade didn't even bother to search inside it for a usefully lockable room.

Directly opposite was the old court building. It was the opposite end of the architectural spectrum: solid, stone-built in a sort of polygonal fortress shape. It had been damaged in places but stood mostly intact. Cells in the basement would have held prisoners before trials during the two centuries before the Times.

Major Halthrop stood smiling outside the glorious monument, hands on his hips. 'This is perfect. How apt that we can hold Dira here, before his trial.'

Jane squinted at the major in the bright sunshine, having just exited the building and forgotten to put her sunglasses on quickly enough.

Darren asked, 'Shall we take him down inside there, then?' Terry had already pulled Dira off the quad bike and handcuffed his wrists together again. Halthrop didn't answer but gestured into the doorway.

Jane followed them inside and showed her boss the rooms she had found that could work as living quarters for the four of them whilst guarding Dira for the next forty-eight hours. Three internal rooms were sufficiently isolated from the broken exterior windows that they would be comfortably away from the elements. Spare beds were brought up from the cells in the basement – Halthrop wanted the militia to feel like they had more luxury than their prisoner.

He took a table and chair down for Dira but could not return the man's armulet. Aluen had not ruled out the possibility that he might still be able to shut off the audiopts remotely, or even trigger the Doughnut servers to send more of the hallucinations.

Dira had calmed down and spoke coherently. 'What do we do, then? Two days in here, whilst your group just hangs around waiting, is that it?'

They looked at each other through the cell's still open door. Halthrop nodded. 'Yep, that's pretty much the extent of it. We'll take you out for a bit of a walk a couple of times a day, but the things you're accused of mean that we can't take any chances. Mostly you'll be locked in here, I'm sorry to have to say.'

Dira continued to speak softly. 'You know, I really didn't do any of those things. I hope Aluen and Ali Dally and the others can work through the network and find out what Smith did to the feeds to prove it.'

'I would tell Highnam's Kangaroo to hold off on your trial until the infotechs had answers for us on that, but your attack on Jack and Vicky in the tractor shed happened when the system was switched off.'

'It was off for detection, but not for transmission. Because the system isn't designed for transmission, I assume they must not have shut that down, because he managed to send Vicky the illusion of me attacking them. That was all him too.'

Frank knew he didn't want to get into this discussion. It wasn't his place to make judgements, that was purely in the purview of the Kangaroo meeting. His gut also told him that this was more deception, and that they had the right man in custody. The convolutions of what was real and what was not did make for a truly intriguing scenario, though. The permutations fascinated him. *What a weapon of war the hallucinatory feeds would be.*

Halthrop replied. 'I don't think we mentioned it before: Truvan made a voice recording of the deal you made with him.'

For the briefest of moments, Dira paused, then he continued in the same stride. 'Major, I may be manipulative, but what I said to Truvan was just talk. I was trying to get him to help me catch Smith. Plus, I'm angry that Smith's chosen to implicate me for some reason. At that particular moment, I probably did want to kill him. But his capture was the only thing that took me to the shed last night. I wanted to catch Smith to hand over to you. Which I did successfully. You do have him in custody, don't you?'

'Kangaroo will sort out the truth from the lies, hopefully with the help of a complete KangaReview from the sifters. But in the worst case, we'll have to include witnesses to whatever we can confirm is actually real.'

Dira chuckled. 'If you can independently confirm whether or not it's real, then you don't need the witness. And if you can't, then what the witness says has no guaranteed basis in fact.'

Halthrop put his hand onto the door's outside handle. 'Well, I'm just the policeman. I'll get you and Jack to Kangaroo, and they can make judgement with whatever information can be provided. A woman died, so they won't just say, "There's no telling what went on, everybody goes free." People will want some kind of justice.'

'Well, I hope you'll remind them that, in the absence of information to the contrary, then the audiopt feeds give a complete and correct record. I don't understand where this fantasy, that I'm somehow involved, has even come from.'

'I'm impartial. Catch and return to Kangaroo, that's my job. I won't try to influence their judgements one way or the other. We'll bring some food later.' As he closed the cell door and turned the heavy lock, Halthrop wondered if Kangaroo would be able to function without testimony from him and his team. He set great store by the separation of powers in any government. The town meetings in any Kangaroo formed both their judiciary and legislature at the same time. With the sifters and the Brigade acting together as the executive branch, he believed that the Covenants of Jerusalem were being properly implemented and supported.

The next day, Halthrop left the other three to guard Dira, while he visited Jack at the Doughnut. En route, he worried about Jack being held in custody in Dira's basement cage. Frank's gut was consistent in its reassurance that Jack was innocent of all the crimes and Dira was the one that should be punished.

He kept arguing with himself, though, about the dangers of treating Jack differently. The major knew that defending the system was the best way to ensure justice for all. It was not his place to judge, as he had made plain to Dira the previous afternoon. The upshot of that should be that he treat all suspects in exactly the same way.

He kept chasing away a niggling concern, *What if I've got it all wrong?* He'd allowed Jack to spend the two days before his trial, largely unsupervised, in the cage that protected against anyone seeing what he might be up to. He wiped a finger across his moustache, left then right. *Thank goodness we smashed up the computers in there.* Nonetheless, he decided to confirm with Asa and Tony that they were monitoring Jack closely, to ensure he didn't access any of the Doughnut's systems.

Jack was dozing in the narrow bed at the far end of the cage. They had cleared up the debris of Darren and Terry's smashing spree enough to make a path in and out for Jack.

Halthrop was pleased to see that Jack had not acquired an armulet. He suggested Tony take a break upstairs.

'How's the leg?'

Jack pulled himself up to sitting. 'Doc tells me it's as good as I deserve. I'm not entirely certain what she meant by that, but she's been keeping my wound clean and checking that the splint is doing its job. So, OK, I think. As good as I deserve, I suppose.'

Halthrop nodded and carried a chair over. 'I just wanted to run through the plan for tomorrow. Asa's going to transport you to Highnam Court for Kangaroo. They're still gonna hold it in there, so I hope the surroundings don't prejudice anything. I appealed to Lloyd Lloyd about it, but he's adamant.'

Jack nodded but said nothing.

'The meeting starts at three, so I've asked Asa to make sure you get there by noon. We'll arrange a meal for you there, and you'll be able to get in and get comfortable well before anyone shows up.'

Jack nodded again, watching Halthrop's face closely.

'You and Dira are both going to have to be on the stage at the same time. Well, all the time. I've got Terry and Jane and Darren lined up to keep the two of you on totally opposite sides of the space, and Darren and Terry will be guarding him closely.'

'Father and son on opposite sides but both accused of the same thing.'

Frank paused for a few seconds. 'You had no idea he was your father before?'

'No, none at all. We worked... well, not together, he was infotech for Newnham rather than for me... but even so, we were fifteen years in really close proximity, and he never gave me even the slightest clue. I can't even work out if it's true, or some even bigger, convoluted part of his plan.

THE MIND'S EYE

'If he were my father, why in Malthus' name did he never tell me? Why stay away from me, when we worked just two floors apart?' Tears were coming from Jack's eyes. He wiped them away with the blanket, seemingly annoyed with the tears themselves.

'Whatever his plan is. I'm going to spend some time later doing a big search of my history and my mother's and grandmother's. I'll see if I can find my father, and see whether or not it's Dira.'

'I'm afraid that will have to wait. For the integrity of Sunday's Kangaroo, I've instructed Asa and Tony that you are not allowed to access any infonetwork device before they take you back to Highnam.'

Jack stuttered, 'Wh-What? You don't think I did any of this do you?'

Halthrop held up a palm towards Jack. 'I don't make any judgements. I get you to Kangaroo and your actions will be judged by everyone.'

Jack sounded angry. 'I don't mean, "Tell me about how you're going to uphold the third Covenant." I mean, what do you actually think?'

Halthrop's face went through a number of twitches. 'Honestly?' He paused for another cheek twitch. 'I don't have enough reliable evidence to say what went on. My gut tells me you're innocent. But this whole business has taught us all about the need to find reliable evidence before believing anything.'

Jack's voice became more of a wail. 'But we know each other. You understand what kind of a person I am. I couldn't hurt anyone – I just couldn't do any of these things.'

'I want to believe that. I think I do. But I have these niggling doubts. First: you did blow up this place before, so you are capable of big crimes. Secondly, a year and a half starving and alone on that island could have messed up anybody's mind. I hope it's not the case, but I can't rule out that you might not be the same person we left on Steep Holm. Sorry, Jack, I don't think I believe you're anything other than a victim here, but there's no actual evidence I can point to. In many ways, I'm very relieved that my position in this whole thing means I specifically don't have to work out who did what.'

Jack face combined confusion with worry. 'What are you going to tell Kangaroo about all of this?'

'Yes, I am concerned about how to undertake my role properly. Lloyd Lloyd has asked me to present a summary of whatever evidence we have. I need to do that as dispassionately as possible, but I know that in my heart I feel like I have to decide who is guilty and who is innocent. I know I'm going to struggle to present everything in a balanced way with no sort of implication to the villagers about how they should judge it all. I really hope Aluen and the others manage to find confirmation of something. Anything, just as long as we can state for sure that it's true and real.' He was wringing his hands together. 'This whole thing is just so impossible.'

'What does she think? Are they getting anywhere? Have they found the hack? Can they use that to find all the things he did?'

Halthrop shook his head. 'I'm sorry, I came down to see you first. I'm going to meet with her and the others in a few minutes.' The major stood up and turned to leave.

Jack pulled his blanket up and hugged himself with it. He spoke quietly. 'See you tomorrow, then.'

At the threshold of the cage, Frank turned and gave a small nod. He said nothing and left.

THE MIND'S EYE
Chapter Thirty-two
25th March 2091, 3pm
Kangaroo Hall, Highnam village

Jack stared across the stage towards Dira, who sat, flanked on either side by Darren and Terry. Lloyd Lloyd was a hunched version of himself. The normal striding confidence was less obvious as his newly developed kidney infection had become quite serious. He had refused to let anybody else run the Kangaroo meeting. Major Halthrop sat next to Jack on the left side of the stage, wearing a cleaned and pressed version of the Brigade uniform. Jack himself was nominally guarded by Jane. He had absconded from banishment, and the Brigade might well have to return him to Steep Holm at the end of the day.

Normally larger than life, on this occasion, Lloyd Lloyd did not fill the chair at the front of the stage. 'People, please,' he croaked.

Highnam Court's old orangery was packed with Highnam's population. The weather was hot and sunny. All the doors had been opened, and many villagers were outside on the lawns. Lloyd Lloyd's voice barely scratched the hubbub of conversation. Jack searched the crowd for familiar faces. Asa and Tony stood beside George Kendrick, well away from Marisa's husband Jonty Leone.

Halthrop left Jack and approached the village Spokesperson at centre stage. 'Would you like me to do the loud voice stuff? I can relay whatever you'd like me to say.'

Lloyd Lloyd nodded and put his hand up to the crowd.

The major managed to use a voice that was not shouting but still stentorian. 'Attention please, good people.' He stood slightly behind Lloyd Lloyd and indicated the man using an open hand.

'Thank you.' His voice was quiet but had regained its composure. 'Major Halthrop may have to do some of the talking for me today. I am not very well. The major has been instrumental in bringing the suspects to you here today. He knows more of the full story, I think, than anyone else. And he's completely impartial.' He turned as best he could to look up to Halthrop's face. 'Perhaps, Frank, you could outline the sequence of events for everyone, could you?'

Halthrop slid a finger and thumb across either side of his moustache and took a step forward. 'Good afternoon. Today's Kangaroo meeting will be somewhat unusual, and not least because I am having to stand in for –'

'Oh, Malthus, look out!' The cry was from a woman in the middle of the audience, as she pointed towards the internal entrance doorway.

'Quick, everybody, run!' Another shout came up from nearer to the open sliding doors, but the man was also pointing sideways towards the same entrance.

As one, the crowd turned to look at the doorway – the actual door had been destroyed in the fire, and the full house meant that that were several people close together in the space. A buzz of confusion rose up.

The two who had shouted held up arms pointing at the space, and a third person, close to the first shouted, 'That was Jack Smith,' and also raised their arm to point at those standing near the vestibule. He then turned around to point at Jack on stage. 'But he's there now. How did you do that? Have you invented a teleporter or something?'

Major Halthrop held out both arms, centre stage, and commanded, 'OK, OK, let me explain.' He made a big show of lifting his armulet towards his mouth and spoke loudly enough for everyone to hear. 'Thank you Aluen, that seems to have worked well. Wait, out.' Dropping his arms again, Halthrop continued to the crowd, 'Sirs, madam, can you tell everyone what you just witnessed, please?'

To highlight the difficulties of the misinformation in the case on trial, Aluen had caused a replay of the hallucinatory audiopts transmission from the night of the fire. The investigators had found some of the fake realities' storage locations on various Doughnut servers, and Halthrop had hit upon this idea as the way to explain the problem to the Kangaroo meeting.

The three witnesses had been standing in the exact same spots as Tony, Asa and Lloyd Lloyd at the moment of ignition the previous Tuesday. In the most vivid way, the three had seen a reconstruction of the first crime. Halthrop fed some questions to lead them through the vision and convince the assembly that this problem was real. In his preparation notes, he had underlined the word real and added an exclamation mark.

'Why is the hall not on fire again?' Frank had struggled with the difficulty of impartiality throughout his preparations. He had written several times in his notes, *Defend the system, not the person.*

After some shrugging and mini discussions in the audience, Halthrop continued by answering his own rhetorical question. 'Because that was not real. The Jack Smith behind me is real. The one our three friends just saw run in and throw the flaming torch was a counterfeit, a vision. It had no substance. When the fire was really lit, the criminal did come in and throw the torch down, but they were disguised by the vision.'

Lloyd Lloyd interrupted him to suggest that the meeting should pause for a moment for everyone to remember Marisa Leone.

Jack saw Marisa's husband staring directly at him. Jack bowed his head to break eye contact and kept it down until Halthrop began speaking again.

'Now, take care here,' Halthrop instructed the crowd. 'The most crucial thing to take away from this meeting is that over the last week, none of what we can see and hear from the audiopt records can be trusted – they were hacked. We think this only happened on limited occasions, but the overall point is that it is not possible to accept our usual standard of evidence: the audiopt records.'

This caused more consternation in the crowd, and Halthrop had to give them a full two minutes before trying to bring back order. Jack saw him put his hand on Lloyd Lloyd's shoulder to reassure him that it was best to just let them have their discussions. The assembly broke into conversation again. Lloyd Lloyd tried to hush them, but his voice was almost non-existent.

Halthrop spoke up again. 'Please, everybody, let me explain, because it is even more problematic than that.'

A heckler called out, 'What could be worse than hacking the audiopts?'

Jonty Leone turned to where the shout had come from. 'My wife is dead! I'd say that's worse.'

Silence fell across the room.

Jack could see that the atmosphere of the Kangaroo meeting did not support the theory that he had been framed. He sat forward in his seat and stared across at Dira. *How could a father do this?* Why *did you do it?*

Major Halthrop held up both hands in a pacifying gesture. 'Please, if you'll let me tell the whole story, you will be able to come to some sort of conclusions about how to rule on these things. But it's complicated enough that you need to know all parts of it.' He paused briefly but had the attention of the room.

'I know this sounds crazy, but we have confirmation from several of the techs at the Doughnut that this is in fact what happened. Indeed, beyond that, some individual audiopt feeds went off for a period. They just go blank for a while, right in the midst of other people whose feeds remained on throughout. This is also supposed to be impossible but seems to be part of the same set of attacks on the system. What it means for us today, is that we will have to allow firsthand eyewitness testimony from the night we switched off the audiopts.' He hit a surge of oratorical strength. 'Your scepticism is good, though. Eyewitnesses can be flawed, so I am glad that you are up to the task of disinterested analysis of what they tell you. I am confident that together you can work out how to serve justice for Marisa, and for Lloyd Lloyd.' Halthrop looked across to Dira. The man was staring across the stage behind the major, straight at his son. Jack felt a twinge in his broken leg. It was stretched out in front of him, held stiff by the yellow inflatable.

'The infotechs are confident that they can close off the hacking loophole in the software, so the system is back to normal now. Before we bring up the witnesses, I want to show you some of the audiopt contexts that led us to realise that we must not use them as evidence today.'

Aluen had put together a synchronous pair of audiopt feeds which they now played to the room as side-by-side 3D projections, with the timestamps clearly showing the exact same date and time for both. The first was Lloyd Lloyd's observation of Jack entering the room they were in, throwing the flaming torch and running out. The alternate reality showed a man's hands and a saucepan as he cooked a seagull on a stovetop.

Once the two paused after twenty seconds, Halthrop confirmed with the women in audience below him, 'Is that what you saw a few minutes ago?' She gave a faltering but positive reply.

The major waved his hand to indicate the other half of the projection. 'This one is the real Jack Smith, who had remained in exile on Steep Holm right up until he was framed for the fire.'

Jonty called out. 'Come off it, that could be anybody. It's even named for somebody else. Are you saying the system doesn't know who anybody is now either?'

'Right, look, you're right; this isn't enough evidence to prove the hack. One of the problems is that when the fake feeds are distributed, other feeds are also switched off. That's the idea, so you believe the fake ones, and there's no distraction from the real live feeds. He intended it this way, but hadn't reckoned on Jack using that other man's armulet.' Halthrop waved at the image of the saucepan frozen in the air.

'This next pair of videos definitely should show the issue, though.' He teed up another pair of identically timestamped feeds. Aluen had also supplied the records showing the drowning of the mystery man from Newnham, which Dira had viewed with her three months previously.

Having played them through, Halthrop said, 'This took place in Newnham, and it is the belief of the Newnham sifter that in fact the man who drowns never existed. He was inserted, fake, into the optic and auditory nerves of these two men.' He pointed at the two who had witnessed the drowning.

'But this woman never sees the man.' Halthrop replayed the feeds from Liss Peng and Anton Belling and pointed at the area in space where Ms Peng failed to see anybody.

THE MIND'S EYE

'Now, in that instance they saw somebody where nobody was present. In some cases, though, the feed has been hacked to show somebody different from the actual criminal. So Lloyd Lloyd suffered his injuries, but he and Marmaran Truva witnessed the wrong person – their minds were fed false sights and sounds.'

Again, the crowd descended into chaotic small conferences.

To belabour the point, he rhetorically asked the audience which of the two events had actually happened – was it Peng's view or Belling's view that was actually real?

The murmurings of the crowd made it plain that they were still unconvinced, or at the very least they were utterly confused. Halthrop followed up with further points. He showed Vicky Truva arriving at Steepholm and meeting Jack at the beach. Jack looked across to Vicky. She stood with her father and brother to one side of the room. It looked to Jack as if the light was better there as her face shone.

'You can see from the timestamp this is barely twelve hours after the fire, and Jack is already here, a journey of many hours from Highnam. If you watch the footage further, it also shows that he was ill from malnourishment, barely able to travel.'

Jack could see the mood of the room getting away from Halthrop. He hadn't even introduced Dira as the perpetrator yet. A female voice called out, 'I've been to Weston-super-Mare in a hurry – you can easily make that journey in time.'

Jack wondered if Halthrop's nodding at this point would be the turn that sealed his fate. After banishment had previously seemed to fail to stop him, Jack felt sure Kangaroo would sentence him to execution if he couldn't turn this around.

'Indeed,' the major responded. 'But that meeting is at, what, eight in the morning?' He pointed to the timestamp floating above them in the air. 'And Lloyd Lloyd suffered his attack, here in Highnam, at 9.30am. That journey is impossible.' The room fell silent for only the second time that afternoon.

Jack leant back slightly and looked at Dira. The man had not reacted; his focus was still directly on Jack.

Halthrop pressed for home. 'Now, further to that, there is direct experience of an induced vision that was suffered by my own Brigade members, including myself, and Truvan Truva, who was with us at the time.'

A few people near the Truvas turned to look at Truvan. He stood passively and did not make any kind of expression to confirm or deny his involvement.

Halthrop continued, 'Truvan and I were searching an underground bunker near Cheltenham. My lance corporal was guarding the door.' He indicated Darren, who was staring at his own feet. 'You can see he is large enough that nobody could pass him in a doorway without being noticed.' A couple of the audience chuckled but stopped quickly.

'Truvan and I saw Vicky Truva and Jack Smith rush past us in the dark space, and we chased the sound of their footsteps along a corridor and up the stairs to the same door that Darren was guarding. The two had vanished without Darren seeing them at all. My other two men were blocking the only alternate possible route, and Jack and Vicky did not pass them either. They simply disappeared.' Halthrop paused theatrically. 'As if they were never there.'

After another pause, he continued. 'In fact, they were never there. We were induced into seeing a vision of them by a feed from the audiopt system transmitted into our brains.'

THE MIND'S EYE

The silence lasted another couple of seconds, before the room exploded into chatter and even some shouts of dismay. As the conversations continued, Jack caught Vicky's eye. She gave him a little smile but almost immediately turned to talk to her father.

Jack saw Lloyd Lloyd mouth the word 'now' up to Major Halthrop.

'Kangaroo,' he almost shouted to take control of the floor again. 'You have seen that the feeds are not to be trusted, but it is clear that this place was burnt down, causing the death of Mrs Leone, Lloyd Lloyd was attacked, the Bristol Brigade headquarters was blown up, Jack Smith here was attacked, and he and Vicky Truva were both kidnapped and threatened with murder.

'If we cancel all audiopt surveillance evidence as unreliable, you then need to hear from eyewitnesses. But...' he let quiet reign for a moment '...only eyewitness accounts from the times when the audiopt system was down, so that we know they were not witnessing fake feeds.'

Halthrop turned towards Jack. 'Jack, please tell your peers what happened to injure your leg.'

Dira interrupted before Jack could even start. 'The feeds were on at that time.'

'Yours weren't,' Jack retorted.

'Which just goes to prove that I was in my basement workshop, where the feeds never work.'

'Stop, stop!' Halthrop intervened. 'Please do not speak out of turn. You will all get your say, but we need to keep everybody here clear on what you're talking about, and on the order of events.'

He turned to face the room. 'People, Dira...' He extended a straight arm sideways. '...is an infotech for Newnham Kangaroo. He has worked at the Doughnut for more than twenty-five years, during which time he has learnt everything there is to know about the infonetwork and the audiopt surveillance network. By all accounts, he is probably the most experienced and capable technician in the place.

'He has a large basement workspace. This includes a large, metal caged area, which, whether by accident or design, is impervious to the audiopt's radio waves detection system. This means his feed record is littered with blank periods. On many occasions, we cannot say where he is, or was.

'Furthermore, it has become clear that he has also used his knowledge of the systems to develop programs that will create these visions I've been explaining. Remember, the entire system has been compromised.

'However, it is true that Jack was attacked during the time when the system was on, so we will move on from that crime.'

He beckoned Vicky to come up to the stage. She moved up the half dozen stairs to end up at the very front of the stage, near to Dira and his guards. 'And later, at a point when the audiopt system was definitely switched off – under the supervision of other technicians at the Doughnut, and with the express permission of your Spokesperson – Vicky Truva was knocked over the head and awoke tied up in the tractor shed of Ellie Smith's old farmhouse.'

Highnam's rumour mill had already spread most of the stories surrounding this case. Jack was unsure whether Vicky's story would progress things.

She explained all that Halthrop had said in introducing her and finished with the story her kidnapping. She finished with a detailed account of how Dira was about to attack her with a large rock when Jack had fought him off, and Dira had run away.

THE MIND'S EYE

The man she accused jumped to his feet this time. 'That's not true! Why are you doing this?' He turned to the audience. 'I was kidnapped alongside Vicky. I managed to untie myself, and I leant over Vicky to try and untie her too, when he attacked me.' Dira pointed across the stage at his son. 'My leg was crushed when he blew up the Doughnut – I can hardly walk properly – so I had real problems trying to get away from him. I don't know why, but they have some sort of vendetta against me.'

Jack scanned the confused faces in the crowd. They looked backwards and forwards at the various parties on the stage. The murmuring in the audience worried him: Dira had reminded them that the biggest crime ever was previously proven as Jack's doing. To this Kangaroo court, he was a well-known terrorist.

Major Halthrop turned towards Dira. 'Enough, please sit down.' The major waited until he complied. 'Thank you, Vicky. Please do return to your place.'

Dira leapt up again and shouted. 'What she witnessed wasn't real either. They may have switched off the audiopt detection that night, but the system could still transmit.' Dira pointed an accusing finger across the stage to Jack. 'He arranged another fake vision, so she thought I was attacking her. That wasn't real – it was Jack attacking her. He faked the audio and video to look and sound like me.'

Major Halthrop signalled Darren and Terry, who manhandled Dira down to his seat. Terry put his hand over the prisoner's mouth, and Darren stood large between him and the crowd. Dira whipped his head to one side to shout, 'I'll never get justice. You see how they won't let me te–' Terry had covered his mouth again, but Dira bit him, and the hand retracted immediately. 'See how they treat me, they don't want you to hear the truth, I can't–' Darren had pulled off his camouflage cloth cap and shoved it into Dira's mouth.

Halthrop advanced to where Dira struggled, gagging. 'If you refuse to follow the procedures, we'll have to gag you properly. I promise you will get your say, but we must do this in an orderly fashion.' Dira settled, and the major pulled the cap from his mouth and handed it back to Darren.

Dira made to start arguing again, but Halthrop raised a finger and it silenced him.

THE MIND'S EYE
Chapter Thirty-three
23rd March 2091, 3.30pm
Kangaroo Hall, Highnam village

Jack wondered whether Dira's outbursts would have served to make him more or less believable in the minds of the assembled villagers. Would his claims that he was being silenced and railroaded actually take hold?

Major Halthrop turned back to the throng of Highnam villagers. 'Well, you have conflicting claims there, so now I would like to play you an audio recording. This was made by Truvan Truva, during the period when the audiopt system was off. I think it is the most compelling and conclusive evidence we have for you.'

The major played the recording that Truvan had made of Dira offering to kill Jack. When it finished, all eyes were on Dira. He remained seated but protested again. 'I didn't mean that.'

Halthrop intervened. 'OK, this is probably the right moment to hear from Dira himself. Please, sir, explain yourself to Kangaroo.'

Darren and Terry shepherded him towards the front of the stage, and Dira stood at an angle, so he could still look and point across at Jack. 'That recording – that is real, I accept that, but it was all just talk. I know Truvan hates Jack, and I wanted to get him on board to help, so I pretended that we would hurt Jack. I knew that would motivate Truvan and get him to help us catch him. We had to catch him to stop this crime spree. I'm so sorry about your wife, Mr Leone. It was exactly that that made me so desperate to stop him.' The tête-à-têtes in the audience were, this time, mere whispers. Most people could not take their eyes off Dira.

Dira avoided engaging Truvan, but turned a little more towards Jack. 'I'm so sorry, son. I don't know what drove you to these terrible crimes, but I feel so bad that I was no real father to you. If only I had been there for you – been a real father – maybe you wouldn't have gone down this path. Probably, you wouldn't have caused the first explosion in 2089 either.'

All eyes had shifted to Jack. He squirmed in his seat, which sent shots of pain up his broken leg. He couldn't think how to respond, and finally just croaked, 'Stop it!' Tears slipped down his cheeks. Jack knew these would reinforce the idea that he was guilty, but he couldn't stop them. He pictured Dira holding the photo of Clara with her wine glass raised. *How is this being a real father?* He leant forward and put his face in his hands.

Halthrop waved to Darren, and he and Terry dragged Dira back to his seat. Frank stepped over to Jack and placed a hand on his shoulder. He bent over and whispered, 'I'll take the other witnesses now, so you can compose yourself. You can speak at the end.' Jack did not raise his head from his hands but nodded in place.

Jack sat back up and wiped his face. Lloyd Lloyd spoke into the major's ear at the front of the stage, and they pointed together at various people in the audience, to agree the order of those left to call up to speak. He noticed that they did not point at Truvan Truva, but nobody else could hear the discussion between Frank and Lloyd Lloyd.

Marmaran, Tony and Asa individually presented their movements and recollections of the night of the kidnappings. Their stories built up a coherent picture of Jack as an injured victim. Marmaran included emotionally loaded details about his daughter's trauma at the hands of the kidnapper, but Halthrop interrupted twice, to remind the meeting that

THE MIND'S EYE

Marmaran had not witnessed the kidnapping and was only recounting what Vicky had told him. None of the three men had actually encountered Dira in real life at all, prior to that moment.

Truvan was not to be called up, and Dira protested about this. Halthrop responded with a reminder to everyone that Truvan had provided the audio recording of his discussion with Dira. He continued by asking, 'This Kangaroo must be utterly fair. Truvan Truva, do you have anything you would like to offer the meeting of your interactions with Dira on Thursday night?'

Truvan looked at his feet and shook his head. Jack was astounded. He peered over to try and gauge Truvan's motivations. This would be the perfect opportunity for Truvan to remind everyone about the death of his twin, and to poison the meeting against Jack. Had Vicky persuaded, or maybe threatened, her brother in some way? Jack wondered if Truvan had refused to participate, because he knew that Dira was actually the criminal, and he couldn't bring himself to engage in a way that might actually help Jack. He smiled at his image of Truvan squirming on the horns of this dilemma.

Halthrop asked Jack to present his evidence. They brought a chair to the front of the stage, and Jane helped him up from the side bench to sit there. It was positioned badly, so Jack had to really twist in order to look at Dira. He began by addressing the expectant faces in the crowd.

'You can see my leg here is severely injured.' With turning from the audience, he pointed backwards and right, towards Dira. 'That man smashed it with a metal bar.'

As a communal intake of breath went up, Major Halthrop stopped him. 'Jack! We have established very clearly that we are limiting evidence to the period when the audiopt system was completely off. Please only speak of that time.'

Jack held up a placatory hand. 'Apologies, but I'm just so angry.' Jack didn't actually get angry, at least not in a way he recognised as what people called 'anger'. He was more confused about how this whole situation had come about, and why his father would want to frame him. However, Jack had watched Frank carefully, and he had seen a lot of old videostories.

He put on the body language and voice of a wrongfully accused victim. 'During that night, I was recuperating in the Highnam clinic. At some point in the small hours, I was violently dragged from my bed with a bag tied over my head. I passed out from the pain, and when I awoke, I was in my grandmother's shed, tied to a tractor, alongside Vicky, who was also tied up. Dira was there, and he started ranting and talking about murdering me and pretending he'd saved Vicky from me.'

'This is all lies!' Dira shouted.

Darren cuffed the man on the side of the head with a soft hand. Halthrop wagged a finger at Darren and then turned it to Dira, who was glaring at his blond guard.

Jack let the audience see the scene play out and then took up his story again. 'When she pointed out that the audiopts were off so he wouldn't be able to fake the feeds believably to look like he had saved her, he then changed tack and said he would just have to kill us both. He had a large rock raised high above our heads all the time. I was really scared.' Jack paused as he heard Dira wrestling with his guards some more.

'It was only then that I discovered he was my father.' Jack's voice cracked at the word 'father', but it wasn't any kind of theatre. He lost his thread, but the pause only heightened the tension in the room. The only thing that could be heard in that moment was birdsong floating in from the gardens. 'I had never known he was my father.' Jack turned in

THE MIND'S EYE

his seat as much as he could and cried out, 'Why did you keep that secret from me? We worked so close together for fifteen years, and you never said a word.' A few tears returned to Jack's eyes.

Dira froze. He said nothing in reply.

Jane assisted Jack back to the side bench, from where he looked across at Dira, who stared at him. It was no longer the malicious glare he had maintained throughout the Kangaroo meeting. Jack couldn't tell exactly what Dira's expression said. He reckoned it was somewhere between confusion and curiosity.

He had no clue as to how the Kangaroo might rule. Jack thought that the people were convinced about not believing the feed records. He was less sure that the evidence against Dira had been presented in such a certain way. The man had a vaguely plausible counterargument for each point. But what would Kangaroo do in the face of such serious crimes, with so little certainty about who was responsible? He worried that the assembly would throw its collective hands up in the air and convict both of them. Or neither of them. Or stick with Jack as the easy answer – 'He did it before, it must be him.' He had intended to include a renunciation of the Doughnut explosion in his testimony but had forgotten. He hoped his emotional appeals and his appearance injured in a splint, would sway Highnam in his favour.

Lloyd Lloyd tried to stand up but was too weak. Halthrop leant forward to hear his instructions. 'Your Spokesperson says we should make some decisions about what to do with all of these crimes and bits of evidence. Lloyd Lloyd has some ideas, but he asks if there are any suggestions from the floor.'

Jack could not pick him out in the crowd, but he heard Asa call out. 'Jack Smith is innocent. Free him from exile.' A handful of concurring shouts followed, but it was by no means a majority.

Lloyd Lloyd tugged at Halthrop's trouser leg. After a brief confab, the major said, 'Let's just wait on that decision for a minute. We need to judge who was responsible for the crimes of this last week. Bristol Kangaroo has agreed that Highnam should rule on all the crimes together, including the explosion at our Brigade HQ. So, now, Lloyd Lloyd asks you to vote on whether you believe it was Dira. The Doughnut's sifter and infotech investigation found programs on their servers to both manipulate audiopt feeds, and their records, and also to simply delete individual feeds. Who actually used these programs, and when, has been deleted from the servers. Dira has worked there for twenty-five years. Jack was banished to Steep Holm, by this very Kangaroo, and my Brigade left him there with no boat. Vicky found him there again at the same time as Lloyd Lloyd's attack. But the audiopts can be manipulated. So, it is down to you to decide on who committed the serious crimes in Highnam and Bristol.'

Jack considered the wording. It sounded like Halthrop was leading the crowd to a particular answer. Jack smiled, not at the prospect of being freed, but at the irony of the major's prior words about not getting involved. He seemed to be going against his own principles. *We're going to have to discuss this later.*

'We'll consider sentencing afterwards. For now, please raise your hand if you believe that Dira is the criminal that committed the arson, explosion and attack on Lloyd Lloyd.'

The meeting was split. With Jane's help, Halthrop came to a total of hands raised in the room and outside the open doors. Lloyd Lloyd received the electronic votes of those who were attending the meeting by armulet. The Spokesperson was the only person who knew how many people attended the

THE MIND'S EYE

meeting via armulet, and so the final interpretation of what made a majority fell to him. Jack worried that his illness might affect his faculties.

They whispered a discussion and then Major Halthrop announced, 'By a margin, this Kangaroo declares that Dira is guilty of the arson, and hence the death of Marisa Leone, the explosion at Bristol Brigade headquarters, and Thursday's attack on Lloyd Lloyd.'

Terry had obviously been pre-programmed with instructions for this outcome. He flourished the metal handcuffs and hammed up the ceremony of placing them on Dira's wrists. The man did not resist and just stared at Jack throughout.

Halthrop addressed the meeting again. 'During the course of this investigation, Jack Smith was instrumental in assisting us. He was first to establish that fake feeds were being sent to people's eyes and was no end of help in identifying Dira as the culprit and monitoring his whereabouts.'

Jack felt a little embarrassed at this. He was not convinced he had been able to keep tabs on Dira much at all, but he remained silent and wondered how Frank might continue.

'In my opinion, he is very much the sort of citizen that Highnam should be proud to have as one of their own.'

Truvan shouted, 'Stop! He killed my brother. Don't forget Bailey, don't make his death be for nothing. Smith tried to destroy our way of life. And he crippled that man.' He had stretched as tall as he could and pointed over nearby heads towards the newly cuffed prisoner.

Marmaran had to reach up to put a hand on his son's shoulder. He pulled him back down off his tiptoes and spoke out himself. 'What are you proposing, Major?'

Asa's voice rang out again. 'Free him! Freedom for Jack Smith!'

Halthrop held out both hands, palms down. 'I am not a member of this Kangaroo, so I can only advise you as another human being, albeit one quite familiar with crimes and misdemeanours across our region, and indeed across many Kangaroos. I have spoken with Lloyd Lloyd, and he is in agreement with my suggestion.' Most eyes flicked to their seated leader, who was nodding as sagely as he could manage, and then back to the speaker.

'In terms of sentencing Dira, I propose a straight swap. Jack returns home from his exile, and Dira is sent to live on Steep Holm.' The room buzzed. Jack spotted Vicky hugging her father. Beside them, Truvan's face was both aghast and angry at the same time.

Dira's eyes never left Jack. They made Jack's skin itch; he fidgeted in his seat but knew he could not get up and move. He wouldn't look across at his father.

After several minutes to consider, Halthrop pulled the meeting back to order. He asked for alternative suggestions to his sentencing proposal, and two gained traction amongst the people.

There was a minimal volume of support for a proposal that Dira should be executed. Jack suspected that this had more support than it sounded but few people were willing to vocalise support for a death penalty. No suggestion regarding Jack's future was made in this argument.

Truvan called for them both to be exiled to Steep Holm together. In doing so, Truvan also proclaimed the father-son relationship between them must mean both were dangerous. This caused more confusion. Halthrop pointed out that Dira had threatened to kill Jack, so if they chose exile for both, he would recommend Beaumont Island, a second uninhabited one near to Steep Holm. Their family connection muddied the waters on this option. Jack could tell people were thinking less about choosing an objective punishment than how the relationship might have led to the whole situation in the first place. He could make out mutterings along the lines of 'Apple not far from the tree' and 'Bad seed.' He heard his grandmother's name a number of times as well.

After some procedural discussion with the Spokesperson, Halthrop called for a vote between the three options. Jack's outcome in the execution scenario had not been clarified, but he reckoned he would be returned to exile unless the swap idea won the vote.

With three options, the voting was more complex to count. There was no obvious standout choice, and Jack knew that those attending via armulet would not get caught up in any mob mood that might prevail in Kangaroo Hall. It took Jane, Halthrop and Lloyd Lloyd nearly fifteen minutes to collate everything and agree what to announce.

'People of Highnam Kangaroo, you have found Dira guilty and have now made a clear decision on his sentence. He will be banished to Steep Holm island in place of Jack Smith, for the rest of his life. Jack will be free to return and live here, should he so choose.'

Some cheers went up around the room, but it was not clamorous. Vicky smiled continuously. She hugged her father again and spoke to her brother whilst holding his hand. Truvan appeared implacable. He spoke quietly to his sister, whilst glaring at Jack.

Jack dared not look at Dira and continued to scan the members of the meeting. A few gave him a thumbs up, some were focussed on the opposite side of the stage, and most held conversations with those around them. Jack's leg wouldn't have made it easy for him to get up, but he didn't feel like he could even try. Jack felt as if his skeleton has vanished. His whole body just flopped down in his chair. He had no control and couldn't lift any part of himself. All of the weight of unknown worst-case scenarios was gone.

Lloyd Lloyd attempted to wish everyone well and close the meeting, but his voice was gone. Major Halthrop took the mantle and announced that everyone could leave. Few actually did move towards the exits. Mostly, they continued their animated conversations.

Jack decided he must face down his father. The man would be gone very soon, and he needed to have looked Dira in the eye and asked directly about his motivations. He turned, but the other side of the stage was empty. Darren, Terry and Dira were all gone. They must have left by the small door at the side of the stage.

Vicky reached the top of the stairs again and advanced behind Lloyd Lloyd's chair towards Jack. Her smile was stuck. She even struggled to talk normally as her lips were immovably stretched. She reached her arms forward, and Jack's strength returned with a whoosh. He stood up to receive her hug with a sudden insatiable buoyancy. From melting into the seat, his body was now floating on air.

'I can't believe it.' She repeated again, 'I can't believe it.'

Jack had no words to reply.

'This is so crazy. If he hadn't appeared and committed all those crimes, you'd still be stuck on that island forever.' She hugged him even tighter and then released him and stepped back slightly. 'But instead, you're coming home. I can't believe it.'

Jack's legs wobbled slightly. Vicky must have thought it was his broken one causing pain – she held his arm and helped him lean back to sit down. She sat next to him and took to

THE MIND'S EYE

watching the rest of the villagers. Jack looked at her enthralled face, watching the little groups of people chatting. Some were serious, but most had lightened, and there was occasional laughter in the conversations.

Major Halthrop helped Doc get Lloyd Lloyd out of the chair and down the small staircase to the main floor of the hall. She had a wheelchair for him, and his wife wheeled him out, accompanied by the doctor in admonishment mode.

Frank then turned and moved across the stage to Jack and Vicky. He waved Jack to stay seated and shook his hand in place.

'Congratulations.'

'Thanks, I'm still a bit shocked. Not really sure what to do now.'

'Well, when we take Dira to Steep Holm, we can bring back anything you want from there.'

The sound of his father's name brought another wobble to Jack's body. He needed to find out why Dira had been so intent on destroying him. Visions of Ellie, and of Clara's photograph, roiled through his head. Jack needed to know so much more about Dira than just the recent crimes. He felt like there was a hole in his entire existence that he had never noticed before. 'Can I speak to him before you take him away?'

Halthrop looked sidelong at Jack. He didn't answer for a long time, and Jack was squirming inside. 'I'm sorry, Dira's already said he doesn't want to see you.' He put his hand on Jack's shoulder and repeated, 'Sorry.' Halthrop turned and walked away.

Jack's mouth hung open as he watched the major's back recede.

Chapter Thirty-four

27th March 2091, 10am
Grannie Ellie's house

Jack heard his front door open and close.

'What are you doing? You should be resting.'

At the sound of Vicky's voice, he turned his head to try and look back. He was on his side, on Ellie's kitchen floor, legs stretched out and leaning into a cupboard to try and clean it. His right leg remained in the bright yellow plastic splint.

'Oh, hello.' Jack felt the strange knot in his stomach again.

Vicky moved around into his sightline. 'Put that down and let me help you up.'

'Hold on, Doc said you're supposed to rest too. There's no telling how badly that bang on the head may have damaged your brain.'

She waved a dismissive hand. 'I passed all my cognitive tests just now. Doc says you and Dad should keep an eye on my moods and conversation, but unless there's more symptoms, I should be OK.'

They manoeuvred Jack up and into a wooden chair at the small kitchen table. Without further comment, Vicky started to fill the electric kettle with water.

'The electricity isn't powerful enough for that. I need to get up on the roof and clean the solar panels.'

'You'll do no such thing. That leg needs recovery time. You need to rest. I'll get some of the neighbours to come and help us sort this place out for you.'

He knew there would be no use in arguing. 'There's still some embers in the stove. You should be able to perk that up and heat the water on it. There's no new coffee though; it'll be years old.'

She smiled and, after transferring the water to a pan, went through the process of revitalising the fire in the range. Vicky sat opposite Jack, and they looked at each other in silence for a while.

'How have you found moving back into this place?'

They hadn't seen each other since the trial. That had only been two days earlier, but Jack felt like he had not seen her for weeks. 'With my leg, it's pretty hard to do anything. Even sleep.'

'Must be pretty weird coming back to this house after so long. And without Ellie being here.'

Jack shrugged. 'Yeah, I guess it is. I haven't really thought about it properly yet.' He stopped for a moment, picturing his grandmother standing across from him at the kitchen sink. 'But I've been sleeping in my old bed. Eventually, I expect I'll want to take the bigger bedroom, but it doesn't feel right at the moment.'

She nodded and put her hand across the table onto his. 'It's hardly surprising. You've had so much upheaval to try and take in the last few days. Discovering Dira, returning from exile, and moving back in here after so many years, and without Ellie lighting the place up.'

Jack looked towards the sink and the window to the rear garden. He imagined his grandmother holding a flower in one hand and secateurs in the other. She was wispy and looking out through the window to the March sunshine. The apparition seemed to disperse the light like a dust-laden sunbeam. Outside the window, Dira's face appeared. Jack jolted, and the chair screeched back a little on the stone floor.

'What is it?'

He turned to Vicky. 'You don't see him?' Jack pointed to the window, but the face was gone.

'See who?'

Jack slumped in the chair. 'Sorry. I've been having visions of my fa… of Dira, all the time. He doesn't do anything, but I get waves of fear when I see him. I don't know what it is. Or what to do.'

Vicky squeezed his hand silently and stood to make coffee.

He watched her back and almost inaudibly said, 'I missed you.'

She turned her long face to smile at him. 'You mean just now, or over the last year and a half?'

'Well, both of course.' He grinned. 'But I was talking about the last couple of days. Since Kangaroo. I was hoping you'd visit sooner.'

She turned completely and placed a cup in front of Jack before sitting back down. 'I had to keep tabs on Truvan: make sure he's calmed down and isn't going to come over here and cause any trouble.' It was Vicky's turn to gaze out of the window. 'I did a lot of thinking too.'

Jack missed the cue – he was now distracted by thoughts of Truvan attacking him in the night. 'Is he OK? I mean, he isn't talking about coming round here, is he?'

'I think he can control himself.'

Jack was not convinced but did not argue. He tried to change the subject so he wouldn't think about Truvan or Dira anymore. 'Good, that means you can come and visit every day.'

She fiddled with her cup and then looked up at him. She did not speak.

Jack faltered. 'If you have time, of course. I mean, I'll be really busy trying to fix up this place with a broken leg, but please do visit anytime.' The pace of his speech increased. 'I'm thinking that once I've aired and cleaned everything and got stuff going again in the vegetable garden, I'll see if I can go and work at the Doughnut. I'm thinking that they'll need a replacement for D...' Jack stumbled over saying his name. 'For Dira. I'm not sure I know enough just yet, but I worked there for fifteen years, so I should be able to pick up the technical side of things pretty quick, I hope. That reminds me, I must call Aluen and suggest it. Otherwise, she'll get somebody in before I'm ready to go back. I hope she can survive OK with some sort of temporary support till then.'

Vicky squeezed his hand again. 'I could help you fix this place up.'

Jack paused. 'Yes, please. That'd be great. Only if you have time to keep coming over. I mean it's not far, but I'm sure you've got stuff you need to do at home.'

She smiled and squeezed more firmly. 'Maybe I'll stay over occasionally. With that splint on, you won't be able to get anything done at all.' She leaned over and gave him a kiss.

Jack wasn't too sure what to say. His mind was reeling from the kiss. He was saved by his armulet sounding. Vicky had given him Grannie Ellie's armulet back, and Tony had presented him with a new leather strap for it. The videocall was from Major Halthrop.

'Connect call. Project image.' The man's face appeared in front of them, emerging from the table.

'Jack, my man, how are you?' With their original suspect now exonerated by Kangaroo, Halthrop felt himself free to be more friendly. He had always had a sneaking respect for Jack, despite their first encounter being a consequence of Jack's blowing up the Doughnut.

'I don't really know. It's all taking a lot of getting used to. And I can't do very much with my leg, which means I can't

get through cleaning the place up and making a home of it.'
He looked over to Vicky's face, and she puckered her lips silently. Jack blushed and hoped the major couldn't see the whole scene.

'How is the leg?'

'Doc says I messed it up pretty badly fighting with Dira. At least another month in this splint, she reckons.'

'Oh dear, that is a long time.'

Vicky announced her presence. 'I'm going to help him.'

'I can't say I'm surprised.'

Jack stared at the projected face: neat, blond hair and his hallmark moustache. Vicky tittered quietly. He looked up to her face, but she was also staring at Frank's blue eyes.

'Well, she wasn't allowed on Steep Holm, so we had to wait until now.' Jack and Vicky flashed their eyes at each other.

'I don't think I should disturb you two for very long. I just called to let you know that we deposited Dira on Steep Holm yesterday afternoon. As you suggested, we removed the armulet you left. And we buried the two skeletons. Right thing to do, really. Bit late, but better late than never.'

'Oh yes, well done. Sorry, I never even thought to do that. Did you leave him more ways of growing or catching food? I came close to starvation a few times. In fact, I would probably be dead by now if Vicky hadn't come to save me.' The two of them gave each other moony eyes again.

'Yes, fishing rods and nets, new material to make a polytunnel, and some proper gardening tools. You were right that all those ones in the barn were pretty much rotten.'

'Did you leave him one of those knives like you gave me? That was the single best thing I had.'

'We don't have any more.'

Jack was silent. He looked at the ceiling.

'Right. I'll come and visit you sometime, but for now, take it easy and get better.'

'Thank you, Major.'

Vicky chimed in, 'Bye.'

The image vanished and their coffee cups were all that remained.

Epilogue
20th April 2091, 11.45am
The Doughnut

Jack watched the air above the cracked concrete wobble with refraction. The sun baked the courtyard inner circle of the Doughnut's hole. The giant building had a perfect sun trap in its centre, and the reflections from the steel and glass of the walls seared the ground.

With the building's climate control, Jack was comfortable in a constant twenty degrees. The window tinting meant he didn't even have to squint much, despite the intensity of the light reflected from the white and silvered surfaces outside.

Jack had already decided he preferred working as an infotech to working as a sifter, and he had only returned to the Doughnut four days earlier. His injury still forced him to limp up and down the stairs; it had been easiest for everyone for him to set up in Dira's old basement workspace.

Not that that had been easy. With his bad leg and the month-long gap that Newnham's sifters had been without their second infotech, expediency ruled the decision. But Jack was regularly visited by distracting thoughts. Imaginations of his father plotting at the same desk he now worked at did not make for smooth sailing in his tasks. Working adjacent to the server hall he had blown up in his failed attempt to revolutionise society added to his distractions. He wondered about his father stuck in the rubble of the explosion. The visions continued to haunt Jack. They were especially disturbing in Dira's own lair. Fortunately, the apparition never did anything. He just appeared near to Jack, staring at him.

THE MIND'S EYE

In technical terms, Jack had quickly come to realise that, whilst many infotech tasks were simple plugging in and testing whether recycled hardware functioned, actual diagnosis and repair of faulty equipment was much more complex. He was managing to look up the manuals and ask other infotechs, but everything took a long time.

He turned from the window and walked into Aluen's office.

'Ah, there you are. I was just about to come and find you. You've been offline all morning, so I wasn't sure if you got my message.'

'Yes, sorry, I was working in the cage, and time ran away from me.'

Aluen scowled. 'We should dismantle that cage. We can't continue with periods when the audiopts don't work.'

Jack nodded. 'Not a problem, I'll get onto that. But everything always takes longer than you think. I tell you, I have a new-found respect for the infotechs. I mean, I respected their work before, but I had no idea just how much they – we – actually have to know. Don't worry, the cage is on my list of jobs.'

'I suppose when everything just works, you have no real idea the depths of complication that actually make it all happen.'

'Yes, I've come to envy the simplicity of what Vicky has, tending to animals and vegetables.' Jack made a rueful smile, but Aluen's face showed that she knew he was only a little envious. She didn't need to articulate her understanding that he loved complexity and the challenge of learning. She'd said it out loud before.

'Me too,' she said through a little smile of her own.

'Right, sorry it took me so long, but I'm here now. What is it you need?'

'Well, it's a bit of a sensitive one I think, so say no if you don't feel like you're the one I should be asking to do this.'

'OK.' Jack's answer was drawn out. His voice tone went down and up slowly, and it took him more than two seconds to say the two letters.

Aluen looked him straight in the eye for another few seconds. 'Before you came to work here, we had a team of four infotechs, randomly chosen, and tasked them to work on closing the hacks that enabled us, and Dira, to shut down the audiopt system.'

Jack already knew this. 'Right.'

'Well, they reckon they have done that job, and they also reckon they fixed three other possible hack entry points in the system.'

'Right.'

Aluen paused again. 'I want you to break into the system.'

'What?' Jack thrilled at both the idea that he should attempt such a challenge, but also that he had a colleague with similar thinking to his own about taking down the surveillance network.

She immediately dashed his excitement. 'I'm wanting you to test for flaws that remain so we can close them too. I realise it might take a while given that you're still learning the infotech stuff, but I'm not expecting that we're up against any deadline.'

Jack mulled the idea over for a minute. He was not considering whether or not he would accept, as that was already a certainty; he was musing on how he should play the role.

'Are you authorised to ask me to do this?'

'Authorised by whom? You know very well that nobody actually runs this place. We all just get by doing our own thing

THE MIND'S EYE

and sharing ideas where they come up. So, whatever you find we'll also share with the other sifters and infotechs, and hopefully we can seal up the system tight.'

'I think what I'm asking, though, is what protection I'll have from punishment by Kangaroo if anybody finds out and thinks I'm just trying to blow things up again. We saw with Dira's crimes that I'm a natural scapegoat in many people's eyes. I'm not sure I want to take that risk.'

Aluen had stood up to chat with Jack. She sat down in her chair and leant back, looking at the ceiling. 'Hmm.' She folded her arms across her chest and her head leaned slightly to one side.

'Well, of course, there'll be the feeds record for this conversation. So as long as people don't think that you and I are in cahoots and have made this conversation to cover our tracks, I'd hope that'd be sufficient to convince anyone that you're searching for holes in order to plug them rather than to exploit them.'

Jack gave a nonchalant shrug. 'Yes, I suppose that should do it.' He waited a beat and then added. 'I do feel rather like I'm on my last chance though. If this somehow went wrong, I daren't think what punishment they might mete out.'

'I tell you what: I'll have a conversation with the Newnham Spokesperson. When she confirms it's OK, then we've got real evidence that we are working with the best intentions.'

Jack shrugged again. 'That sounds like it should do the trick.'

'Just don't shut the system down by accident!'

Jack chuckled loudly. 'Don't worry, I'll be very careful.'

'Right, well that's twelve o' clock, so I'm off home. I'll leave you to get started on that. I don't think there's anything else on your jobs list at the moment, is there?'

'What? I've got a ton of things to do. We just spoke about the cage, but I'll be surprised if I even get to that this week.'

She held up her hands in surrender. 'I'm kidding. Just add it to that list of jobs.'

'I can't guess at how long it might take.'

'Well, as it's something where we're expecting no outcome, I'm not quite sure how we'll decide when to stop, but I guess if we chat about how it's going once a week – does that sound OK?'

'I'll say yes, but I don't know either whether that's likely to be useful. But I can report more or less often about what I find, as I find it. I think with such a nebulous task, we're just going to have to play it by ear. But I'll put together a plan that breaks down the various major sections of the whole system and try attacking each one separately.'

'Well, you never know, attacking more than one part at a time might be the way that makes it break down.' She laughed and pointed at him. 'Just don't make it break down!'

He smiled. 'Yes, boss. See you later.' He turned and walked back to the staircase.

On his way back down, Jack took the long route and passed through the adjacent, destroyed server hall. At the adjoining doorway, he looked back and forth between the twelve-screen workstation in the cage and the twisted shells of giant computers. A smile forced its way onto his face at the thought of the lengths he had been to, particularly to avoid audiopt detection, in the making of the bombs for his ill-fated attempt at forcing the surveillance feeds offline.

Even with Dira's fake feeds and violent crimes, the populace had still not seen fit to dismantle the audiopt system. 'Third time's a charm,' he mused aloud, as he sat down in front of the screens.

THE MIND'S EYE

* * *

Find more books by this author at
mileshudson.com

Printed in Great Britain
by Amazon